The Winter of Second Chances

Jenny Bayliss lives in a small seaside town in Kent with her husband, their children having left home for big adventures. She went back into education when she was thirty-nine and gained a first-class degree in Creative and Professional Writing from Canterbury Christ Church University. Jenny likes long walks along the seafront and baking days, especially when it's cold outside. She is a stationery-obsessed coffee-lover, who doesn't believe in saving things for best and shamelessly wears party dresses to the supermarket. *The Winter of Second Chances* is her second novel.

Say hello to Jenny on Twitter @BaylissJenny.

Also by Jenny Bayliss

The Twelve Dates of Christmas

The Winter of Second Chances

JENNY BAYLISS

PAN BOOKS

First published 2021 by Pan Books

This paperback edition first published 2021 by Pan Books
an imprint of Pan Macmillan
The Smithson, 6 Briset Street, London EC1M 5NR
EU representative: Macmillan Publishers Ireland Ltd, 1st Floor,
The Liffey Trust Centre, 117–126 Sheriff Street Upper,
Dublin 1, D01 YC43
Associated companies throughout the world
www.panmacmillan.com

ISBN 978-1-5290-2710-5

1 3 5 7 9 8 6 4 2

A CIP catalogue record for this book is available from the British Library.

Typeset by Palimpsest Book Production Ltd, Falkirk, Stirlingshire
Printed and bound by CPI Group (UK) Ltd, Croydon, CR0 4YY

Visit **www.panmacmillan.com** to read more about all our books
and to buy them. You will also find features, author interviews and
news of any author events, and you can sign up for e-newsletters
so that you're always first to hear about our new releases.

For Lindsay and Jo with all my love xxx

Chapter 1

Annie was almost home when she realised she'd left her phone at the restaurant. It was September and the night air was nipping at her jacket collar, letting her know that summer was on the wane. The gentle rhythm of her rubber-soled boots on the pavement was as soothing as the tick of the old carriage clock that used to sit on her parents' mantelpiece.

The high street was quiet. The pubs had long since expelled their patrons and the lights in the flats above the shops were all but extinguished. Even a town as busy as Leaming on the Lye had to sleep sometime. Annie wandered slowly back the way she had come. She was completely alone aside from the flash of a bushy red tail as a fox disappeared down an alleyway, no doubt hoping to find a loose bin bag or discarded kebab.

Annie liked this time. After the heat and rush of the kitchen during service and then the laborious cleardown, when the last customers had departed, full-bellied and ruddy-cheeked from the house wine, came the quiet. The front of house staff left first, carpets hoovered and tables laid ready for lunch service the next day, leaving just the kitchen staff, tired yet strangely elated at having got through another crazy night.

When the last pan was dried and the floor mopped, Annie would let them go, listening as their animated conversations drifted out of the courtyard and into the sleeping streets beyond. Since the twins had left home, her chefs had become like her surrogate children. And then she was alone. The calm after another hard-won day washed over her. She was too tired to dwell on things and that was just the way she liked it.

Up ahead, towards the mall, a man in a leather jacket staggered under the weight of his companion, who leaned listlessly against him, drunkenly singing 'Hit Me Baby One More Time'. Annie walked on and soon she was standing back outside The Pomegranate Seed, the restaurant she and her husband Max had run for the last fifteen years.

Annie unhooked the latch on a tall gate to the side of the building. A steep path led down towards a small courtyard and kitchen garden, with raised beds and cold frames to the right, and to the left, a crooked flight of stone steps down to the kitchen door.

The security light was on the blink again and the gravelled passage was in almost complete darkness, save for the dim phosphorescence of the harvest moon. But it didn't trouble Annie: she knew every dip in the path, every leaning nuance of the ancient stone steps – this was her domain.

She fumbled for her keys, then let herself in. The kitchen hummed with electrical appliances; the green lights atop the industrial fridges and freezers punctuated the blackness of the still-warm kitchen. Annie located her phone quickly on the vast stainless-steel worktop by way of the red message light that pulsated from it. The cold light from the screen spilled out into the sleeping kitchen. It was a message from Max:

Sorry, love, going to be late. Jude's fallen out with Petra again, so I'm going to sink a few pints with him. M xx

Annie rolled her eyes. Petra seemed to throw Jude out of their flat above the pub on an almost weekly basis. She shoved the phone into her pocket and was about to leave when she heard a noise coming from the restaurant. She froze. *Shit!* She cocked her head in the direction of the restaurant beyond and strained to listen.

She couldn't make out voices but there was definitely somebody moving about in there. She opened her phone to see what time Max had sent his message; with luck she could catch him somewhere between sober and useless. As Annie's finger hovered over Max's name, the last bar of her phone battery blipped out and snapped her back into darkness.

Bugger, bugger, bollocks! Annie cursed silently. The dull thud of a glass being dropped onto the rush matting of the restaurant floor thrilled her to attention. Her heart thrummed, eyes wide against the dark, as her breath came hard and fast. And then she did the thing that always made her shout at the actresses in horror movies: she crept slowly towards the noise.

Her intention was to sneak behind the bar and use the restaurant phone to call the police. The sticking noise her rubber soles made against the vinyl flooring seemed to fill the black corridor with a sound like Velcro strips being ripped apart. Annie pulled herself up onto her tiptoes and teetered on.

As the dim outline of the doorway to the lounge area came into view, Annie got down on all fours and crawled the last few feet.

The lounge area consisted of two long velvet banquettes and low tables – also known as tables eight and nine for the

3

purposes of the staff – where diners could enjoy drinks and canapés before being escorted to their tables in the restaurant beyond. Annie was squeezed between the open dishwasher and two metal barrels with plastic pipes that led up to the drink pumps. There was a pervading smell of stale beer and drain at this level.

Over the drone of the drinks fridge and the wine chiller, Annie could make out heavy breathing. It was closer than she would like. Now what was she going to do? She couldn't very well call the police with the robbers on the other side of the bar.

She had to do something, she was not about to let some thieving arseholes make off with her hard-earned cash. If they wanted what she had, they'd have to work twelve-hour shifts like she did.

Annie had heard somewhere that if a predator in the wild approaches you, you can scare it off by running at it, full pelt, and yelling at the top of your voice. Spurred on by outrage and an increasing need for the toilet, Annie decided to test the theory. She slipped the electric fly swatter off a nearby shelf and set it to 'zap'. After several abortive counts of three, she took a good lug of air and leaped out from behind the bar, shouting and screaming. She slapped her palm against the bank of light switches on the wall and light flooded the lounge. Still fully embodying the banshee spirit, Annie swiped wildly in the direction of the intruders with the swatter.

What followed was unexpected. There was a lot of frightened screaming. The sudden change from dark to light had left Annie temporarily dazzled and it took her a moment to register what she was seeing. Sprawled across the banquette at table nine, desperately and inadequately trying to cover her nakedness with cushions – one of which had the words *Keep Calm and Carry On* embroidered across its front – was Ellie, the newly appointed waitress. And stood before her, with a fast-drooping erection and a blue bar towel held up against his nipples, was Annie's husband, Max.

Later, as Annie lay back against the crisp white pillows in the hotel room, she would think of all the clever, cutting things she could have said to her husband in that moment.

'It's not what it looks like!' Max had said.

Behind him, Ellie sat very still, eyes wide like Bambi, as if she thought by not moving, Annie might not be able to see her. In an ideal world Annie would have whipped back smartly with something along the lines of:

'Ah, I see you're training young Ellie in the finer arts of customer service.'

Or:

'Don't tell me: there was a blackout and all your clothes fell off and Ellie was so frightened you had to put your penis into her vagina to calm her down?'

But what Annie actually said, when faced with her naked husband screwing the naked waitress half his age, while she, his long-suffering wife of twenty-six years, stood before him deflated, with crow's feet around her eyes and an electric fly swatter hanging loosely by her side, was, 'Gup . . . Gup . . . Ubber . . . Affphoof.' Then she'd stumbled backwards, zapped her own thigh with the swatter and let out some wee.

Chapter 2

Annie slept surprisingly well, considering she had just entirely changed the course of her life, and woke before dawn on a strange sort of high. She called Marianne, her head chef at The Pomegranate Seed, filled her in on the situation and handed her the responsibility of the kitchen.

'What a shitbag!' said Marianne. 'Don't worry about a thing, I've got this. How long do you think you'll be gone?'

'I haven't really thought that far ahead yet,' said Annie. Her heart began to pound as she realised she had no plan beyond the next two days, for which she'd booked a hotel room. 'Can you remind Max to feed Mrs Tiggy-Winkle?' Annie asked. Mrs Tiggy-Winkle was her cat.

'Are you sure you're okay?' asked Marianne.

'Don't I sound okay?' said Annie.

'Well, yes,' said Marianne. 'You sound a bit too okay. A bit manic. Like you've taken speed or something.'

Annie laughed. The sound was high-pitched and she heard a note of hysteria in her voice.

'I'm fine!' Annie said, a little too brightly. 'Really! Absolutely fine!'

She looked around her hotel room knowing that every

room in the building would be identical: generic 'modern art' canvas above the bed, satin silver bed runner to break the expanse of white linen, a brown faux leather chair in one corner and walls painted in a pale grey, which would no doubt be called something ridiculous like Husky Shimmer. There was a desk along one wall with a hairdryer, a travel kettle and two cups on a plastic tray, and above it a flat-screen TV. It was the travelling salesman's home from home, the hen party haven, and now a wronged wife's bolt-hole.

'Do you want me to come over?' asked Marianne.

'No, no. Don't be silly. Somebody's got to run the kitchen.'

And then, almost as if her voice was speaking without her brain's permission, she found herself saying, 'They were on table nine, you see. I chose that sofa. I picked the colour out of a book of swatches. And the weird thing is, when I caught them, I kept thinking, *What about the velvet? Semen is a hell of a stain to get out.* That's mad, isn't it? What kind of a woman worries about semen stains when she walks in on her husband screwing another woman?'

There was silence on the line for a moment.

'Your silence suggests you think I'm bonkers,' said Annie.

'Sorry,' said Marianne. 'I got sidetracked there. I was trying to remember which supermarket sells a product that claims to remove semen.'

'From velvet?'

'From anything, I think.'

'Good Lord!' said Annie.

'And if it doesn't work, we can always get it reupholstered.'

'I don't think I'll ever be able to look at table nine without feeling completely humiliated.'

'Then we'll skip reupholstering and go straight to burning!' said Marianne. 'We'll have a ceremonial burning of table nine in the street.'

'I'm not sure burning sofas is very environmentally friendly,' said Annie.

'We could build effigies of Max and Ellie and burn them along with it. Like the ultimate closure!'

'You've got a dark side, Marianne,' said Annie. 'My kitchen is in good hands. The staff will never dare to cross you.'

As she ate breakfast in the hotel restaurant she complimented herself on how well she was handling everything. She felt fine, she really did. And then she got back to the hotel room and found ten missed calls, seven texts, a dozen messages on Facebook Messenger and an email, all from Max. Annie didn't read them. She was suddenly very tired. She didn't want to think about all the things she was supposed to be thinking about: the business, finances, the twins, Max, Ellie, the end of her life as she knew it. Annie turned the volume on her phone down low, and got back into bed, where she stayed for the next two days.

Her phone buzzed on the bedside table. She let it buzz until it died away. And then it buzzed again immediately. Annie sighed and reached languidly over and looked at the screen. It was Peter. She answered it.

'Hello, love,' she said.

'Hey, Mum,' said Peter. 'Alex is here with me. We've got you on loud speaker.'

'Hi, Mum,' said Alex.

'Hello, darling. Where are you?'

'At mine,' said Peter.

'I came down after work,' said Alex. 'I can work from here tomorrow.'

'Oh, that's nice,' said Annie.

'Well, we heard we'd become the product of a broken home, so—'

His sentence was cut short by a scuffling sound followed by an aggrieved 'Ouch!'

'We're calling to tell you we support your decision,' said Peter.

'Should have done it years ago!' said Alex.

'Oh!' said Annie. 'Well. This is unexpected. Who told you?'

'Grandma,' said Peter.

'Of course she did,' said Annie.

Max's mother would have been champing at the bit to tell the boys before Annie got the chance. She imagined her as a sort of ageing racehorse in a twinset, leaping over her mahogany nest of tables and upsetting the faux Tiffany lamp to get to the phone. It was no wonder Max was such a prima donna; whatever his faults were, as far as her mother-in-law was concerned, they were down to anyone but him.

'I'm sorry you had to hear it from someone else,' Annie continued. 'I was going to call you, I was just . . .' *Sleeping mostly*, she thought. 'I was just getting my head together a bit and then I was going to tell you.'

'We know about Dad's affairs, Mum,' said Alex.

'Oh God!' said Annie. 'Really? How?'

'Er, we're not stupid,' said Peter. 'We've known for years.'

'Years? Oh God!' Annie groaned again. 'I am so sorry.'

'What are *you* sorry about?' asked Alex.

'I'm sorry that you found out,' said Annie. 'You were children. Children shouldn't have to deal with their parents' shit.'

'Like I said,' said Peter, 'we weren't stupid.'

'Of course you weren't,' said Annie. 'I was the stupid one.'

'Shit happens,' said Alex.

'What a fabulous way to sum up your childhood,' said Annie. Her head was pounding like someone was trying to remove the top of her skull with a melon-baller. 'You'd better start making a parental snag-list and I'll pay for your counselling.'

'Already started,' said Alex.

'It wasn't all bad,' said Peter in a way that was meant to sound reassuring.

'Urrgh,' said Annie. 'This is a nightmare. I'm stuck in a nightmare!'

'Don't get hysterical,' said Alex. 'Sooner or later everybody's parents drop off their pedestal. It's the natural order of things. Helps to make you grow up. Dad just fell off his a little earlier than most.'

'When did I fall off mine?' asked Annie.

'You haven't yet,' said Peter.

'But we remain hopeful,' added Alex.

'We're hoping for something spectacular!' said Peter. 'A drug-fuelled sex orgy with a priest or something.'

'Blimey!' said Annie.

'Let loose, Mum!' said Alex. 'Get pissed. Get a tattoo! Do something just for you.'

'The world won't stop spinning if you get off the ride and walk for a while,' said Peter.

'What did I do to deserve you boys?' she asked.

'You just got lucky, I guess,' said Peter.

'We want you to know that we support your decision one hundred per cent,' said Alex.

'So, you can go easy on yourself, knowing that you don't need to worry about us,' added Peter. 'We don't come into the equation.'

'What we're saying is,' said Alex, 'don't go back. If it's permission you need, then you've got it.'

The call ended and Annie promised to keep them posted on her movements, although at the moment she couldn't envisage herself moving very far. She wondered what it was about *this* affair that had finally forced her out of impotence. The scene flashed before her in all its fleshy glory and she winced. That was why: there was knowing a thing and there was seeing a thing. Actually bearing witness to your husband cheating in full technicolour was like a sucker punch to the eyeballs; Ellie's perfect pointy nipples were going to haunt her for the rest of her days. Annie pulled the duvet back over her head and went to sleep.

Chapter 3

When she had once again exhausted the supply of tiny coffee sachets in the room, Annie went down to reception to ask for more and to book herself in for another four nights at the hotel.

'Um, do you have another card?' asked the receptionist, her cheeks blotching pink.

'Another card?' asked Annie.

'Yes. This one doesn't appear to be working.'

The receptionist handed the business bank card back to Annie. Annie was flummoxed. She knew there was money in the account – quite a bit actually.

'How odd,' said Annie and she handed over the card to her and Max's joint savings account.

The receptionist gave a hesitant little cough, her cheeks blotched darker.

'This one doesn't seem to be working either,' she said, trying not to meet Annie's gaze.

'That doesn't make any sense.' Annie took the card back and looked it over as if there might be a clue in the shiny plastic. 'I can't understand it.'

'Is there perhaps any reason why your cards might have been stopped?' asked the receptionist awkwardly.

A sudden dawning broke through the clouds of confusion in her mind and Annie came over first hot and then cold as white rage consumed her. With a calmness she didn't feel, Annie pulled out her personal credit card and handed it over.

'I'd like to use this instead, please,' she said.

As she walked back to her room, she was dizzy with anger. She called Max. He didn't answer. When his smooth, crooning voice said, '*Hey, this is Max Sharpe, leave a message and I'll get right back to you. Beep,*' it was all Annie could do not to bite the phone in half. She took a deep breath.

'You froze me out of our accounts!' she yelled into the mic. 'Unfreeze them now, Max, or so help me I'll . . .' What would she do? What could she do? 'I'll make you sorry!' she finished with what she hoped was a vague enough threat to be menacing.

She was livid. She wanted to throw things and smash stuff up, but this wasn't her house, and the furniture was nailed down. Instead, she lay prostrate on the bed and fantasised about what she'd do if she was at home right now: she'd empty his expensive aftershave down the toilet and replace it with pine floor cleaner, maybe scratch *FUCK YOU* into his vintage vinyl Smiths records with her fingernails, and very possibly fill the toes of his beloved brogues with cat food.

Annie had become pregnant with the twins at just seventeen and she and Max had married the same year. With her parents' support she was still able to enrol at catering college and do her chef's training. She got a job as a line chef in a Michelin-starred restaurant and worked her arse off to make it up through the ranks to sous chef and then head chef. It was tough but she was driven.

Max, charming, hardworking and everyone's friend, had risen quickly from waiter to manager of a successful gastro pub. In the moments when the couple weren't working or dealing with the demands of raising twin toddlers – usually in the scant time between their heads hitting the pillows and sleep – they fantasised about opening their own place. They had a lot of shared dreams once.

Annie's parents had died far too young. Although she had a family of her own by then, their deaths left her feeling like she'd been orphaned; she felt cheated by the lack of time she'd had with them. Her mum was only sixty-five when she died suddenly from an aneurysm, and her dad died soon after, of a broken heart. Annie used her inheritance to buy The Pomegranate Seed building. They lived in the flat above and built up the restaurant below, with Max managing front of house and Annie running the kitchen and doing the lion's share of the childcare.

There were times when she would cry from sheer tiredness but then Max would steal her away to the stockroom and sweep her into a Hollywood embrace, and she would be restored. Max could do that: he could make her feel like she was his entire world, and they were on an amazing adventure together. But Max's powers worked in reverse too; just as easily as his words could build her up, so too they could knock her down, so that she felt small and worthless and afraid of what she would be without him.

A restaurant critic for the *Guardian* had once described her and Max as 'a dream team' and in many ways they were. While Max schmoozed the patrons out front, Annie excited and delighted them on the plate. Glossy magazines ran features on them, and Annie was frequently asked to share recipes for special holiday issues. They had a lot going for them; far too much for Annie to throw it all away over a little thing like infidelity. *Relationships are messy*, she would tell herself, *no marriage is perfect*.

When the boys grew up and left home after university, Annie took on more work. They converted the upstairs rooms of The Pomegranate Seed (their old flat) into a coffee lounge. The restaurant opened for lunch and dinner and the coffee lounge opened from breakfast till teatime. Annie was busier than ever, and more successful than ever. She never had a moment to herself. All these things helped her swim against the current of self-doubt and kept her too tired to address the notion that her marriage had been failing almost from the time it began.

Annie breathed in and out, long slow breaths to centre herself, as she lay prostrate on the hotel bed, picking over the carcass of her marriage. Enough was enough: she'd spent too long running and going nowhere; she was jumping off this hamster wheel. There would be no more hiding, no more excuses, for her or Max. Her children had grown and flown and there would be no better time to rebuild herself. Annie had ripped the blinkers off, and she was ready to face the music.

Chapter 4

Most of the tables in the hotel restaurant were occupied by families with young children; crayons and character backpacks littered the floor and the ignorable muzak melodies were almost lost beneath their cacophony. Annie sipped her wine. She was the only woman eating alone. She didn't mind. Being by herself used to be a rare treat when the boys were small. Since they'd grown up, being by herself had become her state of being. A man in a cheap suit a few tables down, also eating alone, consistently tried to get Annie's attention, raising his glass and winking at her every time she looked down that end of the restaurant. Annie smiled weakly and ignored him. As she scoured the dessert menu, another man approached her table and asked if she'd like some company. She politely declined and the man sloped off, shrugging his shoulders, and went back to propping up the bar. She was just scraping up the last of her 'triple chocolate delight' when another man-shaped shadow fell across the table. Annie was about to insist that she *really* was more than happy to share a meal with herself, when she caught sight of the shadow's shoes: two-tone, well-worn brogues. Max's shoes.

'Hello,' said Max.

His face was all angst. He looked down at her imploringly with his big blue eyes. Annie realised she had frozen with the dessert fork halfway to her mouth. She laid it down, unable to eat the last mouthful of her pudding, which pained her slightly.

'May I sit?' asked Max.

Annie gesticulated towards the chair opposite hers and Max sat. He looked tired. Contrite. His blond hair, greying attractively at the temples, was fluffy and uncharacteristically unwaxed. His beard was almost entirely grey with flecks of white at the sides and at the edges of his moustache. She resisted the urge to stick her fork into his forehead – but only just.

'You froze me out of our bank accounts.' Annie's voice was quiet but loaded.

Max looked nervous.

'Come home and we can work it out,' he said.

'What you did cannot be *worked out*. Not this time. Unlock the accounts; that's my money too and you have no right to take control of it.'

'I was frightened. I didn't know what you might do.'

Annie took a deep breath. The couple at the next table were eating chocolate fudge cake and Annie was filled with an almost overwhelming desire to scoop it up and squidge it in Max's pleading face.

'Just unlock the accounts, Max.'

'I will, I promise. But we need to talk,' said Max.

'You had one job,' said Annie.

Max put his head in his hands. One of his elbows was resting in a splodge of ketchup. She didn't tell him.

'What did we agree after the last time?' said Annie. 'What did you promise?'

'I know. I know!' said Max from behind his hands.

'Don't fuck the staff!' said Annie.

The couple on the table to the left looked over, the woman's eyes bright with curiosity, but she swiftly returned to her mixed grill when she was met with Annie's stare.

'I'm sorry,' said Max. 'It was a slip-up. It'll never happen again. I promise.'

'You've made me look like a fool,' said Annie. 'And yourself look like an arsehole.'

'It didn't mean anything,' Max sobbed quietly. 'She's nothing!'

'That's even worse,' hissed Annie. 'That poor girl! For God's sake, Max, if you're going to ruin what little was left of our marriage, at least do it for something more than nothing.'

'What do you want me to do?' asked Max. 'Tell me what to do. Anything. I'll do it.'

'I want a divorce,' said Annie.

'No, Annie. Please. I'm sorry. I'm so sorry. Please,' said Max.

'It's over,' said Annie. 'I'm done.'

Chapter 5

When her extra nights at the hotel were done, Annie rolled over, pushed her arm out of the duvet, grabbed the hotel phone and called reception.

'Hello, how can I help you?' came a female voice.

'Oh, hello,' said Annie. 'This is Mrs Sharpe in room 208. I'd like to book another three nights in this room, please. Just charge it to the card I used for the last two bookings.'

'I'm sorry,' said the receptionist. 'This room is booked for tonight.'

'This actual room?'

'Yes.'

'You have no other spare rooms in this hotel?'

'Oh yes, madam, we have other rooms. We could move you into one of those,' said the receptionist brightly.

'No,' said Annie. 'I don't want to move. I'm already here and settled. But if the arriving guests haven't requested this actual room and all the rooms in the hotel are identical, then you could put them in the room you want me to move into and they will never even know they've been allocated a different room.'

'But we have a system,' said the receptionist, less brightly.

'But *I'm* already here and *they* won't know the difference,' said Annie.

'But *this* room is booked out,' said the receptionist.

'Look,' said Annie. 'I'm a reasonable woman. Ask anyone. Ask my cheating husband! I am the most reasonable woman you could ever hope to meet. But I am not moving from this room; you'll have to come in here and carry me out.'

'I'm just going to put you on hold, Mrs Sharpe,' said the receptionist.

Annie was treated to a tinny rendition of Beethoven's *Fifth Symphony* down the line, while the receptionist presumably decided whether to call the police or the psychiatric team. After a few minutes another voice came over the line.

'Thank you for holding, Mrs Sharpe,' said the voice. 'I'm the shift supervisor. That's another three nights in room 208 booked in for you.'

Annie thanked the patient supervisor and apologised for being a pain in the arse and explained that she had recently found her husband having sex with a waitress half his age on a velvet banquette and it was making her behave rather oddly. When she put the phone down, Annie pulled the duvet back over her greasy head and slept for another nine hours.

When she woke, there was a note pushed under the door, which read: *Delivery outside.*

Curious, Annie opened the door and found a bottle of wine and a box of chocolates with a small card attached.

Dear Mrs Sharpe,
I thought you might need these. Sorry about your cheating husband.

Best wishes,
Sally (the supervising receptionist you spoke to this morning)

Annie was deeply touched. Her eyes filled with tears. It occurred to her in that moment that she didn't really have any friends, not of her own; she'd never had time to make any. And if she had, there would have invariably been sharing and she would have had to confess that her husband was a manipulative, serial cheater, and that was a shame she preferred to keep to herself. She spent many hours a day with Marianne and they got on very well, but they'd never met each other outside of work, probably for the reasons above. She had Mrs Tiggy-Winkle, of course, but she couldn't answer back and was aloof at the best of times. As Annie stood between the compact, windowless bathroom and the built-in wardrobe, trying to ignore the smell of her unwashed body, it occurred to her that Sally, the hotel receptionist, was the closest thing Annie had to a friend and she'd only spoken to her on the phone from beneath her duvet.

Annie began to sob. And once she'd begun, she found it very hard to stop. By the time the late-night movie started, Annie was out of both tissues and tears. She opened the box of chocolates and poured the wine into the glass from the bathroom; she finished the wine before the movie ended and fell asleep with the empty tumbler still in her hand and a dark chocolate coffee cream in her mouth, which melted and dribbled down her chin and onto her stale pyjamas.

Chapter 6

Annie woke the next morning with a hangover and yet she felt lighter than she had done for several days.

She peeled off her pyjamas and stuffed them into the waste-paper basket. Then she brushed her teeth – twice – climbed into the shower and let the hot water wash away the despond-ency of recent days. She imagined the gloom personified, clinging to her skin like a rind which cracked under the shower pressure and peeled off in sheets, slipping down her body before gravity pulled it down the plughole and away.

In the midst of all the uncertainties she now faced, there was one thing of which Annie was clear: she wasn't ready to let the credits roll on her story yet. She was only forty-four, goddammit! She caught sight of herself in the mirror as she dressed. Certainly, her bottom was rounder than it used to be. And her boobs were more pendulous than pert, but all in all she wasn't in bad shape. The extra weight acted like a sort of chubby-cheek Botox which helped to plump out wrinkles that might have otherwise appeared on her face, and with a little help from her Warm Russet hair dye, she could easily pass for forty – well, maybe forty-two. Her large round eyes were the colour of warm honey; Peter said they reminded him of one of the rabbits from *Watership Down*. She had a pert nose, a heart-shaped face and high cheekbones, and her thick wavy hair hung in soft layers around her face. Annie smiled at her reflection as she pulled on fresh jeans and a jumper that still smelled of fabric softener. *Today is not a day to mope*, she said to herself. *Today is for finding somewhere to live.*

She left the hotel at lunchtime with four appointments to see flats booked in that afternoon. As she passed the reception desk, a voice called out, 'Mrs Sharpe! There's a delivery for you.'

The receptionist smiled as she produced a huge bouquet of flowers from beneath the desk. Annie smiled back graciously and thanked her. She didn't need to look at the card to know who they were from; they reeked with the stench of a Max Sharpe charm offensive.

This was how it would start: the wooing. No one did remorse like Max. He could be so utterly woe-filled that anyone would think it was he who had found his spouse bonking the accountant, the jeweller and, in this case, the waitress, and not the other way around.

He would make grand gestures and even grander promises. Alongside these, he would attack her sensibilities: what about the children? The restaurant? The house? He'd kill himself, is that what she wanted?

Their lives and livelihoods were inextricably linked, so that as a younger woman, with small children and a business to keep afloat, Annie was too exhausted to seriously consider all the logistical and emotional untangling that leaving would entail.

The first affair was the worst. After the second one, Annie retaliated with a revenge affair. It didn't last long and Max never found out about it. She'd thought about telling him, just to hurt him, but that wasn't really why she'd done it. She'd done it to even the score; it also made it easier to excuse herself for staying if they'd both cheated. The crux of the thing was, she had loved him back then.

Annie had spent long resentful nights trying to decide if a full-blown love affair was worse than a one-night stand. She came to the conclusion that the longevity of the encounters didn't matter; ultimately there was no time limit that made putting your dick in someone that wasn't your wife okay.

Though she had allowed herself to be wooed and cajoled into giving things another try, a steady erosion had begun after the first affair, and with each unaccountable lateness, unfeasible excuse or unnecessary errand which followed, the thinning of their marriage became more acute.

Annie met the estate agent outside the first flat. She had been able to pick him out from the crowd as he strode along the street towards her: his grey suit jacket, undone and flying open, tie swept back over one shoulder and the kind of swagger that suggested he'd closed seven deals before break-fast. He shook her hand and introduced himself as Phil. Phil carried a briefcase and wore an earpiece, and would spontan-eously burst out the word 'Mate!' before holding his hand up to Annie – in the manner of one stopping traffic – and launching into a conversation with the person in his ear.

The flat was essentially a beautifully decorated bedsit with a view of the pretty town below and a monthly rent that made her say 'Pardon?' twice when he told her. The second flat was situated just off the main high street. The smell of stale urine in the narrow passage that led to the front door suggested that this was a popular cut-through after pub closing time. Phil wasn't overly pleased by Annie's reticence towards his offerings and warned her that they would be snapped up by someone else if she dragged her heels. She assured him she wouldn't and that if someone else did snap it up, then it simply wasn't meant to be. Phil looked at her like she had just walloped out one breast and shaken it at him; clearly, he didn't go in much for trusting in fate.

Jackie – the second estate agent – was about Annie's age but had a far smaller bottom. Annie soon found herself telling Jackie about her marriage breakdown. It was strange: she couldn't seem to stop telling people about it. As someone who had previously been a very private person, she found it odd that she was suddenly struck with the urge to overshare with anyone who would listen. It was, she supposed, a strange kind of therapy.

The building was a grand Victorian villa, slightly run-down but not so much as to lose any of its charm. A cloud of grass smoke plumed out of the first-floor window and floated down over the two women.

'That takes me back!' said Annie.

'You and me both,' said Jackie.

'Maybe we should knock and ask for some,' said Annie.

'I can't afford the calories from the munchies that would follow,' said Jackie.

And that's why you've got the smaller bottom, thought Annie.

Before they'd even reached the second-floor flat – Jackie kept up a lively conversation as they climbed, while Annie concentrated on breathing and tried not to go into cardiac arrest – their ears were assaulted by a pounding music so loud it shook the stairwell. The two women turned on the stairs and went straight back down them.

The next flat was in a 1960s block, uninspiring but practical and close to the town.

'It's just such a big step,' said Annie.

'Not really,' said Jackie. 'Rent it for six months and see how you feel. Or rent it for six months and spend that time looking for something you'd really like. You've made the biggest leap by leaving your husband and restaurant, the rest is easy!'

'It doesn't feel easy,' said Annie.

'That's because you're thinking about it too deeply. This is a stepping stone. Six months is nothing.'

'I'll think on it,' said Annie.

'Don't think too long!' said Jackie.

Chapter 7

It was early evening and the sun was low in the sky but the air held its late summer warmth. Chairs and tables were still laid out in the street in front of the cafes and bars, and people seemed to be enjoying the after-work sun with a glass of wine and friends.

Annie sat at a round bistro table which looked out over the bandstand and the quaint little run of shops beyond. The waiter took her order, and Annie absent-mindedly picked up a discarded copy of the local paper that lay on one of the chairs.

Dusk was beginning to eddy around the patrons of the bar and Annie pulled her jacket around her shoulders. A mischievous breeze sifted through the little market square, lifting scarves and fluttering napkins. The breeze tugged at the corners of Annie's newspaper; it slipped between the pages and lifted them open. Annie looked around for something to act as a paperweight and found a flat grey pebble underneath the table. She turned it over in her hand and saw it had been painted with the words: *Everything will be all right.* She smiled. The painter could have had no idea who would find their random pebble, but it made her feel instantly better.

She was about to fold the paper back up when something

at the bottom of the right-hand column of the page caught her eye.

It was a small advertisement, outlined in bold black lines:

Winter Guardian Required

Annie read on:

> Live-in guardian required to act as custodian
> of secluded beach apartment and small (closed)
> business premises over the winter months. This is
> an unpaid position and the custodian will be
> responsible for all utilities but the rent is free.

As a woman with a serious lack of cash flow, *rent-free* was an enticing prospect.

The ad gave no address or hint as to where this secluded beach might be but there was a phone number, and Annie found herself punching in the numbers before she'd fully registered what she was doing.

'Helloo!'

'Oh, hello,' said Annie. 'I'm calling about the ad in the paper for a winter guardian?'

'Ach, how lovely!' said the woman. She had a strong Scottish accent and the kind of creamy voice that made you want to lie back and have her read you a story.

'I've had that ad in the paper for over a month!' said the woman. 'You're the first person to call. I was beginning to give up hope.'

'Well, I'm very interested in having a look.'

'Please!' said the woman. 'Please do! I'd said to myself, this is the last week I'm going to put the ad in and if nobody calls, then it's just not meant to be.'

'When can I come to view?' asked Annie.

'Tomorrow?' said the woman.

'Perfect!'

'Could you bring some I.D. and could I ask you to email me a reference, please?'

'Oh,' said Annie. 'Yes, of course.' She was sure Marianne wouldn't mind writing her a reference.

'And just a couple of bank statements, if you don't mind. It's just so that we know you're financially able to cope with the job.'

'We?' asked Annie.

'My nephew and I,' said the woman. 'He's helping me with the details.'

The apartment was at a place called Willow Bay, so-called because – according to the woman with the soft story voice, who introduced herself as Mari – a smugglers' ship named the *Willow* had sunk there in a storm in 1502. Annie was intrigued.

When Annie arrived back at the hotel, the receptionists were changing shifts. The lady relinquishing her responsibility for the front desk smiled as Annie entered the lobby and Annie saw her name badge read 'Sally'.

'Hi,' said Annie. 'I'm Annie Sharpe. Thank you so much for the wine and chocolates. It was really kind of you. It was just the tonic I needed.'

'You're welcome,' said Sally. 'There's not much that booze and chocolate can't fix.' And then, emboldened by her foray into the world of flat-hunting, Annie did something quite out of character.

'I'd like to buy you a drink,' she said. 'Have you got to rush off?'

Sally beamed at her and backed her wheelchair out from behind the desk.

'There's nothing that can't wait!' said Sally.

The conversation was easy. Annie had already blurted out most of the excruciating details of Max's infidelity over the phone to Sally, so there was no need for polite coyness now.

Annie guessed that Sally was a bit older than her, with cropped dark hair and an elfin face. As they chatted Annie discovered that Sally had been divorced twice and had a grown-up son and daughter. Her current partner was a *wonderful* woman called Susan but neither of them were keen to go down the marriage route again.

'There is nothing quite like that feeling when you find out your beloved has cheated on you,' said Sally, as they settled into their second glass of wine. 'It's like being punched in the chest. Knocks the wind right out of you.'

Annie nodded.

'And how stupid you feel!' said Annie. 'Like, how did I not know? How did our *greengrocer* guess and I didn't?'

'The greengrocer knew?'

'About the second one, yes. He kept seeing Max ducking in and out of the flat above the bank, from his shop window. He'd known my parents; I guess he felt loyalty-bound to tell me.'

'I love a loyal greengrocer,' said Sally, which made Annie guffaw into her wine. 'And yet you went back for more! I kicked my first husband out the moment I found out. That was it. Over. Nobody does that to me.'

'God, you're so together,' said Annie.

'It's not about being *together*,' said Sally. 'It's about knowing your worth. I was worth more than being cheated on. My mum drilled it into me as far back as I can remember. She said, "Sally, people are going to try to take advantage of you because of your chair. Know your worth, my girl."'

'Your mum sounds amazing,' said Annie.

'She is,' said Sally. 'Hard as nails and soft as playdough!'

'My family didn't do divorce,' said Annie. 'I mean, that's not the only reason I stayed, but my mum and dad had me much older in life and they were very religious; they believed in for better or worse like it was an actual law.'

'Screw that,' said Sally.

Annie sighed and rubbed her temples.

'I don't know,' she said. 'It was just too complicated not to be with Max. And I guess a part of me was too proud to admit that I'd failed.'

'*You* failed?' Sally spluttered. 'This is classic learned behaviour derived from societal misogyny.'

'Blimey!' said Annie.

'Unbelievable!' Sally was on a roll. 'He breaks his vows and you're the failure? This is why we need feminism. Women have been programmed since the dawn of time to take responsibility for men's failings. Stop shouldering the blame for your husband's shortcomings. In fact, let me just take that from you right now.'

Sally leaned across the table, grasped Annie by the shoulders and then let go, throwing her arms up into the air with a flourish as if she were batting away a hornet.

31

'There!' said Sally. 'I hereby remove all feelings of failure associated with your husband's roaming penis.'

Sally dusted her hands off over the side of the table, ceremonially removing any remnants of blame.

'Right!' she said. 'Gone. What's next?'

Annie gawped. It was the strangest thing, but she actually did feel as though an invisible weight had indeed been removed.

'You're amazing!' said Annie.

'Far from it,' said Sally. 'I'm just aware of the things I don't have control over: one of them is my legs, the other is people's behaviour.'

'You should do public speaking,' said Annie.

They ordered more drinks and some olives and bread to share; Annie, never normally one to miss a meal, realised she hadn't had dinner and was beginning to feel the effects of the house wine.

'So, are we talking classic shotgun wedding here?' asked Sally, spearing an olive with a cocktail stick.

'Pretty much,' said Annie. 'I had to have my dress let out three times before the wedding and even then, I looked like I was smuggling two bear cubs under my gown. Twins,' she said by way of an explanation.

'How old were you?'

'Seventeen,' said Annie.

'Wow!' said Sally. 'Married at seventeen! How very twentieth century of you.'

'What about you?' asked Annie.

'I was twenty-five,' Sally replied. 'The first time. He was thirty. We had a good run, until he started an affair with his podiatrist, silly sod. Joe, my eldest, was five when we divorced.

And then I met Pete on a single parents' holiday in Corfu. It was all a bit of a whirlwind; marry in haste repent at leisure, that sort of thing. And then along came Susan.'

'Were you always bisexual?' asked Annie. 'Oh my God, I'm so sorry, that's such a personal question. It must be the wine, I promise I'm not usually so blunt. Just forget I asked that.'

Sally laughed.

'Susan likes to say that she *turned* me,' said Sally, raising one eyebrow. 'But with hindsight I think I probably was bi. We just didn't have a name for it back then. Joe says we sound like an inclusive reading book for primary schools: *Sally and Susan Love Each Other Very Much.*'

When the bell went for last orders, Sally ordered a taxi and Annie ordered a toasted cheese sandwich and a packet of crisps to take back to her room. The women swapped phone numbers and Sally made Annie promise to tell her how she got on with tomorrow's viewing.

Annie had just settled into bed when her phone pinged with the sound of an email.

Dear Ms Sharpe,

My name is John Granger, I am Mrs Mari Chandler's nephew.

My aunt has asked me to send you directions of how to get to Saltwater Nook, which I shall detail below.

Should you decide to take up the residency agreement, I think it only fair to stress that this is a short-term arrangement. The building is being sold in the new year and your lease will not be extended. This is not a sitting tenancy and you will be expected to move out by the date provided at the time of sale.

I would ask in the meantime that you treat your guardianship of my aunt's property with due respect. I will undertake random spot checks of the property during the winter to ensure that the building is being reasonably maintained. Any action that is deemed to be in breach of this agreement will result in immediate termination of your tenancy.

I thank you in advance for your understanding in this matter.

Kind regards,
John Granger

Annie bristled. Even allowing for the fact that cadence could be tricky to interpret through text, this email felt rude. Who on earth did John Granger think he was? Who did he think she was? Some sort of serial squatter? She read the directions he had promised at the bottom of the email and somehow even they contrived to irk her. How someone could make *at the roundabout take the second exit* sound like he was telling you to kiss his arse, Annie couldn't fathom, but John Granger had managed it. Annie huffed as she reached out to turn off the lamp. 'Sitting tenant indeed!' she blustered and pulled the duvet roughly over her head.

Chapter 8

It was a bright morning and the air was charged with the woody scent of the changing season. Harvest was full upon the land and the leaves on the trees mirrored the colours of ripening squashes and pumpkins.

Annie drove out of the west Kent bustle, through the leafy Weald, with its miles of orchards and converted oast houses, towards the coast. She had never lived close to the sea, and the idea of it felt like an adventure.

She began to get glimpses of the ocean to her right: snatches of brilliant azure peeping between mossy hilltops. Annie followed the signs and found herself, at last, driving through the quaint little village of Willow Bay. Whitewashed cottages with wisteria climbing the walls, and wildflower gardens, crisped at the edges by the sun, swayed in the sea breeze. There were two pubs directly opposite one another – The Sunken Willow and The Captain's Bounty – and both had that look of charming decrepitude on the outside which promised a good home-cooked Sunday roast within. The thatched roof of The Captain's Bounty drooped significantly on one side and the wall beneath it looked as if it had been partially swallowed by the flower bed. And The Sunken

Willow, Annie thought, was most probably only held upright by the thick mass of dark green ivy which smothered three sides of the building.

The road curved sharply to the left and a sign – hand-painted – read: *Caution! Steep Hill. Check brakes!* Annie swallowed. How steep could it be?

The road narrowed as it descended. To the left of her, cottages seemed to cling to the climbing hillside, their pretty landscaped gardens trickling down to precarious driveways carved out of the crag. On her right side, dropping down away from her, were equally tenacious houses nestled in the cliff face, half shrouded by trees, their chimneys peeking out above towering rhododendrons.

Soon tarmac was replaced by the crunch of shingle as Annie pulled, at last, into a clearing at the bottom of the hill and parked, as she had been advised by Mari. She climbed out of the car and was greeted by the clack and hiss of waves on stone. A warm wind whipped her hair about her face and Annie quickly pulled it back into a ponytail.

Beyond the small parking area were several stone steps leading up to a promenade. Behind her were dunes sprouting long grass and old rockfalls which had become part of the landscape, and beyond them, a thick mass of thorny brambles scaled the hillside from where Annie had just emerged.

To the left, the promenade curved for maybe half a mile before disappearing from view around a jutting cliff.

There was a smell of warm seaweed on the breeze and Annie tasted salt on her lips. She shielded her face with her hands against the sun and followed the path round with her eyes. In the distance, set back a little from the promenade, Annie could make out a two-storey building, with a gabled roof and what looked like a fenced garden to the rear.

'Surely not!' she said to herself. 'Surely no one lives there!'

She took a deep breath of fresh sea air and began to walk along the promenade in the direction of the dwelling in the distance.

As she got closer Annie was able to pick out more details of the building. It looked like the old Victorian double-height fishing huts she'd seen on the beach at Hastings. It was cladded in black wood but as it came more into view, she could see the bottom third was exposed stone and at some point it had clearly been converted into a habitable dwelling. A tin chimney poked up through the pitched roof, which was tiled black to match the shiplapped walls. A thin wisp of grey smoke escaped the chimney and curled into the sky. Annie hurried her pace.

She could find no door on the beach side of the building, only a hatch and three large windows, shuttered and locked. The door to the side was utilitarian, the only feature the gold circle of a Yale lock with no discernible means of getting attention other than knocking. A few paces back the way she had come was a set of concrete steps, which led down from the promenade to more shingle and the garden she had seen in the distance.

Annie went down the steps and tramped alongside a peeling picket fence that had seen better days. The garden was laid with shingle but it had been cultivated to make a pretty courtyard: lavender and rosemary bushes were dotted about the space, interspersed with clumps of low-growing thyme, herbs and hebes. The spiky seed-heads of alliums on long woody stems bobbed above the shrubs like low-slung planets. The breeze picked up the scent of herbs and the familiar smells washed over Annie like a balm. A flight of stone stairs led up to a Victorian-style front door, with stained-glass panels and matching panels above the door. To one side, a piece of driftwood was attached to the wall with the words *Saltwater Nook* painted in a flowing script. This was it!

Chapter 9

Annie rang the doorbell and moved back down a couple of steps to wait. After a moment or two a high-pitched voice called, 'I'm coming!'

After three or four more minutes, there came the sound of locks being drawn back and the front door opened to reveal a tiny woman, no more than four foot six at a guess. Her long white hair was drawn up into a loose but neat bun on the top of her head and her cheeks looked like pink velvet. She smiled when she saw Annie and her pale grey eyes crinkled at the edges like crepe paper.

'Helloo, my dear!' said the woman, ushering Annie inside. 'I'm Mari. You must be Annie. And right on time too!' she trilled. 'Now, just wait one moment . . .'

Mari pulled a mobile phone out of her cardigan pocket and held it up to her face, squinting. Then she squinted at Annie. Then back at the phone.

'Lovely,' she said, putting the phone back in her pocket. 'It is you! My nephew sent me a photograph of you and I wasn't to let you in until I was absolutely sure the picture matched the person. And it does! So, come on in. I've just put the kettle on. Come, come!'

'How exactly did your nephew come to have a picture of me?' Annie asked.

'Ach, just a wee bit of interweb stalking, my dear,' Mari replied. 'Instaface or one of those other socially mediocre things you young things are all into.'

Annie was not keen on the idea of the *nephew* delving through her internet profile, but she did appreciate being lumped in with the 'young things'.

'You have a lovely garden.'

'I do what I can,' said Mari. 'It's not the easiest place to grow a garden. But the herbs have a wonderful depth of flavour; it must be the salty air.'

Annie liked Mari and her strange house on the beach instantly. She had wanted to get away from it all, and this place was away from everything.

Annie followed Mari into a long, thin whitewashed corridor, sparsely decorated, with framed photographs in black and white of bearded men in roll-neck jumpers, stood proudly beside tatty-looking fishing trawlers. A set of iron hooks held a pair of binoculars and a bright yellow sou'wester. A pair of black wellington boots and a basket lay below. Mari pointed to a pile of logs beside the door that reached the ceiling.

'You'll be needing those,' she said. 'And then some. I've already put in an order for more; Fred will deliver them near the beginning of October.'

They moved on down the corridor. Mari brushed her hand along a padlocked door on the left.

'You won't need to worry about this,' she said – a little wistfully, Annie thought. 'This used to be the tea room but I had it decommissioned a few years ago. It was just too much for me in the end. I keep it locked.'

'Did it do well?' asked Annie.

'Oh aye,' said Mari. 'It had a good run. Still, better to leave them wanting more than outstay your welcome.'

'Is there anything you'd like me to do with it while I'm here?' Annie asked. 'Do I need to check it for any reason?'

'No, dear, let it sleep,' said Mari. 'Unless there's a big storm, in which case I'd ask you to check the shutters are secured on the outside. And prop some extra sandbags against the door.'

On the far wall by the staircase was another door.

'Kiosk,' said Mari when they reached it. 'I don't open it past the first of September, until Easter. If I reopen at all,' she said quietly. 'But, if you get some sunny days near the end of the month, which isn't unheard of, and the beach looks busy, you're welcome to open up. There's a good coffee machine in there; only a year old, Italian. I have it regularly serviced, so it's all in working order. You can use the unopened coffee beans in the storeroom until you run out and then it's down to you to buy more.'

'The storeroom?' asked Annie.

Mari pointed behind her to a door under the stairs.

'Cellar,' said Mari. 'If you want to keep anything down there, keep it off the ground. If the tide rises too high, the cellar floods. It's not flooded for the last few years; not since the council started building up the beach defences each year at any rate. But I don't like to take it for granted. All this climate change makes me nervous. There's a tunnel down there, leads to an outcrop near the cliffs,' she went on. 'Used to be used by the smugglers but we bricked it up and stacked it with sandbags to try and keep the flooding at bay.'

'Smugglers! Wow!' said Annie, ignoring the part about climate change and the inference that she might get swept away. 'What a fantastic piece of history!'

'Aye, it was all blaggards and moonshiners round these parts,' said Mari. 'There's a big freezer down there with ice cream and cones on the shelf above.'

'Oh, I don't think I'll be opening the kiosk,' said Annie. 'I'm not looking to start a business; I'm trying to leave one behind.'

'Suit yourself,' said Mari. And then she added, 'There's another chest freezer down there and a smaller one, both for personal use; keep them topped up. If the winter turns bad and the hill gets cut off, you'll be glad of them!'

They climbed the stairs. Mari leaned heavily on the handrail for support, her breathing laboured; not, Annie thought, by the climb so much as by her knees, which Annie could see were causing her pain. Mari pushed open the door at the top of the stairs and ushered Annie into a bright little sitting room. A long chintz two-seater sofa sat opposite a high wing-backed armchair upholstered in a raspberry and cream tartan; a small coffee table piled high with books sat to the side of it. In one corner was a wood-burner, with a black flue which ran up the wall and through the ceiling, and in the other a small flat-screen TV sat on a leather trunk. The walls were lined with shelves which housed books, stacked higgledy-piggledy where sheer volume made neat and tidy impossible, and stuck everywhere were small yellow post-it notes with little scribbled messages.

A cushion-clad window seat was framed by two large sash windows facing out across the ocean.

'What an amazing view!' said Annie.

'Isn't it,' said Mari. 'It's never the same twice. I've lived here over eighty years and I've never tired of looking at it.'

'Won't you miss it while you're away?'

'I dare say I will. But I won't be too far from the ocean,' said Mari. 'I'm going to stay with a friend who has a house in Cornwall. It's close by the sea. Not as close as this, mind, but it's only a short walk away.'

'More of a home from home than an escape from winter,' said Annie. 'I thought you'd be off to Spain or somewhere.'

'Ah, well, maybe next year,' said Mari. 'This is a practice run. My nephew's idea really. Last winter was too much for me; there's winter and then there's seaside winter! I'm not as hardy as I used to be. Sometimes the weather was so bad I couldn't get out for a week at a time, though my friends in the village are very kind and I didn't want for anything. My friend June, in Cornwall, lives on a high street; everything's on the doorstep. It takes me an hour to climb that hill.' Mari motioned with her head towards the hillside. 'And that's on a good day. But with the January wind against you . . . Like I said,' Mari continued, almost as if Annie wasn't there. 'I'm not as hardy as I used to be. The locals kept an eye on me, along with my nephew, but I don't like fuss. I don't want to be cosseted like some decrepit creature that's past its usefulness. I want to be able to look after myself for as long as I can.'

'Still,' said Annie. 'It's nice to know people are looking out for you.'

Mari smiled.

'John's a good boy,' she said. 'I don't say he's not. But he forgets I used to change his nappy! I daresay if his mother was alive he'd be fussing over her instead. But she's not, God rest her, and sometimes his extravagance drives me to distraction. Look at those,' she said, gesturing towards the windows. 'Triple glazed! Triple! Did you ever hear the like?'

'Were the old ones draughty?' asked Annie, only just noticing that the room was bereft of any of the sounds of the blowy shore outside.

'Whistled like a sheep farmer!' said Mari. 'The draught could blow-dry your hair from the other side of the room.'

'I suppose he thought these would be warmer,' said Annie.

'Oh, they're that all right,' said Mari. 'It's like being sealed in a Tupperware! The boy is terrified I'll catch pneumonia. That's what killed my sister, you see; his mum.'

'Well, then it's understandable he'd want to keep you warm,' said Annie.

'Fuss, fuss, fuss,' was Mari's reply.

One of the shelves was taken up with framed photographs, different sizes and shapes, huddled together and fighting for space. A picture of Mari – a few years younger – looking up adoringly at a grey-haired man. And dotted between pictures of Mari and her husband were images of a dark-haired child, grinning widely throughout a pictorial history of his life: from buckets and spades and Spiderman trunks, to a twenty-something cradling a bundle of pink, to a man in his forties, arm strapped proudly around a young girl in a graduation cap. Mari saw her looking and smiled.

'That's my John,' she said. 'He was always a bonny chappie. Handsome devil, don't you think?'

Annie smiled. He wasn't her cup of tea; a bit too rugged-looking for her tastes. But there was something about his cocky grin against his dark hair and beard that made her want to smile back at the image. He was not at all what she would have imagined from his snooty email.

'He seems very nice,' said Annie, in what she hoped was the appropriate response to a proud aunt.

Mari nodded briskly as one does when a correct answer has been made and walked out of the sitting room. Annie followed her into a narrow hallway. Directly opposite the sitting room was the kitchen and further down the corridor were two more doors. The one next to the kitchen was slightly open and gave Annie a glimpse of an avocado-coloured bathroom sink. By process of elimination then, the door on the other side, next to the lounge, must be the bedroom.

Chapter 10

By now the kettle in the kitchen had begun to whistle feverishly. Mari lifted it off the hob and poured the boiling water
into the waiting teapot, which she then covered with a knitted
rainbow tea cosy. The kitchen overlooked the garden. It was
small but perfectly functional. The cupboards had been
painted a pale green and there was a little curtain in a ditsy
floral fabric strung between the two cupboards either side
of the boxy butler sink. Like the sitting room, the walls above
the lower units were shelved and covered in a hotchpotch
of mismatched crockery, cookbooks and different sized jam
jars filled with herbs and spices and stacked like an old
apothecary.

The tiles were straight out of the 1970s: bright orange
sunflowers and yellow daisies on beige and biscuit back-
grounds. But what really held Annie's attention was the black
range oven, which hummed in the corner. Mari saw her
looking.

'Beautiful, isn't she?' she said. 'As you may imagine, we
don't have mains gas here, so this little beauty heats the
house and hot water as well as cooking dinner. It's oil
fuelled; you probably saw the tank outside? John makes sure

she's serviced every year and there's a winter supply of oil being delivered next month, so even if we go into an ice age, you'll be snug as a bug till spring.'

'Wow,' said Annie. 'I've never cooked on a range before.'

'Do you cook much?' asked Mari.

'I'm a chef,' said Annie. 'Was a chef.'

Was she still a chef? Did it still count if you weren't cooking for a living? Now what was she?

A hand brushed her arm and broke her reverie.

'Are you okay, hen?' asked Mari. 'I lost you for a wee moment there.'

'Oh, crumbs! Yes, sorry,' said Annie. 'It just occurred to me, I have absolutely no idea what I'm going to do with my life.'

Mari handed Annie a mug of strong tea and offered up the sugar bowl, which Annie declined.

'Then it seems to me,' said Mari, 'that this position is just what you need. A little hiatus from the business of normality to get your head straight.'

Mari ushered Annie back into the lounge and gestured for her to sit on the sofa, while she took the armchair.

'Now, why don't you tell me what it is that has brought you here?'

It was a strange sort of interview. Mari asked a series of leading questions which Annie found herself only too willing to answer. She told Mari about the restaurant and Alex and Peter and inevitably – suffering as she was at the moment with some sort of oversharing virus – she found herself telling Mari about Max's affairs, and table nine, and the *Keep Calm and Carry On* cushion which didn't cover her usurper's perfect young breasts.

Mari listened. Too well. Annie wished Mari would intervene or cut her off, since she didn't seem able to stop by herself. But Mari sat back in her chair, nodding and drinking her tea, and said soothing things at appropriate times like, 'Aww, you poor wee thing' and, 'Goodness me, you have been through it!' And when Annie reached the point in her story where she'd answered Mari's ad in the paper – the point at which, to Annie's mind at least, her story stopped abruptly because the rest had yet to be written – she leaned back on the chair and took a long swig of tea and watched a seagull drop a pebble from a great height down onto the stones below.

'Well, dear,' said Mari. 'I feel like my little house will be safe in your hands.'

'You do?'

'Yes. I can't think of a better guardian for my home than one who's lost her own.'

'Oh, I haven't lost it,' said Annie. 'I just don't want it anymore.'

'That's the spirit!' said Mari. 'Truth be told, we're in a similar position, you and I. My nephew wants me to sell the place. Thinks a property developer would jump at the chance to get his hands on this land.'

'Surely your nephew can't force you to sell?' said Annie.

'Force isn't the right word,' said Mari. 'Like I said, he's a worrier. He'd like to see me somewhere a bit more populated. For *safety*! If he had his way, I'd be living in one of those retirement villages with twenty-four-hour warden control and a panic button around my neck.'

Annie didn't think this sounded like a bad idea. Mari had to be well into her eighties. How long could she realistically stay living somewhere this remote? All the same, Annie wondered how much of selling to a developer was for Mari's benefit and how much for her nephew's personal financial gain; beach-side land must be at a premium. Instead she said, 'Don't let anybody force you into something you don't want to do. If you don't want to sell, don't sell. Your nephew will have to respect your wishes.'

'Ach, don't you worry about me, hen,' said Mari. 'He's a big softy underneath it all. Now, I'll leave instructions on how everything works and days for bin collections and things. Paul, the window cleaner, comes the third Monday of every month and I'll leave this month's money in an envelope. I've taken the liberty of making a few notes that might be helpful with orientating yourself with the Nook. I have to write notes for myself these days . . . I get a little absent-minded . . . Now then, let me see, what else . . .'

'So, I've got the position then?' Annie asked.

'Yes, dear,' said Mari. 'I've never left my home with a guardian before, so I'm not exactly sure of the protocol.'

'I've never been a guardian before, so we're both learning new things!' said Annie. 'I won't let you down.'

'Of course you won't!' said Mari. 'How soon can you move in? I'm packed and ready to go. I had a good feeling about you. I called my nephew last night and he's coming down tomorrow to take me to the train station.'

Can't wait to bundle you off so he can sell your home from under you to property developers, thought Annie.

Mari was bustling about the little sitting room, pulling papers out of seemingly random books on shelves and stacking them in a pile on the coffee table.

'If you're leaving tomorrow,' said Annie, 'that gives me a day to get my things in order and I'll move in on Sunday, if that's okay?'

'Perfect!' said Mari. 'I wouldn't want the place left empty for too long. Being so close to the sea, the house can get a little damp if it's not lived in. But if you're moving in straight away, I can leave the range on for you.'

Mari picked a black china cat from one of the shelves, unscrewed its head and tipped a set of keys from out of its body into her hand.

'Here,' she said, dropping the keys into Annie's outstretched palm. 'They're all labelled. There's rather a lot, I'm afraid, what with the kiosk and the tea rooms, and the flat, but I like to keep them all locked, you see, for extra security. These are my only spares. I've got a set, John has a set and now you have a set. He may pop in from time to time just to see you're okay,' Mari went on.

'It'll be nice to meet him,' Annie lied. 'He obviously means a great deal to you.'

'He's a good boy,' said Mari. 'He's been like a son to me. Now, I'll leave my number in Cornwall and my nephew's number with the instructions,' said Mari.

Annie smiled and thanked her while Mari continued to fuss around the small sitting room.

'You can park by the garden fence; that's what John does,' Mari went on. 'He's got one of those four-by-four thingamies, makes light work of the shingle.'

'That's very kind of you,' said Annie. 'Thank you.'

She drank the last bit of her tea and stood to leave.

She put out her hand and Mari took it. Her hand felt small

and frail in Annie's; the skin was loose around the slender bones and her fingertips were rough from a lifetime of hard work. Annie found herself feeling protective of this slight, elderly woman and the home that she held so dear.

Mari stood and watched Annie to the garden gate.

'Good luck!' Mari called. 'And bring jumpers!'

Annie smiled and waved.

'Don't worry about a thing!' she shouted back.

She felt pleased with herself and – dare she say it – really quite positive about the next few months. She had just bought herself some time to decide what she would do next, and not having to pay a deposit or a month's rent in advance was excellent news for her credit card.

The breeze teased some wayward strands of hair loose from her ponytail and Annie felt like a romantic heroine, embarking on an adventure. She felt inclined to have a little gallop – there was, after all, no one around to see her – so she thrust her arms out to the side and let the wind ruffle her bingo wings as she erupted into a kind of lolloping jog. She would *find herself* in this place by the sea; how could she possibly not in such perfect, dramatic surroundings? Her spirits soared. 'This is the start of something wonderful!' she shouted. A seagull swooped in low, coast-bound from the ocean, chanting its unmistakable song of the sea, and shat on her head.

Chapter 11

Having used a whole pocket pack of tissues, Annie's hair was still very much stuck together with cack as she revved her engine all the way up the hillside and pulled into the car park of The Sunken Willow.

The landlord looked up from his newspaper as she entered the bar.

'Shat on?' he said.

'Very much so!' Annie replied.

A woman sat at the far end of the bar, nursing a pint of ale. She looked up from her book and over her glasses and said, 'Happens to the best of us.'

Annie smiled uncertainly.

'I'll just go and clean up a bit, and then I'd like to order some lunch, if that's all right?' said Annie.

The landlord, a tall bespectacled man with grey thinning hair, nodded and pointed towards a sign which read *Mesdames*.

'Thank you,' said Annie.

A broad black woman in a billowy orange blouse with a clichéd barmaid cleavage emerged from a doorway behind the bar and stood beside the landlord. Her long black weave was pulled up and wound around her head in two mounds like a cottage loaf. She looked at Annie.

'Shat on?' she said.

Annie grimaced.

'Yes,' she said. 'I'm just going to clean up a bit.'

'Wait on,' said the woman. She ducked back out of the door and returned seconds later with a bottle of shampoo and a towel, which she handed over the bar to Annie.

'Residential hazard,' she said. 'I always keep a bottle of shampoo handy for the afflicted. I'm Pam,' said the woman. 'Landlady. That there is my husband Bill. And propping up the bar is our daughter, Emily, on her lunch break.'

The woman in the glasses raised her pint and nodded in Annie's direction, her impressive afro bobbing gently of its own accord.

'Now off you pop,' said Pam. 'And get that shit off your bonce and we'll talk about getting you some lunch.'

'Thank you,' said Annie. 'Thank you so much. I feel disgusting! I'm Annie, I'm going to be looking after Saltwater Nook—' She didn't get to finish.

'You're the lady Mari found!' said Pam.

Annie had been under the impression it was she who had found Mari, but she smiled and said, 'Yes.'

'It'll be strange without her here,' said Pam. 'She's been here longer than most and outlived the rest. But it can be rough down there and she'll be better off with a friend to share the winter days. You know the history of the place, don't you?'

Annie was distracted; she touched her hand to her head and felt her hair hardening. Pam saw her and threw her arms in the air.

'Oh, look at me!' she said. 'Talking about history when you've got a head full of shit!' And Pam bustled Annie round to the ladies' toilets and pushed her inside.

'You'll have to wash it in the sink,' she called as she backed out the door. 'But it's a good size and you'll dry off quick enough if you park yourself by the range to eat.'

The range did indeed kick out some heat and Annie's hair dried while she tucked into a bowl of homemade mackerel pâté and half a loaf of toasted sourdough. She messaged the boys her new address on their group chat.

Do you need a hand packing? asked Peter.

What about moving all your stuff in? asked Alex. You can't get everything in your little car. You'll be backwards and forwards all day.

I'll be fine, Annie reassured them. I'll only take what I need. The place is fully furnished, so it's just a case of packing a few clothes really.

You can't move all by yourself, Peter wrote. That's miserable. Let us come and help you. Alex, is Greg around at the weekend? We could use his muscle.

Greg was Alex's partner.

No, he's got a rugby tournament. You'll have to make do with weedy me.

Honestly, boys, Annie typed. I'll be fine. It's no big deal. You can come down in a couple of weekends and see the place when I'm settled in. xx

Next, she had to speak to Max. She didn't want to speak to Max. But she needed to go to the house and pack and she wanted to make sure he wasn't home.

'You've found a place?' Max sounded surprised.

'Yes.'

'Already?'

'Yes.'

'Where is it? Is it close by?' he asked.

'You don't need to know where it is,' said Annie. 'It isn't close by.'

'What if there's an emergency?' said Max.

'You've got my phone number; if there's an emergency, I'm pretty sure you'll call me rather than come around to my house to tell me! Have you spoken to the bank about the accounts?'

'I'm working on it.'

'Work harder.'

'It all feels so final,' said Max.

'Divorces usually are,' said Annie.

'Don't say that word!' said Max. 'Take the time you need but don't say it's over. Please, Annie. I can make this right.'

'You can't make this right, Max. Just . . . just please be out while I pack.'

Annie closed her eyes and rubbed her temples with her free hand. She didn't feel like a romantic heroine anymore. She felt the full weight of her middle-aged life hanging from her shoulders like wet sandbags.

As she was paying at the bar, Emily came to stand beside her.

'You're moving into Saltwater Nook,' she said.

'Yes, I am, on Sunday.'

'Are you friend or foe?'

'I'm sorry?'

55

Emily slid a flyer along the bar to Annie, entitled SAVE SALT-WATER NOOK AND RECLAIM YOUR HISTORY.

'It should belong to everyone,' said Emily. 'No one person should get to decide what happens to our joint history. There are two choices: stand for what's right or stand with John Granger.'

Emily's focus on her was intense and Annie could feel herself shrinking from her steady glare.

'Um, I don't really have an opinion right now,' said Annie tactfully. 'Until yesterday I didn't know Willow Bay existed, let alone Saltwater Nook. I'm afraid you'll have to do without my input for the time being.' She smiled, hoping to pacify Emily's fervour.

Emily seemed to accept this. She nodded towards the flyer.

'Make sure you read it,' she said. 'You're involved now. There's no room for sitting on the fence.'

Annie left, having promised to do her homework, and wondered what she had got herself into. *Too late to back out now*, she thought. And besides, where else was she going to find a place to live that didn't require rent?

Chapter 12

The house was empty as promised when Annie let herself in on Saturday morning. The familiar smell of Max's aftershave hung in the air and the foot towel in the bathroom was still damp, so he hadn't been gone long. She hadn't loved Max as a wife should for a long time, but in twenty-six years she had grown accustomed to him: to his little ways, his scent, his coughing in the mornings, his snoring gently reverberating through the bedroom wall.

After the second affair, they had taken separate bedrooms; Max's need to wrap himself around her as they slept was no longer adorable and his farting in bed had lost its charm. They'd still had sex occasionally, but Annie told herself that she was merely using him as a tool to satisfy her primal urges.

Mrs Tiggy-Winkle stretched out on the bed while Annie packed.

'I'm sorry to leave you, Tiggs,' she said. 'Let me get sorted and I'll come back for you. I think you'll like your new home, there are plenty of places to explore. You'll be a seaside cat instead of a town cat, how do you like that?'

Mrs Tiggy-Winkle rolled onto her back and stretched before pulling herself back into a coil and going to sleep.

With the last box loaded into the car, Annie took one final look around the place. She heard the key turn in the lock and the front door close softly. *Oh shit!* she thought. Mrs Tiggy-Winkle, who had been padding along beside Annie on her farewell tour, retreated into the airing cupboard.

'Coward,' said Annie as Tiggs's ginger tail disappeared between the louvre doors.

She heard Max's footsteps walking from room to room downstairs and finally the creak of the tread on the stairs. He saw her and planted himself at the top of the stairs, one hand on the wall, the other gripping the newel post, casually blocking her exit.

'I couldn't let you leave without saying something,' he said. 'And now I don't know what to say.'

'I think it's all been said before.'

'I guess I'd always hoped we'd find each other again,' said Max.

'Not in the places *you've* been looking,' Annie retorted.

Max looked at the carpet.

'I don't want to fight,' he said. 'I came to tell you again that I'm not giving up on us. We've been through too much. You hate me now and I don't blame you, I hate me too. But I'm going to make it right.'

'I don't hate you, Max,' said Annie. 'Hate requires much bigger feelings than I have for you. And you can't make this right. It's too broken. Let's just move on with our lives and stop pretending we shouldn't have called time on us ten years ago.'

'Did you say goodbye to Tiggs?' asked Max.

'Yes,' said Annie. 'I'll come back for her in a few weeks.'

'You can't take her,' said Max.

'What do you mean, *I can't take her*? She's my cat!'

'She's my cat too,' said Max.

'You don't even like her!'

'I do like her,' said Max. 'She just doesn't like me. Maybe we'll bond over your desertion.'

'You deserted our marriage long before I did!' said Annie, her hackles rising. This was precisely why she hadn't wanted to see Max.

'I don't want to do tit for tat with you,' said Max quietly. 'It's painful enough without petty insults adding to the sting.'

It was remarkable how Max always managed to climb up to the moral high ground even when his ethics were in sinking sand. Annie concentrated on breathing and resisting the urge to push Max down the stairs.

'You don't want to do tit for tat?' she asked incredulously. 'I leave you because you cheat and so you freeze me out of my own bank accounts. I'd say you are well and truly in tit for tat territory!'

'I'm trying to undo it. I've been calling the bank to get it reversed. It'll take a bit of time.'

'Let me pass,' said Annie in exasperation.

Max didn't move. She could feel his eyes on her.

Her heart pounded. She didn't look at him. It was a familiar fear. She'd always told herself that his behaviour wasn't abusive because he didn't hit her. But deep down she knew that was wrong. Max's psychological manipulation was insidious – he might not leave bruises but that didn't mean there weren't scars. She had to make a stand.

'Let me pass, Max,' she said again. 'This isn't going to make it any easier. I'm not going to change my mind.'

Max dropped his hand and moved aside to let her pass.

'I'll kill myself!' said Max as Annie started down the stairs.

She'd been expecting it but it still winded her when it landed. Annie breathed deeply and turned slowly to look up at him. She couldn't be shackled by his threats any longer. It wasn't fair. He'd been using those three little words on her like a cattle prod for as long as they'd been together, and each time he said them Annie would let herself be lassoed back into the pen, for fear of the consequences. She couldn't let herself be held to ransom any longer. She'd paid enough.

With as much calm as she could muster, Annie looked him in the eye and said, 'This is on you, Max. You are responsible for your own actions. If you kill yourself, you will devastate your children and probably be the death of your mother. But your blood won't be on my hands.'

The forcefulness of her words shocked her. Max stared down at her, his expression stunned and confused. Annie held his stare, trying to fix her face into something that resembled unmovable resolve. It wasn't easy with her heart thundering against her ribcage. Max broke away first and Annie turned, unsure whether her quivering legs would be able to carry her down the stairs. Her hand trembled as she felt for the bannister, gripping it hard to steady herself. She fumbled with the front door; the air felt as though it was being sucked out of the hallway. The catch gave and Annie stumbled out of the house, pulling the door shut firmly behind her. She pulled the fresh air into her lungs and propelled herself towards her car.

She sat for a moment, gathering herself, breathing shakily. She'd done it. He'd pulled out his trump card and she'd called him on it. For a moment she was hit with a wave of sickness and her hand was on the door handle, ready to go back into the house and leave things better, to placate him, to check that he wasn't gathering all the tablets in the house just to spite her. But she breathed through the initial panic and it passed.

Chapter 13

Annie pulled up outside The Pomegranate Seed and steeled herself for her second emotional wrench of the day: saying goodbye to her staff. The hum of voices and growl of the coffee machine from above signified that the coffee lounge was in full swing with its morning revellers. The restaurant was quiet, aside from the clink of glasses as the bar staff prepared for service.

Annie walked on down to the kitchen. She heard the hive of activity before she saw it. The radio blasted out tunes and Marianne blasted out orders above it. Annie's stomach gave a twang. She would miss this. She would miss the chaos and the mania; that fire that whooshed through your veins as the orders came in one after another after another, until you felt like you would drown in dockets. That camaraderie that only comes with all of you working together, with diligence and speed, sweating and cursing and laughing at the face of the mountain you've yet to climb.

She stood outside the kitchen. Listening. Knowing instinctively what was happening on the other side of the wall: what had been prepped and what was yet to do, where on the list of chores and tasks they were at this exact time of the day.

As she soaked in the sounds of her kitchen for the last time, a feeling of completeness came over her. She had instigated the activity within; she had taken a bare room and filled it with her passion and chosen other people whose passion matched her own to help her bring her ideas to fruition. She had designed and nurtured every element and now it was full grown; an independent body which ran by itself, because of her. She would miss it. But she could leave knowing that she had made something durable enough to go on in her absence.

Her entrance into the kitchen was met with hugs and high spirits. She gave her team one last pep talk and read them the riot act.

'I may not be here in body,' she said as they gathered around, just as they used to for the morning briefing. 'But this joint is still my baby and I expect you guys to keep it going for me. And I will be checking up on you!'

There were 'ooh's and 'ahh's at this.

'So that means no cutting corners with the flaky pastry; I'm looking at you, Flash!' said Annie, pointing to a tall gangly youth with a tattoo on his cheek. Flash grinned and pretended to look about for someone else she might be talking to.

'Or rushing the caramelised onions,' said Annie. She moved her gaze to a spotty sous chef who blushed and giggled. 'What is our onion mantra?'

'*The slower the sweating, the sweeter the onions!*' came the chorus.

'And don't cook the shit out of the vegetables,' said Annie. 'Say it with me!'

'Snap, not pap!' came the military-style response before the team dissolved into laughter.

After she had dismissed her chefs back to their work stations, she and Marianne went over the final copy of the autumn menu.

'It should be him going,' said Marianne.

'Don't complain,' said Annie. 'You've got a promotion out of it!'

'Yeah, but still,' said Marianne.

'I'm looking forward to some time out,' said Annie. 'I need it. It'll be good for me.'

The morning was sunny with the faintest nip in the breeze. Annie had checked out of the hotel so early that the night staff were still on reception. She was sad not to have seen Sally before she left, but she had her number and was determined to use it.

She arrived in Willow Bay while the residents were still enjoying a Sunday lie-in. The two pubs were dark and quiet and squirrels and blackbirds had appropriated the beer gardens.

Annie meandered down and around the steep hill in second gear, acutely aware that her car was three times heavier than the last time she'd driven down it. As she rounded the corner at the bottom of the hill, she saw a car already parked in her spot beside Saltwater Nook's garden.

Oh hell, she thought. Surely Mari's nephew wasn't here to check up on her already? But as she drew closer, slowly negotiating the car along the shingle path, she recognised Peter's old Honda Civic and her heart leaped. She swallowed hard in an effort to push down the lump in her throat and blinked quickly to clear the tears that were making her vision wobble.

Alex and Peter unfolded their long legs from the small car, stretching and yawning as the sea breeze snapped at their shirts. They were non-identical twins, but unmistakably brothers. Both boys had dark hair and big eyes like Annie, but they'd been blessed with their father's height and chiselled features. Alex wore his hair cropped short; his black beard was professionally trimmed with neat sharp lines that framed his cheekbones. By contrast, Peter's shoulder-length hair was a mass of dark curls that whipped about his face in the wind. His square jaw was hidden beneath a thick unruly beard that gave him a distinctly biblical look.

Annie's composure was lost to the wind as soon as she got out of the car. She hugged them each in turn and they mocked her tears as she knew they would. On the back seat of Peter's car she saw her patchwork quilt, the bread maker, the slow cooker and her red enamel Le Creuset casserole dish: beloved things she'd reluctantly had to leave behind due to lack of space in her car.

'How did you . . . ?' Annie began.

'We spent the night with Dad,' said Peter. 'Got a takeaway after service. He helped us pack your things.'

'Really?' said Annie.

'I think he's trying to be a gracious loser,' said Alex.

'I see,' said Annie, instantly suspicious.

'How on earth did you find this place?' asked Alex. 'It's in the middle of bloody nowhere.'

'Don't you like it?' asked Annie, turning away from the wind and pulling her hair into a ponytail.

'He's craggy because there were no independent cafes open for him to get an artisan coffee,' Peter mocked.

'You can't walk twenty paces in Soho without finding somewhere that serves coffee at any time of the day,' said Alex.

'We managed to find a Costa open in Dover,' said Peter. 'I thought Alex was going to weep with relief.'

'I can't deal with the morning without at least a double-shot macchiato inside me,' said Alex. 'And since someone had taken the coffee machine' – Alex looked pointedly from Annie to the sleek black and silver machine on the back seat of her car – 'I had to make do with some instant shite that Dad found in the back of the cupboard.'

Peter raised his eyebrows. 'Looks like someone needs another coffee,' he said.

'When did my babies become such big-city sophisticates?' Annie asked. 'Whatever happened to the little boys who liked to dance around the lounge to "Livin' la Vida Loca" in their Ninja Turtle underpants?'

'Alex still does,' said Peter.

'At least I wear underwear,' said Alex.

'Okay,' said Annie. 'Let's get this stuff up to the flat and I'll make you both some coffee. I haven't been to the shops yet, so I've got no food to offer you, I'm afraid.'

'We bought almond croissants,' said Peter.

'Perfect,' said Annie.

Chapter 14

'Woah!' Peter exclaimed as one by one they huffed and puffed into the flat laden with boxes and bags. The lounge seemed even smaller with the twins stood in it. 'That view is awesome,' Peter continued.

'Oh my God, Mum,' Alex called from the kitchen. 'This kitchen is seriously retro-chic.'

Peter joined him, setting down the coffee machine and plugging it in, while Annie checked the cupboards for mugs.

'Or is it that it hasn't been decorated since the seventies?' asked Peter.

'You have very little appreciation of style,' said Alex.

'I disagree,' said Peter. 'My style is just different to yours.'

'Hobo-chic?' said Alex.

'Unpretentious,' said Peter. 'Just because my flat isn't a carbon copy of *House Beautiful* magazine . . .'

'I'm surprised you've even heard of *House Beautiful*,' said Alex.

'I've seen it on your poncy velvet coffee table,' said Peter.

'That's a footstool, you neanderthal,' said Alex.

'You both have lovely taste,' said Annie, handing each of them a mug of coffee. 'Life would be very dull if we were all the same.'

'That's been your stock response to every argument since we were born,' said Peter, smiling. Alex grinned and took a swig of his coffee.

'And there is still barely a situation it doesn't apply to,' said Annie. 'Now, drink up and help Mummy move into her new bachelorette pad.'

Alex and Peter grimaced, and Annie laughed. She realised how much lighter her heart felt just from seeing them. In the spring they would turn twenty-seven and Annie found it hard to comprehend that she had children who were close to thirty years old, when in her head she was still twenty-four. Alex was a graphic designer and serial monogamist, living in a minuscule but trendy flat in Soho with Greg, the latest love of his life. Peter worked as a gardener at Eltham Palace and lived in a shared house in Greenwich. His girlfriends were so frequent and fleeting that Annie had stopped bothering to learn their names. Her sons were intelligent, successful men in their own right. But when they were together, particularly when they were with Annie, they seemed to revert back to their child selves, squabbling and sparring for her attention.

It didn't take long to move in. The killer was lugging the boxes up the stairs to the flat several times over. Alex had bitched and whined so much on his third ascent that Annie had considered gagging him with his linen scarf. Peter jogged up and down with apparent ease, which did nothing to promote good humour in his brother. At eleven o'clock, they stopped for a break and Annie was grateful for the almond croissants. Although, as it turned out, Mari had very kindly stocked the fridge with milk, cheese, a bag of samphire, bacon, ham, hummus and tofu. The two drawers at the bottom of the fridge brimmed with vegetables and salad. A yellow post-it note stuck to the top shelf read:

> *To get you started. Wasn't sure if you were a normal person or one of those vegans, a lot of young people are these days, so I thought I'd hedge my bets!*

By mid-afternoon, Annie's clothes were hanging in the single wardrobe and the quilt, sewn by her mother, was draped over the small double bed. With her make-up and toiletries hidden away in the bathroom cabinet and a few framed photographs of the boys strategically placed in spaces which weren't occupied by books or vintage china, Annie put the kettle on the stove and surveyed her new home.

'Not bad, eh, boys?' she said.

'It's perfect, Mum,' said Peter.

'Just the place to recoup and regroup,' said Alex.

'So, who's for tea and bacon sarnies?' Annie asked.

'Sorry, Mum,' said Peter. 'We've really got to get going.'

'I promised Greg a roast dinner after his rugby tournament,' said Alex. 'And Peter's got a date.'

'The ballerina didn't make the cut then?' said Annie.

Peter grinned sheepishly and shrugged his shoulders.

'You know me, Mum,' he said.

Annie rolled her eyes.

She was always sad to see them go. But today had been an unexpected bonus and so she couldn't complain. Still, the flat felt empty when they were no longer filling the space with their long limbs and witty commentary.

Annie ran her hands over the bumpy walls of her new, very old home. 'Hello, Saltwater Nook,' she whispered. 'I'm your new guardian.'

Chapter 15

The sun was high in the sky, glinting off the water like a million silver knife tips and pouring in through the lounge window. Mari had left the flat spotless. Upon inspection of the cupboards Annie found tins, chutneys and dried goods: pearl barley, red lentils and rice. There was another post-it note stuck to one of the cupboard fronts:

There's plenty of fish in the freezer downstairs. If you are a fish eater, please use it. Ely calls once a week with his catch. You don't have to buy but I can never say no.

Intrigued, Annie made her way downstairs and down again to the cellar. She had the sense that were she to lick the cold stone walls, they would taste salty. She resisted the urge to test this theory, though she cooled her hot red cheeks by turns against the cold stone and wondered about installing a chair and a lamp down there for when her perimenopausal hot flushes became too much to bear. Annie tugged the light pull and the arch-ceilinged cellar became dimly illuminated. A white salt line ran around the bottom two layers of stones

71

in the wall. The plug sockets were all placed above head height and the freezers and free-standing cupboards stood on brick-built perches, two feet off the ground. To the left of the staircase, a pile of sandbags gave away the location of the old tunnel entrance. The arched stone frame remained but the middle had been filled with much newer red brick. Annie's curiosity twitched to see the old smugglers' tunnel beyond the wall.

The freezer was bounteously stocked with local fish such as speckled pollock, orange-spotted plaice and mackerel. Already Annie's mind began whirring with meal ideas. After years of creating recipes and cooking for the masses, she finally had the time to cook just for herself. By the time she finished her shifts at The Pomegranate Seed, she didn't have the energy to cook. So, while her customers enjoyed her bouillabaisse or venison in red wine with shallots and dauphinoise potatoes, Annie would often wind up with beans on toast.

The kettle was whistling furiously by the time she emerged from the cellar. As she pulled a chintzy mug down from the shelf, she noticed a yellow exercise book with *A Guide to Saltwater Nook* handwritten across the front and then below, in a different pen but the same hand, was written *For Annie*. She finished making her tea and then took herself into the sitting room.

Annie began to leaf through the book. Mari was nothing if not thorough. In addition to the instructive post-it notes that dotted every switch, appliance and cupboard, she appeared to have handwritten a manual, which advised and informed of tasks that needed to be done, month by month, around the building and garden to ensure *the smooth running of the place in winter.* The book opened with a letter, stuck into the first page with a square of sticky tape.

Dear Annie,

When I began writing this notebook I didn't have a face or a name to write it to, just a hope and a prayer that someone would read it. I suppose I wrote it as a kind of call-out to the universe; I hoped that the act of putting my thoughts to paper would work as a summoning spell, to guide the right person to us – to me and the Nook, that is. And here you are.

I hope you don't mind or find it too fussy that I have taken the liberty of writing these notes. In many ways they are as much for me as they are for you. I began writing them back in the spring, when I knew I wouldn't be spending another winter here. I did not know then who would be guardian to my little home but I hoped for someone just like you. I am lucky that way: fate has a way of knowing what I need and when.

Please don't see this as a list of rules or compulsory tasks. It is simply a guide to the things that make living here easier and, dare I say it, more pleasurable during the winter months. Adherence to it will also make my restoration to the Nook in the spring – should I decide to come back – a smoother affair but that should not make you feel under any obligation.

Take from these notes as much or as little as you wish. And feel free to add to them anything which you find useful. I am not too proud or too old to learn new tricks, though there is every chance that I may forget them as fast as I learn them!

You might want to get in a few provisions for the bairns on Halloween. The locals know that I won't be here but some might come down anyway – for the sake of tradition.

Don't let the seagulls bully you. Show them who's boss, or at least that you are their equal. They are beautiful birds when you get to know them.

Above all, take care of yourself, my dear. I think you need Saltwater Nook almost as much as it needs you. I may be an old woman but I see more than most. Fate brought you here for a reason. The rest is up to you.

With love,

Mari

Annie flicked through the pages. September seemed to be mostly battening down the hatches for the onslaught of winter: checking the paint is good on the outer shutters of the old tea room, and cleaning them of dead bugs and general dirt that may have gathered between the panes and the shutters. A general tidy-up around the garden:

Cut back any of the tender herbs you might want for drying. The woody herbs will be fine to harvest as you wish throughout the winter, though you might want to pull the sage and thyme tubs up to the porch for shelter. Cut back the lavender when the flowers have begun to dust the pebbles like lilac confetti.

A quick skim through the October pages offered further general maintenance tips about cleaning out the range and checking the fuse box, and gave the arrival dates for deliveries of oil and logs:

Sweep out the log store ready and make sure the roof hasn't sprung any leaks; wet logs are of use to neither man nor beast.

A large chunk of the October notes was devoted to Halloween, which Annie determined to read nearer the time. But for now, she decided to treat herself to a pub lunch. With a fancy for a glass of wine, or three, Annie left the car outside Saltwater Nook and decided to tackle the hill.

Chapter 16

The tide was in and white horses lathered themselves over the tips of black rocks which sat just below the surface of the waves. Beyond them, markers showed the edges of the safe swimming zone.

A few couples walked with their dogs, one or two runners passed Annie by as she walked, and she said hello to all of them, starting as she meant to go on and assuming that these would become familiar faces in the months to come.

Beyond the path that led up the hill, two fishermen had set up camp on the beach, sheltered by cliffs which arched over as if their middles had been hollowed out by a giant ice cream scoop. The fisherman in the blue knitted jumper and orange waterproof trousers stood up from his stool as Annie drew nearer, and waved.

'Halloah!' he called. 'Are you the young lass who's looking after Mari's place?'

'Yes,' Annie called back. 'I'm Annie.'

'Good to meet you, Annie,' said the fisherman. 'I'm Ely, I expect we'll be seeing a lot of each other over the next few months.'

Annie laughed.

'So, you're the man responsible for my well-stocked freezer!' she said.

'That I am,' he said. 'Plenty more where they came from if Neptune smiles favourably on us.'

Ely smiled and waved once more before resuming his seat on the tiny stool that didn't look equipped to cope with his bulk.

Annie walked on, the sharp incline of the hill becoming visible via glimpses through the trees and brambles which clung to the rocky cliff face.

'Hello there!' A tall woman with an infectious smile, alabaster skin and unfeasibly rosy cheeks came from behind Annie and tapped her on the shoulder. 'Couldn't help over-hearing your convo with Ely,' the woman went on. 'We were walking behind you, trying not to eavesdrop but ended up, you know, eavesdropping!' She was wearing a long-sleeved striped top underneath a padded gilet, skintight jeans and floral wellies.

'I'm Samantha,' said the woman. 'And this is Tom.'

Tom smiled warmly and held out a hand for Annie to shake, his other hand still holding Samantha's. Annie wondered how long they had been together. Was hand-holding one of those things that eventually got lost in the business of married life, along with kissing during sex and putting the loo seat down? She wondered if she and Max had *ever* held hands when out walking? Maybe they hadn't been one of those couples.

'We own Willow Bay Stores,' said Tom. 'Whatever you need, we stock it,' he said proudly. Tom was as long and lanky as Samantha. He wore a Barbour jacket over a check shirt, tucked into his jeans. His dark skin and jet-black hair contrasted with

Samantha's pale complexion and blonde curls; they looked more like a celebrity couple than shopkeepers.

'And we do parcel drop-offs and collections,' added Samantha.

'Good to know,' said Annie. 'I'm Annie. You probably heard, I'm looking after Saltwater Nook for Mari over the winter.'

'She's an amazing lady,' said Samantha.

'Absolute legend!' added Tom.

'How are you settling in?' asked Samantha.

'Good, I think. I literally just finished unpacking, so I guess the verdict's still out. I'm just off to one of the pubs to get some dinner.'

'Oh!' said Samantha. 'The Sunken Willow stops dinner at three o'clock, you'll never make it in time!' Samantha looked stricken.

'And The Captain's Bounty doesn't start serving till six o'clock,' added Tom.

'Oh, damn,' said Annie. 'I really fancied a roast too.'

'Wait a mo,' said Samantha brightly. 'I'll call Pam.'

Samantha whipped out her phone.

'Hi, Pam,' she trilled down the phone. 'I'm with Annie, the lady who's looking after Mari's place . . . Oh, did she?' Samantha laughed. 'It's happened to us all.'

Annie guessed Pam was telling Samantha about her bird-shit-hair incident.

'Listen,' Samantha continued. 'Would you mind putting a roasty dinner by for her? She's not going to make it up the hill before you stop serving. Great!'

She turned to Annie, still with the phone to her ear.

'Chicken or pork?' Samantha asked.

'Um, pork, please,' said Annie.

'Did you hear that?' Samantha said into the phone. 'All the trimmings?' Samantha looked at Annie again.

'Yes please,' said Annie. She didn't know what all the trimmings entailed but she figured she'd be wanting them by the time she'd climbed the hill.

'Brilliant. Thanks, Pam, you're a superstar!' said Samantha.

'Legend!' Tom called into Samantha's phone.

Samantha slipped her phone back into her pocket.

'All done,' she said. 'It'll be waiting for you when you get there.'

'At The Sunken Willow,' added Tom.

'Thank you so much,' said Annie. 'That was really kind of you.'

'If you want to throw yourself into village life, the pubs are the best place to start,' said Tom. 'They're kind of the heart of the community.'

'And our shop is its arteries,' added Samantha proudly.

'We came down from London three years ago and I can't think of anywhere else I'd rather be,' Tom said, and Samantha nodded in agreement.

'Welcome to Willow Bay!' Samantha trilled as they headed down a set of steps and onto the beach.

Chapter 17

Annie began to climb, crossing driveways that snaked down to the houses hidden in the hillside.

Within minutes she was sweating and panting. She peeled off her jumper – a charming fair isle affair, in olive greens and dusky pinks that she had felt suited her new position of intelligent, financially secure (when she got her money back) single woman of a certain age living on the coast – and tied it round her waist. The cool air felt wonderful as it landed on her damp neck.

The gulls' cries still dominated the skies but here they were joined by the chirrups of other birds: the warbling coos of woodpigeons and doves, the sharp, high-pitched whistle of starlings, jostling for position in the trees above.

There was a smell of woodsmoke in the air and somewhere, in one of the gardens hidden behind the dense wall of yellowing rhododendrons, someone was listening to a tinny radio.

Annie's shadow bobbed along ahead of her, as if encouraging her to keep going. No wonder it took Mari an hour to climb this hill, she thought. The trees here arched over and sheltered Annie from the sun, and the dappled light that filtered through picked out golds and reds in the smattering of leaves on the ground. After another five minutes, Annie reached the summit of the hill and stood with her hands on her hips. She felt triumphant. She looked at her watch; it had taken her forty minutes. She mentally challenged herself to have smashed that time out of the park by the time she left Willow Bay next spring.

The change from high summer to autumn was reflected in the busy front gardens. Japanese anemones waved for attention, craning their cherry-blossom pink heads above the spent nigella flowers. Reedy hollyhocks listed drunkenly, their blousy blooms replaced with brown papery seed-heads that looked as though they would jangle like morris dancer bells if you shook them.

Annie thought about her kitchen garden back at The Pomegranate Seed. The squash would be ripe, the courgettes all but finished. The new menu would be in full flow. She would miss pulling the parsnips for winter soups and stripping the sprout trees for the hundreds of Christmas dinners they would cook in December. But she had weathered change before: when her parents had died, so close together in time that the pain was still raw when the next wave of grief crashed over her. When the boys went off to uni and later when they truly left home to begin careers and build their own lives. Yes. She had experienced greater upheavals than the loss of a kitchen garden. Strange, she thought, that these were the things she missed and not the husband she had equally left behind.

The Sunken Willow was significantly busier than it had been on Annie's last visit. It was dark and invitingly warm. The smell of the open fire mixed with the rich scents of roasting meats and the earthy notes of cauliflower cheese made Annie's stomach growl.

Annie spotted Pam's ample cleavage at the pumps through a gap in the crowd before she saw her face. One of the patrons moved his head and Pam's face came into view. Pam met her eyes.

'Annie roast pork!' Pam called.

'Hi!' said Annie.

People were beginning to notice the stranger in their midst and Pam, sensing her patrons' curiosity, said loudly, 'Everybody, this is Annie. She's looking after Mari's place for the winter.'

This announcement was met with lively greetings, glasses raised in her direction and multiple offers of drinks. Annie smiled and said, 'Thank you', took rain checks on drinks and hoped that the population of Willow Bay didn't think her surname was 'Roast-Pork'.

'Emily, love. Do me a favour and take Annie round to the restaurant, would you?' Then she turned back to Annie. 'Emily will take you round and Bill will bring your dinner out in a minute. What can I get you to drink?'

Annie was parched from her walk up the hill.

'I'll have a large glass of Zinfandel and a pint of iced tap water, please,' said Annie.

'Right you are,' said Pam. 'I'll bring it through.'

Annie followed Emily through the bar, down a couple of steps and into what must have been the oldest part of the pub, judging by the lilt of the stone walls, which served as the restaurant. Families were finishing up their puddings and sipping coffees.

Emily stopped at a table situated in a nook by the window. Annie slid onto the bench, festooned with cushions embroidered with stag heads and thistles. To her surprise, Emily took the Windsor chair opposite her.

'Did you have a chance to read the pamphlet yet?' she asked.

Dammit! thought Annie. What with the move, she'd completely forgotten where she'd even put it.

'Oh dear. Sorry, no, I haven't.'

Emily shuffled her chair so that her legs were fully under the table and folded her arms.

'There's a lot of history in Saltwater Nook,' said Emily. 'And the bay,' she added.

'So Mari said,' Annie replied. 'She didn't have time to tell me much. It was all a bit of a blur really: her moving out, me moving in.'

'You know he wants her to sell the place?' said Emily.

'Who?' asked Annie.

'John, her nephew,' said Emily.

'She mentioned it,' said Annie, non-committally.

Emily leaned back in her chair.

'This is the first winter Mari has spent away from the bay since she arrived here as a thirteen-year-old runaway,' said Emily.

'Goodness!' said Annie. She wasn't entirely sure what response Emily was looking for.

'Whose idea do you think that was?' Emily surveyed Annie through her horn-rimmed spectacles, her fingers tented in front of her face.

'Hers,' said Annie. 'She told me she couldn't face another winter here.'

'That's what she told you,' said Emily. 'But how do we know he didn't cajole her into leaving?'

Annie had to admit this thought had passed through her mind.

'And what would be his reason for that?'

'To get her out of the way!' said Emily. 'Distract her with a holiday and then BAM!' Emily smacked her hand down on the table, making Annie jump in her seat. 'Get her to sign away the deeds to her house. Goodbye, historical gem. Hello, overpriced boxy beachside apartments, sports cars and *The Real Housewives of Willow Bay*!'

'Now, now, Emily,' said Pam.

Pam set Annie's wine and water down on the table. Annie swigged gratefully from first the water then the wine and then the wine again. Emily was rather an intense welcome party.

'Emily runs the Willow Bay library, just down the road. And the local history society,' said Pam.

'We can kiss our history goodbye if Granger gets his way!' said Emily.

'Don't you be filling Annie's head with your conspiracy theories,' said Pam. 'John's a good man.'

'Doesn't change the fact that a massive piece of Willow Bay history will be lost!' said Emily.

'I don't say it won't be a tragedy,' said Pam. 'But it's not in our hands.'

'Isn't the building listed?' asked Annie.

Bill arrived with Annie's dinner. Curls of meat-scented steam rolled up from the plate and Annie's mouth watered.

'Mari never applied for listed status because she didn't want local government to have an opinion on things she might want to do to her own property,' said Pam.

'Which means whoever she sells it to can knock it down without repercussion,' said Emily. 'The plain fact is that history should belong to everyone, not just one person. Our campaign is to have Saltwater Nook turned over to the historical society. We will maintain it for generations to come and turn it into the Willow Bay museum.'

'Is there much call for a Willow Bay museum?' Annie asked.

Emily eyed her like a tiger about to pounce on a deer and Annie got the distinct impression she had managed to make an enemy on her first day of residence. Pam stepped in quickly.

'Oh my goodness, Willow Bay is full of history, absolutely riddled with the stuff,' Pam said jovially. 'We have a long history of shipwrecks and smugglers, even some sunken treasure! They say there were British soldiers living in the tunnels beneath the cliff and your new home, during the Napoleonic Wars, gathering intelligence from boats in the night. If the walls of Saltwater Nook could talk—'

'But they can't,' broke in Emily. 'Which is why we have to be their voice and protect it from villains like John Granger.'

'I don't think you give John enough credit,' said Bill.

'Dad!'

'You're looking at it from a purely academic perspective,' said Bill. 'But John's got to think of Mari. You want Mari to sign the Nook over to the historical society and that's all very noble but what happens to Mari? Her money's tied up in that place.'

'Oh, he's not doing it for Mari,' said Emily. 'He's doing it to line his own pockets. History is bigger than just people!'

'Some might say it's *just people* who make the history,' said Bill thoughtfully.

Emily snorted. Annie wished they would all bugger off, so she could hoover up her dinner. If they didn't sling their hooks soon, she was likely to plunge her face into the food and start devouring roast parsnips.

Pam squeezed Emily's shoulders and planted a kiss on her head.

'Come on, Emily, my love,' she said. 'Let's leave poor Annie here to eat her dinner and give the local politics a rest.'

Emily stood and went arm in arm back to the bar with Pam.

Bill placed a cruet set on the table and said, 'Enjoy!' before he too left her in peace at last with her much anticipated dinner.

Chapter 18

Happily stuffed and having received phone calls from both Alex and Peter to say they'd each arrived home safely, Annie headed out of the pub. As she pulled open the porch door, she was confronted by a man wiping frantically at a grey slick of bird shit on his head with a supermarket receipt.

'Happens to the best of us,' she said as she let him pass. He grimaced at her and as the door squeaked closed behind her she heard Bill's voice ring out through the pub.

'Shat on?'

Annie parked herself on one of the benches on the lawn and listened to the birds noisily settling down to roost in the trees.

The Pomegranate Seed was closed on Mondays, so the waning of a Sunday (one of their busiest days of the week) was always plump with the promise of liberation. Habitually, she felt that promise now and then reminded herself that it wasn't just Monday she had off but Tuesday, Wednesday, Thursday and Friday . . . It was a lot to comprehend. What would she do with all that spare time? Even days off from the restaurant were filled with chores and menu planners and all the things that needed to be done in order that she could hold down a fifty-hour-a-week job *and* avoid a visit from a TV crew from *Britain's Grimiest House*.

She thought back to when Alex and Peter were little. Annie would drop them off at school or nursery, with hugs and kisses and lunchboxes full of all the *right things*. Then she'd race home to get the house straight before work at eleven. At three o'clock, she would dash back to the school gates to pick them up. A play in the park, help with homework, cook dinner, do bath and story-time, brief the babysitter and head back to the restaurant by 7.15 p.m. to oversee the dinner service.

School holidays were a whirlwind of guilt and self-loathing. As a woman, you couldn't afford to excel in just one thing; you couldn't *only* be a great parent, or *only* have a great career, you had to be great at *all* the things you did, or society would deem you a failure.

'You're amazing!' people would say. 'I don't know how you do it!'

And Annie would think, *If only you knew what a fraud I feel most of the time*. She was forever waiting for them to realise that she was making it up as she went along. Boisterous melodies from a live folk band burst out of the open door to The Captain's Bounty along with the smell of roast beef and potatoes cooked in duck fat, rooting her back in the present. The joyous sounds of banjo and fiddle seemed to suit the landscape. It was a little after six; obviously The Captain's Bounty's turn to feed the masses. Annie determined to test The Captain's hospitality soon.

It was still light. There were a couple more weeks before the evenings would start drawing in earlier. But it was cooler now than it had been at the same time even three weeks ago and Annie was glad of her sweater. She walked slowly down the hill, soaking in this beautiful place that was to be her home for the coming months. And she felt . . . well, she felt lucky.

Chapter 19

The next morning, Annie was woken by a strange squeaking sound and the tinny clatter of metal. She was momentarily disorientated until she remembered where she was and then she pushed the discombobulation of sleep aside and opened her eyes. The wallpaper was a festival of pink tea-rose posies tied together with lilac ribbons in repeating patterns around the walls. The morning light permeated the cream jacquard curtains. Annie stretched and rubbed the sleep from her eyes – carefully so as not to encourage more wrinkles than was necessary.

There came another metallic clatter. Annie padded out into the hallway in her blue scotty-dog pyjamas, scratching her bird's nest head as she went. She yawned loudly as she walked into the sitting room and came face to face with an unfeasibly tanned man looking in at her from the other side of the glass.

Annie screamed and threw a scatter cushion hard at the window. The cushion thumped dully against it and flopped onto the window seat. The tanned man looked down at the cushion and then up at Annie, bemused. Annie dashed back into the hall and stood with her back to the wall, panting. Her brain clicked back into gear and she realised it was the third

Monday of the month, which meant the man at the window was Paul, the window cleaner. *Jeez! Where is the time going?* she wondered.

Annie mussed her hair into what she hoped was more beach-tousled than sweaty-bed, straightened her pyjamas and walked back into the sitting room, with as much dignity as she could muster. Paul was laughing, hands held up – one holding a squeegee – in surrender, in a way only a person supremely confident at the top of a ladder could do. He had a friendly face. His skin was the colour of a well-roasted chicken, and a career spent outside had given him wrinkles around his eyes and mouth that deepened into well-worn creases when he smiled.

She found herself laughing at him laughing at her and quite forgot that she wasn't wearing a bra and that her boobs grazed the bottom of her ribcage beneath her baggy pyjama jacket. She had a sudden urge to twirl her hair around her fingers, and a strange stirring in her tummy-hugger pants reminded her that she hadn't had sex in a very long time. And, more to the point, that she would like to remedy that as soon as possible. *And why shouldn't I?* she thought. *I'm forty-four, not dead!*

Paul motioned down towards the ground and raised his eyebrows. Annie gave him a double thumbs up and wondered if she'd always been this uncool. As Paul began to dismount the ladder, Annie dashed into the bedroom and hurriedly put on her bra. She scooted into the bathroom and performed the quickest of tooth brushes and squidged a blob of toothpaste onto her tongue for extra freshness; she didn't want to frighten him off with morning breath.

Several unboltings later, Annie wrenched open the front door and felt the fresh morning air burn her minty tongue and whistle through the gap in her pyjama top. Paul the window cleaner leaned casually against the mailbox post. He wore a white T-shirt – wet down the front – and old straight-cut stone-washed jeans. His hair was a mess: a tangled windswept mass of blond and grey, with coarse stubble to match. Annie expected him to snap open a can of Diet Coke any second. He broke into a wicked grin when he saw her.

'Hello!' he said. He walked over to the steps and leaned against the handrail; one foot rested on the bottom step. When not scaling ladders, leaning seemed to be his thing. It was difficult to descend the steps with any kind of sex appeal whilst wearing hedgehog slippers and a pink fluffy dressing gown with cat ears on the hood, but Annie gave it her best shot.

'Hello,' she said, hoping she didn't have a toothpaste moustache.

'Mari found her brave victim then,' said Paul.

'Victim?' asked Annie.

'Have you ever spent a winter on a beachfront?'

'No,' admitted Annie. 'But how bad can it be?'

'Spoken like a true towny,' said Paul. 'It can get pretty wild!'

'I think I can handle it,' said Annie. *Oh my God! I'm flirting!*

'I'm sure you can. Is it just you?'

Forward! she thought.

'Yes,' said Annie. 'Just me.'

Paul grinned. If a star sparkle had pinged off his teeth at that moment, Annie would not have been surprised.

'Good,' he said. 'I'm Paul.'

91

'I know,' said Annie. 'Mari told me you come every third Monday. To clean the windows, I mean,' she added as if she needed to clarify.

Paul laughed, a deep gravelly laugh, and Annie began to feel very hot inside her animal-themed nightwear. She wasn't sure if it was the flirting or the menopause.

'Yes,' he said. 'I *always* come on a Monday!'

The heat spread up her neck to her cheeks.

'Smashing!' she said.

Smashing?? What kind of response was that?

'I'd be happy to show you the delights of Willow Bay if you need a welcome guide,' said Paul.

'I've been to The Sunken Willow,' said Annie.

'Okay,' said Paul. 'In that case, why don't I take you on a tour of the rest of Willow Bay on Saturday afternoon and we'll finish with a meal at The Captain's Bounty?'

'Sounds good,' said Annie.

Wait, is this a date? Oh my God, it sounds like a date!

'I'll pick you up at three o'clock?' Paul asked, breaking Annie's inner monologue.

'Great. And then you'll have come on a Saturday too!' said Annie and instantly wished she could be swept away by a large wave.

Paul laughed.

'Lucky me!' he said. 'Well, I'd better finish off.'

Annie looked at him dumbly.

'The windows?' said Paul.

'Windows!' said Annie. 'Finish off the windows, of course. Great. I'll probably get dressed. Will get dressed. Obviously. I don't just stay in pyjamas all day, that would be weird. I'm going now. I'll see you Saturday. I won't have pyjamas on then. I'm going. Bye!'

Paul smiled. Annie turned and climbed back up the steps to the front door, her hedgehog slippers slapping and flapping on every stair.

'By the way,' Paul called, as Annie pushed open the door.

She turned.

'What's your name?' he asked.

'Annie,' she said.

'Good to meet you, Annie,' said Paul before swaggering out through the gate, a damp cloth hanging out of the back pocket of his jeans.

Annie pushed the door closed and leaned against it. She was sweating. Every part of her, from the inside out. Even her eyebrows were sweating.

She called Treena.

'Treena's Beauty Parlour!' trilled Treena.

'Hi, Treena, it's Annie Sharpe.'

'Annie!' said Treena. 'Crikey, it's been ages!'

'Yeah,' said Annie. 'I've been remiss in the body hair department lately.'

'I thought you'd found another lady,' said Treena.

'Oh no,' said Annie. 'I've just been au naturel for a while.'

'Word is you've left Max,' said Treena.

'As usual, the *word* is right. Max and I have split up.'

'I'm not sorry to hear it.'

Treena was privy to, and chief keeper of, all the secrets in the high street. If MI6 had had a mind to train her, she could have been the greatest spy the secret service had ever known. There is an intimacy between a woman, legs akimbo, on the bed and the beautician brushing hot wax onto her vulva that makes her feel able to divulge her innermost worries and confidences. A good waxing lady is like a spatula-wielding counsellor. Annie had burst into sobs many times on Treena's table and not just from the eyewatering pain of having her body hair ripped out by the roots.

'Can you book me in before Saturday?' asked Annie.

'Course I can, my love,' said Treena. 'What needs doing?'

'Everything,' said Annie. 'Tash to toes, please.'

'Date, is it?'

'Not exactly,' said Annie. 'But I'd like to be prepared.'

'I'd better block out the whole afternoon,' said Treena.

Chapter 20

Annie spent the next few days familiarising herself with her new environment. She began by heading right from Saltwater Nook, away from the direction of the hill. Here the promenade swept round for about a quarter of a mile until it ended abruptly in a set of iron railings. Beyond them were jagged rocks that led up to the grassy cliffs above. A little before the railings there were steps down to the beach and from the beach you could carry on round – tide permitting – to where the headland jutted out in a peninsular to form the bay. Mari had said that the tunnel, which supposedly led to the cellar at Saltwater Nook, began in a cave at the furthermost point, before the cliff turned the corner and fell out of view. Even at low tide Annie guessed you could expect to get your feet wet trying to reach it. On the other side of the peninsular there was no beach to speak of for a mile or so; only rocks and towering cliffs like ancient sentries.

Curious, Annie headed down the beach towards the edge of the headland, wearing a pair of wellies and carrying a torch she had found hung on the back of the bedroom door. The pebbles crunched satisfyingly beneath her boots; empty mussel shells and lank brown seaweed littered the beach. The sky that morning was the colour of lead and the water was a molten mirror image, darkly rippling and swollen with a promise of menace.

The tide was about as out as it was going to go but she was still splashing through puddles. Deeper pools shimmered in hollows between the rocks and here the seaweed was alive and waving beneath the surface of the water, its fronds brushing against the plump anemones – like raspberry wine gums – which suctioned themselves to the pool-sides.

The cave mouth was tucked away, completely invisible from the shoreline and just big enough for a small row boat or dinghy to sail into unnoticed at high tide. The mouth was angled as such that someone watching from the promenade would assume the boat had simply passed around to the other side of the peninsula. *Perfect for smugglers*, thought Annie.

Annie looked back once and turned into the dark cave. There was surface water here and it ran down in rivulets, joining and pooling together like quicksilver, pulled by the call of the sea. The sharp echo of drips and constant tinkle of running water was loud in the small space, as though she was miles below ground, instead of toe-deep in a cave mouth.

She flicked on the torch. One side of the cave was chest-high in rough warty limpets, before it smoothed out into chalky undulations. The other side was formed of natural ledges, which ate into the cave – plenty high enough for a smuggler to hole up in, till low tide, without fear of being swept away. She shone the torch around as she made her way further in. She couldn't make out where the tunnel was meant to begin. Even with her torch, the way forward just seemed black. She looked back. The glimmer of daylight seemed small and far away; she must have walked in a curve. Her nerve was beginning to wane. If she should slip or get stuck in here, no one would know she was missing and she didn't know exactly how long low tide lasted or how quickly the sea would rush back in to claim the cave.

Reluctantly she turned back the way she had come. She would venture here again when she had a better understanding of the tides. The torchlight fell on something on one of the higher ledges. Annie moved towards it, keeping her light on the spot. It looked like a battered old rucksack, dirty with time but with snatches of fluorescent orange and blue still visible beneath the grime. Her heart kicked up a notch. Had she discovered a bag of jewels or a shipment of heroin? Was she likely to get shot if it was the latter? Maybe this tunnel was used by modern-day smugglers too! Unable to quell her inquisitiveness, she picked her way across the mossy rocks and began to scramble up the slippery ledges to the bag. She reached up, standing on tiptoes, and her fingertips brushed one of the fabric straps which dangled over the edge when a voice snapped, 'Leave it!'

Annie stopped dead. When her heart began to beat again, she gingerly brought her arm down.

'Okay,' she said in a voice that she hoped sounded calm, compliant and non-confrontational. 'I'm going to go now. Please don't kill me. I am not at all interested in whatever it is you're doing here.'

She began to climb carefully back down the rocky ledges, her hands and knees shaking. 'I'm leaving now,' she soothed. 'I haven't seen anything.'

She plopped back down onto the pebbles and crunched her

way as quickly as she could towards the hole of light ahead. Her heart pounded in her ears; she could feel her pulse thrumming in her forehead as though it too was trying to escape. She wanted to look back to make sure whoever it was wasn't following but she dared not; if he was coming up behind her, it was better that she didn't know about it. *Shit, shit, shit, shit,* she thought. Her hand shook and the torchlight trembled accordingly.

She rounded a curve and the cave mouth beckoned with an ethereal light which poured in from outside. Annie let out an involuntary gasp of gratitude. In another moment she was stumbling back out into the sultry morning, breathing hard and hoping to God there would be somebody else on the beach. Her feet slipped and slid as she scrambled up the mounds of pebbles, which collapsed beneath her wellingtons and pulled her backwards as though she were perpetually trying to run the wrong way up an escalator.

Chapter 21

A wet Border Collie bounded along the beach with two women in tow. Annie was flooded with relief. She quickened her pace to put space between her and her would-be attacker and close the gap to the women.

'Hello there!' shouted the older of the two. She was a broad woman and looked as though she'd been born to wear her blue Barbour jacket and beige corduroys. 'Everything all right? You look like you're trying to escape the devil himself!'

Annie stopped scrambling long enough for the dog to leap up at her and send her sprawling onto the pebbles. The Collie, thinking it was a game, bounced expectantly beside her prone figure.

'Podrick!' the woman shouted. The younger woman laughed.

'Sorry!' she called. 'He's a bit overenthusiastic. He's still in training.'

'For what?' said Annie, pulling herself up to a sitting position. 'Law enforcement?'

The women reached Annie and the older woman held out her hand. Annie took it and was pulled to her feet with a force that took her by surprise.

'Sheep dog,' said the woman. 'I'm training him up for my daughters.'

Annie brushed herself down.

'You looked as though you were running from something,' said the younger woman. 'Is everything okay?'

'There's a man,' said Annie, still slightly breathless. 'In the cave.'

The daylight was diminishing the threat she had felt in the cave, and the presence of other humans squashed it further. With hindsight she wondered if her fears may have been a tad hysterical, heightened by Mari's talk of 'blaggards'.

The women looked at her and exchanged glances with each other.

'Did you get a look at him?' asked the younger woman.

'No,' said Annie. 'I heard him. There was a bag, you see, on a ledge . . .'

'Alfred?' the younger woman asked her friend.

'More than likely,' said the older.

'Who's Alfred?' asked Annie. 'Should I be concerned? I've just moved down here. I don't want to be on the wrong side of the local criminal element!'

The younger woman laughed. It was a sweet laugh which matched her sweet little face and her flowery dress and cardigan.

'Alfred's not a criminal,' she said.

'Alfred is Willow Bay's homeless person,' said the older woman with candour.

Annie felt her eyebrows rise.

'Maeve!' said the younger woman. 'You make everything sound so . . . so brutal!' She turned to Annie. 'Alfred is homeless by choice, kind of. He's sort of a nature man,' she said. 'Believe me, we've tried to get him into sheltered accommodation, we've had the council out to see him about support . . .'

'Says he's too long in the tooth,' said Maeve. 'Started coming quite a few years ago. Jolly good company when you get to know him. Stays for the summer, goes back to the city for winter.'

'Too long in the tooth?' asked Annie.

'To live indoors,' said the younger woman. 'He says he's lived under the sky too long; he can't cope with being an "inny".'

'You make it sound almost romantic,' said Annie.

'She could make dog turds sound romantic,' said the older woman. 'Just moved here, you say? I'm Maeve. This is Gemma. You've met Podrick.'

At the sound of his name, Podrick, who had been very interested in a dead crab along the way, came bounding back up the beach.

'I'm Annie,' she said, ruffling Podrick's fur.

A crunching sound behind her made Annie turn as a figure emerged from out of the cave. A hood pulled low over his eyes partially concealed his face, but she could make out a hooked nose and a wild black beard. He wore a long black wax jacket that grazed the tops of his boots and carried the dirty rucksack on his back. Seabirds flocked around him as he strode up the beach, the pebbles seeming to lie compliant under his feet.

'Alfred!' called Maeve.

Alfred waved his hand in response but didn't turn or break his stride.

'You nearly scared this poor woman to death!' she shouted.

'Sorry,' came the voice beneath the hood. 'No harm intended. Probably shouldn't be so quick to meddle with things that don't belong to her.'

He climbed the steps to the promenade, scaled the iron railings with ease and dropped down to the other side, picking his way effortlessly though the boulders until he had disappeared around the curve of the cliff, the birds following in his wake.

'Bit of a backhanded apology,' said Annie.

'He's all right,' said Maeve. 'Just a bit rough and ready is all.'

'How does he survive?' asked Annie.

Gemma replied: 'He does odd jobs and gardening for the pubs and general handyman work around the village, so he does all right. The pubs quite often pay him in meals.'

'There are worse things to be paid in,' said Annie.

'Quite,' said Maeve.

'The gulls seem to like him, does he feed them?'

'No,' said Gemma. 'He protects them, makes sure their nests in the cliffs stay untouched and looks after them if they break a wing or something. That's what I mean by "nature man" – he's kind of a wildlife caretaker.'

The clouds that had been threatening to drop their load all morning suddenly did so. A curtain of cold water collapsed from the sky; the blue-black surface of the sea danced as though a swarm of piranha frenzied beneath it.

'Oh my God!' screeched Annie.

Gemma was squealing and covering her head with an ineffectual cotton neck scarf. Maeve remained unmoved, as though refusing to let the rain see it was making her wet.

'Quick!' shouted Annie. 'Come back to mine.' She pointed over to Saltwater Nook.

The women looked at one another as a shared recognition dawned. They followed without speaking, and Podrick leaped about them, excited by the sudden change in the weather. The rain pummelled Annie's skin pink as she fumbled with the keys at the front door. Her expensive anti-wrinkle cream had run into her eyes and stung like a bastard, so that she was half blind and squinting when she finally found the right key and the three women and one wet dog stumbled into the lower hallway.

Maeve shut the door on the rain and Annie flicked the light on. Pools of water were collecting at their feet as their saturated clothes expunged what they could no longer hold.

'I'll get the kettle on,' said Annie, making for the stairs.

'I can't bring Podrick up,' said Maeve. 'He's soaking.'

As if on cue, Podrick, who had been investigating the bottoms of the skirting boards, suddenly shook himself and sent a spray of water up the walls and over the women. The cramped hallway was already becoming infused with the odour of wet dog. Annie had an idea.

'No problem,' said Annie. 'We'll go in here!'

Annie found the appropriate keys and set to work on the door to the disused tea room. Truth be told, she'd been waiting for an excuse to go in and have a look around.

Chapter 22

The room was dark, the windows covered on the outside by wooden shutters. Annie ran her hands along the wall for the light switch and flicked it. A strip light in the ceiling buzzed angrily like a disturbed bee and flickered into life.

'Well I never!' said Maeve. 'It's just as I remember it.'

Aside from a couple of boxes of Christmas decorations and an old door lying up against one wall, the place looked as though it had just been closed down at the end of a working day. Mismatched wooden chairs stood upside down on battered pine tables – three smaller and one long bench table which ran almost the length of the sea-facing window. Six old nautical oil lamps in mottled brass sat along the windowsills, covered in a rind of dust. Along the wall by the door they had just come in through was a short counter, a small chiller and a myriad of shelves behind them. The till on the counter was pre-electric.

'I never came in here,' said Gemma. 'It had closed down before we moved to the bay. We always make good use of the kiosk in the summer, though.'

'It's tiny!' said Annie, comparing it mentally with The Pomegranate Seed.

'Did a roaring trade, though,' said Maeve. 'Got too much for her in the end.'

'Couldn't she have hired some help?' asked Annie.

'She had help,' Maeve replied. 'But she wanted to retire. Didn't want the hassle that goes with running a business.'

'Fair enough,' said Annie. 'I've spent half my life running a business. And then one day you wake up and realise that so much of what defines you is in *the business* that you're not sure who you are without it.'

'So that's what you're running from,' said Maeve.

'Maeve!' said Gemma. 'Put your filter back in. Sorry, Annie.'

Annie was about to protest that it was fine when Maeve cut back in.

'Oh rubbish,' she said. 'Any fool can see she's running from something. What are you? Mid-forties? So, I ask you: why is a middle-aged, articulate woman, with a clear line where her wedding ring was recently removed, hiding in a glorified beach hut?'

'Easy there, Marple,' said Gemma. 'I'm so sorry, Annie. She lost her filter when she hit her sixties and nobody's been able to find it.'

Annie laughed.

'It's fine, honestly,' she said. 'Maeve's not wrong. Though it's more of a retreat than a hiding place.' Annie took a breath. She figured if she told her story now, she wouldn't have to tell it again; small villages being what they were, gossip spread quickly. 'I've walked out on my failed marriage and left behind my half of the business.'

'What was the business?' asked Gemma. 'If you don't mind me asking.'

'I'm a chef,' said Annie. 'I own The Pomegranate Seed restaurant in Leaming on the Lye.'

'The Pomegranate Seed!' said Gemma. 'I know that place. I took Brian there for our anniversary last year. It's been in all the foodie magazines. Gosh, is that you? Your food is amazing!'

'Do stop gushing, Gemma,' said Maeve.

'No, please,' Annie laughed. 'Let her gush.'

'Cheat, was he?' asked Maeve.

'Honestly, Maeve,' said Gemma. 'You're like a bloodhound.'

'There's not much that could induce a woman to leave behind a successful business,' said Maeve. 'Women are practical like that. So, either he cheated, or she did.'

Gemma slapped her head.

'Maeve!' said Gemma. 'This is why you don't get invited to parties.'

'He cheated,' said Annie. 'And I left.'

There was a lull in the conversation and Annie looked around the room. The pictures on the walls – framed posters of old 1920s and 30s adverts for ice cream, cocoa and soap – had cobwebs strung between their frames like lace hammocks. A copy of *Country Life* lay on the longest table as though just read and discarded. Annie ran her thumb across the dusty cover to reveal the date: 1992.

'How old is Mari?' Annie asked.

Maeve sucked air in through her teeth and frowned as she mentally calculated.

'Ooh, she's got to be in her nineties,' she said. 'Well into them too, I'd say.'

'Good Lord,' said Annie. 'She doesn't seem it.'

'Never had children,' said Maeve by way of explanation. 'Except her nephew, John, he was hers as near as dammit. But none of her own. It's the kids that kill you.'

'Charming!' said Annie. 'And how many have you got?'

'Five,' said Maeve. 'Two daughters and three sons. The youngest one's thirty now but it's still like herding cattle when they're all together. I reckon they've taken five years each off my life.'

'What a bastion of gentle parenting you are!' said Gemma.

'This one has her kids in bed with her and her husband,' said Maeve with a nod of her head in Gemma's direction.

'It's called *attachment parenting*,' said Gemma.

'It's called a rod for your own back!' said Maeve.

'What about you, Annie?' asked Gemma. 'Any children? Is that okay to ask? I never know if it's an insensitive question. You know? Not very feminist.'

'Oh, for pity's sake,' said Maeve. 'She's either got them or she hasn't. And if she hasn't, she either didn't want them, couldn't have them or left it too late.'

'I swear to God, Maeve, you're going to get us banned from places one of these days,' said Gemma.

'I've got two grown-up boys; twins,' said Annie quickly to try and stop the situation escalating. 'I started early,' she added, smiling at Gemma in a way she hoped would put her at ease.

Maeve and Gemma continued to verbally spar with one another, as they took chairs down from tables. There was a good-naturedness about their arguing, and Annie sensed a deep affection between the two women.

A gust of wind rattled the shutters and the rain followed

with renewed gusto, sounding like a thousand tiny hands smacking the paintwork. Annie shivered and remembered that she was still soaked through. Rain dripped steadily off the ends of her hair and onto her sweater.

'Right,' said Annie. 'I'll get that kettle on.'

'Jolly good,' said Maeve. 'Mine's a tea with milk and two, leave the bag in.'

'Got it,' said Annie. 'Gemma?'

'Coffee would be lovely, please,' said Gemma. Her teeth were chattering. 'Milk but no sugar.'

'I'll see if there's an electric heater upstairs I can bring down,' said Annie. 'And towels, I'll bring towels.'

'Don't worry about the heater,' said Maeve. 'I've found this old beauty!'

Maeve pulled an old Calor gas heater into view. She blew the worst of the dust off the rungs and rubbed the rest with her coat sleeve.

'Off you go,' said Maeve. 'Gemma and I will have us a table sorted for when you get back.'

Podrick weaved in and out of the tables, picking up cobwebs in his wet fur and leaving paw prints on the dusty floor.

If Annie didn't know better, she would say this room had been breathing shallow, biding its time while it waited for her to find it. She shook herself – *silly, rooms don't breathe* – it was just an old forgotten space, someone else's history that she was romanticising. And yet, Annie felt a warmth in this place that not even the dust and neglect and the very obvious draughts could hamper.

Chapter 23

While the kettle came to the boil on the stove, Annie disrobed and shrugged into fresh tracksuit bottoms and a fleece hoodie. She made herself and Gemma a coffee from her fancy machine and set Maeve's tea to brew, while she went from cupboard to cupboard looking for snacks. She found an unopened packet of Hobnobs and added them to the tray. She tucked two towels under one arm and draped two blankets from the airing cupboard around her shoulders, before gingerly making her way down the stairs with the laden tea tray.

She pushed the door open and was engulfed by the smell of burning dust and the unmistakable scent of the Calor gas heater. Already the warmth from it was spreading through the forgotten space.

Gemma jumped up from her spot by the heater and took the tray, setting it down on a small central table, now dust-free and streaked with wet. Three chairs, also dusted, sat round it. Annie handed out towels and blankets and took a seat.

'Now then,' said Maeve. 'How do you feel about book clubs?'

'Book clubs?' said Annie. 'I've never had the time to join one. I've always fancied the idea, though. Are you part of one?'

'No,' said Maeve. 'We want to start one. A Victorian book club, revisiting the classics. This place would be the perfect venue. What do you say?'

'Maeve!' said Gemma. 'You're so brusque!'

'What do you mean?' asked Maeve. 'There's no point pissing around the bush, is there? Either she wants to be part of the club or she doesn't.'

Gemma threw her arms in the air in frustration. Annie pondered.

'I'm not sure Mari would be happy for me to use the tea room,' said Annie. 'I'd have to ask her first.'

'Ask her then,' said Maeve. 'I'm not suggesting you host a Roman orgy! Mari won't mind, she's a good sort. Loves a book. We'd be inviting her to join if she were here.'

'How many of you are there?' asked Annie.

'Two so far,' said Gemma. She was smiling really hard, as if her friendliness could cancel out Maeve's asperity. 'Three, if you join,' she went on. 'Four would be better. Maybe you know someone who might be interested?'

Annie considered the proposal. She supposed Mari wouldn't mind. After all, how wild could a book club get? At worst she'd end up with her tea room spring cleaned. And if winter by the sea really was going to be as arduous as people kept telling her, then maybe it would be good to have something to look forward to.

'Okay,' said Annie. 'Let me check with Mari. And I'll say a tentative yes in the meantime.' Sally's face bloomed into Annie's mind. 'I have an idea for our fourth member too.'

Gemma clapped her hands. 'Amazing!' she said. 'It's going to be so good. I'm so excited! I can get Molly to babysit and if we do it on a Wednesday, it won't matter if I'm late back as she doesn't have college on Thursdays. She can sleep in the spare room and I'll drop her home in the morning when I drop the kids off . . .'

'Gemma!' said Maeve. 'Calm down.' She said this as though addressing a dog. Podrick looked up from his place by the heater, one ear cocked, before nestling his head back down on his paws. 'Her husband's been back at sea for nearly two months now,' Maeve addressed Annie. 'She doesn't get out much.'

'It's true,' said Gemma. 'I don't. When Esme started school in September, I didn't know whether I was crying with relief or sadness. Sometimes I think I made a terrible mistake giving up work to be at home with the kids.'

'How old are they?' Annie asked.

'Lennox is seven and Esme is four and a half.'

'Tough ages,' Annie sympathised. 'Too big to be babies and too small to be in any way independent.'

'I catch sight of my work suits in the back of the wardrobe sometimes and I can't believe it was me that used to wear them. I hardly remember who that woman was. It was my decision to stay at home, but I look at women who kept their careers when they had children and I feel like I've let the side down.'

'I often thought I'd made a terrible mistake by *not* giving up work to be at home with the kids,' said Annie. 'I'd see women like you and think I'd denied my boys something precious.'

'It's the guilt,' said Gemma. 'Guilty if you do and guilty if you don't. I worked in pharmaceuticals, so it was a lot of travelling. And what with Brian being away for months at a time . . .'

'And were you both men, we wouldn't be having this conversation,' said Maeve. 'You want to judge yourselves? Judge yourselves by how a man would feel in the same situation. I guarantee you'll have an easier time of it. Now, back to the matter in hand.'

'I say we choose a book now,' said Gemma. 'And then, Annie, you can ask your friend tomorrow and we'll meet here next Wednesday at, say, seven thirty to discuss?'

'Provided Mari agrees,' said Annie.

'Oh, she'll agree,' said Gemma. 'Ooh, it's so exciting!'

'Gemma, don't squeak so,' said Maeve. 'It's like being friends with a guinea pig.'

'Aren't book clubs usually monthly?' Annie asked.

'Well, usually, yes,' said Gemma. 'But I really can't wait to get started. And if we meet, say, every couple of weeks, just think how many books we'll get through . . .'

'Like I said,' butted in Maeve, 'she doesn't get out much.'

'I'll bring wine,' said Gemma, ignoring Maeve.

'Of course you will,' said Maeve. 'I'll bring the car.'

'And I'll make some nibbles,' said Annie. She was finding Gemma's enthusiasm infectious.

'What's going to be our first book?' asked Maeve.

'Ooh, I've got one!' said Gemma, her hand in the air.

Annie and Maeve looked at her expectantly.

'*The Woman in White*,' she said, 'by Wilkie Collins. I watched it on TV and I've been meaning to read it ever since.'

Annie shrugged. 'Works for me,' she said. 'I'll pick up a copy from the library tomorrow.'

'I'll download it,' said Maeve. 'Listen to it while I'm walking the dogs.'

'That's cheating!' said Gemma.

'Poppycock!' said Maeve. 'It doesn't matter which way the words go in, so long as they go in.'

Gemma and Maeve left, having devoured the packet of Hobnobs between them. Gemma had the school pick-up and Maeve – a retired sheep farmer as it turned out – had to go and help her daughters, who now ran the farm between them, to fix a fence that had blown down in last night's wind. Annie texted Mari about the book club and received a swift response in the positive. Then, since she had nothing more pressing to attend to, she set about cleaning the tea room.

Chapter 24

Beyond the counter, set into a wall of shelves, was a door which led to a galley area and the kiosk – also shuttered and dark – which housed the coffee machine, a small portable hob on a butcher's block, an old butler sink, a reasonably new dishwasher and a table-top oven. The coffee machine was as good as Mari had promised and whether out of chef's habit or sheer inspiration, Annie found herself daydreaming about the possibilities presented by the kiosk and tiny tea room as she worked.

Sooner or later she'd have to sell her half of the business. And then what? She didn't know if she wanted to run her own restaurant again. But equally, she'd been her own boss for too long to work for someone else.

These were the thoughts that followed her around as she cleaned and dusted down someone else's history. Had it been hard for Mari to give up the tea room? Or had it been a relief? Annie stood back, resting her hands on top of the mop. The spider hammocks were gone, and the peach complexions of pre-war children advertising Pears soap and Cadbury chocolate were warmer now they weren't smiling through a film of grime. The incessant buzz and harsh light of the fluorescent tube in the ceiling rather spoiled the effect of what would otherwise be a lovely place to enjoy a cup of coffee, and Annie decided she would invest in some candles to light the room for the book club.

It wasn't a fancy room but Annie figured that with the shutters thrown open and the windows looking out onto the ocean beyond, it didn't need to be fancy. She imagined cold blustery weather outside and the warm scent of coffee within. She looked towards the dozens of newly cleaned empty shelves and pictured them filled with bags of coffee and stacked cups and Kilner jars of homemade granola and cookies.

Stop it! she said to herself. *This is a temporary stop, nothing more! By March it'll either be a museum or a pile of rubble.* But the thoughts kept coming, almost as though the space was whispering its possibilities in her ear.

The rain had finally stopped, and Annie decided the place could use some fresh air. She let herself out of the tea room via the door at the far end and walked around the outside of the building to the kiosk. On a separate fob, clearly marked, were the keys to the padlocks securing the shutters. Annie pocketed the padlock and pulled back the peeling wooden shutters to the kiosk, fastening them on the hooks either side of the wall. Then she locked herself back inside the tea room and flung open the kiosk windows. The wind blew in cold and fresh and the building seemed to breathe in response, as though waking up from a sleep.

Annie ran her gaze over the coffee machine and switched it on, just to see. The machine whirred satisfyingly into life and Annie busied herself looking for the bags of coffee Mari said she had left.

'Are you open?'

Annie jumped up from beneath the counter to find a man and woman, about her age, looking in at her.

'Oh,' said Annie. 'Um. Yes. Yes, why not!'

'Oh fantastic!' said the woman. 'I'll have a mocha and, Aiden?' She turned her make-up-free face, with its English rose complexion, to meet his. 'Latte?' she asked.

The man smiled at her. 'Lovely,' he said.

'Right you are,' said Annie. She'd found the unopened bag of coffee beans and a tub of hot chocolate but milk was going to be an issue. In the corner by the marshmallows, she spotted a multipack of long-life barista oat milks.

'I don't have any fresh milk at the moment,' said Annie. 'How do you feel about oat milk?'

'Fine with us,' said Aiden. 'Our daughter is dairy intolerant, so we're no stranger to the crazy milks!'

'You must be Annie,' said the woman. 'I'm Raye and this is Aiden. Pam's told us all about you. We're the landlords of The Captain's Bounty.'

'I hope you'll be visiting us soon,' said Aiden jovially. 'We'll be jealous if you don't!'

'Actually, I'm coming for dinner on Saturday,' said Annie.

'Oh fabulous!' said Raye. 'You must leave room for Aiden's tiramisu – it really is something.'

Aiden and Raye looked more like they should be reading runes and selling dream-catchers than running a pub. Raye wore her sandy hair in long dreadlocks and green Dr Marten boots peeped out from beneath her striped Ali Baba trousers. Aiden's pale skin was striking against a backdrop of dark corkscrew curly hair – Annie wondered if their heads stuck together like Velcro in bed – and he was dressed in faded black skinny jeans and a rainbow Baja hoodie. They could have come straight from Glastonbury Festival.

Annie tipped the beans into the grinder, answering questions over the subsequent noise about where she'd come from and what had brought her here.

'Crikey!' said Raye. 'I hope our homespun pub grub won't be too much of a comedown. Pam didn't mention you were a chef.'

'If the smell of your Sunday roast is anything to go by, I should be in for a treat,' said Annie as she rifled around for cardboard takeaway cups and rinsed the metal milk jug out.

'Will you be open all season?' Raye asked.

'I didn't know I was going to be open now,' Annie laughed. 'You might be my first and only customers.'

'Oh, I wish you would,' said Raye. 'It would be great to be able to get a decent coffee after a wintry walk. We come down here to blow the cobwebs away between opening times.'

Annie knew well those precious snatched hours between the end of lunch service and the beginning of dinner.

'Don't bully the poor woman,' said Aiden. 'She's only just moved in.'

'I'm not bullying her,' said Raye. 'I'm just saying there's a lot of people who would appreciate being able to grab a coffee down here out of season.'

'Do you think so?' asked Annie.

'Oh God, yes!' said Raye. 'It's all very well catering for the out-of-towners all through the summer but what about the people that live by the sea all year round?'

'Don't get her started,' said Aiden.

117

'I mean it,' said Raye. 'Go to any seaside town past September and it's tumbleweed city, everything's boarded up, like a zombie apocalypse.'

'I told you not to get her started,' said Aiden.

Annie laughed and handed over the coffees.

'Well, you've given me something to think about,' said Annie. 'That's six pounds, please.' She had no idea of Mari's pricing structure, so she used the one from the restaurant.

Raye handed over the cash and Annie was grateful for it; if there was a card machine in the place, it was well hidden.

'See you Saturday,' said Aiden as they headed back in the direction of the hill.

'Unless you decide to open again beforehand!' called Raye over her shoulder. Annie saw Aiden give Raye an admonishing nudge and Raye raise her hand in an expression of *What?!*

Annie had six more customers during the following hour and a half it took her to finish cleaning and familiarising herself with the kiosk and its contents. She found a mobile card machine beneath the counter and a plastic cash tray. Every single customer asked whether she was planning to open through winter and Annie deftly avoided giving a straight answer.

'Maybe on sunny days,' she said non-committally to a man with an impressive King Edward moustache.

'It's the wet days we could do with it,' he grumbled.

By the time Annie was finished the little tea room was pine fresh and aglow with bleachy newness. Annie treated herself to a double-shot mocha before closing the place up again and heading back up to the flat. She sat in the armchair gazing out of the window at the clouds waltzing across the sun, their shadows dancing light and dark on the ocean below. She sipped her coffee and understood why Mari had never left. Annie felt she would never be bored of this view. The restaurant seemed very far away, both in distance and in time. She wondered if, with hindsight, she had mentally withdrawn from the restaurant as she had from her marriage. She thought about Max and realised that she wasn't even that angry with him anymore about the cheating – well, at least not enough to want to set fire to him.

Chapter 25

Something woke her. Annie rolled over and checked her phone: 3 a.m. The storm was wild enough to be heard even through Mari's triple glazing but the sound which woke her hadn't come from outside. Annie lay very still, straining her ears. There it was again. A clatter. It wasn't in the flat but it was in the building. Maybe one of the shutters had come loose in the wind. She lay there wondering what to do. *What if it isn't a loose shutter? What if it's an intruder? Damn!* she thought. *I'm going to have to go down there and check it out.*

Annie pulled her dressing gown around her and slipped her phone into the pocket. She scouted silently through the flat for a weapon – just in case – but there was none. *What kind of woman lives alone without at least a baseball bat for defence?* she wondered. Annie settled for an umbrella with a reasonable spike on its end, and a rolling pin. She opened the door to the flat and pulled it closed as quietly as she could, leaving it on the latch in case she needed to scoot back inside in a hurry. The narrow staircase was cold. The wind whistled through every crack and beneath door frames and blew chill around her naked ankles. The rain pelted against every part of the building as though demanding to be let in.

At the bottom of the stairs, Annie listened again. She turned her head first towards the kiosk, then the tea room and then the cellar. To her relief the cellar was quiet. A shuffling sound drew her gaze sharply to the tea room door. What was that? A fox? A rat? A person? The key was poking out of the lock, just as Annie had left it. Her arms had gone stiff with tension. She shook them out, stowed the rolling pin under the arm which held the umbrella – spike forward – and turned the key as quietly as she could.

There was a ruckus behind the door, like a chair being dragged across the floor. *How big is that rat?* she asked herself. In one swift movement, Annie pushed open the door and slammed on the light.

'Who goes there?' Annie yelled. She wasn't sure where this came from; she blamed it on reading too many classic crime novels.

There was a scream and what looked like a pile of dirty laundry and blankets flew into the air. Annie shrieked and hurled the umbrella harpoon at the blankets, followed by the rolling pin which made a thud as it hit its mark. There was a yelp and a man's voice cried, 'I surrender! Please don't hurt me!'

Annie's heart pounded. She'd used all her weapons so she grabbed a large Kilner jar from the shelf and brandished it towards the voice.

'Who are you?' she said. 'What do you want? I know kung fu!' This was a lie.

'It's Alfred,' came the voice from beneath a brown army blanket. 'I only came in here to sleep.'

'Where's the other one?' asked Annie.

'What other one?' asked Alfred.

'The one who screamed,' said Annie.

'That was me,' said Alfred, still speaking from beneath the blanket.

'It sounded like a woman,' said Annie.

'Well,' said Alfred gruffly, 'you took me by surprise.'

'Come out from under there,' said Annie.

'Don't throw anything else at me,' said Alfred.

Annie lowered the Kilner jar.

A dirty hand reached around and pulled the blanket down to reveal a scowling man in his sixties. His hair was too long to be tidy and his black beard needed a trim, but the hook nose unmistakably belonged to the man she had seen stomping up the beach after she had accidentally stumbled upon his hiding place in the cave.

'What are you doing in here?' asked Annie. She put the jar back on the shelf. 'You frightened the life out of me!'

'I told you,' said Alfred. 'I came in here to sleep. The weather's bad and the tide's too high for me to stay in the cave. I'm sorry if I scared you.'

'That's okay, I think my heart rate is returning to normal,' she smiled. 'Do you often sleep here?'

'Only when the weather's bad, like tonight,' said Alfred.

He was well spoken; a Northern twang clung to the ends and beginnings of his words. Despite the fright he'd given her, Annie felt sorry for him: she wouldn't want to be outside in this storm.

'Mari knows,' said Alfred.

'She didn't mention it to me.'

'It's an unspoken agreement.'

'How did you get in?'

'Mari gave me a key to one of the shutters,' said Alfred. 'And the window latch gives with a little jimmying.' He lifted one hand to reveal a silver key swinging between his thumb and forefinger.

'Ah, that explains it. For a moment I thought I had a Houdini on my hands!'

'Nothing so exciting, I'm afraid.'

Alfred began to shift onto his knees.

'I'm going to get up,' he said. 'Please don't launch any weapons at me.'

Annie smiled and held her hands up.

'I am unarmed.'

The rolling pin clattered onto the floorboards and rolled under a table as he stood. He leaned the umbrella up against a table leg and set about folding his blankets and stuffing them neatly into the shopping bag he'd been using as a pillow.

'What are you doing?' asked Annie.

'I'm leaving,' said Alfred.

'You can't go out in this!' said Annie. 'The weather's terrible.'

As though to strengthen her point a gust of wind hit the shutters like someone was outside battering them with a canoe.

'Just stay,' said Annie. 'If it's all right with Mari, it's all right with me.'

Alfred smiled hesitantly. It wasn't a face that was used to smiling. His leathery cheeks concertinaed into deep lines that travelled up past his eyes and along his weather-beaten forehead.

'Are you sure?' he asked.

'Absolutely,' said Annie. 'Do you need anything?'

'No, thanks,' he replied. 'I've got everything I need.'

What you need is somewhere to live! Annie thought to herself, but she said, 'Okay then. Well, goodnight.'

This time Alfred really smiled; the lines in his face deepened so that it looked like it was swallowing itself. But his eyes twinkled and Annie couldn't help but smile back.

He retrieved the rolling pin and handed it back to Annie, along with the umbrella. Annie smiled sheepishly.

'Sorry about that,' she said, tucking the weapons under her arm.

'No apology needed. Goodnight,' said Alfred. 'And thank you.'

Annie nodded. Alfred began to pull blankets back out of his bag.

Back upstairs, the warmth of the little flat washed over her and Annie felt a pang of sorrow for the things that made Alfred feel he couldn't cope with being an 'inny'. She made herself a cup of camomile tea, plucked Mari's guide to Saltwater Nook from the bookcase and settled back into bed.

Annie opened the handwritten book and flipped through the pages. At the beginning of the section marked *September* was a side note, which read:

Alfred:

Around this time of year, Alfred will occasionally let himself in of an evening when the weather is particularly squally. He is homeless. Something happened to him a long time ago that caused him not only to lose his home but to feel like he didn't belong in one. He is a good man, of that much I am sure, and a man of nature too. He is as in harmony with the world as the birds are the air.

He's no bother and there's nothing you need to do for him. I'd go so far as to say he'll thank you for doing nothing for him. He's a proud man in his way. Alfred is an all-weather friend with a practical hand you'll find yourself mighty grateful for. He has a key to the padlock on the furthest set of shutters and he's happy enough to jimmy the window slightly to let himself in; the lock on the window is loose anyway.

He sleeps in the old tea room. It's dry, if a little draughty, and about as close to being in a house as he's ever likely to get. I don't mind saying I feel better about thunderstorms when Alfred's downstairs. When winter sets in proper, he'll be on his way and you won't see him again till the hyacinths bloom.

Annie placed the book on her bedside table and determined to pay it some proper attention, lest she find herself in store for more surprises along the way.

Chapter 26

When Annie left Saltwater Nook the next morning in search of a copy of *The Woman in White*, the air was so bitingly fresh it took her breath away. She had woken up early and taken a mug of tea downstairs for Alfred, but the tea room was empty; he must have left before sunrise.

She shivered until she was a third of the way up the hill and then the chill turned to sweat. She repeated *It will get easier* in her mind like a mantra, over the sound of her ragged breathing and the screaming ache in her thighs. It was good to have goals.

The library stood just off the main street and backed onto a park, with woods beyond. She decided to call Sally quickly while she waited for her cheeks to fade back from beetroot purple to radish pink.

'Annie! Hi!' came Sally's voice. 'Good to hear from you. How's the new pad?'

'It's great actually,' said Annie. 'I think I really struck it lucky with this place.'

'Good,' said Sally. 'And how's your brain? Any clearer?'

'It's a work in progress,' Annie replied. 'Listen, I know this might sound weird but would you fancy joining a Victorian book club? I don't quite know how it happened but I seem to be hosting one.'

Sally laughed.

'Shit the bed, Annie, you really can't say no to anything, can you!'

'Apparently not,' said Annie. 'But in this case, I think my being a pushover might be a positive thing.'

'I agree,' said Sally. 'Count me in. My last book club had to be disbanded due to irrevocable political differences.'

'Blimey!' said Annie.

'Yes,' Sally mused. 'All got a bit messy towards the end. We should never have pitted the Brontë sisters' works against each other. Still, you live and learn. And you'd hardly know Olivia's nose had even been broken now!'

Annie hoped the Victorian book club wouldn't induce quite such passions. Gemma would be all right, but Maeve and Sally had feisty potential.

'So, what's the first book?' asked Sally.

'*The Woman in White*,' said Annie.

'Ah, good old Wilkie,' said Sally. 'That's quite a tome! I read it a few years ago. I'll dig it out and refresh my memory. When's the meeting?'

'Next Wednesday evening,' said Annie. 'Do you drive? Or will you get a lift?'

'I'll drive down.'

'Okay, great, I'll text you directions. When you get to the bottom of the hill, instead of turning off onto the shingle, just drive straight along the promenade and stop when you reach the building. There's a door to the old tea room on that level which will be much easier with your chair.'

'And it's okay to just drive along the promenade?'

'Yes. I emailed the council this morning and they said vehicles are allowed for access.'

'How wide is the promenade? My car has a side ramp, I don't want to be stuck in the car if the walkway is too narrow.'

'It's thinner in some places than others but up by the cafe, where you'll be parking, is its widest point. Maybe eight meters?'

'Oh, that's plenty of room. I'm not greedy.'

'Will you need help, with the ramp or anything?'

'Nope, it's all good. The biggest danger is getting lost and rocking up at the wrong tea room.'

Annie laughed.

'Don't worry about that, you can't miss me, there is literally nothing but me and the abyss. You'll see when you come down.'

'Where on earth have you moved to?' asked Sally, laughing.

The library lobby was plastered with flyers advertising everything from art classes and church times to private tutoring. In pride of place at the centre of a large cork board was the Willow Bay Historical Society manifesto, and surrounding it were details and times of meetings and agendas. Annie noted that almost every meeting featured a 'Save Saltwater Nook' slot.

She wandered into the library and spied Emily methodically returning a stack of books to their rightful homes. Annie caught her eye and waved. Emily gave a curt nod.

'Hi,' Annie whispered. She didn't want to be shushed by Emily. Emily looked like the kind of librarian who shushed patrons as a matter of course. 'I'm looking for *The Woman in White*,' she said.

Emily pointed to the Classics section.

'You know, Wilkie Collins wrote *The Woman in White* just along the coast in Broadstairs,' said Emily.

'I didn't,' said Annie. 'That's interesting to know. What a lovely stroke of serendipity.'

'This coastline is steeped in history,' said Emily. 'Be nice to keep it that way.'

Annie smiled enigmatically.

'You know, you could be our woman on the inside,' said Emily, 'gathering intel and garnering support for the cause from the people who use the beach.'

'Oh, I'm not sure I should get involved. It feels like a conflict of interests, what with me being a tenant and all.'

'You think you won't be out on your ear the second Granger gets his money?' said Emily.

Mari had promised Annie the place was hers till the spring. Would John Granger honour that? Annie couldn't be sure, but what she did know was that starting a campaign against John Granger was unlikely to help her case.

'Regardless,' said Annie. 'I don't think it's a good idea.'

After checking out her book, Annie made her way round to the Willow Bay Stores.

'Annie, hi!' called Samantha. 'Tom's just bringing in the Willow Farm delivery. We've got parsnips and an early sprout crop. Winter's on its way!'

'Ooh, lovely,' said Annie. 'I'll take some sprouts. They'll be my first ones since February.'

When Tom emerged from out the back laden with boxes of veg, Annie helped herself to a scoop of Brussel sprouts and a bunch of raw beetroot.

'Did you want to put your name down now for a turkey for Christmas?' asked Tom. 'I know it seems early but the farm likes to get an idea of numbers.'

This pulled Annie up short. Christmas! What *would* she be doing for Christmas this year?

'Can I have a think about it?' said Annie. 'My plans are somewhat fluid at the moment.'

'Sure,' said Tom, smiling. 'No worries. Sam and I will be sampling the Christmas delights at The Captain's Bounty this year.'

'He doesn't want to cook,' called Samantha. 'Lazy bugger!'

'You cook it then!' said Tom. He was smiling over at his wife.

'He's only saying that because he knows I can't cook,' said Samantha. 'My talents lie outside of the kitchen.' She winked at Annie and Tom shook his head, chuckling.

'Seriously, though,' said Tom, 'you could do worse than booking yourself in at The Bounty for Christmas lunch, you know, if you're going to be on your own . . .'

Annie promised to give it some thought. Christmas felt like a big balloon of a holiday, looming up suddenly between buildings and around corners to leer at her aloneness.

Chapter 27

By mid-afternoon on Saturday, Annie was waxed and ready for her maybe/maybe not date with Paul. The skin around her bikini line still resembled a plucked goose but she supposed, if it came to it, at least it was better than the coir welcome mat she'd been sporting before.

It had been years since she'd been on a date – decades in fact – and she was nervous. The last time she'd dated, the most pressing issue had been whether or not her kissing partner's braces would tangle with her own. Deep and meaningful conversations centred around what was happening in *Party of Five* and whether Britpop or Grunge was cooler. The idea of dating with nigh-on thirty years of baggage trailing behind her felt almost insurmountable.

Annie had dressed in a pair of baggy teal corduroy dungarees with a thick jumper that had diamonds and stripes woven into the knit. She had pulled her hair up into a red polka dot headscarf and worn her most comfortable desert boots. She loosely resembled a Land Girl but having always been big of boob and round of cheek, this kind of casual style suited her. She finished the ensemble with red lipstick and a dousing of perfume around her neck in the hopes that Paul would get close enough to give her a sniff.

Paul was as easy-going as their first meeting had suggested, which was just as well since Annie was sketchy about first date protocol. Right from the start he set the tone for informal, unpretentious conversation, and without the pressure of having to appear witty or profound, Annie had relaxed into being with him.

There wasn't much about Willow Bay that he didn't know; nor indeed, it seemed, were there any people who didn't know him. If Annie's presence at Saltwater Nook hadn't been known by the entire village before their date, it certainly was now. She could only imagine the gossip. And what's more, she didn't care. The idea of being regarded as a strumpet was infinitely more interesting than her previous moniker of long-suffering wife.

'I'm a carpenter by trade,' said Paul. 'A boat builder. I used to travel from yard to yard around the coastline, wherever there was a contract going.'

'What kind of boats did you build?'

'Fishing trawlers mostly,' said Paul. 'Yachts and the occasional houseboat.'

'No cruise ships then?' asked Annie.

'Nope, no cruise ships. Although I've had a few commissions for suites on some of the big liners.'

'What made you give it up?' asked Annie.

'It gave me up,' said Paul. 'Boat yards were closing down up and down the country; contracts became harder to find. And to be honest, I got tired of chasing them. When my dad got sick, I came back here to look after him. I never left.'

They were weaving leisurely in and out of the moss-covered gravestones in the oldest part of the churchyard of St Andrew's. The church was on the tour. Apparently, the vicar of St Andrew's in the late eighteenth century was not averse to storing smuggled contraband in the crypt to be shared out – for a reasonable price – among his Willow Bay flock.

'Do you keep your hand in with the carpentry?' Annie asked, running her fingers along the rough stone arch of a crumbling tombstone. She was enjoying herself: she felt grown-up and yet younger at the same time.

'Oh yeah,' said Paul. 'I fitted out the Willow Bay Stores and the bar and pews at The Bounty are mine. Every time someone wants a new kitchen, I get called in. Alfred lends a hand with the bigger jobs; he can turn his hand to anything.'

'What's Alfred's story?' Annie asked. 'Maeve and Gemma seemed to think he didn't want a home. That can't be right, can it?'

'I've known Alfred for years and even I don't know the exact details. I think Mari knows but she'd never tell. All I know is he lost his family when he was fourteen in a house fire. He boomeranged around children's homes until he was eighteen, spent a bit of time at Her Majesty's pleasure, before finally giving up on society.'

'Oh my God, poor Alfred. I can't even begin to imagine the mental scars that kind of tragedy would leave. Fourteen! It doesn't bear thinking about.'

Annie thought of the twins at age fourteen, still childlike in so many ways.

'I doubt there was much in the way of therapy or grief coun-selling in those days,' said Paul. 'And I'm not sure being pinballed about the care system would have been much fun either.'

'No,' Annie agreed. 'It goes some way to explaining how he's ended up where he has, I suppose.'

They were quiet for a time as they wandered amongst the final resting places of Willow Bay's oldest residents.

'Now this,' said Paul, stopping beside a ship's anchor laid in the centre of the cemetery, 'is the actual anchor from the actual sunken *Willow* . . . supposedly.'

'Wow,' said Annie. 'So, it's a kind of memorial?'

'That and an insurance policy,' grinned Paul. 'The villagers thought if they rested the ship's anchor on holy ground, it might tether the lost sailors' souls and stop them causing mayhem around the bay. Being that they'd driven them to a watery grave, they were somewhat jumpy about spectral retribution!'

'That's a touch grizzly,' said Annie.

'We Willow Bayers like a bit of macabre.'

'You really love it here, don't you?'

'I couldn't ask for more,' said Paul. 'My dad left the house to me. And between the window cleaning business and the carpentry, I make as much as I need. Being my own boss means I can get out on the water whenever I like.'

'Do you fish?'

'Me?' laughed Paul. 'No, I leave the fishing to Ely and his boys. It's the surf that calls my name.'

'You surf?' asked Annie.

'Kitesurfing, windsurfing, you name it,' said Paul.

Annie got the impression Paul was trying to impress her. It was working.

Chapter 28

'Penny for them,' said Paul.

Annie blinked and realised she'd wandered to the end of the gravel path that wound through the graveyard and was standing inside the wooden lychgate.

'Sorry,' said Annie. 'I was lost in my thoughts.'

'Anything I can help with?' asked Paul.

'I was thinking that you seem to have the work–life balance thing sorted,' said Annie. 'I've never been very good at balance. I'm on the lookout for tips.'

'Well, you're headed in the right direction,' said Paul.

'How can you tell?'

'You're here, aren't you?' said Paul. 'You left behind something that wasn't working and struck out on your own. You're finding your balance.'

'You make it sound like more of a determined effort than it was,' said Annie.

'Then what was it?' asked Paul.

'Running away,' said Annie. 'Spur of the moment.'

'You need a perspective adjustment,' said Paul. 'Every action can be seen as either a positive or a negative. You need to retrain your mind so that your reactions to your actions are positively charged.'

'Like, *a smile is a frown turned upside down*?' asked Annie.

She smiled at Paul and he laughed back at her.

'In its most basic terms, yes,' said Paul.

'Where do you learn this stuff?' asked Annie. 'Do you have a guru sitting cross-legged in your living room?'

'I've read a lot of books and smoked a lot of weed,' said Paul.

Annie tried not to let the shock show on her face. She'd never really got into the whole weed scene. She certainly hadn't indulged since she'd had the twins. Well, that wasn't strictly true: she'd smoked some once with Max after the twins' fourth birthday party. It had been a disaster: she became paranoid and convinced herself that she was having a deep-vein thrombosis and was going to leave her children motherless and spent the next hour begging Max to let her call herself an ambulance. That had been her last foray into the murky world of drug use.

'Should you be smoking weed and climbing ladders?' Annie asked.

Paul laughed.

'It's strictly recreational,' said Paul. 'I like a smoke, the way you probably like a glass of wine. Contrary to popular belief, it doesn't have to be the devil's gateway to heroin.'

He was smiling wryly at her. Annie felt suddenly very uncool. She imagined her eighteen-year-old self, drawing a square in the air with her fingers and then pointing at Annie, a look of disappointment on her young face.

'Oh God, no, of course not,' said Annie. 'I've smoked weed before. Loads of times.'

She had no idea why she'd said this. Paul was looking at her with an expression which exuded both amusement and pity, like one might give a chihuahua in a tutu. She inwardly slapped her forehead hard. Paul's grin widened to a smirk.

'Are laughing at me?' she asked with mock chagrin.

'I'm trying really hard not to,' said Paul.

Annie gave him a playful nudge. It was all becoming rather flirty, she thought with no small pleasure.

'I didn't have time to experiment with drugs,' said Annie. 'I was a parent at seventeen.'

'Well,' said Paul, leading her away from the churchyard to a wooded area set back from the path. 'You're a big girl now.'

He pulled a pouch of tobacco out of his jeans pocket and to Annie's horrified delight, began to roll a joint.

'It's the middle of the day,' she whispered. 'In public!'

Paul laughed softly and guided her to a fallen tree, motioning for her to sit down. Annie sat on the prostrate trunk and craned her neck to see around them. There was nothing but trees.

'It's a Saturday afternoon,' said Paul in a soothing voice. 'We're not working. To my knowledge, neither of us is planning to handle heavy machinery anytime soon, and we are nowhere near any of the public.'

He lit the joint. The pointed end curled and blackened and drifted to the ground. Paul sucked hard, the tip glowed orange and crackled. He breathed in, held it for a long moment and then exhaled slowly. The creamy smoke plumed into the air, thick and pungently fragrant. He held it out to Annie.

'It's not strong,' he said. 'Think of it as an aperitif.'

Annie hesitated and then took the spliff from Paul. She

tentatively sucked, pulling the fragrant smoke down into her lungs and trying to suppress the spasms that urged her to cough. She held her breath for a moment and let it go. Her head swam a little but not unpleasantly. She passed it back to him and let the sensation wash over her.

'Woah,' she said, feeling kind of spongy, as though she might melt into the tree trunk like candlewax.

Paul grinned as Annie took another drag.

'I feel so . . . funky,' she said.

Paul chuckled.

'Funky?'

'Yeah,' said Annie. 'And smooth like a peach, only wobblier like goo.'

'Man, I wish I was in your head right now,' said Paul.

By the time they left, having shared the joint sixty–forty in Paul's favour, Annie's limbs felt deliciously soft, the grass beneath her feet a thick bouncy underlay that cushioned her every step. She found it impossible not to keep giggling in a high-pitched 'squeee' sort of way, especially when everything around her seemed so hilarious: that squirrel was definitely strutting like Mick Jagger and she was pretty certain the herring gull on the church roof had just screeched 'Fuck off, Melvin!' to the gull on the flagpole. Paul decided it would be best to do a couple of laps around the village before reintroducing Annie to society, so that by the time she entered the pub, she was relaxed and rampantly peckish.

Chapter 29

'Hi, Raye,' Annie called over the bar.

If Annie had had to guess what The Captain's Bounty's interior would look like, it would have been exactly this. Strings of multicoloured fabric birds with tiny bells between them hung down the black wooden joists which punctuated the long dark pub. The uneven plaster on the walls was painted a deep Moroccan orange, which burst like a warm sunset between the wonky criss-cross of beams. A visual anthology of Willow Bay's nautical history decorated the walls: black and white photographs of fishermen past with their boats, sat beside paintings of clipper ships, coastal maps and cottages – some of which Annie recognised from her hazy village tour.

A band was setting up in a cleared space opposite the bar. Raye gave a cheery wave and Annie saw her nudge Aiden conspiratorially. Paul rested his hand in the small of Annie's back and guided her towards the far end of the pub, to a table for two by the fire. For Annie, a woman sex-starved and mildly stoned, a hand in the small of the back was practically foreplay.

They started the meal with salt and pepper squid that melted in the mouth, and aioli.

'Oh my God, I'm so ready for this,' said Annie.

'That's called the munchies,' said Paul, a knowing smile playing at his lips.

'I am a chef, you know,' said Annie. 'I don't need to be stoned to appreciate good food.'

'No,' said Paul. 'But maybe it takes your appreciation to another level.'

Annie wanted to argue but she was too busy eating to speak. Paul chose beer-battered Dover sole and thrice-fried chips for his main and Annie had pan-fried plaice with hassel-back potatoes and samphire. She would have dearly liked to have sampled Aiden's famous tiramisu but in the event of the evening taking the turn she hoped it would, she didn't want to be too full of mascarpone to enjoy it.

The throne-like wooden benches on which they sat had high backs and floral motifs had been cut out of the wood, so that the light filtered through them and danced patterns on the table. Annie ran her hand idly over the undulating wood. She saw Paul watching her.

'You made these,' she said.

He smiled. Not his cocksure grin but a softer smile.

'I did,' he said. 'The benches and the bar. They're all me.'

'They're beautiful,' said Annie. 'You're an artist.'

Paul's smile widened and he looked down at his plate.

'I'd best get you drunk before you start finding flaws in my work,' he said.

Annie laughed.

'I didn't have you down for modesty,' she said.

'First impressions can be deceiving,' said Paul.

Annie had a warm feeling inside her that was more than

weed and wine. The evening passed in a pleasant haze. The folk band played with the right amount of wistfulness and hope to fill the atmosphere with positively charged phero-mones. The flames danced in the hearths and the regulars, merry with hooch and warm of feeling, danced on the flag-stone floor. Annie danced with Paul, her bashfulness soon unwoven as the music plucked at the stitches that bound her. His arms felt nice wrapped around her, the heat from his palms splayed out across her back.

'Thank you for a lovely tour,' said Annie, as they meandered back through the quiet dark streets.

'You're welcome,' said Paul.

The cold night nipped at Annie's fingers but her body felt warm and the air between them was thick with expectation. They had reached the end of the path by which they must decide whether to continue the date, or end it on a delicious goodnight. Annie's heart was racing. She wasn't sure which outcome she was hoping for but she felt giddy with the excite-ment.

'Would you like to come back for a coffee?' Paul asked.

'Yes,' said Annie, and the decision was made.

Chapter 30

Annie lay very still. She hoped Paul was still asleep. She had woken after a fitful snooze and lain awake thereafter, pondering as the black slash of night between the curtains was slowly diluted by the encroaching dawn.

The benefit of having sex with the same person for years, even when that person is a lying cheat, Annie thought, is that you are comfortable with each other's bodies; you know theirs almost as well as your own. You know what they like and vice versa. More importantly, you both know what it takes to get the job done to both parties' satisfaction; what it lacks in passion it gains in functionality. The grey morning light draped itself across the slow breathing mound beneath the black and white striped duvet cover. Annie tried to sigh quietly. Having sex with someone new was fraught with logistical dilemmas. You couldn't anticipate which way they would lean, for example, or whether your hips would knock, or their chest would crush your ribs. It had been a somewhat disappointing experience.

There was more slapping of flesh than she remembered from her last sexual encounter; at times it sounded like a sea lion clapping. At one point their stomachs, wet with the sweat of exertion, had somehow suctioned together and then farted out a languorous raspberry as they parted. The sticky, ungainly parts of sex were funny with a partner who was as comfortable as an old slipper but far less so with a stranger. But it wasn't even that which had been the problem. The spark that had fizzed wildly between them throughout their date had simply sputtered and died between the sheets. There was no gasping, other than when Paul had leaned on her hair and pinned her head to the bed. No mewling, like the women in sexy novels seemed to spend so much of their bedroom-time doing. Just the awkward sound of their laboured breathing and the wet slapping of their skin and the farting of their stomachs. She'd managed to cobble together an orgasm but she'd had to visualise Poldark really hard to get it. The biggest grunts of the whole affair came as the pair tried to disentangle themselves afterwards. With disappointment, Annie reconciled herself to the fact that she and Paul were sexually incompatible.

The mound in the bed snorted and stretched.

'Are you awake?' Paul asked.

'Yes,' said Annie.

Paul shifted. The light from his phone cast a beam across the ceiling.

'What time is it?' asked Annie.

'Seven fifteen. Do you want some coffee?'

'No, thanks.'

Silence blanketed the room. Annie wanted to get back to Saltwater Nook. She wanted to have a shower and brush her teeth. She hadn't seriously considered that a sleepover might be on the cards and, as such, she hadn't come prepared. She baulked at the idea of putting yesterday's knickers back on and breathed shallow in hopes that her morning breath wouldn't reach Paul's side of the bed.

'I'm going to go,' said Annie. She sat up, twisting the duvet about her as she reached across the floor and raked her discarded clothes towards her. 'I think the walk of shame is best done earlier rather than later.'

'I can drive you,' said Paul.

'I'd like to walk,' said Annie.

'I'm sorry about last night,' said Paul. 'I don't understand it, it was like . . .' He trailed off.

'The oomph was absent?' Annie offered.

'Exactly,' said Paul. 'We should have been great.'

'We should have,' said Annie.

'It wasn't you,' said Paul. 'I think you're amazing, you're sexy and funny . . .'

'It wasn't you either,' said Annie. 'Maybe some people just aren't meant to have sex.'

'Do you think we're so similar that we cancelled each other out?'

'It's an interesting theory,' Annie laughed. 'I guess this makes us just good friends?'

Paul nodded, and shook her outstretched hand. 'Just good friends.'

Annie's legs felt decidedly stiff as she tramped down the hill and she smiled as she noted she had probably used muscles last night which hadn't seen a workout in quite some time. Now the initial disappointment had worn off, she felt a certain peace about her lacklustre encounter with Paul. She'd had no expectations after all. She wasn't looking to start a relationship. She wasn't even looking for a fling. She had simply wanted a bit of fun, a bit of attention, to feel a warm body against hers and feel the flutter of flirtation. Well, mission accomplished. Annie reasoned that having bad sex with Paul was actually the best thing that could have happened. What if the sex had been amazing? Then they would have felt bound to have more and more sex and eventually they would have found themselves pursuing a relationship, which was exactly what Annie didn't want. *Yes*, thought Annie, *hurrah for humdrum humping*.

Chapter 31

High in the sky the seagulls were circling and, even after this short time, Annie knew there must be a fishing boat out on the sea. Sure enough, a glimpse through the trees showed Ely's trawler bobbing gently just out past the buoys. It was funny, she thought, how quickly she was getting used to life on the coast; how familiar it all felt, almost as though she had lived a past life in Willow Bay and returned to pick up where she had left off, like one of Willow Bay's ghosts.

The sea today was a mixture of deep green and lapis blue, like the body of a blue-bottle fly.

Annie let her gaze travel slowly and land on Saltwater Nook. She stopped dead. Max's car was pulled up next to hers beside the rickety fence. Her cheerful mood deflated. She was too far along the promenade to turn back and, if she did, where would she go? She supposed she could walk back up to Paul's house, she was sure he wouldn't mind. But she didn't really want to revisit the scene of crimes against coitus just yet.

Max got out of the car and gave her a cheery wave. Annie groaned. *Goddammit*, she thought as she waved a heavy arm in response, *the man's a bloody psychic vampire, coming round here and siphoning off my perfectly good Sunday mood.*

'Hi,' said Max. He was smiling nervously.

This used to melt Annie's heart. Now it made her want to slap his stupid lips off. He reached an arm out and moved forward tentatively as though to hug her. Annie stepped back and his face fell. She tried not to care.

'Which of our children caved in and gave you my address?' said Annie. 'I know I haven't told anybody but them where I'm staying.'

Max shifted his weight from one foot to the other and hugged his arms to himself.

'Chilly this morning,' he said. 'I think the weather's turning.'

'Which one?' asked Annie.

'Don't be mad,' said Max.

No one in the history of ever had started a conversation with that phrase unless they'd done something that was guaranteed to make the other person mad. Annie said nothing. She stared at him and waited. Max looked at the floor and dragged one foot back and forth along the shingle, making a groove in the pebbles.

'When the boys came to help you move in,' said Max, still not looking at her, 'I, um, checked the GPS on their phones.'

Dammit! He was stalking her via stalking their children.

'Do you not see how devious that is?' asked Annie. 'Not to mention creepy.'

'Some might call it caring,' said Max. 'I still care about your wellbeing. I wanted to make sure you were safe.'

'And is your mind at rest now?' asked Annie. 'If you really cared about my wellbeing, you wouldn't have made me penniless.'

Max shrugged his shoulders.

'It seems like a nice area,' he said, ignoring the barb about money. 'A bit remote for my tastes.'

'Luckily, your tastes are no longer my concern,' said Annie.

'You're out early,' said Max.

She was caught off guard. She hadn't expected her walk of shame to be interrupted by her husband.

'Oh, well, yes,' she said. 'It's a nice morning for a walk.'

Max looked at her.

'You've got make-up all down your face,' he said.

'I came out before my shower,' said Annie. 'I wanted to catch the sunrise.'

Max stared at her for a long moment and Annie met his gaze squarely.

'You didn't go out early at all, did you?' said Max. 'You didn't come home last night!'

Annie pulled her shoulders back.

'So what if I didn't?' she said.

'You've barely been here a week,' said Max.

'Don't you dare judge me, Max Sharpe!' said Annie. 'Don't you even dare. You've got some nerve.'

Max backed down instantly and hung his head.

'I understand,' he said in a quiet voice. 'You're trying to spite me. And you've every right to.'

'I am not trying to spite you!' said Annie. 'How big is your ego?'

This wasn't strictly true. Although revenge hadn't been foremost in her mind when she'd climbed into Paul's bed, she couldn't deny that she'd taken a good deal of satisfaction from having sex with someone so soon after leaving Max. But it had been more than that. Paul's hands on her body had felt cleansing; Annie had got her wobbly body out in front of a relative stranger and he'd been only too happy to ravish it.

Annie realised Max was still looking down at her. His eyes were bright with hurt and, to her surprise, smouldering. Annie realised with horror that she had unintentionally made herself more desirable to her husband than ever before. *Oh shit!* thought Annie to herself. *Now there'll be double wooing.*

'I've brought you something,' said Max. His voice was low; gentle yet coaxing. Annie knew this voice. She knew all his voices.

'Divorce papers?' she asked. 'Access to my own bank accounts?'

Max flinched. If they gave out awards for looking hurt after behaving like a bastard, Max would win, hands – and pants – down.

Max opened the passenger door and pulled out a wicker cat basket. A hissing sound came from inside. Mrs Tiggy-Winkle pressed her ginger face against the barred door. She looked severely pissed off.

'Tiggs!' cried Annie.

Mrs Tiggy-Winkle let out a mournful meow.

'I thought you might like some company,' said Max. 'She was always more your cat than mine.'

Annie took the basket from Max.

'Thank you, Max.'

'I brought her a litter box and a few packets of her favourite food. I wasn't sure if there were any shops nearby.'

'That's very thoughtful of you.'

'Shall I help you in with these things?' asked Max.

'No, thank you,' said Annie. 'If you could carry the bags to the steps, I can take it from there.'

'It's no bother,' said Max, pulling three large shopping bags out of the back seat of his car.

'I'm sure it isn't. But as we've already discussed, I haven't been home all night. I'd like to get in and get cleaned up. But thank you for the offer.'

Annie didn't want him in her house. This was her place. Unsullied by Max in any way. Max didn't push it. He followed Annie through the little gate, along the garden path and up the steps to the front door, stopping three steps lower than Annie.

'It's a lovely spot,' said Max.

'Yes, it is,' said Annie. 'I like it very much.'

'You'll be bored,' said Max. 'I know you.'

'Maybe you don't know me as well as you think,' said Annie.

'I want you back,' said Max.

Annie pulled the keys out of her handbag and set about unlocking the various deadbolts, determinedly ignoring Max's comment. She pushed the door open and felt rather than saw Max crane his neck to see past her.

'I mean it,' said Max. 'I'll prove it to you.'

'I wish you wouldn't,' said Annie. 'Just pop the bags down there, thanks.'

Max did as he was told.

'Thank you, Max,' said Annie. 'Well then, goodbye.'

Max climbed the last few steps so that he was level with Annie and dropped the bags onto the welcome mat. He leaned in to kiss her cheek but Annie turned to place Tiggs's basket in the hall, leaving Max to recover his balance awkwardly.

'I'll see you soon,' said Max.

'Mmm-hmm,' said Annie, purposely non-committal.

Max stepped back down and Annie could feel him looking at her.

'Well,' said Annie. 'Thanks for dropping by. Don't make a habit of it.' She smiled sweetly.

'What's happened to you?' Max asked.

'I don't know what you mean,' said Annie.

'You're so feisty. I like it.'

'I've always been feisty. You just stopped noticing.'

'I'm noticing now,' said Max.

He had a glint in his eye, like a shark sensing blood in the water.

'Good for you,' said Annie. 'Say hello to Ellie for me.'

Max opened his mouth to speak but Annie closed the door firmly and locked it for good measure. Annie ferried Mrs Tiggy-Winkle and her luggage up the stairs. She stood to the side of the kitchen window so that she was obscured from view and waited for Max to leave. When at last she heard the crunch of wheels on shingle, she relaxed.

A reproachful meow broke Annie's reverie.

'Sorry, Tiggs,' said Annie.

She unhooked the latch and the door to the basket swung open.

'Welcome to your new home.'

Mrs Tiggy-Winkle unfolded her puffball body out of the basket and stretched first her front legs, then her back. She allowed Annie to make a brief fuss of her, then padded nonchalantly out of the room, tail held high, to explore the rest of Saltwater Nook.

After Annie had showered and changed into something suitably sloppy, she went down to the freezer in the cellar and took out two mackerel fillets for herself and a bag of sprats as a treat for Tiggs. As she began the flight of stairs back to the flat, something by the doormat caught her eye. Annie doubled back on herself and stooped to pick up a piece of lined paper, carelessly torn at the top and folded over into a note. She opened it.

> Dear Ms Sharpe,
>   I came to call on you this morning to see how you are settling in but unfortunately you were not in. I am sorry to have missed you.
>   Yours sincerely,
>   John Granger

The note seemed innocuous enough and yet Annie couldn't help feeling it was somehow critical of her being out when he called. *Don't be ridiculous*, she told herself. *You're just feeling over-sensitive after your run-in with Max.*

They spent the day amiably pottering around the flat. Annie sat in the armchair, with her feet on the footstool, reading *The Woman in White* until her eyes began to cross. Tiggs catnapped in various locations until she found the afternoon suntrap on the window seat and settled down until dinner time. When the sun began to set, turning the sky to ripe apricot as the great orb disappeared down below the waves, Annie and her house-mate had dinner together: Mrs Tiggy-Winkle on the floor and Annie on the sofa, watching *Antiques Roadshow*. For the first time in more years than she could remember, Sunday felt like a magical precursor for the week ahead.

Chapter 32

Annie pulled up next to the picket fence and hauled the bags out of the boot. She'd gone to the nearest town to pick up supplies ready for the first book club meeting on Wednesday; she liked to get ahead of the game. She had bought scented candles for the tables and two seaside-inspired lamps, with puffins and crabs printed on the shades, so that they wouldn't have to use the flickering strip light which gave off grisly crime scene vibes.

Since Gemma was keen to bring wine, Annie decided to make a non-alcoholic hot apple punch as a complement, reasoning that the smell of cinnamon and mixed spice heating on the little hob would also create a sense of warmth in the chilly room. She was planning to cook some mini pesto tartlets to have hot, along with antipasti and a big bowl of fancy crisps. Preparation, planning and list-making were some of Annie's greatest joys and starting a new life required a whole new level of rumination which she was only too happy to embrace.

It was late in the afternoon. It had been chilly all day, the pale sun masked behind smoky cloud, and now even that scant light was starting to fade. The air was clammy and she could feel it clinging to her hair as a woolly grey fog slipped over the rocks and blotted out the landscape. Annie shivered and felt grateful for the little waft of smoke spiralling out from the chimney of Saltwater Nook signalling warmth within. As she hauled her bags of shopping up the garden path, she saw a wicker hamper sitting on the top step in front of the door. She climbed the stone steps and stooped to read a paper parcel tag tied to the basket handle:

With love, Max
Eternally sorry

Oh, for fuck's sake, thought Annie, *what now?* She hoped it wasn't some bizarre love token, like his severed finger. She unlocked the door and pushed her shopping inside, then crouched down and undid the leather straps which fastened the hamper and lifted the lid. Inside were two beige plastic baskets made to look like wicker, a DVD of *The Lost Boys*, a sachet of southern-fried seasoning and a small cool-box containing a pack of six fresh chicken drumsticks and a bag of frozen French fries. A bottle of cream soda lay in the bottom, along with a packet of butterscotch flavour Instant Whip and a pint of milk.

Oh, he's good, she thought to herself. *He's pulling out the big guns this time.* She tried to remain unmoved by the gesture but it lit a scene in her mind from a long time ago. It was her friend Claire's seventeenth birthday. A few friends gathered in her lounge to watch a rented video of *The Lost Boys*. Annie was sat on a cushion on the floor. Max was next to her. Max wasn't her boyfriend but she fancied him in that desperate way that only teenagers can: all-consuming, breath-stuttering, electric passion that torments and exhilarates. She remembered the intoxication of his nearness. How she thought her heart would explode out of her chest as his warm hand reached for hers and held it. Her friends whooped and shrieked as Corey Haim speared a vampire through a stereo on the TV. But Annie didn't care about *The Lost Boys* anymore because Max Sharpe, the hottest boy in the sixth form, was leaning towards her. In that moment she felt her whole life had been a mere prelude to French kissing Max on Claire Smith's living room floor. As the credits rolled, Claire's mum served up southern-fried chicken and chips in baskets, washed down with cream soda and a good helping of butterscotch instant whip, and Annie and Max became an item.

Shit, thought Annie, *how does he do that?*

'Hello!'

Annie jumped, startled, and almost lost her footing, clinging to the handrail to steady herself.

'Holy shit!' The memory bubble popped and Annie suddenly felt the cold mist seeping through her clothes.

'Sorry!' Paul laughed. He was grinning up at her from the bottom step. 'I didn't mean to startle you.'

'Oh, that's all right,' said Annie. 'I was lost in my own little world. How are you?'

'I'm good,' said Paul. 'You?'

'Fine,' said Annie, still distracted by the hamper.

'I've brought friendship flowers,' said Paul. He waved a bunch of late-flowering hydrangeas. 'I don't want things to be awkward between us. I think we get on really well.' He paused. 'It would be a shame for one night to stop us hanging out as friends.'

Annie smiled. *He's such a grown-up*, she thought. *How refreshing.*

'I completely agree,' she said. 'As a matter of fact, how would you like to have dinner with me?'

'Great!' said Paul. 'When?'

'Tonight,' said Annie. 'Come on in and I'll make a start.'

'What's on the menu?' Paul asked.

Annie held aloft one of the plastic baskets.

'Chicken in a basket,' she said.

'Whoa,' said Paul. 'How could anyone refuse an invitation as retro as that.'

It seemed to Annie that the best way to tamp down the flame of an old memory was to recreate it with someone you had absolutely no desire to have sex with. She guessed – as she coated the drumsticks in their bright orange southern-fried crumb – that Max was parked in a layby up in the village, waiting for Annie to call him and ask him to share the hamper with her for old times' sake. The thought of him poised, phone in hand, gave her no malicious pleasure but neither did it make her feel guilty. *This is progress*, she thought.

'I haven't seen this in years,' said Paul, making smacking noises with his lips as he licked the sticky coating from his fingers. *The Lost Boys* was playing in the background and had reached the scene where Michael was being traumatised by a carton of Chinese noodles which had inexplicably turned into worms.

'But you eat dinner out of a fake basket on a regular basis?' said Annie.

'If it's not in a basket, I won't eat it,' said Paul.

'I'm glad you dropped by,' said Annie.

'Not as glad as I am,' said Paul. He stuffed another handful of fries into his mouth. 'So, your ex is hell-bent on winning you back?'

'Until he realises he's fighting a lost cause,' said Annie. 'The trouble is, I've always given in, in the past. It's like a child having a tantrum: if you give in, you set a precedent and next time they'll scream longer because they know eventually you'll give in to their demands.'

'Sounds like you've raised the bar pretty high,' said Paul.

'Unintentionally, yes,' said Annie.

'Do you still love him?' asked Paul.

'No. Not for a long time. Not the way I should anyway. I love him like a pet that shits on the carpet but you clean it up and forgive it because you're used to it and you haven't got the heart to rehouse it.'

'Oh my God,' said Paul. 'That is the worst description of love I have ever heard. That right there is why I've never married. No one's ever going to reduce me to an analogy of an incontinent animal.'

Annie laughed.

'He doesn't like to lose,' said Annie. 'He's got a big ego but it's easily dented.'

'What will you do?' asked Paul.

'I'll keep doing what I'm doing,' said Annie.

'Sharing his romantic gestures with other men?' said Paul.

Annie smiled.

'I can't give him any reason to think there's doubt on my part or hope on his,' said Annie.

'It's sort of sad really,' said Paul.

'It is,' Annie agreed.

Chapter 33

Annie was up early as usual. She made two mugs of tea and took them down to the tea room, but Alfred had already left. She was sorry to have missed him again. He'd stayed a few times during the last week and she'd only managed to catch him once to give him a drink before he went on his way. She found herself uneasy that he went out into the cold dark morning without even a hot drink inside him. She had begun to leave snacks in the tea room before she went to bed, just in case he hadn't managed to get anything to eat that evening. At first, she'd worried that he might take offence, but the food was always gone when she came down in the mornings. Last night she had made extra when she cooked her own dinner and left a portion of mushroom and spinach lasagne out for him; she was gratified to find the plate scraped clean this morning.

She threw open the shutters on the kiosk and opened the window. An easy breeze blew in, fresh and friendlier than last night's wind, as though it had exorcised its anger in the storm and wanted to be friends again. There were a few dog-walkers out and the beach was populated by green-wellied fishermen, hopeful that the churning tempest had driven the fish closer to shore. Annie switched on the coffee machine. People would come or they wouldn't, but if she was going to be down here anyway she may as well be open. She had stocked up on milks and syrups and contacted the coffee supplier about a delivery. She'd only opened the kiosk a couple of times but each time she had, she'd had steady custom. She had been humming and hawing about whether to give the kiosk a proper try, rather than opening it sporadically as the mood took her. A conversation with Alex had decided it for her:

'I thought you wanted to cut loose for a while,' said Alex.

'I did. I do. But—'

'But you can't help fantasising about starting a new business,' Alex cut in.

'I'm not sure I'm cut out for not working at all. I get fidgety. And there's something about this place. I don't know how to explain it.' She paused for a moment and Alex waited. 'It inspires me,' she said finally. 'It makes me want to build something, something that's just mine.'

'Well then, you've answered your own question,' said Alex. 'Stop dipping your toe in and make it happen.'

Annie had her first customer at a quarter past eight and she informed them, and all those who came after, that from now on she would be open every day bar Sunday. A six-day week didn't entirely fit with her original 'taking a step back' idea, however, she decided she wouldn't open past half past two in the afternoon, thus giving her what felt like acres of free time.

Between customers, she took the chairs down from the tables in the tea room and set a scented candle on each one. Along the middle table, at which they would sit for the book club, she ran a line of tea lights and positioned her new lamps. When it became clear that it was going to be a busy day for coffee, Annie brought her ingredients for tonight's snacks downstairs and baked them in the small oven in the cafe kitchenette.

Her phone lit up as she was rolling out the pastry for the tartlets. It was a text from Max. She hadn't thanked him for the hamper; she didn't know the etiquette for gifts from estranged husbands – any message would open a dialogue she didn't want. Where Max was concerned, it was easier to ignore than engage.

Did you find the hamper I left the other night? I didn't hear from you, so I wasn't sure if you'd got it. I put the perishables in a cool-box in case you spent the night elsewhere. I hope you enjoyed it. Do you remember that night? I'd like for us to go back. Start again. Like when we were mad for each other. I meant what I wrote. x

Annie sighed. It was the same as always: sentimental words sandwiched between thinly veiled passive aggression. She replied right away to prevent a follow-up call.

I did find it. Thank you. And yes, I do remember. The baskets were a nice touch.

She dared not say more. She added no kiss at the end. Max needed only the scantiest crumb of encouragement and he'd be like a Jack Russell down a rabbit hole.

Chapter 34

The candles were lit, the tartlets were warming through in the oven and the Calor gas fire glowed merrily in the corner. As she added the ingredients for the hot apple punch to the saucepan Annie began to feel nervous. She barely knew any of these women. What if they didn't get on? What if they decided they didn't like her? What kind of impression did she give as a newly single, newly unemployed woman stumbling around her forties, undecided as to whether she should wear leather trousers or fair isle cardigans, or both?

The warm apple and cinnamon added their perfume to the vanilla-scented candles, and Annie shook crisps into bowls and set them on the table. Sally was the first to arrive.

'Oh, this is lovely,' said Sally as Annie closed the door behind her.

'Sweet, isn't it?' said Annie. 'It's like a time capsule.'

'It's great,' said Sally. 'Are you going to open it up? It would make a fab little bistro in the evenings.'

'Maybe,' said Annie, inwardly fist-pumping herself: opening the tea room was her latest planning fantasy and it was nice to hear the idea positively mooted by someone outside of her own brain. 'Would you like some non-alcoholic punch?'

'Yes please,' Sally replied and moved a chair away from the table and inserted her own in its place. She plonked her copy of *The Woman in White* on the table and grabbed a handful of crisps. 'So, how's it been?' she asked. 'New place and all that?'

'The place is great,' said Annie. 'I love it. I know already it's going to be a huge wrench to leave here in the spring. There's something about it that seems to wrap you into it. I feel' – Annie stopped, pondering the right word for how she felt – 'ensconced,' she said. 'I feel ensconced.'

'That's really good news,' said Sally. 'I am genuinely pleased for you.' She shoved in another crisp. 'I won't lie to you, when I first spoke to you, that day on the phone, I was seriously worried about your mental health.'

'So was I,' said Annie. 'I think I needed to reboot.'

'Everyone gets body-slammed by life at least once,' said Sally. 'But look at you now! You've got a nice little place – in the arse end of nowhere admittedly – and you're back on top of your personal hygiene, it's all good.'

Annie laughed.

'I have to admit, I didn't expect to be quite so settled so soon,' said Annie.

'And what about the ex?' asked Sally.

'Not so settled,' said Annie.

'Those shelves look well stocked,' Sally said, casting a look around.

'Yes.' Annie smiled. 'I may have opened the kiosk. I'm just trying it on for size.'

'Well, it's good to see that the stupid husband didn't squash your entrepreneurial spirit. Well done, you!'

There was a trilling outside followed by a deeper snappish voice and a knock at the door. Annie ushered Gemma and Maeve into the tea room and quickly shut the door on the chill outside. Gemma was waving a bottle of wine above her head like she'd just entered a dorm-room party.

'She's been insufferable all the way here,' Maeve complained, taking her Barbour coat off and chucking it onto the bench along the window; the candles flickered in protest.

'I'm excited,' trilled Gemma. 'Our first book club meeting. Oh, Annie, I love what you've done with the place, it looks so cosy.' She caught sight of Sally and stretched out her wine-free hand. 'Gemma,' she said. 'You must be Sally. It's lovely to meet you.'

'Maeve,' said Maeve, shaking Sally's hand when Gemma had put it down. She inclined her head back towards Gemma who was cooing over the pesto tartlets. 'She'll be asleep by ten,' she said. 'She has the temperament of a Labrador puppy.'

Sally laughed.

'So, you've decided to open the kiosk proper then,' said Maeve. 'I'm glad to hear it.'

'News travels fast,' said Annie.

'The Willow Bay hotline never sleeps,' said Gemma. 'It'll be lovely to be able to buy the kids hot drinks after a cold walk.'

Annie poured drinks and laid the tartlets out on the table. The candles settled down to a gentle quiver as everybody took their seats. Each woman had their copy of the book in front of them, except Maeve who tapped her head, saying, 'It's all in here.'

Gemma had brought a notebook with gold-edged pages, which she smoothed open with her palms.

'I've been making notes while the children do colouring in,' she said.

'Right,' said Maeve. 'Let's begin.'

The women shuffled in their seats and ran their hands over their books as though divining inspiration from the jackets.

'It was long,' said Sally. 'But not as long as it seemed when I read it at school.'

'But not boring,' said Gemma.

Sally nodded.

'No, the explanations and descriptions seemed pertinent.'

'And at least not *all* the women were drips,' said Annie.

'I assume you're referring to Marion?' said Maeve, leaning back in her chair. 'Unusual for a male writer of the time to write a woman of such gumption and not have her fainting all over the place.'

'I hate that,' said Gemma. She put her hand to her forehead and feigned a Victorian swoon. 'Oh, I do declare,' she said in a wispy voice, 'I just caught sight of Julian's sock-suspender!'

'Laura faints all over the place,' said Sally. 'Made me want to slap her with a wet cod.'

'All delicate and self-effacing,' agreed Annie. 'Why wasn't Walter in love with Marion? She was much more interesting.'

'Because Victorian men didn't want interesting women,' said Maeve. 'They wanted china dolls with vaginas.'

'I've known a few twenty-first-century men like that,' said Sally.

'Why are Victorian women always written like that?' asked Gemma. 'They can't go out in the drizzle for fear of catching a chill, which will undoubtedly result in a fever and near death.'

'I always thought that about Jane in *Pride and Prejudice*,' said Annie. 'She trots out on a horse in the rain to see Bingley and spends the next three weeks at death's door.'

'If I'd have been Bingley,' said Maeve, 'that would have put me right off her.'

'If you'd have been Bingley, you'd have had her put down like a lame horse,' said Gemma.

Maeve nodded gravely.

'It's interesting that Marion could only be brave and intelligent because she was manly,' said Annie. She flicked through her book to a piece of paper poking out of the top of the page. 'Wilkie describes her as swarthy with a masculine jaw and a full moustache. He's basically written Marion as Magnum P.I.'

'I noticed that too,' said Gemma, flicking through her notes. 'Why couldn't she have been sexy and pretty and still be clever and brave?'

'If she'd been sexy, she would have been evil,' said Sally. 'Because men found sexy women tempting and therefore those women must be bad.'

'And if she'd been pretty,' said Maeve, 'then she'd have been too meek to be clever and been killed by rain: undoer of good women all over nineteenth-century Britain.'

'And everyone knows,' said Annie, 'that only men can be clever and heroic.'

'Or swarthy women with full moustaches,' said Gemma.

'What did you think of Walter?' Annie asked.

'Typical hero,' said Sally, in a bored voice. She waved a hand dismissively as though batting Walter out of the room.

'And, therefore, completely uninteresting,' said Maeve.

'Oh, I don't agree,' said Gemma. 'Why must a kind and honourable man be classed as boring? I hate that whole damaged hero crap. I don't want my daughter to grow up chasing after arseholes; I want her to meet someone nice, like Walter. There's a lot to be said for being nice.'

'I'm with you,' said Annie. 'It feeds into the *I can change him* mentality. We shouldn't be chasing after badly behaved, ill-mannered men. And we shouldn't allow ourselves to be kept keen by men who treat us mean.'

The women had polished off most of the tartlets between them and Annie refilled the crisp bowl, as they continued to dissect *The Woman in White*.

'Do you think Marion was a virgin?' asked Gemma.

'Wilkie would have written her that way,' said Maeve. 'Or she couldn't have been a heroine.'

'Imagine that,' said Gemma. 'Never having sex in your life!'

'Well,' said Maeve, 'she could have sorted herself out. Just because she didn't have sex with another person doesn't mean she didn't enjoy the pleasures of the flesh.'

'Maeve!' said Gemma.

'What?' said Maeve. 'Oh, you youngsters are all the same: think you invented masturbation. When my husband died, I had five children under the age of eight and a farm to run. I had precious little time to find a man to fulfil my needs, so I used my initiative.'

'Is that what they called it in your day?' asked Sally.

The women laughed.

'And I've been using it ever since!' said Maeve.

'I'm surprised you had the energy,' said Annie.

'It helped me wind down at the end of the day,' said Maeve.

'Sometimes I think I like the idea of sex more than the actual sex,' said Gemma. 'When Brian's away it's all I think about but when he's home, I'm just too tired most nights. I'd like the orgasm without all the rest of it.'

'Which is exactly my point,' agreed Maeve. 'Cut out the middleman.'

'Literally,' said Sally.

'At least you're guaranteed a good time,' said Annie. 'Which is more than can be said sometimes for the real thing.'

Gemma clapped her hands to her cheeks and squeaked: 'I completely forgot: you had a date with Paul!'

'Paul the window cleaner?' asked Maeve.

Annie felt her cheeks get hot.

'Hmm,' she said.

'A date?' said Sally. 'Nice work. How was it?'

'Raye said you were in The Bounty for dinner,' said Gemma. 'And Mrs Spencer said she saw you leaving his house on the Sunday morning.'

'Well, it seems like the whole of Willow Bay knows exactly how it went,' said Annie.

'Congratulations,' said Maeve. 'You're a seventies porn cliché.'

'How so?' asked Sally.

'She slept with the window cleaner,' Maeve replied.

Sally laughed loudly and Gemma choked on her wine.

'Go ahead,' said Annie. 'Laugh it up.'

'Will you see him again?' asked Gemma.

'As friends,' said Annie.

'Didn't float your boat?' asked Sally.

'Let's just say I'd have been better off using my initiative,' said Annie.

'Dildos!' said Maeve loudly over their laughter. 'Dildos are the way forward. Mark my words! Mine's called Fernando. A good strong name; exotic.'

'For Christ's sake, Maeve!' Gemma spluttered.

'You named your dildo?' asked Sally.

'Can we stop saying the word dildo?' asked Gemma.

Maeve ignored her. 'Yes,' she said. 'Technically this is Fernando Mark Three.'

'Blimey,' said Annie. 'You get through them.'

'There's never been anyone since my husband and he died over thirty years ago.'

'You haven't had sex in over thirty years?' Sally looked faint.

'Never had the time to find a man and I doubt I'd find one as reliable as Fernando.'

'Mark Three,' added Annie.

'Quite,' said Maeve. 'I upgraded on the last one.' Maeve wiggled her little finger and winked.

Annie was surprised at how easily her laughter came; she couldn't remember when she'd felt so light in her heart. Being here with these women, so different to her and yet each of them relatable to her in their own way, she felt bolstered by their camaraderie. She was having fun, pure enjoyment for the sake of it. Annie was still on a high when she flicked off the lamps and headed up to bed. Who would have thought a book club could be so life-affirming!

Chapter 35

Annie had begun to think there might be more business at Saltwater Nook during the winter months than Mari had presumed, and she found herself increasingly drawn to the idea of reopening the tea room; these days even the quietest villages expected to be able to enjoy a proper barista-made coffee. She recalled Alex's horror at not being able to get a decent coffee when he visited. Perhaps an artisan cafe was just the thing Willow Bay needed. Maybe wintry day-trippers would be attracted by the prospect of a little city luxury in the sticks.

The morning after the book club, she decided to talk it over with Mari. It could be financially positive for both of them: Mari would gain a steady income from the rent on a previously dormant space and Annie could try her hand at building a new business. Of course, Mari would be back in the spring and Annie would have to find somewhere else to live but she was sure she could find somewhere locally to rent. She knew all these grand ideas would come to nothing if the dreaded nephew convinced Mari to sell. And yet, she couldn't make her mind be quiet. Her phone rang, making her jump.

'Hello, my dear.' It was Mari. 'I'm just checking in to make sure everything is okay.'

'Hi, Mari, it's lovely to hear from you. I was just thinking about you. How are you enjoying Cornwall?'

'I may be a little bit in love with it. But don't tell the Nook.' Mari whispered this last part and Annie laughed. 'We're close by the sea and a two-minute walk to the shops. I won't lie to you, I haven't missed that hill.'

'I don't blame you,' said Annie. 'Whereabouts in Cornwall are you?'

'A little place called Mousehole. Isn't that an adorable name? My friend's house is too large for one person really but just about perfect for two. I have my own room with an en-suite and we meet every morning in the sun room for a pot of tea and some toast.'

'It sounds wonderful,' said Annie.

'And what about you, my dear? How is Saltwater Nook treating you?'

'Very well,' said Annie. 'I hardly remember what it felt like to live anywhere else.'

'Ah, I knew the sea would settle in your bones. It takes a special kind of person to live there, not everyone is cut out for it.'

Annie laughed. 'Well, I haven't done the winter yet,' she said. 'It might still beat me. But I've been opening the kiosk nearly every day,' she went on. 'It's very popular. And I was wondering . . .'

'Yes?' Mari said in that way people do when they already know what you're going to ask.

'Well, I was wondering how you would feel about me doing a trial opening of the tea room? Obviously I would buy all the stock and register it correctly; it would all be above board. I've run my own restaurant so I know all the red-tape stuff, and I'm fully insured but I'll take out an extra insurance for the tea room. And I was thinking that I could give you twenty per cent of anything I make, or I could rent the space from you? Whichever you'd prefer. Have a think about it. You don't need to answer right away—'

'Child, child!' Mari trilled. 'Calm yourself.'

Annie's heart was beating like a bird's. She hadn't realised just how much she wanted this until she'd said it out loud.

'Do as you want with the place,' said Mari. 'It's yours till spring and after that we can negotiate terms. If you make a profit, I'll take my twenty per cent and if you don't, then I won't. Does that sound fair?'

'More than fair,' Annie gushed. 'Thank you so much! Would you mind if I move a few things about? Maybe make a few changes?' Her brain was on fast-forward, mentally rearranging things, one image after another flashing before her eyes.

'As I said, my dear, do as you wish. I'm not precious about it, it's been gathering dust for decades. If you can make it useful again, all credit to you. It's serving no purpose while it slumbers.'

'I promise to be sympathetic to its history,' said Annie.

Mari tsked down the line.

'Sympathy is for those we pity,' she said. 'It doesn't need your sympathy; it needs your oomph!'

Annie laughed. 'Okay, I'll give it my best oomph. I won't let you down.'

'I know you won't, dear. But I should warn you, you may run into opposition from my nephew. As you know, he's keen for me to sell the place. He might not take kindly to a business starting up. Don't get me wrong, there's not a thing he can do about it; I've agreed to it and that is that. But it won't stop him throwing his teddy out of the perambulator!'

Annie felt her chagrin rise at the mere mention of the dreaded nephew.

'I'll watch out for tantrums,' said Annie. 'So long as it doesn't cause problems between the two of you.'

'It won't,' Mari said with parental confidence.

Annie had begun making lists and preparations for reopening the tea room as a coffee shop the moment she had put the phone down after speaking with Mari. So that by the time she had called Paul – in his new capacity as a friend *without* benefits – and commissioned him to do some building, lifting and general handiwork around the place, she had a clear idea of what she wanted to achieve. The whole thing needed to be done on a shoestring, not least because she was still having to draw cash out on her much abused credit card, and also because this was, after all, just a pop-up shop with a very good possibility of it closing down in the spring if John Granger sold the property. Luckily Paul's mates' rates were exceedingly matey and Alfred was on hand as extra muscle and only required food for his services. Maeve had donated a stack of old wood left over from the building of a new barn on the farm and Bill had brought down three unopened tubs of chalk-white paint from when they'd painted their apartment above the pub.

The first thing to address was moving the coffee machine so that it was conveniently reachable from both the cafe and the kiosk. Paul took the partition wall down to make the space open plan and then built a long counter against the far wall, where the coffee machine was re-plumbed into its new position, as was a sink and a five-ring electric hob with a small electric oven (all second-hand), and a microwave (donated by Sally) was set into one of the new cupboards. Beneath the counter he built a series of deep cupboards and plumbed in the dishwasher.

Annie continued to open the kiosk as usual; it was important to keep her customer base happy. And being that it was only a takeaway service, the disruption from banging and drilling was minimal – at least to her customers.

The old nautical oil lamps, which Annie had lovingly restored to their brassy glory, were given to Paul, with her strict instructions, and transformed into a stylish light fitting; the lamps now housed electric bulbs and were attached by a long length of industrial-looking wire. The offensive strip light in the ceiling was removed and the new-old lamps were hung above the counter at different heights, the wire looping between them, as though the lamps were hanging over the side of a fishing boat. Annie had rescued the kitsch floral crockery from the old cupboards and stacked it on top of the coffee machine, where it teetered in a riot of ditsy floral and plush rose petals, like the Mad Hatter's tea party.

Chapter 36

As the days went on Annie fell into tempo with the pulse of running a business on the coast. Come hell or high water – and sometimes the weather at Willow Bay seemed to encompass both – the dog-walkers and the joggers would be out for their early morning constitutionals. Annie would open the kiosk at eight a.m., ready to catch them on their way back, wind-bitten and frozen-fingered and grateful for a hot drink. There was always a lull around nine a.m. and then, between ten and eleven, it was the turn of the Lycra mummies speed-walking their pushchairs and small dogs, in stark contrast to the retired folks – sensibly attired against the cold and steady of pace. Skinny flat whites and tea were the orders of the hour respectively.

During the lulls, Annie would sit in the tea room and read by the Calor gas fire, so as to hear the 'OOOhee!' of customers calling her attention through the window. She opened the shutters on the large picture windows of the tea room to let in the daylight and read *Nicholas Nickleby* – the next book club choice – or Mari's notebook. It felt like a sublime existence, albeit fishbowl-like at times, as curious faces pressed against the glass to see inside. But she supposed it was understandable, after the place being shut up for the last twenty years. On Saturdays and on her lunch breaks Emily stood outside with a placard which read: *SAVE SALTWATER NOOK*. It wasn't a personal vendetta – though it wasn't ideal – and she quite often bought a hot drink from the kiosk when it was really cold and chatted amiably with Annie about how business was before going back to picketing.

Annie walked the length of the promenade almost every day, either first thing to watch the sunrise or when she closed the kiosk at half past two. The weather grew colder exponentially as the days of October ticked by.

Some days there seemed only to be unrelenting rain, driven horizontally by the wind, the sky leaden and so heavy she could feel it pressing down on her shoulders. On these days Annie stayed in, watching the storm from behind the kiosk window, wrapped in a knitted poncho, cradling a mug of coffee while strands of her hair were lifted by the draught in the old window frames.

She had wondered if she might feel lonely but, in truth, she didn't, not a bit. Alex and Peter texted regularly, and she called them each weekly for a proper catch-up. She had the book club and she was feeling more and more a part of the Willow Bay community. The evenings were quiet, but Annie revelled in them; she had spent her entire adult life in a career that demanded her evenings and now she had them back.

On nights when the tide was high and the weather unsettled, Annie knew that Alfred would stay, and she always made sure to leave food and a thermos of hot tea in the tea room for him. Early one morning she stepped out for her walk and found bundles of rosemary tied with string on the doorstep, ready for drying, and the garden neatly chopped back – a job she had been meaning to get to – and she understood that she had entered into a bartering agreement with Alfred: food and shelter for odd jobs.

The transition from autumn to winter was accented by the creeping of early morning frosts, which glittered on the sage leaves in the garden and left tell-tale wet patches on the ground when the sun and salt dissolved it. As per Mari's note-book, Fred had delivered the winter logs and, thankfully, Alfred had been on hand to help Annie sweep the log store and pile them into it. She hadn't asked Alfred to help her, he had simply appeared when Fred's van turned up and set to work. He wasn't much for polite conversation and Annie found his quiet company strangely reassuring. It was an odd sort of friendship, if you could call it that, but it suited Annie as much as it did Alfred.

'Don't you ever worry that the tide will come in while you're in the cave?' Annie asked Alfred as they worked.

'Nope. I know the tides like I know myself.'

'You've never been taken by surprise? By a storm or some-thing?'

Alfred chuckled and shook his head.

'Nope. I respect the sea. I don't ever take for granted that she won't take it upon herself to sweep me out to the depths. I know her moods, and when she's in a tempest I'm wise enough to stay out of her way. She's just like a woman: you've got to know when to worship and when to take cover.'

Chapter 37

The man from the council's environmental health department had been due to drop in today to give her the okay for opening the old tea room as a new cafe business, but he hadn't turned up, so Annie assumed he'd either got lost trying to find the place or been held up on other business. The air was heady with the scent of newly sawn pine and freshly ground coffee. Not having had time to bake for tonight's book club, Annie had bought three boxes of macarons at the Willow Bay Stores, which she would offer with coffees of their choice.

The candles flickered as the book club attendees blustered into the cafe, sopping from the rain that fell in sheets across land and sea. Dripping coats were slung across the backs of chairs to dry, and wet boots made footprints on the floor.

'Oh wow!' exclaimed Gemma. 'Annie, it looks great! Well done you!'

Annie smiled, pleased.

Maeve surveyed the room and nodded.

'Mari would approve. You've done just enough to bring it up to date without losing the essence of the place.'

'Thanks, Maeve. I'm glad you think so,' said Annie.

'You kept the old pictures,' said Sally, pointing to the vintage prints.

'They fit somehow,' Annie replied and Sally bobbed her head in agreement.

'Oh, I do wish you'd have a proper opening ceremony,' Gemma pouted.

'It's only a pop-up,' Annie reasoned. 'If it was a permanent fixture, I might have, but sadly it isn't.'

'The Willow Bay Historical Society aren't best pleased,' said Maeve.

'No,' Annie agreed, biting her lip.

'They'll come round,' said Gemma. 'They just need to see you as a custodian of the history, rather than a hijacker.'

'Your sunshine and rainbows outlook is really quite refreshing,' said Sally.

'Thank you,' Gemma said, unable to flatten out her grin. She held up a bottle of wine. 'Right! Let's get started.'

The women took their seats, Maeve digging out handfuls of crisps from the bowl in the middle of the table with her big rough hands. They each pulled out their copies of *Nicholas Nickleby*, except Maeve who once again tapped her head to indicate that she had the manuscript saved in her brain; Sally's copy was particularly dog-eared.

'That school,' Gemma began. 'Dotheboys Hall. Made me cry, it was so awful!'

'Everything makes you cry,' said Maeve. 'You cry at adverts for cat food.'

'Don't tell me you weren't touched by the plight of those poor children, Maeve,' Gemma admonished. 'Even you aren't that hard.'

'Of course I was,' said Maeve.

'It wasn't entirely fictional,' added Sally. 'It was a crappy time to be alive if you were without social standing or money.'

'When Nicholas whupped Wackford Squeers's arse, I almost yelled for joy,' said Annie.

'Poor Smike,' Gemma lamented. 'What a sad little life. He barely had a glimpse of happiness. All that fear and pain.'

'I think Smike was Dickens's comment on society. Yes, he wound the story up in a neat bow for the most part. But in reality, many people lived hard, short lives. Smike epitomised their plight,' said Sally.

'I agree,' said Annie. 'Dickens was giving a voice to the people who didn't have one. It wasn't the poor who would be reading his work; most of them wouldn't have been able to read, let alone afford the stories. It was the socially buoyant he was trying to reach.'

'What did you think of the female portrayals?' asked Sally.

'Usual drivelling bints,' said Maeve. 'They're either too sensitive or too stupid.'

'I give you Kate and her mother,' said Annie, topping up Gemma's and her own wine glass.

'The virtuous fainting virgin and the prattling self-absorbed windbag,' Sally offered.

'What did you think of Nicholas?' asked Gemma, a little dreamily.

'I think he was too pious to be good in the sack,' said Annie.

'I disagree!' trilled Gemma. 'I think Nicholas showed great passion. Especially for Madeline Bray.'

'But he'd have kept his pyjamas tucked into his socks on his wedding night,' said Sally.

'Maybe he was a little too virtuous?' said Annie.

'Here we go again,' said Sally. 'The eternal good guy versus bad boy debate.'

'Not at all,' said Annie. 'I suppose I'd just be attracted to someone more spirited; someone like John Browdie.'

'He was an oaf!' exclaimed Gemma.

'And a chauvinist,' said Maeve.

'I'm not saying he's my ideal man,' said Annie. 'But if I had to choose a man from this particular book, I would choose Browdie over Nickleby.'

'I can see that,' said Sally. 'He was a good-natured realist.'

'Exactly,' said Annie. 'Plus, I think he's kind of beefy, whereas Nicholas I imagine to be a bit scrawny.'

Maeve chose this moment to clear her throat loudly.

'Speaking of beefy,' she said, and Gemma began to giggle uncontrollably as she leaned across to top up Annie's glass.

Maeve rustled around in a bag she'd brought in with her and pulled out a box. She placed it in the middle of the table. Annie and Sally stared. Gemma continued to giggle. The clear plastic window of the box revealed a large dildo in shades of pastel peach.

'Open it!' chivvied Gemma.

'Me?' Annie asked.

'Yes, you,' said Maeve. 'It's a gift. For hosting the book club. We wanted to get you something practical.'

Sally was grinning and showing all her teeth.

'Were you in on this?' asked Annie.

Sally shrugged.

'Maybe,' she said. 'But Maeve made the choice since she's the expert in these things.'

Since Annie hadn't made a move to open the box, Maeve did it for her, pulling the rubber phallus from its casing and waving it about.

'Here,' she said, pointing to a suction pad on its base. 'It's got one of these.' She licked the suction pad and smacked the dildo down hard so that it stuck to the centre of the table. 'There,' she said. 'You're welcome!'

'Thank you?' said Annie. 'Why does it need a suction cup?'

'So you can mount it,' said Maeve as though Annie was stupid. 'You know. Go on top. Ride it!'

Annie held her hands up to stop any further explanation.

'Right,' she said. 'Got it, thanks.'

'But not necessarily on a tabletop,' said Gemma.

'Safety first,' added Sally.

The dildo stood to attention, leaning ever so slightly to the left. Maeve reached over and squeezed its tip.

'You see, it's got give,' she said. 'Like a real one.'

'Firm but pliable,' added Sally.

'In my experience, realism is best,' Maeve continued. 'I've tried all sorts of dildos – solid, smooth, ribbed, knobbled – but you can't beat an authentic-feeling penis.'

'Maeve, are you sure you weren't in the porn industry?' asked Annie, strangely unable to take her eyes off the rubber willy stuck to her freshly sanded table.

'No such luck,' said Maeve. 'Just a long time single.'

'I prefer the term synthetic penis,' said Gemma. 'Dildo sounds so coarse.'

'You old romantic,' Annie laughed.

Gemma grabbed the box and turned it around, pointing to a photograph of a tall naked man in the act of running his hand through his dark hair, while caressing his erect penis in the other.

'It's a copy of his,' said Gemma delightedly. 'They make plaster-cast moulds.'

'What a claim to fame,' said Annie.

Chapter 38

The four women sat quietly for a few moments, sipping their drinks while they contemplated the large synthetic penis.

'You should name it,' said Sally after a while.

'Ooh,' said Gemma. 'Yes, good idea. You could call it John, since you like John Browdie so much!'

Sally leaned forward with her pen and rested it first on one testicle, then the other, whilst solemnly saying, 'I hereby name thee John Synthetic Penis the First!'

The women cheered loudly and clinked glasses. Maeve excused herself and stepped out into the rain to use the small brick-built outhouse situated to the right of the cafe door. It wasn't exactly ideal having the toilet outside but Annie didn't want to begin any major renovations until she knew whether her gamble to reopen the cafe was going to pay off. The remaining women were just beginning to discuss the suicide of Ralph Nickleby when the door burst open. A large man stood dripping in the doorway, his broad shoulders filling the entire frame. His face was covered by the hood of his coat, pulled low to protect him from the rain, and his dark wet outline glistened in the lamplight.

Gemma screamed and jumped out of her chair. Sally yelled

'Oi!' and Annie made a loud surprised noise that was somewhere in between.

'Who the hell are you?' shouted Annie, trying her best to sound brave and threatening at the same time.

'I've got a gun!' Gemma screamed, forcing her hand into her cardigan pocket and pointing it at the man.

'Gemma, calm the fuck down!' said Sally. Then she turned to face the hooded man and said with a calm that would cut through the angriest of drunks at her reception desk: 'And WHO the FUCK are you?'

The man pulled down his hood to reveal short dark hair, greying at the temples, and a clean-shaven face with a dark shadow where tomorrow's stubble would be.

'Never mind who I am,' he said, wiping the rain from his forehead with the back of his hand. 'What the hell is this? Some kind of porn coven?'

'Are you from the council?' Annie asked, suddenly remembering the no-show from the environmental health man. 'This isn't what it looks like,' she hastened to add, waving her arm to encompass the candles and wine and the dick standing to attention on the table.

Gemma, recovered from the initial shock, squinted up at the man and then grinned. 'Oh, it's you! How are you?' She'd necked a glass of wine and its warmth had clearly bolstered her bravery; she pointed to the dildo and said, 'This is so funny! You're not going to believe this but this is John! Perhaps we should call him Little John to differentiate.'

At that moment Maeve came bowling through the door and knocked the tall, frowning man further into the cafe.

'What's all the bloody noise?' she shouted. 'Can't a woman

do her business in peace?' In another moment, recognition lit her face and she strode over to the man and pulled him into a bear hug.

'John, my boy!' she said, clapping him on the back. 'Good to see you! You've met the others?' she asked, nodding around the room.

'Not officially, no,' said the man through gritted teeth.

Annie imagined her stomach dropping out of the bottom of her jeans and inching away across the floor. *Surely not!* she thought. *Surely this isn't the first impression I give to the man who could potentially ruin my new business?*

'No?' said Maeve, seemingly oblivious to the excruciating scene before them. 'Right then, introductions. John Granger, this is Annie Sharpe; she's looking after Saltwater Nook for your aunt and doing a damned fine job of it so far too. Obviously you know Gemma already and then there's Sally. And together we make up the Victorian book club.'

'And what the hell is *this* to do with a Victorian book club?' asked John, pointing at the phallic table centre.

'Oh, that's just a little something for Annie,' said Maeve, without a hint of embarrassment. 'Single girl and all that. Thought it might keep her out of mischief.'

Sally was managing to keep her composure – just. Gemma was snickering like a drunk schoolgirl. And Annie wanted to swallow her own head. She stood, cleared her throat, and held out her hand as though it was perfectly normal to meet one's landlady's nephew over a candlelit dildo.

'Hello,' she said. 'I'm Annie. It's lovely to meet you.'

John regarded her for a long moment. In this light his eyes looked as black as the eyebrows from under which he held her with a stare that could freeze water. His long nose came to a sharp point, as did his chin. His lips were a thin, disapproving line.

'I'm afraid I can't say the same,' he replied.

'That your name is Annie?' she said, attempting to lighten the mood.

'That it's nice to meet you,' he said, without a hint of humour.

'Look, we've clearly got off on the wrong foot,' Annie reasoned. 'I'll admit this doesn't give a glowing impression . . .'

'Oh, you've made an impression all right,' said John.

'Why don't you pull up a chair. We'll pop Little John back into his box and you can join us for a glass of wine and the remainder of our book club. It'll give you a chance to see that we're not a bunch of drunken harlots.'

'Speak for yourself,' said Maeve.

Annie ignored her and continued, 'Have you read *Nicholas Nickleby*?'

Gemma held her copy out for John as Sally tugged furiously at Little John until he relinquished his suction on the table with a loud pop, whereupon she slipped him back into the box and pushed it under the table.

'I want you out of this property!' said John.

'What?' Annie said. The book club blustered similarly in indignation.

'Now wait just a moment, John,' said Maeve.

'I'm surprised at you, Maeve. I'd have expected you to show a little more respect for my aunt's property.'

'And I'm disappointed in you!' said Maeve. 'How do you think your aunt would feel if she knew you'd treated her guests with such rudeness?'

John began to splutter. 'Her guests? Her guests? Her guests that have turned her home into some kind of sordid sex parlour!'

'You're really not seeing this in context,' said Annie, trying her best at peacemaking.

'I've seen all I need to see,' John said coldly.

He turned to leave, wrenching the door open. The wind caught it, slamming it hard against the wall. The rain blew in in horizontal shards of water. John turned back to face Annie; the light from the room lit the rain behind him so that it looked like shooting stars.

'I want you off this property by close of business tomorrow,' he snarled. And with that passing shot, he yanked the door closed behind him, the force of it blowing out two of the candles.

Gemma opened another bottle of wine and poured a glass for Annie. Annie took a gulp and then another.

'I can't believe it. I've just been evicted!'

'Nobody's evicting anybody,' said Maeve.

'You heard what he said,' said Annie. 'He wants me out by tomorrow.'

'John doesn't own Saltwater Nook, nor did he give you the job to be guardian of the place,' said Maeve reassuringly. 'The only person who can evict you is Mari.'

'Absolutely,' chimed in Gemma. 'And Mari is a very reasonable woman. I'm sure she wouldn't dream of evicting you over such a silly misunderstanding.'

Annie didn't feel reassured.

'We weren't actually doing anything wrong,' Sally soothed. 'I think it's important to keep it in perspective. What we're

JENNY BAYLISS

dealing with is a man who was frightened when faced with four women in touch with their sexuality and his discomfort manifested itself as anger.'

'I'll talk to Mari in the morning,' said Maeve. 'You're not going anywhere.'

Chapter 39

Annie woke the next morning with a knot in her stomach. The thought of having to leave Saltwater Nook left her cold. She hadn't had enough time, she'd barely begun, plus her credit card had taken a bit of a beating getting the place ready to open. She couldn't imagine not being here; not waking up every morning beside the fickle Atlantic Ocean. Not flinging open the shutters on the kiosk to reveal the familiar, eager faces and discussing the weather as the coffee machine limbered up for another day's work.

She lay with the comforting weight of a snoring Mrs Tiggy-Winkle on her feet and the khaki of an October morning staining the curtains. The rain scratched against the window-panes like it wanted to be let in. She had heard the now familiar noise of shutters being adjusted and re-closed as Alfred let himself out at dawn; would her successor look out for him? she wondered. Annie decided she needed to speak to Mari herself. She would not let another egomaniac man bull-doze her life.

Mari answered on the second ring.

'Well, bless my soul,' she declared. 'I am popular today. I've just had John on the phone.'

What a grass! Annie thought, snorting inwardly.

'So, you know about last night,' said Annie. 'It wasn't as bad as it sounds . . .'

'Quite a cackling coven you've instigated by the sounds of it.'

To Annie's surprise, Mari sounded amused.

'It was the book club,' said Annie. 'There were some . . . high jinks.'

'John was reluctant to go into detail but he used the words "sordid" and "sex aid"; are these the high jinks to which you are referring?'

Annie almost laughed but swallowed hard to quash it. She decided it was best to just come right out and say it.

'It was a bit of a joke,' Annie began. 'At last week's book club we'd been discussing my recent singledom and the other members thought it would be a fun idea to get me a, er . . .' Annie stumbled. Was she really going to use the word dildo to a nonagenarian? 'A, um, synthetic penis,' she finished, remembering Gemma's more romantic affectation.

Annie heard a gasp followed by what could only be described as tittering in the background.

'Am I on loudspeaker?'

'Ach, yes, dear,' said Mari. 'My friend June is very interested in the current debacle. It's better than telly!'

From some small distance the voice of the titterer called, 'Do tell us more about the synthetic penis!'

Annie laughed.

'Oh, Mari, I am sorry. I hope you don't think we were being disrespectful. It was just unfortunate timing that your nephew arrived when he did.'

'He called you a sex witch!' said the distant voice.

'I should be so lucky,' said Annie, and Mari and her companion chuckled daintily. 'It was probably the candles that gave the witch vibes,' Annie added.

'Cock by candlelight!' called Mari's friend.

'Oh, hush now,' Mari admonished. 'Annie will think we're a couple of old hags.'

'Well, anyway,' said Annie, trying to steer the conversation away from cocks by candlelight. 'I can assure you, I am in no way abusing your trust. I really hope this doesn't make you change your mind about letting me stay.'

'Oh, tut tut. Not at all,' Mari said. 'My nephew is being overprotective as usual, thinks I'm made of glass; a china prude he'd have me cast as,' she went on. 'Well, I can tell you, I am none of the above. You stay, my girl, and put those plans of yours into action. I'd like to see the Nook be an active part of the community again.'

'The local Historical Society isn't best pleased,' said Annie.

'Ah, young Emily. She is a marvellous woman, full of passion! She's not angry with you, dear, she just wants the bay to keep the Nook. We're all on the same team when you come down to it. Perhaps you are the person to unite us. Have you had any thoughts on a name yet?'

'I've been knocking around The Saltwater Cafe in my head,' said Annie. 'I thought, keep it simple. I've run it by a few people, and they seem to like it.'

'It's the perfect name for it,' said Mari.

Annie ended the phone call feeling as though she'd been given a reprieve on a sentence.

Chapter 40

In the awkward chaos which had brought the book club to an early close, Annie realised they hadn't chosen a new book. She privately messaged Maeve first to let her know there was no need to call Mari, and then messaged the group with a suggestion of *Lady Audley's Secret* by Mary Elizabeth Braddon. She had come across a copy in Mari's bookcase and thought it would be nice – since they were all women – to read a Victorian novel written by a female author. Within moments her phone began to ping with responses.

Gemma: Are you sure you want to continue with it after last night? Is everything sorted with Mari? 🙂

Maeve: What are you talking about woman? Welcome to host at mine if you feel awkward having it at the Nook.

Sally: Best damn book club I've ever been to! Love this book suggestion. Read it at uni for a module on Victorian female writers; scandalous . . . though not as scandalous as our book club. 🙂

Annie: I have absolutely no problem hosting at the Nook. Spoke to Mari. All good. She encouraged us to continue. John Granger can kiss my arse!

Sally: What about plastic John?

Annie: He's not called John anymore.

Gemma: What's he called now?

Annie: Mr Knightley.

Gemma: From *Emma*?

Annie: Correct.

Maeve: So, you like them grumpy then, hey?

Annie: Not grumpy. Honourable.

Sally: But not too honourable, right?

Annie: 😑

Gemma: Can you describe a dildo as honourable?

Maeve: Can we get back to the book club?

Gemma: It's a yes from me. 😊

Sally: Me too.

Maeve: Then we're agreed. Good choice, Annie.

At half past two Annie was about to close the kiosk for the day when a shadow fell across the opening, blocking out all of the light. Annie had her back turned, washing up the milk jugs.

'You're in luck,' she called. 'I was just about to close up. But I'll make an exception.' She turned, smiling, to greet her last-minute customer and came face to face with John Granger. His expression was thunderous.

'I came here to apologise for the way I handled last night, only to find you abusing my aunt's hospitality again!' he said. His thick Scottish accent was laced with anger and the depth of his voice seemed to bounce around the small kiosk.

Annie felt her chagrin rise. She would not be cowed by such a disagreeable man. She wiped her hands dry on her apron and squared up to him.

'Firstly,' she began, her shoulders pulled back and her chin jutting out in indignation, 'I have your aunt's full blessing to open the kiosk whenever I like. Secondly, I have put money in the kitty towards the stock I initially used, and since then I have paid for all the coffee beans, milks and sundries myself. And thirdly, I don't know what impression you are under but I am *not* here under your aunt's *hospitality*! I am liable for all bills and utilities and am employed to oversee and maintain Saltwater Nook until such time as Mari decides to return.'

John Granger rocked back on his heels looking contrite. He blew out a breath.

'I'm sorry. Can we start again?' he asked, posting his hand in through the kiosk. 'I'm John Granger. Not nearly as grumpy as I seem. It appears my aunt has been omitting to tell me the arrangements the two of you have made. You've taken me by surprise – twice. That doesn't happen very often.'

Annie shook the proffered hand gingerly.

'It's not often that I'm described as *surprising*, so we're both treading new ground,' she said, allowing him a small smile. She wasn't sure of him yet.

'Do you even know how to use that thing?' he asked, pointing to the coffee machine.

'I am a fully trained barista,' she replied as haughtily as she could muster. 'Among other things.'

'Oh?' there was note of surprise in John's voice and Annie thought she detected a twinkle of humour in his eyes.

'I am a classically trained award-winning chef and have run a successful restaurant for fifteen years.'

'If it's so successful, why did you leave it?' He raised one eyebrow; he was teasing her. Annie didn't know if she liked it or not.

'That's a bit impertinent, Mr Granger,' she said and gave what she hoped was a Mona Lisa smile.

Just then Raye came bounding up to the kiosk window, seemingly unaware of the human mountain stood in front of it.

'Hi, Annie! Thank goodness I caught you, I was worried you'd be closed already. I've just got back from the cash and carry and I'm gagging for a coffee before we open. Can I have an oat milk mocha, please?' She thrust her reusable bamboo cup through the hatch.

It was only then that she noticed the scowling man.

'Oh, gosh, sorry!' she flustered. 'Were you here first? Trust me, barging in like a fairy elephant!' And then she registered who the other customer was. 'John!' she squealed delightedly and threw her arms around his waist, hugging him tight. 'Great to see you! Are you here for long? You must drop in to The Bounty, Aiden would love to see you. You've met our Annie then? She's an absolute lifesaver, I tell you.'

Annie smiled and John Granger looked uncomfortable.

'It's lovely to see you, Raye,' he said with a warmth that Annie found hard to associate with the same stony face that had greeted her on both occasions they'd met. 'How are you? How's Melody getting on?'

'I'm good,' said Raye. 'We're all good. Melody is loving university life, we'll be lucky if she even bothers to come back for holidays at this rate. We miss you, though; where've you been hiding yourself?'

John Granger smiled then and Annie felt her eyebrows rise in incredulity. She hadn't expected a face with such a propensity for scowling to be capable of such friendliness. His eyes crinkled at the edges with lines that implied he smiled often, though Annie considered that they could equally be the result of frequent glowering. The five o'clock shadow of last night was dark stubble today, tapering to smatterings of white at the sideburns.

'I miss you guys too,' said John. 'Work's just been crazy this last few months. And I've had a few ups and downs with Celeste.'

Raye frowned sympathetically. 'Everything all right now, though?' she asked.

'Yes,' he said reassuringly. 'You know how it is.'

And Raye nodded knowingly. *Trouble with the missus*, Annie thought.

'So, when are you going to give up life in the big smoke and come back here where you belong?' Raye asked.

'One day,' he said. 'One day.'

'Are you getting coffee?' she asked.

Annie raised an eyebrow and couldn't quite hide the smirk that threatened around her lips. John looked at Annie and then back to Raye.

'No,' he said. 'I had to visit a client in Whitstable, stayed the night in a hotel. I've got to get back to London.'

Raye pouted comically.

'But you'll come down for the grand opening on the eighteenth, won't you?' she asked.

'What *grand opening* would that be? Have you finally built that extension to the pub?'

Raye chuckled.

'Sadly not. We're still ploughing pennies into the pot for that one.'

'Well, you just let me know when you're ready for that free design consultation,' said John.

'Thanks, John. As soon as we've saved enough, we'll be on the blower quicker than you can say boutique hotel!'

'So, what's this *grand opening* then?'

'You know!' exclaimed Raye, thumping John playfully on the arm and nodding in Annie's direction. 'The Saltwater Cafe. Annie's worked so hard on the place; though she won't make nearly as much fuss about it as she ought to,' Raye chided, waggling her finger at Annie. 'And what's worse, she won't let us make a fuss about it either, even though we're all desperate to and beyond excited that we'll finally have a coffee shop in Willow Bay!'

John Granger's face darkened. He turned towards Annie. Annie realised that Mari had omitted to mention *all* of Annie's extra-curricular business activities to her nephew. She was surprised he hadn't noticed the new layout in the tea room when he had gatecrashed their book club last night. But then, she conceded, his focus had rather been distracted by the dildo suctioned to the table.

'You didn't know?' said Raye, her smile faltering as she cast a nervous look at Annie, who did her absolute best to smile reassuringly back.

'No,' said John, his mouth pulling into a tight line. 'I didn't.'

'Oh God!' Raye lamented. 'Have I spoiled the surprise? I have, haven't I? Oh, me and my big mouth. Aiden calls me *colander* because I can't seem to keep any thought I have from spilling out. Oops, sorry, Annie.'

'Don't worry,' said Annie, smiling. 'You haven't spoiled

anything. Mari must have forgotten to mention it.' She looked pointedly at John. 'Would you like to see what I've done with the place? Consider it a VIP sneak preview.'

'Thank you but no,' said John. 'I'm in a hurry. Goodbye, Raye,' he said, kissing Raye on both cheeks. 'Tell Aiden I'll be up to see him soon.' He turned and glared at Annie. 'Goodbye, Ms Sharpe,' he said acerbically and stalked off down the promenade towards the whopping four-by-four parked at the bottom of the hill.

Annie willed the gulls that were circling the sky above to crap on his head, but they didn't see fit to oblige.

She finished making Raye's mocha and handed back her bamboo cup.

'Sorry,' said Raye. 'I seem to have dropped you right in it. I guess a cafe opening up doesn't quite fit with his plans to sell.'

'Don't worry about it,' Annie reassured her. 'He doesn't scare me.'

'Oh, he's a darling when you get to know him. Really,' she added, seeing the scepticism in Annie's expression. 'You must have just got off on the wrong foot.'

The man from environmental health finally arrived at about four o'clock. All was in order, as Annie knew it would be. It turned out she knew the agent from The Pomegranate Seed.

'I thought your name looked familiar when I got my list through,' said Stephan. 'The Pomegranate Seed hasn't closed down, has it?'

'No, no,' Annie assured him. 'I'm just trying my hand at something new.'

'You've picked a funny time to open a seaside cafe. End of season and all that.'

'I'm planning to stay open through the winter months.'

Stephan sucked air in through his teeth.

'Are you sure? Most seaside places die a death off-season. It's not exactly a great place for footfall, is it?'

'Well, I'm not expecting to tap into the tourist market,' Annie replied. 'But there's a pretty tight-knit community here who seem keen to have a coffee shop on their doorstep.'

'I hope you're right,' he said. Though Annie could tell from his expression that he thought this was wishful thinking. 'It takes more than warm thoughts to keep a business afloat.'

Annie smiled sweetly as she waited for him to fill out her documents and tried to calculate how many times she'd had the finer points of running a business mansplained to her over the years.

Chapter 41

It was mid-October, and while the days were getting shorter and the weather was distinctly chillier, business at the kiosk was still booming.

Annie had never intended the cafe opening to be a big deal. After all, it was really just a pop-up shop. However, there was something about John Granger's disapproval which led her to abandon her whisper of an opening in favour of a big fat shout, and in double-quick time Annie managed to rustle up a grand opening that Raye could be justified in getting excited about.

With a little persuasion from Aiden, the folk band who had played at The Captain's Bounty agreed to play a two-hour afternoon set outside the cafe. Paul used his charm on the kitesurfing club and managed to rustle up a race in the morning – when the wind was due to be at its strongest that day – to the outer marker, kindly deposited by Ely on his early morning fishing trip. Pam had agreed to cut the ribbon at ten o'clock on Saturday morning to declare The Saltwater Cafe officially open for business. In addition to being landlady of The Sunken Willow, she was also the chairwoman of the Willow Bay Council – with a guiding hand in everything from collections for local charities and fundraising, to the Willow Bay festivities; mother and daughter were quite the powerhouse.

Annie had revelled in organising her grand opening; it played to all her list-making skills. Paul had been an absolute star, ferrying garden tables and chairs down from the two pubs and setting them in strategic clusters along the promenade. The Captain's Bounty and The Sunken Willow had declared they would continue the celebrations throughout the evening with a joint BBQ; Annie was discovering that the residents of Willow Bay needed very little excuse to throw a party.

The weather was due to be cold and windy but bright – just the weather to bring revellers to the beach in want of a hot drink. On Friday night Annie was still working to make sure everything was ready. Maeve had offered to make a lemon drizzle loaf cake and a fruited tea bread to help out, and Annie had made two batches of cookies – oatmeal and raisin and chocolate chip – plus a Victoria sponge, a coffee and walnut cake, and a rocky road to go with her brownies and chocolate fudge traybake. As Annie was dolloping clouds of whipped cream onto the bottom half of the Victoria sponge the phone rang.

'How's the prep going?' asked Gemma.

'Almost done,' said Annie. 'I'm about ready to drop.'

'I'll bet! Listen, I don't want to add more to your schedule but I was talking to the mums at the school today and everyone is wondering, since you're going to open and all, if you'd consider keeping up Mari's Halloween tradition? It would be lovely if you could. Mari always makes Halloween so special.'

Annie mentally kicked herself for not reading Mari's note-book recently. With a jolt, she realised Halloween was just around the corner.

'Well, I'll see what I can do,' said Annie. 'I wouldn't want to ruin a time-honoured tradition!'

'Annie, you're amazing!' cooed Gemma. 'Everyone will be so pleased!'

Annie smiled down the phone and wondered what the hell it was she was going to have to do.

When the last cake was stashed in the chiller, Annie wrapped a sandwich in foil and left it on the table just in case Alfred spent the night. She also wrote him a note inviting him to come along tomorrow for the opening, promising free coffee as payment for all the work he'd done. She had been worrying that Alfred might feel he couldn't sleep in the old tea room now it was reopening. It was important to her that he should still feel welcome, but equally he was a proud man; the merest hint of charity or pity on her part would push him away. She tucked the note under the sandwich, and then with one last look of satisfaction around the place she headed up to bed.

Chapter 42

The weather looked like it would hold. It was definitely chilly – you could smell the cold in the air, fresh and clean – but the sky was lapis blue and the cotton-wool clouds were the pure white friendly kind. Alex and Peter had messaged to wish her luck; Alex late last night – no chance he would be up early after a night out – and Peter this morning after his run. Max had sent her a passive-aggressive text asking her to respect their years in business together by not using recipes she had designed for The Pomegranate Seed.

Annie opened the kiosk early as usual and, to her surprise, Alfred came to wish her luck.

'Why don't you stay for the festivities?' Annie asked as she made him an extra-large latte with four sugars.

'I'm not keen on crowds,' said Alfred.

'Well, so long as you know that you're welcome,' said Annie, not wanting to push it.

'I'll be up at Maeve's place all day, sorting the guttering.'

'I'm surprised Maeve doesn't fix her own guttering,' Annie laughed.

'It's about the only thing she won't do. She doesn't like

heights. Otherwise she probably would. But then I'd be out of a good pie and mash supper.'

'She's a very capable woman,' said Annie.

Alfred grunted.

'Built like a shire horse and just as pig-headed. I appreciate the snacks you leave out for me,' said Alfred, changing the subject. His voice was gruff, hoarse from lack of use.

'It's no bother,' said Annie.

'You don't have to do it just because Mari did.'

'I know. I like to. And besides, you help me with the garden and you were a godsend getting this place ready, so it's payment for services rendered.'

Alfred made a sort of growl that might have been an agreement. Annie handed him his coffee.

'Thank you. You make very good coffee.'

'Thank you. You are always welcome to stop for a morning coffee before you disappear off on your daily travels,' said Annie.

'I push off early,' he replied. Annie knew this to be true; she almost never met Alfred in the mornings, even when she came down to watch the sunrise.

'Well, if you're ever running late and need a caffeine pick-me-up, please do.'

By half past nine people were starting to gather in the general Saltwater Nook area. Emily and a couple of others held placards which read *SAVE SALTWATER NOOK* but they were quietly respectful in their dissent.

Soon, there was a bigger crowd than Annie could have foreseen, and she began to worry about how she was going to cope if all these people stayed for coffee. Pam had to shout to be heard above the crowd when she made her speech, before

cutting the ribbon across the door with due pomp and ceremony.

'I now declare The Saltwater Cafe open!'

A cheer went up.

'I think I speak for everyone here when I say we are delighted
that Annie, with Mari's blessing, has decided to make
Saltwater Nook an active part of our community once more.'

More cheering. And then someone piped up: 'Come on
then, get that coffee machine humming!'

And so it began and it did not stop. As the first wave of
customers filed into the cafe it became quickly evident that
despite not offering table service, there was still not enough of
Annie to go around.

'Need a hand?' Samantha's voice trilled across the crowd.

'Would you mind? Could you work the till?' Annie called.
Annie had splashed out and treated herself to a twenty-first-
century till in the refit.

Samantha pushed her way through the waiting customers
and around to the service side of the counter. She took a
moment to scan her eyes over the till and nodded to herself.

'Right,' she said. 'I've got this, you concentrate on coffee.'

'Thank you so much!' Annie gushed. 'I really misjudged the
numbers.'

Samantha took orders, payments and doled out sundries,
while Annie worked the coffee machine, her arms aching from
many weeks of not doing repetitive physical labour. There was
a party atmosphere in and outside of the cafe; nostalgic
sounds of 1930s jazz and swing played through the speakers
and lent an ambience of calm despite the hubbub. Gemma
grinned and waved from the back of the room. By the time she

and the children reached the front of the queue she looked as though she might burst.

'It's amazing!' she gushed. 'You're amazing! What a turnout. You must be so pleased. Oh, well done, Annie, I'm so proud of you! Samantha, are you moonlighting? Where's Tom?'

Annie laughed.

'Thanks, Gemma. Hi, kids,' said Annie. Esme and Lennox grimaced – they were less than impressed at having spent twenty minutes in a queue. Annie reached into the chiller and pulled out two pieces of tiffin as a peace offering.

'Tom's manning the shop,' said Samantha. 'When things calm down a bit here, I'll go up and hold the fort so he can come down.'

'Poor Samantha, came down expecting a relaxing morning and ended up working,' Annie explained.

Samantha shrugged, smiling, and said, 'A change is as good as a rest.'

Aside from the wait for drinks, the comments were mostly positive. People were delighted by the prospect of there being a cafe on the seafront. Lots of visitors – drawn by the sunny weather – who would not ordinarily come this far down the promenade, said they would definitely be back. But the people Annie really needed to impress were the ones who would be her bread and butter: the locals. Mari was a beloved local legend and Annie was stepping into some well-respected shoes. She made a point of taking coffees out to Emily and her associates, who took them with grudging thanks, and Annie was gratified later to see the banners rested up against the wall, slogans facing inward.

Paul swanned in and out, accepting compliments on his woodwork skills and chatting amiably with everyone. The cheeky winks in the direction of several Willow Bay ladies did not go unnoticed by Annie, nor did their sultry return gazes; Paul's sexual chemistry was alive and kicking with everyone but her apparently.

The kitesurfing race was a triumph. Bill had a megaphone and gave commentary from his position on the patio wall. Someone had opened a book on the race, which added another dimension to the cheers of the crowd. When the race was over, the folk band struck up and the promenade was alive with dancing children, and adults foot-tapping and clapping along to the music. Fleece hoodies and cable-knits were the order of the day; hair was whipped back and forth by the wind and sunglasses enjoyed a final outing in the glorious autumn sun. It felt to Annie as though the weather had given one last blast of summer before winter. She took it as a good omen, as if the sun was encouraging her in her endeavours.

In the midst of it all Annie found herself looking out for John Granger. She wanted him to see how positive the response was, what she had achieved. But he didn't show, at least she hadn't spotted him. But then she hadn't had much time to see any of the proceedings really. From the moment Pam had cut the ribbon, Annie had been practically attached to the coffee machine. Most of the cakes she had made had sold by half past eleven and the crisps and bars she'd bought at the cash and carry had gone by lunchtime. She knew it was a false indicator of what she would need realistically day by day; she was pretty sure mid-November would be a markedly subdued turnout by comparison. But Mari would receive a healthy twenty per cent from her first day's trading, which would be one in the eye for her nephew.

A large bouquet of flowers arrived in the afternoon, causing plenty of tongues to wag. Of course, it was from Max, the gracious deserted husband. Maeve tsked when she saw them.

'A more heartfelt way to show you care would be to not screw other women,' she said dryly.

Sally arrived with Susan, and Susan made all the right appreciative noises about the cafe.

'So, this is where my other half keeps disappearing off to of an evening,' said Susan, smiling.

'Poor Susan gets a blow-by-blow account of book club,' said Sally.

'I'm thinking of writing a sitcom about it.' Susan arched an eyebrow.

Annie laughed.

'Oh crikey, that'll send the Historical Society into overdrive!'

Samantha left to relieve Tom up at the shop and Maeve heroically stepped into her place behind the counter. It took her a few goes to get to grips with the new hi-tech till, but none of the customers were about to complain about Maeve to her face.

'Looking for anyone in particular?' Maeve asked when she saw Annie scanning the groups of people through the window.

'Oh,' said Annie. *Busted*, she thought. 'I was wondering if John Granger would make an appearance. He said he wouldn't but I thought he might not be able to resist spying on me.'

'I think he went to Cornwall for a few days to catch up with Mari and his daughter.'

'His daughter?'

'Yes, Celeste. Must be about twenty-two, twenty-three now?

She went to live there after uni. Does something to do with the Cornwall Wildlife Trust, looking after ditches or some such. She's a good girl. Did work experience on my farm. Feisty like her dad. John is an absolute fool for her, thinks the sun shines out of her backside. But then I suppose we all think that about our kids.'

Oh, so Celeste is his daughter, not his wife, Annie thought. She didn't know why but this revelation pleased her. She couldn't imagine John being anybody's fool but she liked the idea that he had a feisty daughter – someone to give him a run for his money.

'I hope he's not giving Mari a hard time about me opening the cafe,' said Annie.

'Don't judge him too harshly.'

Annie pulled a face and was about to respond when Maeve put up a hand.

'I know you two got off on the wrong foot and yes, he can come across as brash. But his heart's in the right place. Last winter was very hard for Mari; much harder than she let on.'

'But to force her to sell?'

'Did Mari tell you that?'

'Well, no, but—'

'Mari may not want to sell to builders but that doesn't mean she isn't open to the idea of selling. Mari is a romantic and John is a pragmatist but I am given to understand that their end goal is the same.'

Annie reflected on Maeve's words. Perhaps her own wish to stay in Willow Bay and Emily's fervent hopes to save Saltwater Nook had clouded her opinion of John Granger. Admittedly he did himself no favours – he was gruff and overly formal and quick to judge – but maybe his heart was in the right place.

Chapter 43

At four o'clock Raye and Aiden helped the band to pack up their stuff and began to ferry the garden furniture back up to the pubs ready for the BBQ. The last customers finished their drinks and melted away. The chill in the air was beginning to bite without the sun to lend its warmth.

Annie was exhausted; she could feel the armchair and the TV upstairs in the tiny sitting room calling her name. But since both sets of Willow Bay publicans had turned out in support of her new venture, she couldn't very well not show her face at their BBQ.

'Don't you have to get back for Alfred?' Annie asked.

'Back for Alfred?' Maeve exclaimed.

'I thought he was fixing your guttering today.'

'He is.'

'Oh, well, it's just that he said he was going to get a pie and mash supper out of it.'

'He is,' said Maeve again. 'He doesn't need me to sit up there with him while he eats it! Besides, Alfred's like me, not afraid of his own company. All he's got to do is sling it in the microwave.'

'Has Alfred got a key to your house?' asked Gemma.

'Doesn't need a key,' said Maeve. 'I didn't lock the door.'

'Isn't that a bit dangerous?' asked Annie.

'Not really, my cottage is on the farm, there's always some bugger around to notice if something is amiss. And both the girls know how to use a shotgun.'

'How silly of me to worry,' said Annie.

It seemed like the whole of Willow Bay had gone straight from the cafe to the pubs. People spilled out across both pub gardens, down the grassy banks and even mingled in the road between.

Annie wandered among them and was surprised to find that she didn't feel at all like an outsider. As the light faded and the temperature dropped still further, so the outside lights were turned on, chimineas were lit and thick woollen blankets were passed around in abundance; these revellers were clearly too practised to be cowed by little things like the cold and the dark. Annie wended her way through the throng to where Gemma sat, outside The Sunken Willow. Esme was wrapped in a blanket and dozing contentedly on Gemma's lap. At her feet, the scene was mirrored as Lennox, also wrapped in a blanket with his hoodie pulled low over his face, sat reading a comic by torchlight, while Podrick snoozed with his head resting on Lennox's knees. The glow from the chiminea lit the scene. Maeve leaned forward in a striped deckchair, poking the fire with a stick and adding more logs as required. Samantha and Tom sat cross-legged on the grass with a blanket pulled tightly around the both of them. Annie pulled up a deckchair and tugged a blanket up over her chest. The warmth of the fire was welcome and Annie found herself lulled into yawning by the flickering flames.

'I've been thinking,' Gemma began. 'Maybe we should read something a bit ghosty for this week's book club, you know, in honour of it being nearly Halloween and all that.'

'I'm already halfway through *Lady Audley's Secret*,' grumbled Maeve.

'It won't be wasted,' Gemma reasoned. 'We can do *Lady Audley* next time.'

'Said the vicar to the bishop,' Tom quipped.

'I'm not sure I'll have time to read another book by Wednesday,' said Annie.

'I'm not talking about a whole book, just two or three short stories. Still by Victorian writers, so we're keeping to theme. And anyway, the Victorians wrote the best ghost stories.'

As usual, Gemma's enthusiasm was intoxicating.

'Will we even have time to get hold of the books?' Maeve pointed out. Ever the one to bring Gemma's natural boil down to simmer.

Gemma grinned and, manoeuvring the sleeping Esme so that she could get to her bag, she pulled out three copies of a Victorian ghost stories anthology.

'I gave Sally hers down at the Nook earlier,' she said, handing out the books. 'Happy Halloween!'

'Thank you, Gemma,' said Annie. 'How much do I owe you?'

'They're a gift,' Gemma replied. 'I thought we could read three. They're not overly long. I did some research and marked the pages of the ones I thought would be good.'

Annie flicked through the book. A slip of paper marked each story: *The Mezzotint* by M. R. James, *The Old Nurse's Story* by Elizabeth Gaskell and *The Open Door* by Charlotte Riddell.

'I can't wait, a Victorian spook fest!' Gemma gushed.

Annie was rather looking forward to getting started. The idea of reading ghost stories in an old smugglers' haunt was quite thrilling . . . although she decided she would check all the bolts on the doors were secure before she started.

The walk home was chilly, even with alcoholic insulation. They began moving as a mass at closing time and little by little, as revellers turned left and right and trickled away to their houses, the group became smaller, until by the time it reached halfway down the hill it amounted to a small gaggle. When the last person turned into their drive, having been reassured by Annie that she didn't need escorting to Saltwater Nook, Annie was left alone.

The moon appeared white and bulbous from behind a shaggy cloud and lit the way with its cold blue gleam. Annie shivered and walked on. As she rounded the corner at the bottom of the hill, the promenade splayed out before her, empty and silver in the moonlight. The beach was as black as the sea but for the twinkle of moon-rays catching on the tips of the waves. Annie marvelled at the place she now called home. She had somehow stumbled into this life and it almost felt too good to be hers. Today had been a good day; one of the best she could remember for a long time.

Chapter 44

She was woken the next morning by the sound of the doorbell ringing. It punctured her post-wine sleep, continuing relentlessly until she fumbled into her dressing gown and, smarting at the waft of cold air that whistled up the stairwell to meet her, stumbled, grumbling, down to the front door.

'Did I wake you?'

It was John Granger, looking fresh and designer-stubbled in the kind of smart casual attire which Annie had thought only existed in cardboard cut-outs at Zara Man. For some reason his attractiveness annoyed her intensely. *Why is it only gay men or arseholes who know how to dress well?* she wondered. Annie squinted up at him; the grey morning seemed impossibly bright.

'No,' she answered sarcastically. 'This is how I dress on Sundays.' Her naked toes curled backwards against the spiky breeze.

'Right,' John said and he continued to look at her and then away towards his car and then back at her again. Annie frowned at him, waiting for him to speak.

'Do you need something?' Annie asked, hoping to speed whatever this was along. She was braless under her pyjamas and had folded her arms below her boobs in an attempt to make them look less like they were resting below her ribs.

'Yes,' said John. 'No. I, er, I wanted to apologise, again, for my rudeness after the second time I was rude when I had come down to apologise.'

Annie frowned some more.

'Okay,' she said. 'Apology accepted.'

'That's not all,' said John.

'Somehow I didn't think it would be.'

'I don't agree with you opening the cafe.'

'Yes, I did get that impression. But it really isn't any of your business.'

'You don't understand what it is that you're doing.'

'And what exactly is that?' asked Annie.

'Giving false hope to a trusting old lady.'

'I don't see how. From where I'm standing Mari is doing just fine out of our arrangement. She's going to get twenty per cent of everything I make from the kiosk and the cafe without having to lift a finger. If anything, I'm building her a little nest egg ready for when she comes home.'

'She's not coming home!'

'Says who?'

'Says me!'

'Shouldn't Mari decide whether she gets to live in her own home or not?'

'You have no idea of the relationship I have with my aunt or the discussions we've had about her future.'

'Are those the ones where you sell her home out from under her to a business fat cat for mega bucks?' Even Annie was surprised by her brazen rudeness.

John puffed out exasperatedly.

'He's a builder, I've known him for years. Despite what you may have heard, his plans are very sympathetic to the land.'

'But not so sympathetic to your aunt's wishes.'

John ran his hand through his hair and sucked air in through his teeth.

'You are determined to think the worst of me,' he said curtly.

It occurred to Annie that she might not be being entirely fair, but while she racked her brain for something conciliatory to say, John took her silence as confirmation.

'Enjoy your Sunday,' he said, turning to walk down the steps from the front door. 'Perhaps if you would appraise me by my *actual* actions, rather than what you presuppose my intentions to be, you might judge me less harshly.'

'Presuppose?' Annie called after him. 'Who even talks like that? Oh, wait a minute, the 1870s just called, they want their vocabulary back!'

John didn't look back. In three long strides he had reached the gate and let himself out, fastening the latch carefully behind him. He climbed into his Range Rover and drove away.

Annie was struck by how quickly the conversation had turned. Was he right? Was she determined to think the worst of him? It was true that she had felt riled by John from the very first with his snitty email. And now, she found herself stuck in a kind of spite-rut, where whenever she saw his face, she felt overwhelmingly compelled to be rude to it.

Chapter 45

Halloween has always been a big deal in Willow Bay, what with its shady past and dark history. The village itself is named after the Willow, a ship which ran aground on the rocks out past the peninsula on 1 October 1502. Before that it was known, somewhat unimaginatively, as Fish Beach, a rather difficult to reach, out of the way place that didn't get much in the way of visitors. The story goes that there was a ferocious storm which had raged for three days and nights, and on the fourth night, lost and confused by the starless sky and the squalling tempest, the Willow sailed in close to the bay. The villagers ran to the beach waving flaming torches to warn the ship that it was too close but it was too late – either the crew didn't see them or they couldn't change course in time. The Willow sailed headlong into the bay and was dashed against the rocks. The villagers gathered to help (or pilfer the cargo, depending on which accounts you read) but there were no survivors (again, this depends on which version of events you can stomach; there were accounts of sailors being drowned, so they couldn't make a claim on the cargo). Either way, bodies continued to wash up on the shore for days and weeks after.

The villagers were a superstitious bunch. Though the name

had been changed to All Hallows' Eve by then, the old Samhain belief that the veil between the living and the dead was at its thinnest between the last days of October and the first days of November was still very much alive. As you can imagine, the village was gripped by a fear that they would be overrun with the souls of dead sailors, and so they carved scary faces into turnips and swedes and built fires along the beach to ward off any evil spirits which may have been looking for a spot of revenge.

Later on in the dubious history of Willow Bay, the smugglers used the nights between All Hallows' Eve and Guy Fawkes Night – with the lighted fires on the beach and the near constant cele-brations – as a mask to cover their illegal transportation of whisky and tea into the tunnels beneath Saltwater Nook; it was said to be their most prolific week of the year! At an agreed signal, the residents of the houses in the hillside would drop ropes down to the beach from the bottoms of their gardens and the smugglers would emerge from the Saltwater Nook cellar under cover of darkness with their hoard. They tied the ropes around the contraband barrels and the goods would be hauled up through the undergrowth and dished out to be hidden within the village.

And times after, when smuggling was no more and the smugglers had become all but legends, and when the tide was just right, the village children would gather by the mouth of the cave at Halloween – the older ones leading the way and bringing up the stragglers at the rear – and make a candlelit pilgrimage through the tunnels and up into the cellars at the Nook. It was still going on when I came to live here with my aunt. We would bang on the door to the cellar, half wild with fear and excitement, and she would open it up and feign surprise to find us all standing there, cold and wet and smelling of the sea.

'Well!' she would say, 'you'd better come up since you're already here!' and up the stone cellar steps we tramped and into the tea room where she would have made toffee apples and ginger parkin enough to feed the five thousand! We'd play bob the apple and snap-dragon and one of the fishermen would tell the tale of how Willow Bay got its name, making sure to add in plenty of lost souls and shrieking selkies.

Over time the tunnel processions had to be abandoned; there were incidents, I'll say no more about that. And what with the rockfalls, soon nobody went into the tunnels even for dares. Halloween became altogether tamer and eventually it was decided that even snap-dragon was not really in keeping with health and safety – children poking their fingers into bowls of brandy-flaming raisins probably wasn't ideal on many levels. But my goodness, we had fun!

These days the costumes are a little fancier and the ghost stories a mite gentler but the Willow Bay folk still do a braw Halloween. I don't want you to feel pressure to keep the old ways going. Time must move on. And you, whoever you are who is reading this, will have your own ideas about things. But I'll tell you how it's been done up to now and you can choose for yourself.

The children – with their parents these days, of course – begin to call at the houses in the village at the gloaming for their tricks and their treats. Then they gather at the top of the hill for the procession and down they come, all the way to Saltwater Nook. You'll find in the attic some provisions for decorating the place. I used to dish out hot drinks and sundries but not for the last

*twenty years or so – I can't keep up! So now I make sure I've
a bucketload of sweets and the outside of the place is decorated
with spooky things and Ely will frighten the bairns senseless with
the tale of the sunken Willow and ghostly sailors. Legend has it
that the captain's bounty was never recovered and rests at the
bottom of the ocean somewhere around these parts. Children
love a sunken treasure tale. And they go home happily terrified
and no doubt sleep with the lights on for days after, but it's all
in the name of fun.*

Halloween had not been something Annie had seriously
had to consider for years – beyond the obligatory carving of
the jack-o'-lantern; usually she was working. Ever since reading
Mari's notebook, however, she had found herself thinking
about Halloween with a surprising amount of glee; her list-
making senses were tingling. She had picked up a veritable
feast of tooth-shrivelling sweets and had been checking the
internet for decorations. She had her eye on a few things, but
she really needed to check what Mari already had before she
committed.

The attic was reached by a small hatch in the hallway
between the sitting room and the kitchen. Annie hauled the
ladder from the cellar up the stairs to the flat. She pushed
open the hatch and was greeted with a cold waft of dank air.
Annie climbed up and crawled into the roof space. There was
just room enough for her to stand up in places, and beneath
her feet a skinny path of planks ran along some of the beams.
On either side of the planks, balanced across the beams, was
a sea of cardboard boxes. Annie shone her phone torch around
and found, to her relief, that they were all neatly labelled. She

stepped gingerly towards the boxes marked Halloween and set about opening them; she didn't want to drag them all down to the flat if they weren't things she would want to use. She had just taken a vegetable knife to the tape on the first box when the doorbell rang. *Shit*, Annie thought but then she thought, *Fuck it*, and decided to ignore it. She turned back to the box. The bell rang again. Annie huffed exasperatedly but carried on slitting the tape with the knife and pulled open the flaps. The doorbell rang again.

'Go away!' she yelled.

The first box contained Halloween fairy lights: strings of orange plastic jack-o'-lanterns, white grinning skeletons, bats and baubles with black cats silhouetted inside them. Some were indoor and some outdoor but there was enough here for an impressive display. Annie carefully replaced the flaps and pushed the box towards the hatch before going back to open the next one. She was just detangling two flying witches' heads when she heard a knock at the door to the flat. She froze. The main front door to the building was locked, as was the door to the tea room; it must be someone with a key – John Granger! Annie's initial fear morphed into anger. *The bloody cheek of it!* She was sure there must be a law against this sort of thing. The knocking came again.

'Just wait a minute, would you!' she yelled through the ceiling. 'I'm right in the middle of something.'

She began to shuffle, as quickly as she dared, back the way she had come, the planks wobbling beneath her feet. 'Bloody John bloody Granger, acting the bloody lord and master in someone else's house,' she muttered to herself. 'I'm going to give that upstart a piece of my miiiiiiiii . . .' In her haste she over-wobbled on the plank. She tried to regain her balance but it was no good. Gravity and self-preservation kicked in at the same time; she threw her arms out to steady herself but the wood beneath her feet was see-sawing wildly and her ankles were following suit. In another second one foot had slipped off the plank completely. Annie's right foot clumped down hard between the beams and kept on going, straight through the ceiling below with an alarming crunch. She was kneeling on one leg as though waiting for a starter pistol to go off, both hands gripping the plank, her other leg dangling uselessly through the hole above what she could see, looking down, was the kitchen.

Chapter 46

'Oh, buggery shitting bollocks!' she yelled as she tried to heave her leg up. The motion upset the box of fairy lights further down the plank and before she had finished shouting 'Shit on it!' the box had crashed through the hatch.

The banging on the door became urgent.

'Annie! What's going on in there? Let me in! Are you hurt?'

Annie let out a howl of annoyance; she couldn't get her leg back up to the rest of her body. *Of all the bloody people,* she thought angrily, *it had to be him!*

'I'm fine,' she called. There was a jangling of keys and she heard the door to the flat opening. Annie groaned.

'I'm coming in,' said John. 'It's John Granger.'

'Yes, I gathered that,' she called.

'Where are you?'

'I'm in the kitchen . . . kind of.'

She heard John moving below her. *Wait for it . . .* she thought.

'What the hell are you doing?'

'I'm having a fucking teddy bears' picnic! What does it look like I'm fucking doing?'

'What is it with you and decimating my aunt's house?'

She could hear a smirk in his voice.

223

'You're going to have the place bulldozed to make way for your swanky apartments anyway. I should have thought you'd be pleased I'd made a start!'

Silence. Annie raised her eyes skywards. She'd done it again. John Granger brought out the absolute worst in her. She tried to wiggle her leg up again but she couldn't make her foot fit back through the hole without unbalancing herself.

'You're just making more mess,' said John above the pitter-patter of horsehair plaster hitting the kitchen lino.

'Then why don't you sodding well help me?'

'Did you hurt it in the fall or am I okay to manipulate your ankle?'

'No, I didn't hurt it.'

'I'm going to take your plimsoll off,' he called up.

She could hear the hesitation in his voice. Was he embarrassed at the idea of removing a woman's shoe?

'Okay,' she called down.

She felt the delicate tugging as he untied the laces on her Converse high-top and slipped it off. Then a gentle pressure as he took her foot in his hand and began to push upwards.

'Just relax. No, you're tensing up. Relax your foot, so that I can twist it to fit back through the hole. It should be okay now that your shoe is off.'

'Right.' Annie could feel her cheeks burning. This was not her finest moment.

In another minute her leg was back in the same room as her body.

'Do you need me to come up and help you down?' he asked.

'No,' said Annie. 'Thank you. Just give me a minute.' She

remembered the other boxes. 'There are more things up here I need to bring down.'

'Just bring yourself down,' said John. 'You can tell me what you need and I'll get it for you. I put most of the things up there anyway.'

'Okay. Thank you. I'm making my way back now.'

She shuffled backwards along the plank on her hands and knees, somewhat less confident than when she'd arrived in the attic. When she reached the hatch she waggled one leg about, trying to find the top of the stepladder. She felt John's hand grip her ankle.

'Let me guide your foot down to the rung,' he said.

Annie did as she was told.

'Keep coming backwards,' he went on. 'I've got you.'

There was something in the calm of his voice which made Annie feel odd: she believed him.

With John's help her foot found the ladder rung and she manoeuvred the rest of herself down out of the hatch, with about as much grace as a hippo climbing backwards through a hoop. John's hands never touched any part of her but she could see his arms splayed upwards ready to catch her if she fell.

'Thank you,' she said when she was safely back on carpet. 'Sorry about the ceiling. I'll pay to get it fixed.'

They walked into the kitchen together and looked up at the size-seven-foot hole above their heads.

'I can fix it,' said John.

'Well then, I'll pay for plaster and what-not,' said Annie.

'What were you trying to get up there?'

'Mari's Halloween stuff,' sighed Annie. 'It seems like

Halloween is a pretty big deal down here and I didn't want to let everybody down.'

John looked at her quizzically.

'Oh. That's very . . . I'm surprised. I didn't think you'd be . . . I mean, I didn't expect you to be that invested in the traditions of Willow Bay.'

'It means a lot to Mari,' said Annie. 'And, you know, I haven't had much time over the past few years to get into Halloween and so I thought this year I would. New start and all that . . .' She tailed off. Why was she telling him this?

'How do you know it means a lot to my aunt?'

'It's in the book,' Annie replied. 'There's a whole section on it.'

'The book?'

'The Saltwater Nook book that Mari wrote as a guide for whoever became its guardian.'

John frowned and shook his head.

'I didn't know she'd written notes,' and then he chuckled to himself. 'That's just like Aunt Mari, bossy to the last, never leave anything to chance.'

'Oh, it's more than just notes,' said Annie. 'It's practically an almanac. She writes beautifully. It's almost like prose poetry in parts.'

'May I see it?' John asked.

Annie considered him, her head tilted to one side.

'Yes,' she replied after a beat. 'Of course.'

John followed Annie out of the mess in the kitchen – she felt slightly off-kilter with one shoe missing – and into the sitting room. She picked the yellow exercise book up off the coffee table and handed it to him. John took the book and began to leaf through it. He stopped every so often, his finger hovering over the page to read a particular extract before continuing. A wry smile played on his lips as he skimmed over the pages.

'These are some comprehensive notes,' John mused.

'Yes.'

'Almost a manual,' he added.

'Almost,' Annie agreed.

John closed the book but held it in both his hands as though weighing it. Outside the window the October sun danced across the teal water, making it sparkle and wink as though it were trying to convey a message via Morse code. John looked down at the book, then out over the ocean and back again.

'Right,' he said, as though responding to an unseen voice. His dark eyebrows knitted together, his expression pensive, and then he said 'Right' again but made no move to expand on his internal monologue.

Mrs Tiggy-Winkle meowed mournfully – this was pure attention-seeking on her part – as she padded into the sitting room and broke whatever cycle of thought John had been locked in. He looked at Tiggs and she looked back.

'I sought permission first,' said Annie hastily before John saw fit to reprimand her for yet another abuse of his aunt's abode.

'Yes,' he replied absently, still holding the book. 'Of course.'

He crouched down, resting the book on one knee, and made a kissing sound to Mrs Tiggy-Winkle whilst holding his hand out to the yawning cat.

'She won't come to you,' said Annie. 'She's not good with people. Hates my husband.'

John looked up at Annie, one eyebrow raised. His eyes, she

noticed, were blue-grey like the sea when the sky was thick with cloud.

'Is your husband here too?'

'No. I left him behind. I prefer the cat.' She added, 'We're separated,' though she wasn't sure why she felt the need to clarify this.

John's mouth twitched at the corners in what Annie thought looked like a suppressed smile.

'What's her name?' John asked, nodding his head towards the fat ginger cat.

'Mrs Tiggy-Winkle. Tiggs for short. She answers to both.'

'Because she's prickly, like her owner?' John enquired.

'I am not prickly!' *Just rise above him*, she thought to herself. *You are better than this*. 'If you must know, it's because she likes laundry,' Annie continued.

John raised an incredulous eyebrow.

'She likes to sleep on clean washing. When I first got her I kept finding her in the airing cupboard or in the linen basket. So, you know . . . Mrs Tiggy-Winkle; the hedgehog who was a washer woman.'

John nodded sagely.

'Delighted to meet you, Mrs Tiggy-Winkle,' said John.

To Annie's annoyance, Tiggs padded over to John, sniffed his outstretched hand and began to rub her head against his knees as he made a fuss of her.

Traitor, Annie thought.

'She seems to like me,' said John, looking up with a smug expression.

'Perhaps you smell like fish,' Annie retorted, narrowing her eyes.

John laughed softly and the sound was warm and friendly, like a deep purr. Annie pursed her lips.

'Or perhaps it's my animal magnetism,' he grinned.

His Scottish burr added a curling lilt to all his words which Annie found annoyingly pleasant. *Oh my God*, Annie thought, *is he flirting with me?*

'Or maybe you carry catnip around in your pockets to ingratiate yourself with lady cat owners,' Annie said, smiling sweetly.

'Have it your way,' John said. 'I'm guessing you usually do.'

Annie took a sharp intake of breath but when she looked at John he was still smiling amiably and she decided to let that one pass. She had, after all, just made a rather large hole in his aunt's ceiling and he had been surprisingly gracious about it. As though reading her mind, John stood up, leaving Tiggs rubbing herself around his legs. *Tart*, Annie thought at her cat.

'I'll get the rest of those boxes down for you and then I'll have a look and see what I've got in the cellar to fix that hole,' said John.

He saw Annie looking at him.

'I keep a few things here for maintenance,' he explained.

'You don't have to do it now.'

'Trust me, you don't want the north wind blowing through there. It can get pretty feisty down here at this time of year.'

Annie had to admit that she would rather not have wind whistling through a gaping hole in the ceiling. Not to mention the potential for large spiders to extend their creeping grounds down into the flat.

John was surprising her and she found herself in uncharted territory. He could have been an arsehole about the ceiling, but he hadn't – quite the opposite, in fact. And Mrs Tiggy-Winkle had given him her seldom-offered seal of approval. There was no denying he was handsome. Could Annie be warming to John Granger?

Chapter 47

The fixing of the hole took a long time and a lot of sawing, hammering, sanding and swearing. It was nearly half past six by the time John began to pack his tools back into the large canvas tool bag he had brought up from the cellar. Annie wondered if she ought to offer to cook him some supper. She had supplied him with mugs of tea and biscuits throughout the afternoon and, thankfully, his engagement in his ceiling task had prevented the need for any real conversation. This, Annie had decided, was a good thing, since they couldn't be trusted not to argue if they steered away from the basic niceties. However, an offer of supper would invariably require actual talking. Not only this but, Annie realised, it might be misconstrued as something else.

John came into the sitting room. His hair was grey with dust. He'd removed his jumper and rolled up the sleeves on his shirt but kept it tucked neatly into his jeans. He looked like a lawyer who'd walked through an ash cloud. Annie had been through all the Halloween boxes and decided what she would and wouldn't use. Then she had made lists of all the things she would use with suggestions of how and where she might display them to their best advantage.

'I can help you with Halloween if you like,' said John, drying his hands on a tea towel.

Annie frowned.

'Really?' This pulled her up short.

John shrugged.

'Yeah. I've been part of enough of my aunt's Halloween extravaganzas to know how they work. I mean, I know you've got the Saltwater Nook almanac and all,' he said, nodding in the direction of Mari's notebook back in its position on the coffee table. 'But maybe some first-hand knowledge would be helpful.'

'I didn't think you'd . . . Yes, thank you, that would be great.'

'I know what you think of me,' said John.

'Do you?'

'You think I'm just some money-grabbing bastard who wants to stick his old aunty in a home and be done with her.'

'I did think that to start with,' Annie confessed.

'And now?'

'Now I don't know what to think. You're a bit of an enigma; devil or angel, depending on who you talk to.'

'Small-town gossip.'

'No smoke without fire?'

'You know, it's unfair to judge a person when you don't have all the facts.'

'Then why don't you enlighten me?'

'Because I don't have to.'

There it was again: that arrogance that drove her half mad.

'You ask me not to judge your motives and yet you won't help me to understand them.'

John laid the tea towel on the radiator and began to roll down his shirtsleeves.

'Perhaps you could try a little faith in humanity,' he said, pulling on his knitted sweater and sending a small cloud of dust into the air like a halo around his head.

'Oh, I'm afraid I've been disappointed by humanity too many times to rely on blind faith anymore.'

'What a pity,' said John, grabbing his coat. 'I'll be back to paint the ceiling when the plaster has dried out. Thank you for the tea.'

And he left. The tide of their conversation had turned so quickly that they were neck-deep in another misunderstanding before Annie had the chance to think better of it.

Chapter 48

Having a grand opening turned out to be the best start the cafe could have had. Annie opened the kiosk at eight each morning as usual and then opened the cafe door at nine. Her eight o'clockers were not the type to sit and linger; they wanted to grab coffee and go. But many of her later customers wanted to ease into the morning, sitting at the long bench in the window and gazing out to sea, either alone or with friends. Annie had started an Instagram page and already it was being tagged in carefully crafted customer photographs of cups of coffee with the ocean in shot: #coffeebythesea, #saltwatercafe, #beachlife. She wondered if John was on Instagram. She wondered if he had seen all the positive comments and beautiful pictures of the cafe and the stunning vista. She wondered why she cared.

It was gone three o'clock by the time Annie had closed down the cafe. Tiggs raised her head briefly as she entered the sitting room, yawned and then tucked it back under her paws. The air was stuffy, the autumn sun was high in the sky and the little room seemed to soak in all its rays. Annie threw open the windows and went to make some tea.

She returned ten minutes later to find Tiggs sat on the

windowsill, her ears pricked up and the room filled with the sound of Peter Gabriel singing 'In Your Eyes'. It was coming from outside. Annie crossed to the window and looked down. Max. He was wearing trainers, baggy cargo trousers and a long tan trench coat with the sleeves rolled up. Above his head he held an old boombox – circa 1984 – out of which Peter Gabriel's gravelly voice drifted up to her, while Max – uncharacteristically – said nothing but gazed at her, hopeful and pleading as he recreated the iconic John Cusack window scene from *Say Anything*. Max's arms shook slightly from the effort of holding the boombox aloft. Two of Annie's regular customers hurried by and pretended not to notice the grand gesture being performed on the promenade. *Well, that'll be all over the village in no time*, she thought to herself. Annie sighed; how could anyone fail to be moved by such a demonstration? But she knew that to give even an inch would be dangerous. The song finished and Max pressed stop on the tape cassette. He didn't speak, he just placed the boombox on the floor and continued to stare up at her like a lovesick Romeo. Annie leaned out of the window.

'You look like a crazy person!'

'Crazy in love with you!' Max grinned.

'Oh, for fuck's sake,' she muttered under her breath.

'Come round the back,' she called. Max nodded but didn't speak. He picked up his boombox, nodded cordially to two women out walking their dogs and moved out of her line of sight.

Annie opened the front door and sat down on the step; she motioned for Max to sit too.

'Aren't you going to invite me in?' asked Max.

'No, I don't think so.'

Max sat next to her.

'Are you afraid you won't be able to resist me if I come upstairs?'

He had that glint in his eye that used to make her melt. She knew that if she were to let him upstairs now, she would be in for a good time. She gave herself a mental slap.

'No. I just . . .' Annie paused. *I don't want any part of my new life sullied*, is what she thought to herself. The flat was un-Maxed and she wanted it to remain that way. 'I just don't think exes need to come round for cups of tea. Part of being exes is that you chose to be separated.'

'I didn't choose to be separated, you did.'

'*You* made that decision when you *chose* to start fucking a woman more than twenty years younger than me!'

'How many times do I have to say I'm sorry for you to believe me?' he asked.

'It's not about *saying sorry*, Max, you didn't spill coffee on the rug. What you did was bigger than something that requires a quick sorry.'

Max held his hands up.

'I know, you're right, I'm sorry. I'm sorry for all of it. But can't you see how much I want you back?'

'You get an "A" for effort. You are excellent at wooing. It's the after-woo that lets you down.'

'I'll keep it up then, I'll never stop the wooing. I'll be Prince Charming forever.'

'No. I'm not saying I need a lifetime of romance; truth be told, I'm all wooed out. But . . .' She struggled to find the right words. 'This is the part where you shine, Max. No one does romantic gestures like you do. But your attention span is short. As soon as you've won the prize you start looking for the next challenge. Let's say for argument's sake that you win me over; how long will it be before my allure wears off and you're looking for another shiny young thing to covet?'

'Never again. I know I've said this in the past but that was before you'd left me. This has been my wake-up call. For the first time in my life I truly know what I want and it's you, Annie. It's always been you. You're all I want.'

Annie sighed.

'It's a strange word, isn't it?' she said. '*Want*. What you *want* has always been the problem because it wears off. *Want* is craving a biscuit; you want a biscuit but then you eat the biscuit, and it was *just* a biscuit. It's a feeling that passes and this desperation you think you feel for me, this is going to pass.'

'Want was a poor choice of word,' said Max, his expression pained. 'I *need* you Annie. I love you, I love you like I'm crazy with it.'

'But I don't love you anymore. And if you loved me, you wouldn't have slept with Ellie.'

Max's eyes welled with tears.

'Don't say that!' he pleaded. 'I can make you love me again.'

'I don't want to love you again!' Annie shouted in exasperation. 'Loving you is exhausting. It's too hard.'

'Is it that man?'

'What man?' Annie asked. A picture of John Granger bloomed behind her eyes and she shook it away quickly.

'The man whose house you spent the night at the other week.'

Jeez! she thought. *Paul!*

'No,' Annie replied. 'It isn't him, it isn't anyone. Or at least if it is someone else, it's Ellie and the long list of women that went before her.'

Max looked stung but Annie found herself untouched.

'Please, Max,' she went on. 'Save us both a lot of pain and give it up now. We made two great kids, we built a great business and now it's over. I'm going to file for a divorce.'

'I'll never agree to one,' said Max, dashing the tears from his eyes.

'I'm going to file for one anyway. And if you don't get me access to my bank accounts ASAP, I'll be speaking to my solicitor about that too. I might even have a case for suing you.'

Max stood up. Annie stayed where she was. He picked up the boombox and Annie watched him walk dejectedly to his car. He slammed the door shut and revved the engine too loudly before pulling away, the shingle jumping out from beneath his wheels.

Chapter 49

'It'll be such a shame if this place gets flattened,' Gemma lamented. 'I love our book club evenings and having a cafe down here. And Annie, this is your business, not to mention your home. You can't want to see it bulldozed!'

They were supposed to be discussing *The Mezzotint* by M. R. James. Annie had purposely not switched on the lamps for this, their Halloween book club, so that the room was lit only by candlelight. Their figures, huddled around the table, cast long shadows on the walls. The wind whistled through the shuttered windows and caused the candles to flicker. M. R. James's was the last of their short stories to be discussed, although keeping the book club on track was like trying to race ants, each one going off on its own tangent. As usual, the fate of Saltwater Nook and John's part in its demise was a hot topic.

'No,' said Annie. 'I certainly don't. I mean, he's not my favourite person and obviously I don't agree with his plans.' She waved her arm around to encompass the cafe. 'But I have to grudgingly admit that I think John's intentions are well meant, if a little skewed.'

'Blimey,' said Sally.

'Well, that's a turn-up,' added Maeve.

Gemma clutched her heart and said, 'You know what this would be like, don't you? It would be like in *You've Got Mail*, when Tom Hanks's character puts Meg Ryan's character out of business but they fall in love anyway!'

'It would be nothing at all like that,' said Annie.

'But you're warming to him,' observed Maeve.

'I will admit that he might not be quite as bad as I first thought,' Annie said.

Gemma clapped her hands.

'But I generally feel the same about smear tests,' Annie added.

'As tolerable as a smear test,' Sally said dryly. 'High praise indeed. Why can't they sell the place as it is? You know, rather than knocking it down. Seems to me that would please everyone.'

'They tried,' said Maeve. 'But let's face it, Saltwater Nook is a doer-upper. No disrespect to Mari but the place needs work, even with the bits John does here and there. People won't pay top whack for a project. The land is worth more without the Nook on it.'

'What about the rentals market? Airbnb and that sort of thing?' asked Sally.

'Again, it's seasonal. And at the moment it would only sleep two. John doesn't have the kind of money required to convert the downstairs and there we are back again to where we were a moment ago.'

'Then, of course, there's Emily and the historical brigade,' said Annie.

'Oh, I love Emily,' said Gemma. 'She's so passionate.'

Annie raised her eyebrows.

'You do know she pickets the cafe *all day* on Saturdays,' said Annie.

'Well, she works full-time at the library,' chimed in Maeve. 'Saturday's the only complete day she's got.'

'What's her beef?' asked Sally.

'She doesn't want Saltwater Nook demolished, or the land built on. She wants Mari to sign it over to the village and have it listed to protect it,' said Maeve.

'I don't want it demolished either!' Annie protested. 'She should be following John around with her placards.'

'The cafe's so busy, it's the perfect place for her to make people aware of its plight,' said Gemma. 'And in a way, it's good publicity for your business too.'

'That's right,' put in Maeve. 'There's no such thing as bad publicity.'

'Either way, my business is screwed by spring,' said Annie. 'Saltwater Nook will be a historical monument or a block of flats.'

'Then give Emily and John an alternative,' said Sally.

The women were quiet, all thinking about ways that Saltwater Nook could be saved. The wind buffeted the shutters so violently it almost extinguished a candle.

'I need to divorce my husband,' said Annie. 'Anyone know any good solicitors?'

It was enough to draw the subject away from John Granger and his *good* intentions. Sally recommended a firm of solicitors that had dealt with her divorce and Gemma got them back round to M. R. James's story, and it was agreed that his was the most frightening, Elizabeth Gaskell's the saddest and Charlotte Riddell's the most ambiguous.

'I've put the word around at the school and Samantha and Tom and the pubs have taken care of everyone else,' said Gemma as they were getting their coats on to leave. 'I would imagine we'll be with you by about half past six on Halloween.'

'Great,' said Annie. 'I'll be waiting.'

Maeve smiled approvingly.

Gemma moved a couple of chairs for Sally to steer her chair through the gap. 'I would come but I'm working,' said Sally. 'Much to Susan's disgust. Halloween is weirdly a big deal to her. To me it's more about shooing underage drunks out of the lobby before they egg the place.'

'Oh, hey, I forgot to say.' Gemma was holding the door open and the cold wind was rattling the pictures in their frames. 'Can we do a book club on Tuesday next week? I know it's only a week's gap but I've almost finished *Lady Audley's Secret* and I love our meetings. And then Wednesday is bonfire night. So, I'll get to see you all two nights in a row.'

She must have seen Annie's blank expression.

'Oh,' said Gemma awkwardly. 'You didn't know. Not to worry, Annie, there's no pressure, I'm sure someone else can rustle something up . . .'

Oh, for fuck's sake! Annie thought to herself. *What now? Is Saltwater Nook the bloody party capital of Willow Bay?* She would have to tap back into Mari's almanac.

'What sort of thing are we talking?' asked Annie.

'It's normally John's baby, to be honest,' Maeve replied. 'Mari took a back seat a few years ago. John and Paul usually set up some fireworks along the beach. Nothing fancy. Just a bit of fun.'

Annie came over curiously odd and she felt her cheeks flush

despite her best efforts to act casual. She had never considered that John and Paul would know each other. *Of course they bloody would, in such a tiny village!* she chastised herself.

'Well,' Annie said, 'let's get past Halloween first, shall we? But, yes, if everyone else is in agreement, we can do an extra book club next Tuesday and I'll find out if John and Paul have something up their sleeves.' She tried to say this casually but she felt her cheeks burning. Gemma cast her a sly smile and Annie rather wished the whole town didn't know she'd been intimate with the window cleaner.

Chapter 50

The following night Annie was just starting to drift into that halfway place between wake and sleep when a text came through to her phone.

Good evening, Ms Sharpe! I hope you don't mind, I got your number from my aunt. It's John by the way. I left rather abruptly the other day. If you'd like some help with Halloween from a grumpy forty-something man, then I'd be glad to apply for the role. J. G.

A little firework of excitement whizzed around in her stomach. Annie chastised herself and read the text again. She would like some help, especially from someone who knew how Halloween at Willow Bay went. And it might be good for him to be reminded that Saltwater Nook was an important part of the community.

She typed and deleted several messages before she found a tone that was right.

Finally, she settled for:

I don't mind at all. It's probably sensible for you to have my number anyway, in case of emergencies, which I don't anticipate, but then nobody ever does, which is why they are called emergencies.

Yes please to helping with Halloween. A grumpy forty-something man will be a welcome addition to proceedings. Annie

She added and deleted a single smiley face emoji several times before deciding that John Granger was not the smiley face emoji type. She hoped that he would be encouraged by her sign-off to start using her name rather than addressing her as Ms Sharpe, which made her sound like a Dickensian spinster.

She pressed send and laid back against the pillows. She was wide awake now. There was something furtive about late-night texts, and despite herself she felt a thrill of something rising up in her chest . . . Or maybe it was just the garlic mushroom and leek mac n' cheese she'd had for supper repeating on her. Would he reply to her text? Was he even now smiling at her witty response? She reprimanded herself for the consideration. Was he one of those people who replied straight away or left the message hanging for a day? Would he reply at all?

Annie wasn't sure why she was allowing this to take up so much space in her thoughts. She sighed loudly, disturbing Mrs Tiggy-Winkle, who squinted at her disdainfully before going back to sleep.

It wasn't like she fancied John Granger, though he was undeniably attractive – in a scowling sort of way. But just because someone was pleasing to the eye didn't make them pleasing company. His features, she thought, would be considered by most to be agreeable, though his nose was pencil sharp at the tip and he probably had to pluck his eyebrows to prevent a naturally occurring monobrow. His eyes were blue-grey, deep-set with black lashes which were annoyingly long, hiding away beneath a prominent brow. Max had grown a beard as he'd got older, conscious of his weakening chin, whereas John's chin remained distinct, his jawline strong and untouched by the softening of age, shadowed permanently by a beard awaiting permission to grow through. Her musings were punctuated by her inner self wagging a warning finger at her. Annie blew a raspberry at her inner self and checked her phone. Nothing. She tutted at herself. It was clear that she wouldn't be sleeping anytime soon, so she opened *Lady Audley's Secret* at her bookmark and began to read. She was an hour in when her phone vibrated beside her on the bed. She snatched it up.

Great. I'll probably be over late morning. John 😊

Annie placed the phone back down and opened her book again. She realised she was grinning like an emoji. Her phone pinged again. It was John.

If you could only have one drink for the rest of your life, what would it be? 😮

This was such an odd, unexpected question that she burst out laughing.

What? 😄

Just answer the question, Ms Sharpe. ⏱

Annie took a moment to consider, before replying: Tea. I know that's probably terribly boring but there really isn't a situation which can't be soothed or made better by a cup of tea. You?

Irn-Bru. I'm Scottish, it would be treasonous to choose anything else. 😊

Annie gave this three laughing face emojis and a thumbs up.

I'll see you tomorrow.

You will indeed.

Annie was all of a flutter. John Granger really was most surprising. She picked up her book and went back to reading the shocking exploits of Lady Lucy Audley, though her eyes kept slipping to the bedside cabinet where Mr Knightley lay waiting, wrapped in one of her linen scarves, ready for action.

Chapter 51

On Friday morning, John Granger strode into the cafe to be greeted like a prodigal son by Annie's Willow Bay customers and eyed curiously by those from out of town, who were trying to ascertain if he was someone they ought to recognise. Annie was busy at the coffee machine.

'What can I get you?' she asked, noting with pleasure that for the first time he was properly taking in the changes she had made to the cafe. 'I'm afraid I'm clean out of Irn-Bru.'

John smiled at her.

'Can you do a flat white?' he asked.

'Of course!' She determined to make him the perfect flat white.

'It looks good,' John said, nodding to the shelving and the new arrangement, though Annie could see it cost him to say it.

'Thank you,' said Annie. 'I'm really pleased with how it's turned out. I think your aunt would approve.' She saw his jaw clench ever so slightly and felt satisfied. *Can I do a flat white indeed!* she thought.

'I hope it didn't cost you too much. I wouldn't like you to be out of pocket when it sells in the new year.'

Annie saw one or two wry smiles and raised eyebrows around the cafe.

'Nothing I'm not already well on the way to recouping,' she replied sweetly. 'As you can see, business is booming.' A little queue was forming at the kiosk window. 'Mari's been very supportive.'

John smiled. His eyebrow twitched infinitesimally, Annie noticed and grinned inwardly.

'I'm sure she has.'

Annie banged the milk jug on the counter to disperse any milk bubbles and poured the milk into the waiting espresso, flicking her wrist lightly as the coffee neared the rim of the cup to create a perfect feather in the rich crema. She handed John his flat white and wondered if she looked as smug as she felt. John looked at it, one eyebrow raised slightly in what she had come to learn was John's reaction to surprise. He took a sip – no sugar, she noted – and licked his top lip; Annie found her eyes lingering on his mouth and mentally slapped herself.

'Good coffee,' said John.

'I know,' Annie replied.

She turned away from him and continued with her work. It was a steady day and Annie had little time to pay John any real attention, but she watched him out of the corner of her eye. He was sat at the bench which looked out over the sea. He flicked idly through one or two magazines and glanced over the local paper but after a time he became still, and sat sipping his coffee and gazing out of the window. How many times had he stared out at that view? Annie wondered.

As she was loading the dishwasher yet again, John leaned over the counter.

'If you like, I can get started on the decorations for tonight,' he said.

'Oh, thanks, yes, that would be great. If you give me a minute, I'll run up and start bringing down the boxes.'

'It's no bother,' he said in his musical accent. 'You're busy here. I can get them.'

He held out his hand for the keys to the flat. Annie hesitated for a beat too long. John caught it.

'Are you afraid I might stumble across Little John?' he asked with almost a straight face.

Annie felt her cheeks burn scarlet instantly as she remembered John walking in on their book club after she'd just been presented with a large rubber dildo. She recovered herself as best she could.

'He's not called John anymore,' she said with as much nonchalance as she could muster. 'Such a plain name, John, not nearly powerful enough.'

John tried to suppress a smile.

'I see,' he said, his lips twitching. 'And, if it isn't too pertinent a question, what name of great power did you bestow upon it?'

'Mr Knightley,' she said, haughtily and with a completely straight face.

'Mr Knightley?' he asked. 'The stuffed shirt from *Emma*?'

Annie couldn't quite believe that she was discussing the name of her dildo with her landlady's nephew. She wondered how they'd got from Halloween decorations to sex aids.

'Mr Knightley happens to be an honourable man who is very much in love with Emma and aware of his duty of care to her and her father's wellbeing.'

'Well, that's me told!' he smiled. 'Don't worry, I'm not going to be nosing around. I'll just grab the boxes and bring them down. No peeking, I promise.'

He grinned mischievously and winked at her. The gesture was so unexpected that Annie's already crimson cheeks darkened further. She handed the keys to John. He took them and disappeared through the door to the inner hallway. It felt strange that he was so familiar with her home – he probably knew its nooks and crannies better than she did. And yet, this familiarity didn't make her feel uncomfortable or proprietorial; on the contrary, she was finding she liked it. As much as Saltwater suited her, it fitted John just as comfortably.

Chapter 52

The cafe emptied out and refilled and the kiosk showed no sign of easing up either. Annie being rushed off her feet was becoming a recurring theme. The chocolate pumpkin cupcakes she'd made last night were selling like . . . well, like hot cakes; people were buying them in boxes of four or six to take home for Halloween after the school run. Two empty pumpkin shells sat sadly on the shelf below the counter, waiting to be carved.

When John breezed back into the cafe with three large boxes piled one on top of the other, Annie was so busy she couldn't think straight. The fine weather had brought with it an army of wanderers, aiming to enjoy the watery sun while it lasted. She saw John looking around for somewhere to sit and go through the boxes but every space was taken.

'You might have to sit on the stairs,' she called to him over the noise of the coffee grinder. Four more people walked into the cafe and joined the queue.

'All right to sit outside?' a man in a grey hoodie shouted over.

'If you can find a space!' Annie shouted back. 'Thank you all for your patience, I will get to you all as fast as I can!'

There were nods and waves and noises of goodwill at this, as Annie handed out two large paper cups through the kiosk window and turned to the counter to take the next order from inside the cafe. She was going to have to seriously think about hiring someone; it was becoming impossible to serve the take-away customers at the kiosk and the drink-ins inside at the same time. As she handed over the change to a woman in a wax jacket, she felt herself being gently shoved to the side. She looked up to see John looking down at her.

'If I'm here, I might as well help,' he said.

Annie gawped.

'Shift!' said John. And she did.

John took over the till with only minor queries and left Annie to make the drinks. His presence caused much delight in and outside the cafe as locals chatted with him and asked about Mari and Celeste. It was, Annie thought, rather like working with a minor celebrity. His smile was warm and genuine and his low gravelly laugh seemed to rumble around the tiny cafe. He was good at front of house too, Annie noted. Before long, he was dishing out cold drinks and serving up cakes on china plates with little cake forks, even running coffees out to customers outside.

'You're a natural,' said Annie before she had thought to stop herself.

'I used to help my aunty when I was in my teens,' he answered. 'Every summer. This was my summer job.'

'You spent every summer down here?'

'Aye,' he came back, passing two brimming gingerbread lattes over to a woman who seemed to be trying desperately to catch his eye so she could furnish him with a winning smile.

'My mum had six kids to look after and I was the oldest and the naughtiest. So, Mari would have me down here to stay in the holidays. Kept me out of trouble.'

'Were you at risk of getting into trouble?'

He turned back and looked at her. There was that grin again. Just wicked enough to make her want to involuntarily hiccup.

'Oh, I got into *all* the trouble,' he replied.

Annie gulped and made an unsuccessful feather pattern in a mocha that resembled a slug.

'Help yourself to a cupcake,' said Annie as she hurriedly slurped the slug mocha so he didn't see her mistake and set about making another for her customer.

'Don't mind if I do,' said John, reaching into the chiller.

Annie turned her back to him and raised her eyes to the heavens. *What is wrong with me?*

A group of women came in and claimed the larger middle table. Since she didn't yet know all her customers' given names, Annie gave her regulars nicknames by which she identified them. These women, rather unimaginatively, were called 'the swimmers'. Thrice weekly these women of all ages and stature took to the sea – rain or shine – wearing lairy swimming caps and screeching with unbridled joy as the cold water rushed at them. *Rather them than me,* Annie would think as she watched them bobbing about in the surf. Then they would clamour into the cafe, high as kites on all the endorphins that the freezing ocean had released into their brains.

When the swimmers saw John, they hollered and waved in surprise before taking it in turns to come to the counter and give him their order along with a jovial grilling.

'You're not really going to flatten this place, are you?'

'*I* won't be flattening anything, Malory,' John replied.

Annie leaned round his shoulder.

'He'll be letting someone else flatten it for him,' she said.

She saw John's jaw set.

'But it's such a shame, John,' said floral-fleece.

'Unfortunately, things can't carry on the same forever,' John came back. 'Mari needs to sell. I'm sure you would rather see Mari live out the rest of her days in comfort over keeping a glorified fishing hut.'

'There must be another way! It'll ruin the whole ambience of the place. Big bland boxes no doubt.'

'It will be different, Cynthia, but I've known the builder for years. He'll be very sympathetic to the land.'

'And what about poor Annie?' piped up all-weather-flip-flops.

The other women chimed in with her: 'Yes, what about Annie?'

'Annie knew this was a short lease when she moved in,' said John. 'Nobody asked her to start a business.'

Lease? thought Annie. *If only! If I had a proper lease, I might have a legal leg to stand on.*

'And what do you say, Annie?' asked Malory.

'I won't lie to you,' Annie called over the noise of the coffee grinder, 'I love it here. And I love this cafe. But it's not up to me.'

It was as delicate an answer as she could muster whilst her landlady's nephew was helping her for free in a cafe that he didn't want to exist.

'But the history, John,' implored floral-fleece. 'Think of the lost historical value. I'm sure you know Emily is campaigning to have it turned over to the Historical Society.'

'Trust me, I know,' said John. 'Unfortunately, neither me nor my aunt have the money for that kind of philanthropy. We can't afford to just give it away. Believe me, I've tried every way I can think of to find a solution that suits everybody, but the simple fact of the matter is, the land is worth more without Saltwater Nook than with it.'

'What about the local value then?' asked Cynthia. 'Annie's made the place a part of the community again. That's got to be worth something?'

'Aye, it is. But it's not worth more than my aunt's safety and comfort.'

'What do the local council say about building down here?' asked all-weather-flip-flops.

'I've already got planning permission. I've gone through all the proper channels. I love Saltwater Nook. You know I do. I practically grew up here. But nostalgia doesn't pay the bills.'

'We'll be sorry to see it go,' said Cynthia. 'We'll be sorry to lose The Saltwater Cafe too.'

'You've got a few months of me yet,' said Annie.

'I'll drink to that!' said Malory, lifting her hazelnut latte.

'Perhaps you can change his mind?' said floral-fleece, conspiratorially, as though John wasn't standing right next to her.

'I'm not sure he's very flexible,' said Annie. 'I think John is probably used to getting his own way.'

'Is that what you think?' John chuckled darkly. There was a glint in his eye that could have been chagrin or humour. 'You feel you know me well enough to make those kinds of judgements, do you, Ms Sharpe?'

Annie didn't know if they were playing or fighting; there seemed to be a fine line between the two. And yet, there was something about disagreeing with John Granger which she found most enjoyable; his lack of sugar-coating was refreshingly sharp.

'No,' she said, smiling. 'I've just met men like you before.'

'Men like me indeed! How many men *like me* have you met, exactly?'

Annie laughed then.

'Truth be told, not that many actually.'

'Still an enigma then,' he smiled.

'Yes,' said Annie, looking at him quizzically. His eyes were more blue than grey in this light, with a ring around the iris of a dark green that matched the colour of the sea outside. 'I can't make you out at all.'

'Good,' he said.

Chapter 53

When Annie turned the sign over on the door and pulled the shutters closed on the kiosk, the only sounds left to hide behind were the whoosh of the dishwasher and Enya's haunting Celtic melodies playing on Spotify. She had grown increasingly comfortable in John's presence over the course of the afternoon but now they were alone she felt suddenly self-conscious.

'Well,' John exclaimed, pulling his hand through his hair as he surveyed the aftermath of the busy cafe on every table and surface, inside and out. 'I guess it would be rude to leave you with all this to clear up.'

Annie laughed.

'This is nothing I'm not used to.'

'But today you have a willing servant, so you might as well make use of me,' he smiled.

Annie felt her cheeks redden at the idea but recovered herself quickly.

'Even though you wish I'd never opened the cafe?'

'Even though.' John smiled and then said, 'I'm willing to call a truce. Just for today. In honour of All Hallows' Eve and the spirits that lurk about these shores in the dark.'

John crossed the cafe to where Annie stood by the door. He held out his hand.

'I'm opening the cafe tonight, as in open for business as well as for dishing out sweets. Does that affect the truce?' Annie asked.

'You'd be missing an opportunity if you didn't.'

Annie smiled.

'You're a real mystery, John Granger,' she said.

John smiled back at her and winked.

'Good,' he said. 'Truce?'

Annie shook his hand.

'Truce,' she agreed. She went to pull her hand back but he held it for a moment longer.

'Just so you're clear what a truce means,' he went on. 'It means that for the rest of the day we will refrain from being unpleasant to one another.'

'Not once have I been unpleasant without due provocation!' Annie protested. Her heart was beating strangely fast at being this close to him.

'Ordinarily I would beg to differ. But in the spirit of the Halloween truce, I will simply renew my promise to refrain from being unpleasant for the day's duration. Do we have a deal?'

Annie smiled in spite of herself.

'Deal,' Annie agreed, giving his hand an extra shake for good measure.

'Good!' he grinned. He swooped down on the first table he came to and began gathering up cups and cupcake detritus. 'Then let's clear up this shower of shite so we can make a start on those Halloween decorations. Those wee trick or treating bairns wait for no man!' he added in a jovial, extremely Scottish, accent.

Annie could not have been more taken aback if she'd seen Neptune himself grinning out at her from the surf beyond.

'Right,' said Annie when they had cleared down. 'I'm going to make us a well-earned lunch. Would you like a coffee while you wait?'

'That would be lovely,' John replied. 'I'll get cracking on these boxes.' He reached into one of the boxes he had dragged in from the hall and pulled out what was essentially a basket-ball sized knot of black cat fairy lights.

Annie grimaced.

'I'll make it a double shot.'

She furnished him with a large Americano and left him to it. Upstairs, Annie looked through her cupboards and the fridge and tried to find something to cook for an impromptu late lunch. She settled on a vegetable frittata and salad.

Twenty minutes later and laden with two plates of rainbow food, Annie pushed the cafe door open with her bottom and turned to find that John was not there. For a moment, she thought perhaps he'd changed his mind on the truce; maybe he was simply as mercurial as he seemed. She felt strangely deflated. But as she set the plates down on the table, she heard a *tap, tap, tap* followed by a curse in a thick Scottish accent coming from outside. Annie followed the sound and found John sucking his thumb whilst still holding a hammer in his other hand.

'Are you all right?' Annie pulled her cardigan around her. Despite the brightness of the day, there was a distinct nip in the air.

John removed his thumb from his mouth.

'Yes,' he said through gritted teeth. 'I slipped with the bloody hammer.' He inspected his thumb as he spoke. 'The skin's not broken but it's throbbing like a bastard!'

'I don't think I've ever seen a bastard throb.'

He stared at her, his expression amused, though he still nursed his sore digit.

'You're a bit of a smart-arse, aren't you?' he said.

'Only a bit?'

'I'm still deciding to what degree,' he grumbled amiably, looking up towards the guttering.

'This looks great!' said Annie, following John's gaze. A double string of black cat and pumpkin fairy lights looped in and out of each other above the windows which ran the length of the cafe. Another string, of skull lights, criss-crossed from the Victorian lamp post to the signpost which warned of strong currents at the peninsular.

'I've a way to go yet,' he replied. 'Whether I'll have any fingers left by the end of it remains to be seen.'

'Well, give your fingers a break and come in and have some food,' said Annie.

They discussed their game plan as they ate. Annie explained that her next job was to get her half-sack of potatoes peeled, cubed and sprinkled with garlic and rosemary, ready to go into the oven.

'And what about those pumpkin shells under the worktop?' asked John. 'Were you thinking of making them into jack-o'-lanterns or are they a statement of minimalism?'

'Now who's the smart-arse?' asked Annie. 'As it happens, I was intending to carve them and have them outside on the promenade but, as you well know, I have been rather busy.'

'Nobody forced you to open a cafe.'

'Nobody forced me to cater Halloween for an entire village either. But here we are!'

'Here we are indeed.'

Chapter 54

'Checking out the competition?' John asked.

They were seated at the middle table in the warm cafe, carving pumpkins.

'No. I was checking the time on your watch.'

She saw the corners of John's mouth twitch as he repressed a smile. Annie looked up then and saw that it was fully dark outside.

'How long before they arrive?' she asked. She was excited and more than a little nervous. What if her Halloween was a let-down?

'We've probably got about twenty minutes,' John replied, adding the final touches to an impressive cat arching its back at a ghost rising up out of a cauldron. *Shit*, Annie thought. *That's really good.* It made her scary pumpkin face seem rather ordinary by comparison. 'That's very good,' she told him, though it pained her to say it.

'Thanks,' said John, getting up to wash his hands. 'The pumpkin carving was always a big deal with Aunty Mari. I've passed the bug on to Celeste. You must have carved a fair few of these over the years with your boys?'

Annie pondered the strangeness of getting to know someone

as just herself; for so many years she had been defined by her children and her work. But John didn't know about Annie the mother or Annie the chef at The Pomegranate Seed – to him she was just Annie.

'Yes,' she said fondly. 'Alex would always lose his rag because he was a perfectionist and wanted to create a perfect piece of pumpkin art – even at four. He's a graphic designer now, no surprise really – he's still always striving for design perfection. You'd probably get on well,' she added, eyeing his perfect feline carving.

'And Peter? It is Peter, isn't it?'

'Peter was always more chilled out. I always felt secretly guilty that he might have had to be that way because Alex was so high maintenance, but now I think that was just his personality. While Alex was flinging bits of pumpkin around the kitchen in a fit of artistic rage, Peter would sit obliviously carving out his spooky face, his tongue poking out the side of his mouth; that was his concentration face.'

'And what does he do now?'

'He's a landscape gardener. He loves the outdoors.'

'He'd probably get on well with Celeste,' said John.

Lord alive! thought Annie. *I wouldn't let Peter within ten feet of Celeste, he'd probably just try and get her into bed.* But she smiled and said, 'Yes, probably.'

'Right, let's get this place lit up!' said John, drying his hands on a tea towel and grinning. There was a boyish excitement about him that Annie couldn't help but smile back at.

Together they went outside – the cold was like a slap against Annie's skin, the spiky chill finding its way beneath her tea dress and inside her fair isle cardigan. John made some final adjustments before darting back inside to flick the switch, and Saltwater Nook lit up with amber ghouls and pale skulls grinning out into the darkness. Annie gasped.

'It looks great!' she called out as she made her way back to him. 'I think we should leave it like this permanently.'

'We?' John smiled, one eyebrow raised.

'I,' corrected Annie. 'I should leave it up permanently.'

'It's a bit macabre for Christmas, don't you think?'

'All right then. But I'll leave them up till after bonfire night.'

'That sounds like a plan,' said John.

John switched on the inner Halloween lights, while Annie put tea lights inside the jack-o'-lanterns and sat them outside on the patio tables, their spooky carvings glowing out towards the black sea. Annie looked along the promenade and saw in the distance lots of little lights bobbing along in the darkness as the procession made its way slowly towards Saltwater Nook. Her heart leaped at the sight of it and she ran inside.

'They're coming!' she called, breathless with excitement. 'I've just seen them, they're at the end of the prom.' She was smiling so hard she could feel her mouth stretching.

She looked up to see that John was laughing quietly at her.

'Oh shut up!' she said, though her smile didn't extinguish.

'I'm sorry,' John chuckled. 'It's just that I don't think I've ever seen an adult so excited about Halloween.'

'It's my first Halloween party.' Annie smoothed down her dress and raised her head in the air defiantly.

'What? Ever?'

'My parents didn't believe in celebrating evil.'

'Blimey! And I thought my family was weird.'

'Shut up and help me get the spuds into bags,' said Annie.

Together they scooped hot crispy roast potato cubes into little paper bags and lined them up on trays to be dished out to cold grown-ups. The sweets – of which there appeared to be thousands – were tipped hastily into two large plastic cauldrons and a giant plastic pumpkin head.

'Wait one second,' said John, disappearing out into the hallway.

He returned a moment later with a mass of black fabric in his arms which turned out to be a black witch's cloak and hat which he passed to Annie and a long black Dracula cape with a red satin collar, which he flung around his own shoulders.

'Where did you find these?'

'The leather trunk beneath the telly. I wasn't snooping.' He wore a sheepish expression. 'I knew that's where Mari keeps them. I don't know if the hat will fit you; you've got a bigger head than her.'

Annie scowled at him and pulled the witch's hat onto her head. It was a little tight and she was pretty sure it would leave a red mark around her forehead.

'Actually, it fits perfectly,' she said.

Chapter 55

It was absolute mayhem and Annie was delighted. All the children and many of the adults were in Halloween costumes. Annie counted seventeen witches, including herself, and two very sexy witches who made her feel quite dowdy. There were werewolves – large and small – Draculas, a Morticia Adams, a scantily clad nurse – who looked cold to the bone – zombies, ghosts, pirates, a Ninja Turtle and one Disney princess – this was Esme, head tucked firmly inside Gemma's coat, fairy wand gripped tightly in her gloved hand.

Saltwater Nook got a unanimous thumbs up from the Willow Bay Halloween procession, and a lively roar of approval went up when Annie said the cafe was open for business. John dished out sweets into waiting Halloween buckets held in eager chubby hands, and offered round the little bags of hot potatoes to the adults. Annie stationed herself at the coffee machine – mostly hot chocolates and decaf coffees at this time of night, she noticed – and doled out cupcakes and crumbly shortbread.

Maeve stood at the door waving a bag above her head.

'Got a washing-up bowl or something I can fill with water?' she shouted over the noise. 'I've got a bag full of windfalls from the orchard ready for bob-the-apple!'

267

Annie ducked down into a cupboard in the kitchen area and handed a large clear plastic mixing bowl to John, who duly filled it with water and carried it carefully through the packed cafe to Maeve.

'Ah, John, good man. Happy to see you,' she said as she took the bowl from him. 'I'll try my best not to let any of the buggers drown.' And she let out a throaty laugh.

Annie glanced over in time to see Gemma raise her eyebrows.

There was much screeching and splashing outside as heads were bobbed; long hair was held back by parents and grinning children shivered in their sodden costumes, while others waited in line for their chance to dunk their faces in freezing water for a bruised apple.

Annie watched through the window as Lennox tried in vain to catch an apple in his teeth. Each time he came up for air looking more frustrated. Gemma was trying to coax him away from the bowl, but he was determined. As Lennox plunged his head back into the water again, John shouted, 'Hey, kids, is that a witch on her broomstick?' All eyes turned to the sky as John slipped his hand into the bowl and held an apple still below the water. Lennox, with his eyes tight shut, and none the wiser, found the apple and speared it. John surreptitiously removed his hand and wiped it on his cape. The children looked back in time to see Lennox flick his head up out of the water, an apple clamped in his teeth and a look of absolute triumph on his face. Everyone cheered. Gemma – with an expression of deep relief on her face – mouthed *thank you* to John, who smiled. Annie felt something unexpected bloom in her chest.

Pam and, to Annie's surprise, Emily – minus her placard – had come prepared with towels and blankets and set to wrapping the children up like snug bugs in rugs. Bill came up to the counter.

'Annie, love, we usually do the Willow Bay story outside but since you're open, we wondered if you'd mind us doing it in here?'

'Of course not, I'd love that!'

John overheard and came up behind Bill. 'I'll help you shift things about,' he said.

The two men moved chairs and tables to the sides of the cafe and Maeve and Emily ushered the revellers back into the warm. Ely wandered in then and pulled a chair out to sit in front of the counter. The children – knowing the drill – sat themselves down on the floor in a semi-circle around him. Annie switched off all the lamps but one and turned the volume down on the music. The cafe was bathed in the orange glow of the fairy lights and Annie noticed that someone had turned the jack-o'-lanterns around outside, so that they shone into the cafe from out of the darkness. Annie was about to sit down on the floor when she spotted Alfred shuffle quietly into the cafe. She pulled two bags of potatoes out of the oven and took them over to him. He smiled at her and raised a hand in silent thanks.

'October 1502. It was a dark and stormy night, the rain was lashing against the windows, the wind had ripped tiles off roofs and the water poured in through the holes, soaking the folks within. Lightning streaked across the sky and the thunder crashed,' Ely began.

His voice was as coarse as the rocky cliff face, his bushy greying eyebrows fanned out below the rim of his knitted hat and his unkempt beard was matted like brushed felt. Annie got the sense he was hamming it up a bit for the sake of ambience. The children were caught somewhere between rapt and terrified; all except Esme, who sat on Gemma's lap, facing into her chest, watching something intently on her mum's mobile phone, with a set of headphones clamped over her ears.

Annie looked about the little cafe. She wouldn't have imagined so many people would've been able to fit, let alone find places to lean. The room was warm with the heat and breath of so many bodies and condensation poured down the windows. Outside, the wind began to howl and whistle through the old frames, lending the perfect percussion to Ely's performance. Annie had that uncanny feeling again that this was where she was supposed to be; she couldn't explain it, but there was a sense of rightness inside her.

John was standing across the room with Paul, leaning back against the long bench. Paul whispered something to him, and John laughed quietly. He had his arms folded, one leg crossed casually over the over. He looked overly smart stood next to Paul, the ageing hippy. John, having dispensed with his cloak and pointed teeth, wore dark blue jeans, which seemed to make his legs look even longer than they were, with tan Chelsea boots and a knitted round-necked jumper over a shirt. John chose that moment to look up and their eyes met. He smiled at her and her stomach somersaulted. She felt hot beneath his stare and broke away, smoothing her dress down and placing her hands in her lap.

'He's brilliant, isn't he?' Samantha whispered in her ear.

'John?' Annie whispered back absently.

'No, Ely!'

'Oh, yes. Yes. Ely.'

Chapter 56

The sound of hypnotised children breathing through open mouths was like a whisper of spirits.

There was an audible gasp from the children as his story came to an end and the adults clapped and cheered. Annie had goosebumps all over her skin and the hairs on the back of her neck were standing to attention.

'He can really tell a story!' Annie shouted into Samantha's ear over the din.

'I know! It never gets old, every year it gives me the tingles.'

Ely took a modest bow and swigged generously from the silver hipflask he pulled from his pocket. The crowd dispersed quickly; it would be way past most of the children's bedtimes by the time they reached their homes. People called over their goodbyes and shouted 'Great job, Annie!' and 'Just like the old days!' as they left.

'I'd stay to help you clear up,' said Gemma, struggling slightly under the weight of Esme who was clinging on like a limpet. 'But Maeve managed to park at the bottom of the hill and she's offered us a lift home.'

'Don't worry about that,' said Annie. 'You go with Maeve and get those babies tucked up in their beds.'

'Hey! I'm no baby,' protested Lennox.

Annie bent down and helped him with the zip on his coat.

'You are big and tall, Lennox, but you will always be your mummy's baby.'

He seemed satisfied at this.

'My mum calls my dad a big mummy's boy,' he agreed.

'Well, there you are then,' said Annie.

Pam gave Annie a kiss on both cheeks and Annie thought she saw tears in her eyes.

'That was marvellous, Annie. Just marvellous!'

Emily was stood beside her mum.

'I'm glad you came,' Annie said to Emily. 'It was nice to see you minus your placard.'

'Halloween is an important tradition in Willow Bay. You gave it the respect it's due and I can support that. We're not out to claim Saltwater Nook for the sake of having it,' Emily went on. 'We just want it to be in safe hands, protected.' And then, very loudly in John's direction, she added, 'It's good to know that some people respect the history of this village!'

Out of the corner of her eye, Annie saw John wince, but he said nothing.

The last people left, and Annie heaved a satisfied sigh.

'And then there were two,' said John.

Annie had that strange feeling again. The one where she was excited and uncomfortable and yet somehow at ease being alone with him. Invariably he would annoy or surprise her within the next five minutes; possibly both.

'I guess I'd better get this lot cleared up ready for the morning,' she said.

'I'll help.'

272

'Thank you. You don't have to but thank you. You can eat leftover cold spuds and cake as payment.'

'How could any man refuse?'

They set about sweeping and cleaning down and moving the tables and chairs back to where they ought to be, chatting as they worked. Annie made them a hot chocolate each before turning off the coffee machine and cleaning it down.

'I see you've met Alfred.'

Annie's guard was suddenly up.

'Yes,' she said. 'He's a good man.'

'He used to sleep in the cafe when the weather was bad. Mari thought I didn't know.'

'He still does,' said Annie.

'And you don't mind?'

'No, why should I? He's no trouble. Scared the shit out of me when I first found him down here but now I rather like having him around.'

'He's too old to live the way he does. He should be living comfortably somewhere in his old age, not kipping on cold floors and in caves.'

'He's not *that* old,' said Annie. 'What is he? Late fifties? Early sixties?'

'Too old to be sleeping on the streets.'

'Well, yes, I grant you that, there's no good age to be sleeping rough. But he's not on the streets at present.'

'Not here no. But where do you think he sleeps when he heads into the city for winter?'

'I don't know.'

'I'm fairly sure he doesn't have a cafe owner in the city willing to let him camp out on her floor every night,' said John.

'I'm not disagreeing with you. I'd like to see Alfred somewhere safe and warm too but it's not as easy as just finding
him somewhere to live, is it? Gemma said there've been
attempts to house him before that haven't worked out. We
have to respect that Alfred is a complex character with equally
complex needs.'

'At what point does respect become irresponsibility?'

'What do you suggest?' asked Annie. 'We can't force him
into housing! It's more complicated than that.'

'It's easy to be flippant until somebody finds him dead on
the beach from pneumonia.'

'You're talking as if Alfred is my responsibility,' said Annie.

'Not just yours. Mine. Everybody's. Apathy is as dangerous
as ignorance.'

'I am neither apathetic nor ignorant towards Alfred's
plight,' said Annie.

He held his hands up. 'That came out wrong, that's not
what—'

'Do you know what,' said Annie. 'I'm just about sick of men
telling me *how life is*, or what *they* think *my* thoughts on a
subject are. Thank you for help for your help today, but I can
take it from here.'

She held out her hand to take the broom from John. John
opened his mouth to speak but Annie gave him a look that
brooked no discussion. He sighed and handed over the broom.

'You're impossible,' said John and, without another word,
he took his jacket from the hook by the door and left.

Damn, Annie thought. *I guess the truce is over.*

Chapter 57

When she got back up to the flat she fed Mrs Tiggy-Winkle and got into her pyjamas. She couldn't settle. She tried watching television, drinking hot chocolate with brandy and reading *Lady Audley's Secret* to soothe herself, but nothing held her attention. She was even too fidgety for Tiggs to bother with her.

She hadn't wanted to argue with John. He just seemed to push her buttons. She harrumphed as she raked over their disagreement. So far, though bullish and self-righteous, John's only real crimes had been to want to have enough money to look after an elderly aunt in her twilight years, and to suggest a sixty-something man shouldn't be homeless. What had happened here, she surmised, was a classic case of transference: she was taking out her feelings of frustration and powerlessness with Max on John.

Max's passive aggression bordered on abusive; even when she was aware of what he was doing, his words would leave her tongue-tied and impotent, like screaming through duct tape. She'd been frustrated for so long that John's unthreatening, plain-speaking manner seemed to set all her pent-up words free. She knew instinctively there would be no repercussions with John. But feeling safe with him didn't mean she could behave like an arse. In fact, she reasoned, it ought to garner the opposite response. He did still push her buttons, though . . .

'Oh my God!' she raised her hands heavenwards in exasperation. 'Why is he so annoying?' She was offered no response to her pleas, other than Tiggs regurgitating and waking herself up with a start.

'Serves you right for eating your supper like a pig,' said Annie.

Mrs Tiggy-Winkle eyed Annie with contempt and settled back down to sleep.

Annie huffed. 'Oh, all right,' she said irritably to no one at all. She picked up her phone and texted John.

I'm sorry. I don't know why I snapped like I did. Well, actually, I do know but it's too complicated to go into over text. The thing is, my anger wasn't aimed at you and it was unfair of me to go off like that. I'm sorry that our truce ended. Thank you for helping to make my first ever Halloween party so enjoyable. 🎃

In less than a minute her phone pinged.

I'm sorry too. I came off as self-righteous and accusing and that isn't how I meant that conversation to go at all. I guess the skeletons in both our closets were rattling their bones tonight. 💀 Of course you care about Alfred. I took my frustrations out on you and that was unfair of me. 🎃

Annie read and reread the text. *Blimey!* she thought. *He's like a real-life grown-up!* Another text came through hot on the heels of the first.

I'm driving to Cornwall this weekend to visit Mari and Celeste but I'll be back in Willow Bay on Wednesday to help Paul with the fireworks. Perhaps we can talk again. 🎃🙂

Away till Wednesday? Don't you ever work? 😏

To which he replied: Ha! The benefits of working remotely. I work six days a week but pick my own hours. Can usually be found burning the midnight oil.

'Hmmm,' Annie mused aloud. 'A workaholic?'

She texted: In that case . . . don't you ever sleep?

The response was almost immediate: Not enough and lately even less!

Annie desperately wanted to ask why he wasn't sleeping but given how quickly their conversations deteriorated, she decided to keep things light.

Well, you've got a long drive tomorrow, so hopefully you'll get some sleep tonight. Nite nite.

She deleted the nite nite and then wrote it back in again three times; was it too cutesy? Too familiar? Too dismissive?

'Oh, for the love of God, woman! Just finish the text already!' she berated herself. She put nite nite back into the message and pressed send before she could change her mind again.

Sleep tight! J. came the reply.

Just one more thing . . . Annie messaged.

Yes??

If you could only listen to one song for the rest of your life, what would it be?

He came back within seconds.

Spice Girls, Wannabe. Obviously!

Annie laughed out loud. She was still erupting into little guffaws as she settled herself down under a blanket to watch an old *Hammer Horror* on TV, starring Christopher Lee as Dracula nibbling on some prim ladies with jaunty hats and plummy accents. What better way to finish off a perfect Halloween?

Chapter 58

The next morning, it was pouring with rain and her customers were primarily those for whom nothing will come between them and their constitutionals. A couple squeaked their way to the bench by the window and shrugged out of their hardy outerwear.

Annie's phone buzzed with a text. It was from John: a photo of Mari, laughing from beneath a woollen hat and shrouded in many layers, as she sat outside a cafe in bright sunshine, holding up a coffee cup. Behind her the view fell away down to the sea and little fishing boats bobbing on the water. Just at the edge of the picture was a slender hand with black nail varnish, resting lightly on a packet of cigarettes. This, Annie surmised, must be Celeste. The caption read: Just so you know I haven't locked her away in a nursing home.

Annie smiled. She went to the kiosk and hung out of the window far enough to be able to snap a picture of the lashing rain and the sea which looked to be a muddy brown, swelling beneath a gun-metal sky. She sent the photograph with the caption: Bet you wish you were here! And then followed it quickly with: What crazy time of the morning did you leave to be sipping coffee in Cornwall by 11 a.m.?

He messaged back: 5 a.m. Couldn't sleep.

Where do you actually live? Annie asked.

Why? Do you want to send me anthrax in the post?

I was thinking more a horse's head in your bed!

Classic. I live in London, Clapham.

And what exactly is your profession in Clapham?

I'm an architect.

As an architect, aren't you supposed to love buildings?

I know what you're getting at. I've been made an offer I can't refuse.

Can't or won't?

Do you have a better solution?

She didn't so she messaged: Say hello to Mari for me. ☺

Will do. ☺

It was all rather exhilarating, this dance of words, and Annie found herself working with a distinct spring in her step, despite the dismal weather and the constant mopping up after dripping umbrellas and waterproof coats.

Half an hour later another message from John flashed up on her screen and Annie had to stop herself from breaking into a jig right there behind the counter. What was wrong with her? She felt like a giddy teenager.

By the way, there was something I'd been meaning to ask . . .

Yes?? she typed back.

Who do you think would win in a fight between an apple and an orange?

Annie snorted with laughter, earning herself some amused looks from the cafe.

Why, the orange of course! she typed. It could squirt its juice in the apple's eyes. Everyone knows orange juice in the eye is a real stinger.

Just as I thought, John replied.

It was puerile, of course, but it didn't stop Annie from grinning like a maniac. And besides, what was wrong with a bit of silliness? So far as she knew there wasn't an age limit on it.

The Calor gas fire in the corner pushed out welcome heat, the mellow sounds of Harry Connick Jr wafted around the cafe and mixed with the cheerful hum of customer conversation, and Annie found herself feeling a contentedness she could never have imagined two months ago. She felt so at one with the world, in fact, that she took Emily a slice of cake out with her coffee to keep her going whilst she picketed in the rain.

Chapter 59

Annie woke up on Sunday morning heartache-heavy. It was the anniversary of her parents' deaths. They had died exactly a year apart to the day. When her mum had died, her dad had simply wound down, like a clock quietly ticking down to a stop. Last year, she had almost worked through the anniversary. She had been halfway through checking the dates on the fridge foods in the chiller when she'd remembered, and then she'd felt horribly guilty. It had happened like that other years too. Once she'd been doing the school run and the realisation had sucker-punched the breath right out of her. But this year she had woken knowing exactly what day it was.

She lay in bed thinking about them. The grief had become less raw as the years they had now been absent from her life slowly caught up with the years she'd had with them. Today she really felt it, perhaps because she would have liked to ask for their advice and blessing on this huge life change she had undertaken. She had no other family; she had the boys, of course, but she was hardly going to burden them with her worries and regrets. Tiggs padded up to the pillow and meowed mournfully in Annie's face for her breakfast.

'All right,' said Annie, shaking herself mentally as she clambered out of bed. 'Sometimes I think you're more piggy than puss,' she said to the cat, but Mrs Tiggy-Winkle was already leading the way to the kitchen with her tail in the air.

Annie spent some time sitting on the beach, throwing pebbles into the surf and enjoying the satisfying 'plop' sound before they disappeared beneath the waves. The sky was a pale grey cashmere; the weather seemed less antagonistic today and it suited Annie's reflective mood. Her parents had been so proud when she'd qualified as a chef; they'd worried that getting pregnant would ruin her chances of a career, and had it not been for their steadfast support, it might have. Annie wished they were here now so that she could talk to them about the dramatic changes her life had gone through these past months; she would dearly love their counsel – though she was sure they would support her decisions. There didn't seem to be a cut-off point for missing one's parents. Were they watching over her? She liked to think so. On days like this, it was easy to believe that they were.

Her calm reverie was shattered by a voice calling her name across the deserted stretch of beach.

'I know today is always a hard one for you,' said Max, following her through the gate.

'Yes, well. It is what it is,' said Annie.

'I thought you might like some company.'

'Not really,' said Annie. 'But thank you for thinking of me.'

'I found some old photograph albums. I thought we could go through them together. Maybe sort out how to split them. You can have first dibs.' He smiled uncertainly at her.

Annie sighed exaggeratedly. 'Would you like a cup of tea?' she asked. She didn't have the energy to fight him today.

And so it was that Annie and Max spent the rest of Sunday afternoon flicking through old photographs and – to Annie's surprise – laughing over shared memories.

The last of the daylight evaporated and lamps were switched on. In amongst the holiday snaps and obligatory baby bath-time photographs were pictures of her parents: smiling in their garden, playing with the boys, out at restaurants to cele-brate various wedding anniversaries . . . The years rolled back through the yellowing edges of the albums and soon they were looking at grainy photographs taken on disposable cameras, of Annie showing off a gigantic baby bump while Max pointed at it grinning, Annie and Max pre-bump, down the pub, in the park, at the prom.

'God, you looked hot in that prom dress,' said Max.

'It was practically sprayed on,' laughed Annie. 'I didn't think my dad was going to let me leave the house!'

'Whose house did we go to for the after-party?'

'Mandy Shaw's.'

'Mandy Shaw! Crikey, I wonder whatever happened to her?'

'She's a head teacher in Milton Keynes.'

'Blimey. Do you remember the spare room? Under the coats?'

'Worrying that any moment someone would come in and catch us,' said Annie.

Max's laugh was soft and low. Annie felt the danger but pushed it aside.

'I don't remember you being all that worried,' he said quietly, just close enough to her ear for her to feel his breath on her neck.

Annie quickly picked up another black shiny paper envelope and began to sift through the photographs. Pictures of them kissing; blurry selfies, in the days before mobile phones, when you clicked and hoped for the best.

'I'll never forget that night,' whispered Max, taking the pictures from her and letting them drop to the floor. His voice was low and loaded with determination and Annie was suddenly too tired to resist the inevitable. *Fuck it!* she thought. *It's only sex, it doesn't mean anything.* She needed to feel something other than sad today. And then they were kissing; not in the photographs anymore but on her sofa, in the sitting room of Saltwater Nook – desperate kisses amongst the evidence of their shared lives, their former selves frozen in time, staring out through sepia tones. Annie wriggled out of her jeans and Max pulled his top off, she arched her body towards his. The heat of his hands on her skin, his fingers remembering her secrets, their bodies melding easily together in collaborative muscle memory.

'I love you, Annie,' Max whispered as he expertly undid her bra with one hand. 'Say you'll come back to me. Say you love me too.'

His words pulled her up short. Annie's brain re-emerged from the thick fug of nostalgia and her ache for physical contact. *What am I doing?* she screamed at herself. *What the fuck am I doing?* There was no such thing as *just a shag* when Max was on a mission.

'Stop,' said Annie, trying to wriggle out from Max's tentacle-like embrace. The fire running through her veins turned to ice. She felt sick, angry at herself for being so stupid.

'Don't fight it, Annie,' Max whispered, pushing her further down onto the sofa.

She was suffocating beneath his kisses; his body on hers felt like a concrete blanket and she fought against him.

'I mean it!' said Annie. With limbs flailing, like a beetle on its back, she extricated herself from beneath Max and pulled herself up to standing. 'This isn't going to happen.'

She pulled her jeans back on and threw his top at him.

'Annie, baby, come on. You know you want this as much as I do. Stop fighting against the inevitable.'

Annie was struggling with her hands behind her back, trying to refasten her bra. She gave up and stood, slightly breathless, with her hands on her hips, at once exhilarated and disgusted but entirely certain that she was doing the right thing.

'I want a divorce,' she said. 'And I want you to buy me out of the restaurant and I want my half of The Pomegranate Seed building, and the house. And I want you to unlock our joint account right bloody now! I'm entitled to it and I want it.'

Max sat up on the sofa, blinking in the half-light.

'I haven't got that kind of money.' He was trying to play the victim but it came off as whiny.

'There's no mortgage on the restaurant building,' Annie went on. Suddenly she had all the answers. She wondered idly if this was what an epiphany felt like. 'You won't have any trouble taking one out on it. And if that doesn't cover the whole cost, you can ask your parents.'

'They haven't—'

'This is me, remember, Max. I know they've got it, just sitting in a bank account, waiting for you.'

'That's my inheritance!'

'As long as it's yours it doesn't really matter when you get it, does it!'

'They'll never agree.'

'Then it's up to you to persuade them. You're good at that. I'll make an appointment to see my solicitor and get it all drawn up. I'm not asking for anything that isn't already mine. My inheritance bought that place and it's only right that I get at least half of it back.'

Max, realising she meant business, was gathering up his jacket and stuffing the photograph albums back into the bags.

'You can leave those for now,' said Annie. 'I'll sort through them and make copies.'

'I'm sure,' said Max. 'Maybe you'd like to take the shirt off my back while you're at it, since you seem determined to take me to the cleaners and destroy everything I've worked for.'

'Everything *we've* worked for, Max. And I'm not asking for anything that doesn't already belong to me.'

Max wasn't listening. Holding the bags to his chest, like one might hold a duvet to cover their modesty when waking to find themselves with an unfamiliar lover in a strange bed, and an expression to match, Max yanked open the door to the flat.

'And don't forget the account!' Annie shouted. 'I want my sodding money!'

'I'll see myself out,' said Max. And then, leaning in close to her face, he hissed, 'You're a bitch,' before slamming the door behind him.

Annie swiftly locked the door and listened to his heavy footsteps descending the stairs. After the front door had been pulled shut with an almighty and unnecessary bang, Annie crept downstairs and pulled the latch and chain across the door before scurrying back up to the flat and collapsing on the sofa. She wasn't sure if she believed in an afterlife but if it *was* possible for deceased loved ones to influence the living, Annie would put money on her parents lending her their strength from beyond the grave just then.

It felt like a breakthrough: she would never have stood her ground like that before. Not that she wasn't trembling like a leaf right now, but most of that was exhilaration. Today had been a day of remembrance, but it had been a momentous day for moving forward too.

Chapter 60

'Oh my God!' Gemma exclaimed. 'Thank goodness you didn't sleep with him.'

It was book club night and the women were discussing *Lady Audley's Secret* by Mary Elizabeth Braddon; or at least, they were supposed to be. So far, Annie's close encounter with Max had rather eclipsed the naughtiness of Lucy Audley. Every time they got back on track, something would bring them back round to Annie again.

'Annie is reinventing herself like Lady Audley,' said Maeve.

'Without the child abandonment, faked death and attempted murder,' added Sally.

'Imagine if you'd had sex with him.' Gemma was off on her own tangent. 'You might have given all this up and gone back to Max.'

'That would never have happened,' said Annie. 'It was a momentary lapse which actually ended up crystallising what needed to be done. I think I just felt a bit wobbly, what with the day it was and everything, and Max was being all *let's take a trip down memory lane*. It was just so familiar and comforting and I suppose . . .'

'You leaned on him like a crutch,' said Gemma.

'Or a crotch,' added Maeve.

Gemma spluttered into her wine.

'How did you get on at the solicitor's?' asked Sally.

'Really well. You were right, she is great. She doesn't see any of it as being a problem because I'm not asking for more than is owed to me. If anything, I'm asking for less.'

The conversation slipped back to book club business.

'Interesting that Braddon made Lucy blonde and innocent-looking. If the same story were written by a man, would Lucy have a full moustache and sideburns?' asked Sally.

'No,' said Maeve. 'If she was written by a man, he'd have made her a whore. She'd have had dark hair and dark eyes and massive tits! She certainly wouldn't have begged Sir Michael Audley for a platonic relationship; she'd have straddled him the moment she met him and trapped him under her sex spell.'

'Crikey!' said Gemma.

'Is that what happened with Max on Sunday?' asked Sally. Annie stuck two fingers up at her.

'No matter how good a Victorian woman tried to be, if she had sex outside of the marriage bed, she was destined for a sticky end in literature!'

Gemma hid her mouth with her hands and coughed out the words, 'Sex with the window cleaner!'

Maeve laughed.

'And let that be a lesson to you, Annie.' Sally wagged a finger in Annie's direction.

'Oh, you don't need to worry about me,' said Annie. 'From now on my only relationship is with Mr Knightley.'

'Good girl,' said Maeve, as though praising one of her sheep dogs.

Gemma giggled.

'I'm glad to hear he's come in handy,' she said.

The book club disbanded a little before eleven o'clock, with all the women promising they would be back tomorrow night for the fireworks. Annie still wasn't quite sure what the plan was for the evening but she had been given to believe that John and Paul would have it in hand, and she was happy to leave it to them. For her part, she had decided to make a vat of soup and serve it in mugs with sausage stirrers. It meant another long day at work but if it turned out to be as profitable as Halloween, it would be well worth it.

It was a profitable decision and thank goodness for it. Annie's credit card was maxed out and she needed to start paying some of it off before she found herself in a financial hole too deep to climb out of. *Damn Max*, she brooded as the fireworks began. She hated that he had her over a financial barrel. He hadn't answered his phone since their argument and she still had no access to their account. What little she'd had saved in her own account was down to single figures and she cursed herself for being so complacent with their shared money. She fantasised briefly, amongst the whoops and bangs, about taking a leaf out of Guy Fawkes's book and blowing up The Pomegranate Seed – maybe even with Max still in it – and claiming on the insurance.

The flare of the firelighters briefly illuminated the shadowy figures of Paul and John as they lit the touchpapers and then melted back into the darkness. They had been setting up all afternoon down by the cove – poor old Alfred had been evicted for the day, but he had taken it good-naturedly and Annie had plied him with sausage sandwiches to soften the blow.

'Many thanks,' Alfred mumbled as Annie handed him a gingerbread latte. He dropped three sugar lumps into the already sweet coffee and Annie's teeth ached in sympathy.

'Thank you for tidying up the garden, I recognised your handiwork. The borders look lovely.'

'You still haven't sorted that fence,' said Alfred. 'It won't last the winter.'

'No, I know. I've been so busy. Sorry.' Annie marvelled at the strange relationship she had with this grumpy man.

'I'll do it for you when I've finished my other jobs,' grumbled Alfred, with all the resignation of a disappointed father.

'Oh Alfred, would you? That would be marvellous. I'll see if I can get some new fence posts—'

'No need,' Alfred cut her off. 'I'll get the wood. I know what's needed. You'll probably get all the wrong stuff.'

Annie's feminist feathers ruffled but she conceded that he was probably right. What did she know about fences?

'Someone owes me a favour anyway,' Alfred went on. 'I'll get better wood from him than that rubbish they sell in the DIY shops.'

Annie wondered what Alfred could have done to be owed such a big favour but then she reasoned that Alfred used a different currency than most; she wondered again how this lifestyle translated in the city. And then she remembered that he would be gone soon and she felt a niggle of worry for him, sleeping out on the streets in the cold, with all the dangers that sleeping rough presented.

The fireworks weren't half bad. There were a couple of duds which fizzed and died before they'd begun, drawing jeers and claps from the revellers. But other than that, all the

crowd-pleasers were present and correct. The darkness span-
gled and fizzed with lights so bright they left blobs before
Annie's eyes, as she watched with Lennox and Esme – who
were frightened by the noise – through the windows.

Maeve strode in midway through the display, rubbing her
hands together against the cold.

'I hope Podrick's all right,' she said. 'I've left him sedated
with my daughter. Last year was like *The Hound of the* bloody
Baskervilles in my kitchen with him howling all night.' She
turned and saw Alfred. 'Ah, just the man! I've got a leaking tap
I'd like you to have a look at when you get the time. I've
changed the washer and tightened it all up and it's still
leaking. Think it's a two-man job. Would appreciate your
help.'

'I'll come up tomorrow morning,' said Alfred.

'Need a lift?'

'No thanks. I'll catch one up with Fred.'

'Good man,' Maeve boomed. 'The usual okay for breakfast?'

Alfred has a 'usual' at Maeve's place? Annie thought to herself.

'You still got that extra thick bacon?' asked Alfred.

'Absolutely. Can't do without it.'

Alfred nodded approvingly and said no more; the deal, it
seemed, was struck.

'Mind if I help myself to another soup?' Maeve had turned
her attention back to Annie. 'No, no. Don't get up, I can do it.
I'll pop the cash straight into the till.'

As expected, the cafe filled back up the moment the last
firework had fizzled down into the sea. Even with the prep
Annie had put in earlier, there was no way she could keep up
with taking orders and serving.

'Maeve, you couldn't jump on the till for half an hour, could you?' Annie called.

'Not tonight, I'm afraid. Didn't bring my glasses with me this evening. Blind as a bat up close.'

'I'm driving her home tonight,' said Gemma, as though to put Annie's mind at rest. 'Why don't I help you?'

'If you don't mind, that would be great,' said Annie.

Gemma, it turned out, was a natural. Her friendly disposition made her an excellent calmer of out-of-towners who might otherwise have huffed and puffed about the wait. Annie mused that if she were still at The Pomegranate Seed, Gemma would be just the sort of person she would hire for front of house. She picked up how to use the till almost at once and could remember who ordered what without any problems at all. Annie was in no position to be paying someone to help her out but equally, she would lose customers if the service was bad; word of mouth could make or break a small business, as she well knew. Before she could talk herself out of it, she said, 'Gemma, if I were to take someone on part-time, would you be interested? School hours only, of course, so you could drop off and pick up the kids . . .'

Gemma's eyes instantly welled with tears and she threw her arms around Annie, almost knocking the milk jug clean out of her hands.

'I'd love to! Just say the word.'

'It won't be much,' *that's for damn sure*, 'but I'll make sure your hourly rate is above the minimum wage . . .'

'Fine, fine, fine.' Gemma was waving her arms about. 'Just let me know when I can start.'

'Brian won't mind?' Annie asked. The couple had, after all, agreed that Gemma should be a full-time mum.

'He won't mind at all and if he does, it won't make any difference.' She looked at Annie, her eyes big and intense. 'I need this,' she said with barely controlled desperation. 'I need a job.'

'Then it's yours,' said Annie. 'Give me a few days to sort out the finances . . .' *Sell my body*, she thought, *sell a kidney, maybe two.*

'Honestly,' Gemma broke in. 'Whenever you're ready. Just say the word.'

And just like that, Annie had staff.

Chapter 61

Later, when everyone had left and Annie was clearing down, Paul and John came blustering in, bringing the cold with them, blowing on their hands and still laughing at a joke which had begun before they'd arrived. They smiled as they greeted her, and Annie felt strangely self-conscious under their joint attentions, as though she were a scarlet woman sandwich. Memories of her disappointing fumblings with Paul made her cheeks hot. She reminded herself that she was a grown-up and could have sex with every eligible bachelor who passed her door if she so wished. But it didn't diminish the awkwardness she felt. She wasn't sure what worried her more: the possibility that Paul would tell John that they had shared a night of passion, or that he might divulge that it had been rather a damp squib. Annie realised that it was very important to her that John think she was good in the sack.

'What can I do you for?' Annie asked. 'Great fireworks by the way.'

The pair looked pleased.

'I was wondering if you had any soup left I could take away?' asked Paul.

'Sure,' said Annie. 'It's the least I can offer you after such a fabulous firework display. You can eat it here if you like? As long as you don't mind me cleaning down around you.'

'Thanks, but I'll take it to go if it's all the same. I've got an early start, got to talk to a man about a fish,' he said.

Annie looked at him quizzically.

'Ely's son, Steve, wants to push the business forward. They sell locally and at markets, but Steve wants to expand the number of restaurants they supply. I said I'd have a word with a couple of people I know round Broadstairs way.'

'I might be interested!' said Annie. The words were out of her mouth before she'd fully formed the thoughts behind them. She suddenly felt both men's eyes on her: Paul's enquiring expression and John's familiar scowl. 'I've been thinking a bit about bistro nights and maybe hot lunchtime specials each week, depending on the catch and the season.'

She saw John shaking his head. Paul, ever the optimist, said he thought that would be a fantastic idea. Annie handed over the soup and Paul said a cheery goodbye and left.

'Would you like some soup?' Annie asked John, who seemed to be studying the floorboards.

'No thanks. I just came in to see if you needed help clearing down.'

'That's very kind of you. Thank you, I would. Can I get you a drink?'

'A hot chocolate would go down well.'

Annie set about making two hot chocolates.

'Why do you keep making plans for Saltwater Nook when you know I'm going to sell it?' John asked.

'I've got till March,' said Annie in the breeziest tone she

could muster. 'That's four months to see what I can do. A lot can happen in four months.'

'But why this place?' asked John, lifting chairs onto tables.

'Why not this place?'

'But why here specifically? There must be hundreds of empty shops waiting for a new lease of life.'

Annie handed John his drink and began to clean down the coffee machine.

'I can't explain it,' she said. 'This place is special. It's like it's crying out to be made vital again. There's something here, something magical. You feel it too, I know that you do. Which makes the whole thing altogether more sad.' She was looking at him now, the damp cloth still in her hand.

John sighed one of those sighs that was so long, it was as though he had been holding it in for decades.

'I was a little bastard as a kid. When my dad left, I was even worse. My mum used to send me down here to Aunt Mari and Uncle Frank. Without them I probably would've landed up in prison. I can't help thinking that me being such an arsehole took years off my mum's life.'

'I'm sure that's not the case,' said Annie.

'Are you?' he asked sardonically. 'I tried to make it up to her. I sent money home every month. And when she got sick I tried to get her to come and live with me, but she clung on to that bloody shite-hole of a house she'd lived in with my father out of pure stubbornness. It was a hovel: dingy and damp. But she wouldn't bloody move.' John picked at a fleck of peeling paint on the window ledge. 'She wanted to show him he didn't break her.' He barked out a mirthless laugh. 'Misplaced pride. She died there in that house, all alone, and

I don't even think my dad knew she'd stayed there to spite him.'

'And you're worried Mari will stay here out of stubbornness like your mum?'

'Nobody knows how sick she was last year except me. On a good day she can pootle about okay but on a bad day, when her arthritis is at its worst, she can't even make it from the bedroom to the lounge, let alone down the stairs and up that bloody bastard hill to the village. Even with her friends coming in and out and me dropping by every few days, it wasn't enough. And let me be quite clear, my aunt will *not* let me be her carer; she said she'd rather die than have me look after her, and if you knew my aunt, you'd know that's no idle threat.' He rubbed his hand over his forehead and closed his eyes. 'That's not even the worst of it.'

'What do you mean?'

John sighed.

'She's been diagnosed with Alzheimer's. She doesn't want anyone to know. That's what the notes are all about: she's making sure she doesn't forget. The doctor thinks it'll likely be a slow progression, which is some cold comfort, I suppose, given her age. But still. She's going to need help. I want her to have fun with her friend before she forgets what fun is.'

'John, I'm so sorry. I don't know what to say.'

'There's nothing to say. Those are the facts. I'm not going to lose another family member to sheer bloody-mindedness and wasted sentimentality over a building.'

'But this place isn't like your mum's house,' reasoned Annie. 'Everyone loves it. I love it! It's only wasted sentimentality if no one else appreciates it.'

John pulled a chair out from the bench by the window and slumped down into it, his head in his hands.

'Mari's been talking for a couple of years about moving in with her friend June in Cornwall when she's older. Ha!' Another humourless laugh. 'When she's older! For Christ's sake! I persuaded her to give it a try this winter, see how she gets on.'

'And?'

'She loves it there. If it wasn't for this place, I don't think she'd look back. She's under the Saltwater Nook spell, like every other bugger in this village.'

'And you're not?'

'My aunt is holding out for a buyer who doesn't exist; someone who will love this place like she does. But nobody could love it like she does! It's old, it's tiny, most potential buyers would be wanting to extend it by double at the very least, and that's reflected in the price they're willing to pay for it. Better to sell it as a blank canvas with planning permission.'

Annie walked over to him and laid her hand on his arm.

'I don't think you want to sell it to a developer,' she said gently.

John sighed again and she realised he looked tired.

'It's not about me. The plain fact is, if she sells, I can get them both carers, her and her friend, twice a day; live-in carers even, when the time comes. Meals delivered, shopping delivered, cleaners . . . If she sells, I can give her every comfort for however many years she's got left. She looked after me when I needed it, all I'm trying to do is return the favour. It's my inheritance anyway; she's leaving the place to me. And my decision is that the money is used to make her life comfortable.'

'What if there is someone who loves it as much as your aunt does?'

John looked at her.

'Annie, I don't doubt your motives, but love doesn't pay the bills.'

Annie bit her lip. *That's for damn sure!*

'No,' she said. 'But cold hard cash does.'

'What do you mean?'

'Have you actually signed anything? I mean, could you hold your buyer off for a few months?'

'He knew I was honouring Mari's commitment to let you stay until Easter. Why?'

'I own half my restaurant business. I also own half the building and my house. I'm in the process of trying to get my husband to buy me out. I don't know what price you've agreed with your builder friend, but I want to throw my hat into the ring.'

John was looking at her with an even bigger frown than usual.

'Are you serious?' he asked.

'Yes,' said Annie. 'I want to buy Saltwater Nook.'

She hadn't expected to blurt it out like that. In truth, it had been a half-formulated *what if* rumbling around in her head for a while; one of those idle daydreams that recur when you're washing up, or showering, or watching the sea . . . Now she thought about it, this idle thought had been on a permanent loop.

John sat staring at her, his mouth slightly open as if wanting to say something but the words were not forthcoming. Annie was getting to know his face, the myriad of tiny adjustments that made up his expressions: the twitch at the corners of his mouth which could mean stifled amusement or mischief, depending on the glint in his eyes and the crinkles at their edges, which became deep creases when he was incredulous – as he was now. The lines in his forehead formed ridges when he frowned in annoyance and his eyebrows would meet in the middle for chagrin or work independently of one another when he was being cocky or self-righteous, one brow raising itself into a questioning arch. These little facial clues expressed the things his mouth didn't say and very often belied his words altogether. John Granger called himself a realist but Annie knew he loved Saltwater Nook every bit as much as his aunt. If ever there was a man looking for a reason not to sell to builders, it was him.

'I'll need to think about it,' he said finally, smoothing his face to a blank.

'Take your time.'

'And I'll need to make sure the numbers work.'

'Absolutely. I'm not trying to put you out of pocket. I'm giving you the option to sell it as a going concern. But if I can't offer what you need, I'll stand down and you can sell to the developer. All I'm asking for is fair consideration.'

'Right,' said John. 'Right.'

'Can you get some numbers to me? And I'll do some calculations my end, and then we'll see where we are.'

'Sure,' said John. He had the look of a cartoon character seeing stars and Annie couldn't blame him, she felt much the same.

Annie lay in bed that night wondering what on earth she was doing. At this point she didn't have access to a single penny of her money and yet here she was making make-believe offers on a property in the arse end of nowhere. Is this what a mid-life crisis looked like?

She needed to get Max to agree to her terms. More immediately, she needed access to her bloody bank account. If she kept hitting the credit cards like this, she'd end up having to share the cave with Alfred! And there was another problem. She was becoming increasingly concerned about the prospect of Alfred spending winter outdoors. She found herself unable to drop off to sleep each night until she heard the familiar sound of him climbing into the cafe and knew that he was safe. And on the nights when he didn't stay, she would sleep fitfully. It was like having teenagers all over again. She mentally added Alfred to her list of men to worry about.

Chapter 62

Gemma started her training the following Monday and took to the work with ease. Annie wouldn't be letting her loose on the coffee machine anytime soon but that would come in time. In the meantime, Annie was hoping the extra help would mean she could deal with the ordering and baking for the next day during work hours, as opposed to after closing.

'So, you haven't spoken to John since?' Gemma asked.

It was Tuesday afternoon and it had been raining heavily since eleven o'clock. Customers had been arriving in fits and starts. Annie was smoothing shortbread dough into a round fluted tin, while Gemma cleared the decks after the last onslaught of bedraggled patrons.

'Not in person, no.'

Annie and John had been messaging back and forth, sometimes about the cafe, once about the patched hole in the ceiling that still needed painting, twice about which vegetables would win in a fight, almost as though they were friends.

'And he's coming to stay in Willow Bay?'

'That's what he said.'

'I wonder what that means,' said Gemma, sweeping cake crumbs with a dustpan and brush.

'He said he wanted to come down here to think and he's staying in Raye and Aiden's spare room for a bit. He's been crashing at Paul's place but I don't think he can stand sleeping on Paul's sofa for any length of time.'

'Sounds like he's planning on staying for a while. Do you think he's seriously considering your offer?'

Annie had told Gemma about her offer to buy Saltwater Nook. She needed to thrash it out with someone and she knew she could trust Gemma to keep quiet. She didn't want the whole village to know her plans, especially if they came to nothing.

'I guess so,' said Annie. 'I think I took him by surprise. He'd got his head into the redevelopment mindset.'

'I don't think he really wants Mari to sell. That's why he's been so grumpy about it. If he had the money, he'd probably keep it, maybe even live in it himself one day.'

'Why hasn't he got any money?' asked Annie. 'I thought architects were rolling in it.'

'Oh, I don't think so. I think that only applies to people who design new towns and things like that. Don't get me wrong, he's not poor by any stretch of the imagination. But he paid to put Celeste through university so she didn't come out with debts and, of course, before that – though I only know because he confided in Maeve – I believe he was very generous with Celeste's maintenance.'

'Really?' Annie was trying to sound nonchalant.

'Too generous, Maeve said. But you know what *she's* like, she'd think any more than three square meals a day and a new dress once a year is tantamount to spoiling. Celeste once told me that he paid for her and her mum to have a holiday abroad each year.'

'You've met Celeste?'

'Of course I have.'

'What's she like?'

'Oh, she's lovely; clever like her father, quite *edgy* in her dress sense. I've never met her mum, so I don't know what she's like, but Celeste has the same colouring as John. She's got a lot of piercings. Esme was rather taken with the idea.' Gemma's lips thinned into a straight line.

'I think you've got a few years yet before you need to worry about excessive piercings,' laughed Annie.

'Maeve offered to do Esme's ears with her sheep tagger.' Gemma rolled her eyes. 'Esme thinks it's a marvellous idea.'

The more Annie learned about John, the more intriguing she found him. There was a deep sense of honour buried within those rugged good looks. She was curious to meet Celeste – she sounded wonderful; sassy and passionate, like her father. Annie could imagine them locking horns, two strong-willed personalities. What must it be like to be beloved by John Granger? Annie couldn't deny that she'd like to find out.

Chapter 63

Gemma had left to pick up the kids and Annie turned the sign round to *closed* on the door. The rain clouds had finally wrung themselves dry and were scudding across the sky as if eager to reach their next destination before nightfall. She had just finished stacking the clean cups and saucers onto the top of the coffee machine when a knock on the window made her jump. It was John. Annie found herself looking forward to his visits with increasing eagerness and an equal level of disappointment on the days when he didn't come.

'Are you trying to give me a heart attack?' she called through the window.

John grinned and held up a clear plastic bag full of marshmallows.

'What are those for?' she shouted. 'Have you finally gone mad?'

'Come on!' he called through the glass and motioned to the beach.

'I can't, I've got to clean up here.'

'Leave it,' said John. 'I'll help you later. Come on, you've been working all day. Come eat burned sugary fluff with me.' He pointed along the beach where a thin curl of smoke was rising up from the pebbles.

She grabbed her coat and bobble hat, and ventured out into the cold dusk.

The beach was all but deserted. John grabbed two patio chairs from outside the cafe and they tramped down across the beach, their feet crunching and sinking into the loose pebbles as they headed towards a small campfire.

A sharp breeze whistled around her ears and Annie pulled her hat down lower. John positioned the chairs next to the fire and pushed the legs into the shingle to steady them. Annie sat down, sinking a little as she did so, and John joined her, handing her a long metal toasting fork.

'You've come prepared,' said Annie.

'I used to be a Boy Scout.'

'Really?'

'Not for long. They threw me out.'

'You got thrown out of the Scouts? What on earth did you do?'

'Consistent disruptive behaviour; their words, not mine.'

'What would you have called it?'

'Being a little shit.'

Annie laughed.

They spiked a marshmallow each and held them into the flames, twiddling the forks this way and that. Annie was grateful for the warmth given off by the small fire.

'Are you absolutely serious?' John asked. Annie didn't need to question his meaning.

'Yes, I am. I didn't come here with the intention of starting a business. This was supposed to be a temporary stop for me to catch my breath. That's one of the reasons why a short lease was so appealing.'

'And now?'

Annie breathed in the smoky air, so in contrast with the freshness of the cold late afternoon. The waves whispered to the shore as they began to reclaim the beach in a long slow embrace.

'Now I can't imagine being anywhere else,' Annie replied.

She pulled the fork out of the fire and tugged at the brown crisp edges of the marshmallow to reveal the molten sugar within. She licked her fingers greedily, wincing slightly at the intense sweetness that made her jaw ache.

John took a more cautious, measured approach, blowing on his marshmallow before taking a tentative bite. He reached his other hand into his pocket and handed over a folded piece of paper.

'That's the offer from the developer,' he said. 'I understand that it's for a different proposal than what you're suggesting. His takes into account the profit he can make on the land.'

'And my offer will be for a business with dwelling.'

'Exactly. And I will take that into account when you give me your offer. I'm not greedy, I just need enough.'

Annie looked down at the piece of paper in her hand. She didn't want to open it right now, she didn't want to potentially burst this fantasy bubble she was living in, whereby a bright new future was laid out before her. And she didn't want to sour this sweet moment they were sharing. *Reality can wait a little longer*, she thought, as she tucked the paper into her coat pocket.

'You've really thrown me a curve ball,' he said. 'I had steeled myself for selling this place and then you come along and turn everything upside down. I can't decide whether you're heaven-sent or a devil in disguise.'

'Huh.' Annie smiled to herself as she recalled that she had used almost the exact same words to describe John.

She pierced another marshmallow and thrust it into the fire.

'Not one for spontaneity, are you?'

'There's a fine line between impulsiveness and recklessness,' said John. 'In the past my spontaneity led to trouble, so I trained myself to be more measured; fewer people get hurt that way.'

Annie didn't delve. John had alluded to his troubled past earlier and he appeared to be very much carrying the weight of it on his shoulders still.

'It's going to take me a bit of time to get the money together anyway,' said Annie in a bid to show she wasn't trying to give him the hard sell. 'And I am yet to fully convince my husband that I'm absolutely not going back to him.'

'Are you sure there's no possibility?'

'I have never been surer of anything in my life.'

'That's quite sure then. I looked you up, you know.'

'Of course you did.'

'Your restaurant has an excellent reputation. Are you ready to give it all up? You could work something out with your husband whereby you buy him out instead. Make him leave.'

'I need a new challenge,' said Annie. 'That portion of my life is over. I'd been wanting a change for a long time but it was always easier to remain in the status quo.'

'The rock band?'

Annie grinned and shoved him. John's chair tipped but didn't topple.

'Sorry,' he said, smiling. 'Couldn't resist.'

'Try,' said Annie.

'So, you were sticking with the devil you know . . .' John said, leaving the sentence for her to finish.

'And then my husband unwittingly gave me the shock I needed to break free.'

'My aunt told me about the *Keep Calm and Carry On* cushion. That's rough. I'm sorry, really I am. No one deserves to stumble on that,' he said.

Annie laughed and realised that for the first time since it had happened, she actually did find it funny; mortifying but funny.

'I will never be able to look at that phrase again without cringing,' said Annie. 'And have you noticed how it's on bloody everything? Mugs, tea towels, notebooks . . . I am forever destined to be reminded that my husband's mistress had better tits than me.'

Now it was John's turn to laugh; a deep and rumbling laugh that somehow fitted with the wildness of their surroundings.

'Mari said she bet the government of 1939 could never have foreseen that their rousing slogan would be used in such a disrespectful manner,' said John.

They were both laughing now. It felt nice.

'No,' said Annie. 'I'm sure they didn't.'

'For what it's worth, I think he's a fool.'

Annie's heart skipped and it was a heroic effort not to gaze into John's eyes and lose herself.

'Well, you know all about the hideous demise of my marriage,' she said breezily. 'I think that entitles me to know something about you.'

'What do you want to know?'

'Have you and Celeste's mum been separated long?'

'Years,' said John. 'I used to drink. A lot. Especially after my mum died but quite a bit before that too. When I met Dee, Celeste's mum, I was partying pretty hard, which was fine at the time because she was partying hard too. But then Celeste came along, and I realised I had to sort myself out before I turned into my father.'

'So, you stopped drinking?'

'Yes. I underwent what counsellors would call *a lifestyle change*; Dee called it a personality bypass. She could go out and get wasted and then not drink for a fortnight, whereas I was all or nothing. I either drank or I didn't, there was no middle ground. That's not conducive to a stable environment for a baby.'

'Are you an alcoholic?' Annie asked.

'No. But I had potential.'

'So, no more parties,' said Annie.

'No more parties,' John agreed. 'Unfortunately, Dee had fallen for Party John; Sober John was a lot less fun. Like I said, I was all or nothing back then. I didn't want to drink, and I didn't like being around people who did. Dee and I split up when Celeste was about four years old. It was amicable. I had a lot of shit to reconcile and she knew that.'

'And you never drank again?' Annie was racking her brains trying to remember if she'd left any empty wine bottles in the kitchen. She didn't want to give him the impression she was a lush.

'I'm not a teetotaller,' said John. 'But I don't drink very much. I abstained completely for about ten years, until I felt I had the maturity to drink responsibly. I don't think my problem was ever really the drink, so much as my inability to do anything by halves. If I was going to party, I was going to be a legendary partier; if I was going to be sober, I had to be the soberest of the sober. It took me a long time to reconcile all the elements of myself and have them working together instead of against each other.'

'Wow,' said Annie, peeling a piece of hot marshmallow off her chin. 'You are really together. I mean, like, really together! I'm impressed. I'm a fucking disaster.'

John laughed heartily.

'Don't be fooled,' he said. 'That's years of therapy talking. Most of the time my striving to be the best version of myself results in me being a giant arse – you can bear testament to that!' he said, smiling at her. 'And anyway, I think you're being a bit hard on yourself. You walked away from your marriage with nothing and within a couple of months you've launched a new business. Despite the landlady's nephew sticking his beak in and being a pain in the proverbial.'

It was Annie's turn to laugh now.

'It's true I have become well acquainted with the *proverbial* side of your personality,' Annie teased.

'I don't dispute it,' John said, holding his hands up and accidentally sending a freshly toasted marshmallow flying off into the darkness. 'Bollocks,' he added and skewered another pillowy sweet onto his fork.

'I've spent years slogging my guts out,' said Annie. 'Always working harder, always pushing through to the next level, trying to achieve the next award or accolade. I mean, I *never* stopped. And I told myself it was because I had a lot to prove; you don't get up the duff at seventeen without encountering a lot of judgement.'

'So, you proved them all wrong,' said John.

'But if I'm honest, that's not what I was doing. I set myself on fast-forward, so that there was never time to contemplate the idea that my marriage had been a terrible mistake.'

'You were lying to yourself,' said John.

'I just plain ignored it. I felt like I'd made my bed and I had to bloody well lie in it. Unfortunately, Max didn't only lie in my bed.' She laughed humourlessly.

'That's rough,' said John.

'It is what it is,' said Annie with resignation in her voice. 'Wailing and moaning about it isn't going to change anything.'

'But you feel you can make a fresh start here,' said John.

'Precisely,' said Annie. 'Which is where you come in.'

'Make me an offer,' said John, 'and I promise to give it fair consideration.'

'That's all I'm asking,' said Annie.

She smiled at him then, in the glow of the dying fire, and he smiled back; a smile that seemed to warm her bones from the inside.

When the fire had burned down to embers and daylight had given itself completely over to darkness, they cleared away the remains and headed back up to the cafe.

Chapter 64

Annie put on some uplifting Django Reinhardt and turned the volume up, for an energy boost while she and John set to clearing down the cafe. Annie filled a couple of bread rolls with ham, cheese and red onion chutney and wrapped them up ready for Alfred's supper. John pushed the tables to the sides of the room and stacked the chairs on top of them and began to sweep the floor.

The sound of jaunty violins signalled the beginning of the track 'Minor Swing' and Annie called out, 'I love this one!' above the boom of the double bass and the tickle of acoustic guitar. She wiggled to the music as she wiped down the wooden countertop. She looked up to see John coming towards her, his eyes on hers, his broom left to rest against a table. He extended his hand over the counter and Annie took it, coming around to the other side to join him.

'What are you doing?' she laughed.

John didn't speak but led her to the middle of the floor and, still holding one of her hands, he slid his other arm around her waist and pulled her to him. They began to move around the room to the music. Annie laughed and allowed herself to be inexpertly twirled around the makeshift dance floor.

Neither of them were good dancers, but it didn't matter. They laughed and stumbled and stepped on each other's toes as they danced and whirled around the empty cafe. His arms felt solid around her and she knew instinctively that he wouldn't let her fall. He smiled wickedly as he twirled her out away from him and then pulled her back quickly so that their bodies rammed together. Annie shrieked out a giggle and when she looked up at John, he was smiling with such warmth that his whole face seemed lit up from within those deep blue eyes. Annie's breath caught in her throat, but she recovered herself.

When 'Minor Swing' gave way to a more chilled track they slowed to a sway. They were still in one another's arms, slightly breathless, still smiling. For a moment they remained like that, mid-embrace, looking into each other's eyes. Annie's heart, already beating fast from the dancing, began to race. She could feel the heat of his hand in the small of her back; she could smell the musky black pepper notes of his cologne mixed with fire smoke. His dark stubble travelled down his neck to meet the crisp line of his shirt collar, poking out above his jumper. She could see the pulse in his throat quickening, mirroring her own, and she wanted to kiss it. She cast her eyes back up to his to find him looking at her hungrily. For seconds the air between them was taut with painful, delicious anticipation and then he closed the gap; she stood on tiptoe to meet him, a deep longing pulling her towards him. Their lips met; his breath was hot in her mouth. Every part of Annie's body woke up, her synapses pinged, her skin tingled, as spears of desire shot through her stomach and melted in waves of heat.

Her phone began to ring, vibrating angrily on the counter-top.

'Do you want to answer that?' John rasped into her ear before laying hot kisses down her neck.

Annie threw her head back and he kissed her throat, while she clung feverishly to his shoulders.

'Ignore it!' she whispered hoarsely and then his mouth was on hers again. She didn't know how much more of this she could stand. She made a grab for his belt and began to tug at it. Her phone stopped ringing. John moved just enough for her to get to the buckle, while he lifted her dress and began to move his hands beneath it. Then his phone began to ring in his pocket, and they stopped dead. Both of them breathing hard. Both of them knowing there was only one person who would ring both their phones: Mari. Annie let her hands drop and John answered his phone.

'Aunty Mari,' he said, turning away from her, his voice still rough. 'Is everything all right?'

Annie pulled her dress back down and hoisted up her tights. Her heart was still racing; she felt like a teenager caught fumbling behind the sofa.

'Aye, she's fine,' John went on. 'No, we were just clearing down, she didnae have her phone tae hand. Aye, it's all good, I'm settled in at the pub.'

Annie noted how his accent became stronger when he spoke to his aunt.

'I know,' he said. 'You've nothing tae worry about. Annie's got everything under control. No, she hasn't fixed the fence yet.' He gave Annie a wink as he said this. 'Everyone's been askin' aboot you . . .'

Annie busied herself emptying the dishwasher and tried to ignore the throbbing need in her body. When he finally hung up, Annie had cleared down the rest of the kitchen area. John looked at her sheepishly.

'It was just my aunt,' he said unnecessarily, waving the phone as if to confirm it was via that medium that he had spoken to her, as opposed to setting smoke signals on the beach.

'I guessed as much,' said Annie.

She was suddenly shy. She didn't know what to do next. It was one thing getting caught up in the moment and letting passions take their own course, but it was quite another, once one's wits had returned and all the sensible reasons as to why it would be unwise to shag your landlady's nephew came flooding back to you, to continue on that course, no matter how tempting that course might be. John's expression revealed that he too was wrestling with a similar dilemma.

John cleared his throat loudly and rubbed his hands together. Annie swung her arms back and forth, to what end she didn't quite know; she realised she probably looked deranged and clasped one hand in the other in order to stop herself from moving. John threw his arms up in an exaggerated stretch and cleared his throat again.

'Lovely marshmallows,' Annie gushed, as though they'd just come back in from eating them and the whole foreplay on the dance floor thing hadn't happened at all.

'Thanks,' said John, fully embracing this line of conversation. 'I bought them in a shop . . .' He trailed off and then came back with, 'I really should make a move. I've got a breakfast meeting with a client . . .'

'Oh, absolutely. Thank you for helping me clear down. And for the marshmallows.'

'You're welcome.'

'Right then.'

'Right then.'

'Okay, well, I'll just go back and finish up.' She motioned to the sparkling clean counter area.

'I'll head off,' said John, pointing exaggeratedly at the door, as if there might have been some question about him letting himself out of the window instead.

'Bye then, have fun!' called Annie. *Have fun? What the fuck? Why did I tell him to have fun?* Annie's brain shouted at her.

John frowned and cocked his head to one side. There was a crooked smile forming on his lips.

'Erm, yes,' he said. He stood looking at her for another long moment, his eyebrows knitted together, and then he said, 'Bye then. Have fun.' And he left the building.

Annie felt hot. She knew she was blushing furiously. She imagined herself running hard at the wall and knocking herself out; she was sure being unconscious would make her feel better at this point. She turned the volume up on the music in the hopes that it might drown out her mortified thoughts. *Have fun indeed!* Those words were going to haunt her for a long time.

Later, tucked up in bed with a mug of cocoa – containing a generous slosh of brandy – and with hands shaking slightly in anticipation, Annie finally opened the little note containing big numbers from John. They were big numbers indeed. With this offer he could not only afford carers for Mari, he could probably buy the company. But Annie had never been one to baulk at the throwing down of a gauntlet, and she reasoned that John was a fair man, with an emotional attachment to Saltwater Nook. She could work with this; she just had to get Max to agree to her terms before it was too late.

Chapter 65

A ting emitted from Annie's and Gemma's phones as a message came through on the book club chat.

Sally: Sorry, ladies, I'm going to have to bail on tonight. Susan's got the worst cold. I'm playing nursemaid.

Gemma: Oh dear, poor Susan. Why don't we postpone till next Wednesday?

Sally: I don't want you to miss your club just because of me.

Maeve: Poppycock! We're not doing it without you. All for one and one for all and all that!

Annie: Same. Pass my love on to Susan. Hope you don't catch it!

Gemma slipped her phone back under the counter. She liked to keep it handy in case there was any kind of emergency at school with the children.

'Oh well, that's a shame,' said Gemma.

'Yes. Although to be honest, I hadn't quite finished it yet anyway. I was going to have to google the end of the plot.'

'Cheat,' said Gemma. 'You'll just have to *finally* give me the details of your tryst with John instead. I have very little excitement in my life and with no book club to look forward to I need some drama to keep me going.'

'I keep telling you, it wasn't a tryst! Who even uses that word anyway?'

'I do! My husband is away a lot, I read a lot of romantic fiction. Trysts are a prominent feature.'

'We were probably just on a sugar high from all the marshmallows.'

'But you did dirty dancing.'

'It was hardly dirty dancing.' Annie's stomach thrilled at the remembrance of John kissing her throat. 'Well, all right, maybe it was a little bit dirty dancing.' She had suddenly come over rather warm.

Gemma punched the air.

'I knew it!'

'It can't come to anything,' said Annie. 'It's just not practical, for either of us.'

Gemma pouted but didn't push it.

John had had some design consultations in London and had spent the last week at his place in Clapham. It seemed John was as incapable of taking a step back workwise as she was. Their messaging had taken on a much flirtier tone in his absence. But Annie hadn't just spent her time thinking up peppy repartee – not all of it at any rate. She had been doing her financial homework and number crunching, in readiness for John's return.

Annie had anticipated that the developer's offer for the land would far exceed what she could reasonably offer, but she wasn't disheartened. She had something that the developer couldn't offer: she had the expertise and drive to save Saltwater Nook and all the happy memories it contained for John and his aunt.

After a consultation with her solicitor – which resulted in a reasonably threatening letter being sent to Max with regards to his withholding her money – Annie arranged a meeting with her financial adviser and they worked out roughly what settlement she could expect, according to The Pomegranate Seed's last year figures and her halves of the properties she owned with Max. Annie had always kept her eye on the fluctuating market of the hospitality industry, and she knew how much a small business like Saltwater Nook was worth. A local estate agent had given her a valuation for the building as a whole and Annie had put together an offer accordingly. She'd written it down on a piece of paper and it had been burning a hole in her pocket ever since.

Chapter 66

The swimmers had just left, having taken their dip early on account of the forecast looking choppy for later. All-weather flip-flops had cleaned out Annie's supply of tiffin bars for when her grandchildren visited later. There were no other customers at present and by the looks of the empty promenade in both directions, there wouldn't be any more for at least twenty minutes. Annie picked up a basket and rested the handle over her forearm.

'Right, I'm going to collect some stones. You're in charge.'

Gemma gulped dramatically and Annie laughed.

'Call me if you need help.'

'No problem,' said Gemma brightly. 'I want to crack on with getting the sauces and honeys on the back shelf.'

Annie smiled. Gemma was an absolute godsend, well worth maxing out her credit card to pay her wages; she had already transformed the shelving into delightfully chaotic deli displays that drew the eye and encouraged lots of browsing and, ultimately, buying. Annie was going to have to up her orders from her local providers and was already searching for new lines to add to her artisan foods collection. She wondered idly how many credit cards one person was allowed before some higher authority stepped in.

The swimmers were right to have come early: the sky was baby blue with powder-puff clouds but glowering around the cliff edges the clouds were like wire-wool, casting dark shadows over the sea. Annie drank in the cold air and revelled in the chill after the heat of the cafe. She wandered along the beach, scooping to pick up pebbles to her specifications: smooth, oval or roundish, about the size to comfortably fit her palm.

A voice shouted, 'Don't you know it's illegal to steal pebbles from the beach?'

Annie jumped, dropping the pebble she'd been studying. It was John, just rounding the cove. Annie's heart leaped in her chest at the sight of him.

'You're back!' She tried and failed to wipe the delighted smile off her face.

'I am indeed,' John grinned back at her, as he tramped up the beach towards her.

'Where did you spring from?' she called back.

'Just popped in to see Alfred.' John nodded back towards the cave. He was wearing green wellingtons over his jeans and a cream Aran-knit jumper. As he got closer, Annie could see the beginnings of a beard.

'What *are* you doing?' John asked when he reached her.

'What are *you* doing?' she countered.

'I told you, I've been to see Alfred.'

'I didn't know Alfred took house calls.'

'Have you ever tried?'

'Once,' said Annie. 'He chased me out.'

John laughed heartily at that.

'Sounds about right,' he said. 'Now you. What's all this?' he pointed to her basket.

'Positivity pebbles,' said Annie.

'What?'

'Positivity pebbles. I'll leave these in the basket on the bench by the window, with some non-toxic paint pens, and people can write nice messages on them and bury them on the beach for someone to find.'

'Messages like what?'

'Like . . .' Annie looked to the sky for inspiration. 'Like, *have a great day*, or *you are special*, or *sent with love*, or' – she thought back to that day in Tunbridge Wells and the pebble she had found just before she saw the ad in the paper – 'or *everything is going to be all right* . . . the kind of thing that will put a smile on someone's face when they find it.'

'Why?'

'Why not? Think of it as random words of kindness.'

John frowned at her in a curious way, as though she were a mathematical equation to be solved.

'I like it,' he said. 'What a great idea.'

'Not mine, I'm afraid. But I found one, not so long ago when I really needed a friend, and it was just what I needed at that moment.'

'You had a pebble for a friend?'

'Beggars can't be choosers.'

She looked up at John and he suddenly swooped down and kissed her lightly. It was the briefest brush against her lips, but it still made her breath catch. He took a step back, embarrassed.

'Sorry about that,' he said. 'I just suddenly. It was just . . . you looked so wistful. I suppose I just wanted to let you know that you have a friend, if you ever need one. And I think you're lovely. Despite often behaving to the contrary. And I think that maybe someone made you feel like you weren't lovely and he shouldn't have. But anyway. There we are. And I know it's way too complicated for anything to happen between us at the moment, but still, you're lovely.'

Annie could hardly breathe.

'I . . .'

'Annie! Customers!' Gemma was out on the patio, with her hands making a trumpet over her mouth.

'I've got to get back,' said Annie.

'Here,' John said, taking the basket off her arm. 'You go. I'll hunt out positivity pebbles.'

'Thanks,' Annie called back as she ran, slipping on the stones towards the cafe. And then, quite without realising what she was doing, she found herself running back towards John. Running on shifting pebbles isn't easy, it's like running through porridge, and there is no way to be graceful about it. She reached him, breathless and in danger of turning an ankle, and went up on tiptoe to kiss him on the lips.

'I think you're lovely too,' she gasped. She hoped she didn't faint from the exercise. 'Even though you might sell my home and business from underneath me. But there we are. I think you're lovely all the same.'

And with that, she turned and ran, much resembling someone trying to run in a spacesuit on the moon, all the way back to the cafe.

Half an hour later, John strode in with a basket full of pebbles.

'John!' Gemma trilled. 'Lovely to see you. Annie told me you're staying with Raye and Aiden for a while. It'll be nice to have you around the place a bit more, won't it, Annie?' She nudged Annie conspiratorially as she passed her.

'Oh, great haul,' Annie said, looking at the basket. 'Pop them over in the corner there, would you?'

John did as he was told. Annie looked at John and he smiled at her and winked. Her heart stuttered. She felt as though they had found a secret key to something that only they knew about. John was right, of course: though she didn't much like it, their situation made it difficult for them to pursue their feelings right now. But having John acknowledge that her growing affection for him was reciprocated made it easier to bear.

'Would you like a coffee?' Annie called.

'Americano, please,' said John. 'Double shot, hot milk on the side.'

'How's Celeste?' Gemma asked.

'She's great,' said John. 'Up to her eyes in mud and newts most of the time, but that's how she likes it.'

'She's helping to preserve the planet,' said Gemma with her sweet smile. 'Thank goodness for people like Celeste. So, how come you're staying up at the pub?'

'Because I didn't think Annie would appreciate me sleeping in her lounge on the air bed.'

Gemma laughed.

'Oh, of course, I forgot, you always stay here, don't you? Poor John, you've been evicted.'

'Poor John nothing!' Annie called over. She slipped the piece of paper containing her offer for Saltwater Nook under the cup and slid the cup and saucer along the counter for Gemma to pass to him. 'He'd evict me given half the chance.'

'There's still time,' said John.

'On what grounds?' Annie asked, mock affronted.

'Property destruction,' said John.

'Fair point,' said Annie. 'When *are* you going to paint my ceiling anyway?'

John smiled.

'I can come down early next week if you'd like, I'm pretty booked up with work for the next few days.'

'Well, it'll just have to do, won't it,' said Annie. 'Don't you just hate dodgy landlords?' she said to Gemma, who rolled her eyes. Annie's heart was in her mouth as she saw John clock the piece of paper. She watched his expression change. He didn't open it but tucked it into the pocket of his jeans and settled down to read the paper. The tension was infuriating, exciting and terrifying. Annie hadn't felt this nervous since picking up her A-level results. *You'll just have to wait*, she told her wildly beating heart as she busied herself and tried to act like her hopes for the future weren't nestling in a sexy architect's jeans.

Chapter 67

It was Monday, and early enough that the promenade was still sparkling with frost when Annie took her walk. The air smelled crisp and the sea looked sluggish with cold. She felt buoyant as she walked. Today she and Gemma were going to decorate the cafe ready for Christmas and Annie couldn't wait to get started. Max was waiting for her when she got back. The bounce in her step suffered a puncture.

'You didn't answer my calls,' Annie said, walking straight past him to the front of the cafe.

'My phone wasn't working.'

'Bullshit.'

'I've unlocked the accounts.'

Annie felt a sudden rush of relief. The hundred and fifty pounds it had cost her to have her solicitor send Max a letter was worth every penny.

'About bloody time,' she said. He would be expecting a thank you, but she wasn't going to give him one.

Her relief was leapfrogged by worry that Max might have emptied the accounts.

'I take it you haven't removed all the funds?' she asked.

'Of course I haven't! What do you take me for?'

'Do you actually want an answer to that question?'

Max was following her like an obedient Labrador, stopping beside her as she opened each of the shutters on the windows.

'We need to talk about Christmas.'

'What?'

The door to the cafe was sticky and she had to wiggle the key and shove hard on the door at the same time to get it open.

'I want us to have one last family Christmas together,' said Max. 'You, me and the boys.'

'Max, I can't even think about what I'll be doing for Christmas right now.'

The door gave and Annie stumbled inside, Max on her heels.

'Well, you should, it'll be here before you know it. Oh, this is nice!' he said, distracted by the cafe. 'I've not been inside before. It's a bit kitsch for my tastes but—'

'I really don't care for your tastes anymore, Max,' said Annie absently, as she began pulling the chairs down from the tables.

'Give me one last Christmas, Annie. Please! You've lost your faith in me and I completely understand why. But I haven't given up on you. There's not another woman like you.'

'What about Ellie?'

'I told you, that's over. She's history; you're my future.'

'For fuck's sake, Max, where do you get these lines? Have you got shares in a fortune cookie factory?'

'I can't stop thinking about that Sunday, you and me . . .'

'Try.'

'We were so hot. It was like we were kids again; remember when we couldn't keep our hands off each other?'

'Unfortunately, it wasn't just me you couldn't keep your hands off. And if you recall, Max, that Sunday ended with me asking for a divorce and half of all our assets.'

'I haven't forgotten.'

'Well?'

'Just say you'll think about Christmas,' said Max.

This was how he got to her: it wasn't his smooth moves or his charm, it was his ability to wear her down. Invariably she would say anything just to get him off her back.

'I'll think about Christmas if you agree to get a solicitor.'

Max smiled and tucked a piece of hair behind her ear. Annie repressed a shudder.

'Have a good day,' he said.

He headed out for his car, leaving Annie feeling like she needed another shower. Still, at least she could get to her money now. Getting him to agree to her financial terms with regards to selling was going to be a whole other battle. And she was still waiting for John's verdict on her offer.

Gemma's car passed Max's as she pulled into the space he had just left.

'Was that Max?' she asked, climbing out.

'Yes, it was.'

'He's not like I expected.'

'What did you expect?'

'Oh, you know, cloven hoofs and horns,' said Gemma.

Annie laughed. 'The devil has many disguises! He wants us to spend Christmas together.'

Gemma pulled a face.

'How do you feel about that?'

'Bah humbug!' said Annie.

Chapter 68

The positivity pebbles were an instant success. Their appeal spanned all ages, from small children to octogenarians. John arrived at the cafe to find three rows of painted pebbles drying in neat lines along the shelves. Two boys and a girl in blue blazers and ties had just that moment settled down with more of the stones and paint, and two hot chocolates with cream and marshmallows between them.

Annie's heart leaped when she caught sight of John and she had to restrain the urge to jump up and down and clap her hands together with glee. There was something about the way in which John filled a room which made her feel far less than her forty-four years; it was like he gave off a kind of electricity and she wanted to plug herself into it. Today's excitement was doubly palpitation-inducing because they hadn't yet discussed her offer.

Annie mentally tamped down the sixteen-year-old girl who had taken up residence in her brain and tried to smile enigmatically. John was wearing paint-splattered overalls and he plonked an equally painty duffel bag and a large tin of white paint on the floor on the staff side of the counter.

'You're only painting an A4-sized square,' said Annie. 'Aren't you a bit overdressed?' Annie was trying her best not to admit to herself that she was finding the whole dirty overalls thing rather scintillating.

'I figured I might as well do the whole thing or there'll be one super white patch showing up the rest of the ceiling.'

'God forbid,' said Annie.

'Any chance of a coffee to take up?'

'Double-shot Americano and hot milk on the side?' said Annie.

'You remembered,' John said. Annie smiled. John leaned against the counter and surveyed the cafe while he waited.

A fresh Christmas tree – courtesy of the Willow Bay Stores – dripping with baubles and lights had taken up residency in the far corner of the room. It was far too big for the space. Gemma and Annie had rearranged the furniture as best they could, but still, the customers who sat at the far end of the picture window would have their shoulders consistently brushed by overfamiliar fir tree branches. But it looked magnificent and smelled even better.

Wooden painted stars and silver snowflakes on candy-cane ribbons hung at different lengths at the windows, and on the middle of the window ledge a red candle arch held seven glittering LED candles. A thick garland of dark green foliage and red holly berries fell in loose swags to the front of the counter, while above, the cables of the fishing lantern light fitting had been adorned and wrapped around with a string of gold sprayed pinecones. The little cafe oozed a cluttered homespun charm, which was making customers eager to arrive and reluctant to leave.

'They're clearly skiving,' hissed John, nodding his head back towards the three uniformed teens.

'They're from Meadow Grange,' said Gemma under her breath. 'The big secondary over near Margate.'

'Margate!' said Annie. 'These are some committed skivers. It must have been at least two bus journeys and a bloody long walk to get here.'

'You sound impressed,' said John.

'I am a bit. My bunking off never got more adventurous than the local park.'

'And it's much harder to bunk off these days, what with all the security and CCTV everywhere,' added Gemma.

'Still,' said John, 'we ought not condone it.'

Annie and Gemma made agreeing noises but their hearts weren't in it.

'Why only two drinks?' John asked.

'I don't think the boy with the patched elbow had enough money,' said Gemma. 'I felt a bit bad for him, if I'm honest. He looks familiar but I can't place him.'

They all looked over. The two mugs were placed strategically in the middle but the lad with the patch didn't appear to be drinking out of either of them.

Outside it had begun to rain again, fat rain, more like globules than drops. It felt as though every day this week had been colder than the last.

'Okay if I go up and make a start?' asked John, holding up his can of paint.

'Sure,' said Annie. 'You've got a key.'

John disappeared through the inner cafe door. A gaggle of drenched walkers scurried in out of the rain and Annie and Gemma set about preparing their orders. The twinkling lights and the smooth sounds of Dean Martin and Bing Crosby crooning out Christmas tunes from the speakers was just the thing to soothe away the shivers. Annie helped Gemma transport the drinks over to the walkers' table, who made appreciative noises and cupped their hands around the steaming mugs to thaw their cold red fingers.

As Annie made her way back to the counter, the uniformed girl asked, 'Do you live here?' She had thick black painted eyebrows that looked too heavy for her delicate features.

'Yes,' said Annie.

'Bit out of the way, isn't it?' asked one of the boys. He had acne, and a cheeky smile that Annie was sure made him a hit with the girls at school.

'It is a bit,' Annie replied. 'But I like it that way.'

The boy with the patched elbow looked out of the window. The rain was thick and the condensation formed a mist over the glass, so that the sea looked like an Impressionist painting.

'I'd like it,' he said. 'You must be quite new.'

'What makes you say that?'

'I used to come down here all the time with my grandad, fishing. This place was never open.'

'Ah, I see. Yes, I am quite new. Do you know Ely?'

'Yeah, he was my grandad's mate.'

Annie noted the 'was'.

'Did your grandad live in Willow Bay?' she asked.

'Nah,' said the boy. 'He lived with us, just up the way a bit, near Sandwich. But this was his favourite place to fish.'

'How are your positivity pebbles coming along?' she asked.

The girl had painted a large love heart rainbow with the words *Peace and Love* in the middle. The boy with acne had settled on a rainbow peace symbol.

'Oh, lovely,' said Annie. 'Loving the Pride rainbows.' The girl grinned up at her.

Annie leaned over the third truant; she noticed the collar of his white shirt was grey. He had painted his pebble green and written in careful calligraphy *You Are Good Enough*.

'Well,' said Annie, 'I think this one deserves a hot chocolate on the house.'

The boy looked up at her and smiled shyly.

'Thanks,' he said awkwardly.

'You're welcome. If I found that pebble on the beach, it would make my day.'

The boy smiled again, his cheeks flushing.

Annie pulled the marshmallow jar off the shelf and began to heat the milk. Gemma stopped folding napkins briefly to give Annie a kiss on the cheek and then resumed her task.

'What was that for?' Annie asked.

'No reason,' Gemma replied.

Annie delivered the hot chocolate and stopped on her way back to the counter in front of the large picture windows. It was grey outside, as far as the eye could see. There were times, like now, when the rain and mist colluded to shroud the cliffs, and even the promenade, from view, so that it seemed as though Saltwater Nook was alone at the very edge of the world. Annie stared out into the moody nothingness and felt very small and very blessed to be a part of it.

Chapter 69

It was a quiet afternoon: one or two takeaways and an elderly couple who spent an hour or so reading newspapers and filling in the crosswords. The truants kept their presence low-key. Gemma was handy in the kitchen and between them they got all the baking done ready for tomorrow. The cafe was filled with the scent of hot gingerbread and spiced biscuits, and Annie revelled in the feeling of being super organised.

The truants brought their empty cups to the counter, their dried painted pebbles held carefully in open palms.

'Would you like me to hold on to those for you and I'll bury them under the stones for you tomorrow, give the paint a chance to sink in a bit more?'

The teens agreed. They thanked Annie and Gemma for having them, which made Annie feel both warm and fuzzy, and as though she was complicit in their truancy. Annie felt sorry for them with only their blazers to protect them against the elements. They had reached the door when the boy with the patch came back to the counter.

'Can I bring my CV down? For if you ever need someone to work here at weekends and holidays and stuff? I'm a fast learner.'

'How old are you?'

'Sixteen. I'll be seventeen in March.'

Annie bit her lip. She could really do with some help on Saturdays when Gemma was home with the kids and over the Christmas holidays. But was it fair to take someone on for such a short time? Gemma had taken the job on the understanding that it could all be over by Easter.

'What's your name?'

'Billy. Billy Maitlin.'

'I'm Annie. Here's the thing, Billy, this might be a really short lease. I may only have the cafe until Easter.' Billy's face fell. 'But, between now and Easter I am going to need someone to work Saturdays and over Christmas and the February half-term.' Billy's face brightened. 'If I ask Ely about you, will he tell me you'd make a good employee?'

Billy nodded.

'I'm sure of it,' he said. 'I've been out with him loads. I always helped my grandad. Ely knows I'm a good worker.'

'In that case, be here on Saturday morning. Jeans and smart T-shirt will be fine. I'll give you a trial in the cafe and we'll see how it works out. How does that sound?'

'What time?' asked Billy.

'Can you get here for half past eight?'

'Yes.'

'Great! I'll see you, Billy, at half past eight on Saturday morning. Don't be late.'

'I won't be.' Billy's grin seemed to stretch the full width of his face. 'Thank you! I won't let you down!'

He practically skipped over to his classmates.

'Oh, and listen, you three,' Annie called. The teens

turned slowly to face Annie. 'You are always welcome here outside of school hours and your positivity pebbles are beautifully painted. But please don't use my cafe as your bunk-off hideaway.' Annie smiled to let them know that her admonishment was meant in the warmest way but equally, she didn't fancy having the truancy officer staking out Saltwater Nook. They shrugged their shoulders, cheeks colouring up, and smiled sheepishly, mumbling that they wouldn't do it again.

'Nicely done,' said Gemma, nodding approvingly.

'I've had my fair share of dealing with teenagers,' said Annie.

'Good. I'll drop Lennox and his belongings off with you when he turns thirteen.'

'Ha! No thanks. I'd rather eat worms.'

'That bad, huh?'

Gemma looked at her watch. 'Oh shit!' she said.

'Go,' said Annie.

'But we haven't done the clear-down.' Gemma was turning on the spot in a kind of panicked daze but not actually doing anything.

'Just go,' said Annie, laughing as she took her friend by the arms to stop her from spinning. 'Go on, off with you! I can clear down. I don't want Lennox and Esme blaming me for keeping them waiting at the school gates like a couple of waifs.'

'Thank you, Annie. Sorry, sorry, sorry,' Gemma sang as she grabbed up her belongings and headed for the door. 'Take it out of my wages.'

'What wages? You mean, you're not working for free?'

Gemma laughed and pulled open the door, just as it began to start pouring with rain again.

'Love you, bye!' she trilled and was gone, leaving a wet patch where the rain had blown in.

Annie went to make herself a coffee before she began the clear-down. She had just slid the shortbread out of the oven when a message pinged through from Peter which sucked the wind right out of her sails.

Dad tells me you two might be getting back together? I don't mean to be disrespectful, Mum, but WTAF???

Annie felt dizzy. She rocked on the spot. What the actual fuck indeed! This was just like Max. If things didn't go his way, he would simply reorder the facts as he wanted them to be. She texted Peter back with shaking fingers.

I'm sorry, darling. I don't know what Dad was thinking but I can categorically assure you that a reconciliation is not on the cards! x

Peter texted back almost immediately.

Thank God! I thought for a minute I was going to have to come down there and perform an intervention. What gave him the idea?

I can't imagine. Do you know if he said anything to Alex?

Yes, he did. I'm acting as spokesperson as Alex has meetings all afternoon.

You're not upset, are you?

No, Mum. Don't worry. We'd be more upset if you went back to something that doesn't work for you. Love you. x

Love you too. Sorry for the shock. Come visit me soon. xx

Annie stood stock still, the phone still in her hand, her heart pounding with rage. She texted Max with shaking fingers.

How dare you tell the boys that we are getting back together!

A message came back immediately.

I think there is still something worth saving and I know you do too. And I didn't say we were getting back together for sure, I said we might be.

Annie was so angry she felt as though her head might explode. She called Max's number. Of course, he didn't pick up. When it clicked to his smooth answerphone message Annie shouted, 'We are not getting back together, give me my half of the assets and give me a fucking divorce!' into the phone and hung up.

She slammed her phone down on the counter.

'Wanker!' she yelled in frustration.

The door from the hallway opened.

'You called?' said John innocently.

His comedic timing instantly drew the sting out of her anger. She laughed, finding she couldn't stop.

'Sorry,' she said, still chuckling. 'That wasn't aimed at you.'

'Makes a change,' he said, one eyebrow raised.

'I've never called you a wanker.'

'Not out loud, no.'

Annie laughed and conceded the point.

'My husband told my children we are getting back together.'

'Are you?'

'Absolutely one hundred – no, one million per cent never ever. No.'

'That's quite final. Have you straightened it out with your sons?'

'Yes. They're fine. They love their dad, he's a good father, but they're old enough to understand that he wasn't such a good husband.'

'Even adults can struggle to come to terms with their parents' imperfections.'

'Are you speaking from experience?'

'Yes.'

'Alex and Peter are very well-adjusted adults. And I think being twins, they have the added advantage of being one another's moral compass.'

John nodded.

'You know, my aunt thinks you're a bloody miracle.'

'I am!'

'She's pinning all her hopes on you buying this place.'

'So am I,' said Annie.

John rubbed the back of his neck with his hand. Annie noticed his face and hair were speckled with white paint. He looked done-in; his aura was that of a person weighed down by the weight of responsibility.

'The builder is pressing me for an answer. He's had the surveyor's reports back and he's keen to go ahead.'

'But there's nothing official. You haven't signed anything.'

'No, it's a gentleman's agreement. I won't be terribly popular if I pull out.'

'Will it affect your business if you don't sell to him? I mean, could he be vindictive?'

John thought for a moment.

'I don't think so, he doesn't strike me as the type. Maybe I could offer to pay his surveyor's fees, so he's not out of pocket, you know, as a gesture of goodwill.'

'You're talking like you've made your decision already.'

'Let's just say, I'm leaning more one way than the other.'

Annie felt a thrill of excitement in her stomach.

'But of course,' he went on, 'a lot depends on whether or not your husband agrees to buy you out. And how long he's likely to drag it out for. Mari's needs won't wait.'

'I understand,' said Annie. 'I do, really.' She looked up at him and his eyes met hers. He smiled.

'I know you do.'

Chapter 70

Annie invited John to stay for some supper but he had promised to eat with Raye and Aiden; he was drawing up some plans for a loft extension that was to make The Captain's Bounty – planning permission allowing – an inn with a small number of boutique rooms. When John left, Annie went upstairs to inspect the paintwork. He'd done a nice job and the flat had the painty smell of newness. Her mind was whirring with ideas for the cafe and her fingers twitched to get writing plans and making lists in her notebook: a pudding club night, a seafarers' menu, a candlelit bistro evening . . . Oh, if she could just get Max to hurry up and buy her out already!

Mrs Tiggy-Winkle joined her back downstairs in the cafe and mooched about the place, trying out different chairs for size while Annie finished her work for the day.

'Fancy a walk, Tiggs?' Annie asked when she had finished mopping the floor. She needed to walk off some of her excess excitement energy.

Mrs Tiggy-Winkle looked at her with disdain, but Annie had a surprise for the haughty ginger moggy. Alex had posted down a cat lead which Annie hadn't got around to trying out yet. She wrestled her nonplussed pet into the harness, threw on her warmest jacket and scarf and set off into the gloom.

Dusk was laying its gossamer blanket over land and sea, making the cliffs at the farthest end of the promenade from her seem fuzzy and indistinct. Despite the salt-bite of the wind and the cold damp eking into her tights, or maybe because of it, Annie felt invigorated. There was nothing as nice as a walk in the cold when you knew you had a warm home waiting for you at the end of it. This led her to thinking about Alfred. She wondered how much longer before he gave up the coast for a winter in the city. John was right, of course: sleeping rough was no way for anyone to live, let alone an older person. She wondered how she could make Alfred's cafe sleeps more comfortable. Perhaps she could invest in a camp bed that she could keep in the cellar during the day. Annie was so lost in her thoughts that she didn't see Ely loom out of the shadows.

'It's that kind of behaviour that labels you as a towny,' said Ely. He was standing in front of her, looking down with distaste at Tiggs's harness and lead. Mrs Tiggy-Winkle looked up at him and meowed weakly as if she couldn't agree more.

'She hasn't been out since she arrived at the Nook,' said Annie. 'I thought it would be good for her to get to know her surroundings before I let her out by herself.'

'Got its own mobile phone as well no doubt,' said Ely, still eyeing Tiggs.

Annie laughed.

'I'm not quite that bad. But she is chipped.'

Ely looked at Annie as though she was completely off her rocker and shook his head.

'I was just coming to see you. Had a call from Billy's mum, said you'd offered him a job and needed me to be a reference as to his character.'

'Oh, yes, Billy. He's having a trial with me on Saturday.'

'You could do worse than Billy. He's a good boy. Had a tough start. He can be a handful but only when he's not occupied.'

'So, do you think he'd be good at the cafe?'

'He'll work hard and he'll give respect if it's given to him.'

Annie hoped that wouldn't be a problem; customers were not always famed for their respect for staff. Something about entering a catering establishment caused the nicest of people to behave like complete arseholes.

'Well,' said Annie. 'He can have a trial on Saturday, and we'll see how he gets on.'

'Right. I'll be off then, night fishing tonight.'

'In this?'

'It's as good a night as any,' Ely replied. 'You started thinking about the Christmas Festival yet?'

'The Christmas Festival?'

'Don't tell me no one's told you yet!'

'Let's just suppose they haven't,' said Annie.

'It's only the biggest event of the year, aside from the winter solstice and Christmas, and then, of course, there's the Wassailing but that's not till Twelfth Night, so you don't need to worry about that yet.'

For the love of God! Annie thought. *How many parties can one village have?*

'A bit of carol singing or something, is it?' Annie asked.

Ely laughed until he broke into phlegmy coughs. Annie waited for him to recover.

'*A bit of carol singing*,' he stammered, wiping his eyes. 'Well, I suppose there's a bit of that to it. You won't want to miss it. In fact, now that the Nook's open for business again, you'll be hosting it!'

And with that he offered his goodbyes and set off down the beach. The sound of his wellingtons trampling the stones could be heard long after his body was swallowed by the sea mist.

'Well, bugger me!' said Annie. 'I'd better spend some time with Mari's almanac.'

Mrs Tiggy-Winkle shook herself, her fur clumping in the damp air, and let out a whine that could have woken the spirits of the long-departed Willow Bay sailors.

'Come on then, fusspot,' said Annie fondly. 'Home.'

Chapter 71

Winters can feel quite isolating for a small village, after the holidaymakers have left and the weather has set in, so we never give it the chance. You can be frightened by the wild dark of winter or meet it head on and welcome it in, and we Willow Bayers never shy away from a challenge!

The Christmas Festival is always held around the first week of December and is when our Christmas festivities really start. We set fires all along the beach to light the darkness (and, of course, to let Father Christmas know where we are) and we toast in the season with mulled cider and wine. The Ghosts of Christmas Past, Present and Future usually make an appearance; Pam keeps them in the cellars beneath the pub. Did you know Charles Dickens lived nearby? There is carolling and dancing, and last year Raye and Aiden organised a folk band to play in the moonlight, which was wonderful.

Whoever you are, I implore you to throw yourself into the festivities. It's a celebration of the long nights and the deep cold which allows the land to rest ready for spring. I suppose it's a concoction of Christian and Pagan traditions, but we have always embraced the knowledge that as a village we are a melting pot and proud, and our traditions reflect our unique identity.

Annie laid Mari's book beside her and pulled the duvet up closer. She texted John.

You didn't tell me about the Christmas Festival.

You didn't ask.

That's because I didn't know about it!

Well, how was I to know you didn't know?

Fair point. When is it?

December 8 this year. Will you do it?

Will I have a choice?

Sure, there's no pressure at all, just so long as you're aware that if you don't do it, you'll be trashing a two-hundred-year-old tradition and everyone will judge you. 😊

Ah, is that all?

You wanted to open a cafe . . .

I've got one more question.

Fire away.

You're trapped on a desert island, which one book would you want with you?

Raft Building for Beginners.

Hahahahahahaha. Nite nite xx

Sleep tight xx

On Friday afternoon another text came through from John.

Fancy joining me for dinner at The Captain's Bounty tonight? My treat. It's Mexican night. 😊

'Is it a date?' Gemma was practically hopping on the spot, grinning wildly. The Boden-walking-mummies on the middle table pricked up their collective ears.

'I don't think so. I think we both know it would just complicate things.'

'What are you going to wear?'

Annie bit her lip.

'Not sure yet,' she replied in as nonchalant a manner as she could muster. Should she dress up or be casual? Maybe she'd try a casual dress-up.

'Exciting, though,' Gemma squeaked.

'I'm looking forward to dinner. Aiden's a good cook and I haven't had Mexican food for ages.'

'Not the food! The company . . . the date.'

'It's not a date.'

Gemma looked around at the walking-mummies and mouthed, *It is a date!* and received several conspiratorial winks in return. Annie sighed loudly and started grinding coffee for the next order but she couldn't suppress her smile.

Chapter 72

Later that evening, whilst being eyed suspiciously by Mrs Tiggy-Winkle, Annie got ready for her not-a-date date with John. She had settled on a tie-waisted shirt dress in baby wale cord; navy blue with a ditsy print of little red flowers with yellow middles over it. She teamed it with dark red knitted tights and brown knee-high boots. She noticed, as she applied make-up in the bathroom mirror, that her roots needed doing; little twists of grey stood out in relief against her conker-brown hair. She brushed her hair and it shone in the light, greys and all, and bounced and kinked at the sides. With a steady hand Annie painted a swish of liquid eyeliner and managed to achieve a near perfect flick thanks to a helpful tutorial on YouTube. Her hand hovered, holding the lipstick, while she debated whether or not to go the whole hog, and then, spurred on by Tiggs's disapproving glare, she applied a coat of bright red lip stain called Cherry Passion and smacked her lips together, pouting in the mirror. Mrs Tiggy-Winkle left the bathroom in disgust with her nose and tail in the air.

It wasn't overly busy in the bar area of The Captain's Bounty but the restaurant end was full. Annie was acutely aware that this was her second time having dinner with a man in this pub. She wouldn't like people to think she was sampling the local men as well as the produce. She reminded herself that this wasn't a date. They were just two friends – were they friends now? – having dinner together. If you took into consideration that Annie was a potential buyer for his aunt's property, you could even describe it as a business meal; she wondered briefly if she could offset it against her tax bill as expenses. John had said it was his treat but Annie didn't like to take these things for granted.

The air was heavily scented with garlic, sizzling meats, fresh coriander and the ever-present undercurrent of woodsmoke. Annie's stomach growled. She found John at a table for two near a deep-set leaded window. John smiled when he saw her and stood as she drew near. There was an awkward moment when both of them hovered, clearly wondering if they were in kissing cheek on arrival territory or not. They decided yes, each of them seeming to linger a little longer than was necessary. Annie breathed in John's cologne before they parted – somewhat reluctantly – and sat down, Annie taking the chair opposite him. John closed his book – a ragged, yellowing copy of *A Scandal in Bohemia* – and set it to one side. Annie nodded towards it.

'You're a Sherlock Holmes fan?'

'Not particularly. Just this one really. It's my go-to comfort book when I'm stressed.' He picked it up and turned it over in all its dog-eared glory. 'It was my dad's. He read it to me when I was a kid; I didn't understand half of it but I liked him reading it to me.'

'I didn't have you down for a classics fan. I thought you'd be more of a James Herbert man.'

John looked impressed.

'How very astute of you, Ms Sharpe. As a matter of fact, I am a fan of James Herbert. But I like the classics too.'

'You should join our book club.'

'I'll pass, thanks,' said John. His eyes were sparkling with mischief. 'I've seen what goes on at your book clubs.'

'That was a one-off – not at all indicative of our usual run of events.'

'I get the impression it's really a women-only affair.'

'You're probably right. There's lots of feminist talk and bra burning. Once a month we sacrifice a man to Hecate under a blood moon.'

John nodded sagely.

'I thought as much,' he said.

'Was your dad a big reader?'

'Yes. Or at least, I think I remember him reading a lot but that could be my memory adding embellishments.'

'How old were you when he left?'

'I was about nine. You know those stories about men who go out one day saying they're going to buy a packet of cigarettes and never return?'

'Yes,' Annie laughed.

'That was my dad.'

Annie straightened her face.

'Seriously?'

'Seriously. He told us he was going to the off-licence to get a packet of fags and some crisps and he never came back.'

'Oh my God! Did you ever find out where he went?'

'Oh yeah, he had a whole other family in the next town.'

'What!'

'Yep. I shit you not. Some of his other kids were even the same age as my siblings. He'd been leading a double life for nearly ten years and then one day he obviously picked a favourite. And that was the end of that.'

'What did your mum do?'

'She waited for him to come home and she bore the shame.'

'*She bore the shame?*' Annie asked incredulously. 'What about his shame?'

'I don't think he had any.'

'Did you ever see him again?'

'He turned up at my mum's funeral. My brother punched him in the face, I didn't intervene.' His face darkened but then he checked himself and smiled. 'My sister found herself on a double date once with her half-sister. That was an interesting evening!'

'Oh my God!' Annie laughed. 'I'm sorry, I know it's not funny, but it's the kind of stuff you read about in women's magazines. How awful for your sister. Did they stay in touch?'

'As a matter of fact, they did. They're godparents to one another's children.'

'Your family makes my family seem terribly dull.'

'I'd have taken dull. I've spent my adult life trying to make Celeste's home life as uneventful as possible.'

'Ah well, now, there we are similar. I classically stayed in a bad marriage to ensure that my children didn't come from a broken home.'

'How admirable of you,' said John insincerely.

'Wasn't it? After all my years of faking the happy, I have recently discovered that my kids knew exactly what was going on and grew up aware that their dad screwed around and their mum put up with it. What a fabulous advertisement I am for feminism.'

'I think you're being too hard on yourself. We're all just trying not to fuck up our kids in our own way.'

'I worry that by trying not to fuck them up I might have fucked them up more,' said Annie.

'I think your boys have got a lot to be proud of.'

'Do you? That's very nice of you to say so.'

'I'm a nice guy.'

'I'm starting to believe it.'

'What would convince you?'

'If you let me buy Saltwater Nook.'

Chapter 73

They started the meal with a sharing platter of black bean nachos, the fiery chilli quelled by a cooling guacamole with fresh coriander and the richness of the cheese cut through by a sweet tomato salsa. John was interested in Annie's take on the food and fascinated by how she could identify single ingredients from the impossible jumble before them.

The jug of Mexican sangria which they shared was as potent as it was fruity, and the addition of cinnamon and brandy lent itself to the cold November night.

'I thought you didn't drink,' said Annie.

'I don't drink often – Christmas and birthdays usually – but I'll make an exception tonight.'

'I wouldn't want to lead you astray,' Annie remarked, tongue in cheek.

'What a pity,' said John, staring at her in a way that made her want to flash her boobs at him.

By the time their main courses arrived – fish tacos for Annie and beef enchiladas for John – the conversation had moved on to John's various brushes with the law before he found peace in his career and then fatherhood. Annie was feeling warm and relaxed, and like she might tell John all her deepest secrets.

'I'd better not have too much more,' said Annie. 'I've got work in the morning. And I need to be on top form, I've got Billy in tomorrow morning for a trial.'

'Billy?'

'One of the truants that was in the Nook the other day.'

'Is that wise?'

'Why? Because he was playing hooky? Didn't you ever bunk off?'

'Well, I . . .' John spluttered indignantly. 'Yes, I suppose . . .'

'And did that mean you were untrustworthy?'

'No, but . . .' He had the look of a man grasping for answers. He shrugged his shoulders. 'You're absolutely right,' he conceded. 'I've not got a leg to stand on.'

'Ely vouched for him, Billy and his grandad used to fish with him. Besides, I've got a good feeling about Billy. I think he needs someone to give him a chance.'

John looked at her for a long moment and said, 'I think Billy is very lucky.'

The evening had felt as if they were in their own little cocoon, despite the hubbub around them. It was just her and John – his face, his mouth, his deep smooth voice, the curl of his words, his long slender hands, the worry lines on his forehead, the sharp line of black stubble at his jaw. Was it just the booze? she wondered. The conversation between them was easy. It had been a long time since Annie had talked like this with anyone and she didn't want it to stop, she felt as though she could talk with John forever and never get bored. Ridiculous, she knew. And yet here she was, sharing her thoughts and hopes in a way she hadn't done since she was teenager.

When the bell rang for last orders, Annie was shocked by how quickly the time had gone. She was even more surprised when, what seemed like only a moment later, Raye came gingerly to their table and said apologetically that they were closing up. Annie looked around her. The last customers left in a flurry of scarves and coats; a swirl of damp leaves gusted in like a swarm of brown butterflies as they opened the door. And just like that, the spell was broken; Annie was a grown-up again, with responsibilities and saggy boobs.

'I'll walk you home,' said John, getting up from the table.

'Don't be daft. There's no sense you walking all the way down to the Nook, only to have to come all the way back up here. I'm perfectly capable of walking myself home.'

She stood up and felt the carpet shift beneath her feet as though someone were pulling it from the other end of the room. That sangria really packed a punch. She stumbled, just a little, as she bent to pluck her coat from the back of the chair. John put his hand out to steady her. Annie recovered herself, swayed a little on the spot and laughed.

'Maybe I'll get a taxi,' she said.

'Maybe that's for the best. I'll call you one now.'

John whipped out his phone and made the call. He seemed to know the person at the taxi rank. He chuckled and asked the person on the other end of the line how Thea and the girls were getting on.

'Ten minutes,' said John, a moment later.

'I think I'll wait outside.' She was feeling hot and a bit woozy.

'I'll wait with you.'

'You don't have to.'

'I know.'

'I'll just pay up,' said Annie.

'It's done.'

'It's done?'

'I asked Raye to put it on my tab.'

'Let me give you my half,' said Annie, fumbling in her handbag for her purse.

'I don't want half. I wanted to treat you to dinner.'

'Oh. Thank you. You didn't have to do that.'

'I wanted to. Call it a goodwill gesture to make up for us getting off on the wrong foot.'

'Well, thank you. The next time is on me.'

John raised an eyebrow.

'There's going to be a next time?'

Annie realised she'd jumped right into that one. She felt her cheeks flush.

'I don't see why not,' she said, trying to be cool and collected. 'There's bound to be things that need to be discussed at some point and we may as well do it over a good meal.'

John smiled and helped her into her coat.

'We may as well,' he said.

Annie called her goodbyes to Raye and Aiden. John said he would be back in when Annie's taxi arrived and Aiden promised not to lock him out.

Annie shivered as the outer door gave way with a creak and opened out onto a wall of navy blue cold. She pulled her coat closer around her and parked herself on a wooden picnic bench. Across the road she watched the lights go out one by one in The Sunken Willow and imagined Pam and Bill making their weary way to bed. *Bed.* She shivered again, a convulsive full-body shudder. John sat down beside her and she forgot the cold; suddenly all she could think about was his nearness.

It was quiet but for the occasional hoot of an owl and the breeze whistling through the naked trees. The grass was diamond-studded with the glisten of frost.

'I've been swatting up on Mari's notes for the Christmas Festival,' said Annie.

'It's a pretty special night, a lot of fun,' said John. 'It's kind of a last hurrah before the December festivities begin proper.'

'It's not really a last hurrah if there are a load more festivities to come and there's been loads before it, is it?' said Annie. 'It's more of a halfway hurrah.'

'Well, it's the last hurrah before the proper winter hurrahs begin.'

'I have never known a place to have so many hurrahs.'

John laughed.

'You wait till the dark days of January, that's when they really get going!'

'I'm looking forward to it.'

'I'm glad,' said John. 'You suit Willow Bay.'

'I don't know whether to take that as a compliment or not,' said Annie wryly.

'It's a compliment. I promise. Not everyone would embrace it like you have. And everyone thinks you're great. I can't turn around without somebody telling me what a bloody marvel you are.'

Annie laughed.

'How very discomforting for you!'

'I'm getting used to it.'

'My sources inform me that Pam keeps the Ghosts of Christmas in the cellar.'

'She does indeed.'

'Can I ask what form these ghosts take?' asked Annie.

'They're like giant papier-mâché puppets. Provided it's dry, they'll be walked along the promenade to the beach and fixed to bases where they can view the proceedings.'

'You don't do things by halves, do you?'

'Do it right or don't bother,' John replied.

Annie felt John shift on the bench, and she turned herself to look at him. He was looking at her.

'I'm glad it's you who's staying at the Nook,' he said. 'Don't get me wrong, it hasn't exactly made my life easier. A straight-forward, non-cafe-opening tenant would have been easier. But still. I'm glad that the thorn in my side is you.'

Annie was still formulating a witty comeback when John kissed her. Just once. A soft, gentle, tentative kiss. His lips were warm on hers. She closed her eyes. He drew away, tantalisingly just enough that she could still feel the warmth of his breath. It would only take the slightest movement for their lips to touch. Annie leaned forward infinitesimally and their mouths met again, deliciously, lightly. John's hands cupped her face, the tips of his fingers twisting in her hair. His breath came harder and so did Annie's. She felt her body arching towards him; she reached inside his coat and wrapped her arms around him. She wanted to get under his clothes, to touch his skin, to feel his body on hers. John's kisses became deeper, more urgent and Annie let herself be swept up in his passion. Her skin was tingling, her body alive with want. A sudden bright light and an elongated beep broke them apart. The taxi had arrived.

'Right,' said Annie, jumping up. She was dizzy and almost lost her footing.

'Right. Yes,' said John, pulling his coat around him.

'That's my cue,' said Annie.

John nodded and stood. She felt his hand guiding her as they tramped down the grassy bank to the taxi. John opened the back door and Annie climbed in.

'Thank you for a lovely evening,' said Annie. The temptation to pull John into the back of the cab with her was almost overwhelming.

'Thank *you*,' said John. He pushed her door closed and leaned in through the open passenger window to pass the driver a ten-pound note. Then he stood back, raising his hand once as the taxi pulled away.

Annie climbed into bed, still all of a fluster, and flicked off the lamp. She leaned across to the drawer in her bedside cabinet and pulled Mr Knightley from his wrappings. But it was neither Mr Knightley's nor Poldark's image which filled her mind as she shimmied down beneath the bedclothes and closed her eyes.

Chapter 74

Annie woke up the next morning with more than a smidge of a hangover, which she doused liberally with coffee and carbohydrates before taking herself for a walk along the promenade at seven a.m. Ely's fishing boat was already out on the water, which today was a dark navy blue. The swell was languid, making the waves look thick and syrupy. The weather had changed. She could smell the cold; there was a permanence about this chill, as though a deep elemental shift had caused the very fabric of the air to evolve into a new harsher creature. Winter had arrived. As she walked, shrouded in the frosty morning mist, her thoughts returned again and again to the previous evening and she found herself smiling in spite of the bitter breeze.

By the time she opened the kiosk at eight o'clock she had frozen out her muggy head and felt almost human – coffee would sort the rest. Saturday mornings were her busiest at the kiosk. The serious dog-walkers wanted to get their exercise and their caffeine fixes and be back home before the week-enders descended upon the beach.

Billy arrived at twenty-five past, looking rosy-cheeked and windswept. He was shy and ill at ease – despite Annie doing her best to make him feel relaxed – and it was making him clumsy. He dropped a cup within the first ten minutes of his shift and seemed to trip over every chair leg as he stumbled about the cafe, getting it ready for opening. Annie felt sorry for him; she could see he wanted to make a good impression but his nerves were sabotaging his efforts. His complexion swung between deathly pale and blotchy red, depending on the degree of his errors. But despite this, or maybe because of it, the customers took to him instantly. He pulled faces to make the children laugh, charmed the older customers with his attentive manners and brought out the maternal instinct in every woman over twenty-five.

'Relax,' said Annie, when his shaking hands caused more coffee to be in the saucer than in the cup. 'You're doing really well. All these little errors will stop as soon as you calm down.'

'I'm sorry,' said Billy, his cheeks blotching scarlet instantly. 'I just really want this job.'

'Well, you've got the job. So there, now you can stop panicking and concentrate on getting the hang of the place.'

'I've got the job?' Billy's surprise was palpable.

'It's yours,' said Annie. 'Now, clear down table four and I'll have the next order ready for you to take.'

Billy jumped to attention and set off for table four with a spring in his step and an unquenchable grin.

Ely came into the cafe, under the guise of delivering a bag of oddly shaped fresh fillets for which he wouldn't take any money. He nodded at Billy as he passed him; Billy looked up mid-antibacterial-spraying a table and grinned at him.

'How's he doing?' Ely asked under his breath.

'He's doing great,' Annie assured him.

'I promised his grandad I'd look out for him.'

'Then you'll find your job much easier with him being here Saturdays and holidays.'

'I appreciate what you're doing for him.'

'Not at all.' Annie dismissed his thanks. 'I needed an extra pair of hands and Billy came along at the right time.'

They both peered surreptitiously at Billy, who had just filled an old margarine tub with water and set it down under the table for a customer's Cocker Spaniel. The customer thanked him and gave a nod of satisfaction to his retreating back.

'Well, he's tamed our most discerning customer,' said Annie wryly. 'So, the rest ought to be plain sailing. It'll take him a few weeks to get the hang of it but I think he's made of the right stuff.'

Ely nodded and gave an appreciative grunt before heading back to his boat with a large gingerbread latte.

At midday Alfred poked his head in at the kiosk window. He rarely ventured into the cafe during opening hours; too many people, he complained.

'I'm going to get that fence fixed,' he said. 'Weather's turned, winter's here.'

'Oh brilliant, thank you, Alfred! Have you got everything you need?'

'Yes, thank you.'

'Coffee to help you work?'

'Please.'

'I'll bring it round to you. It'll be about ten minutes.'

Alfred nodded and shuffled off out of sight. A woman – *an out-of-towner*, Annie caught herself thinking – watched Alfred leave with something amounting to distaste and took his place at the window; her face was pinched into repulsion as she looked around, as though Alfred's presence had somehow dirtied the immediate vicinity.

'Begging, was he?' she asked.

Annie was instantly indignant.

'He happens to be a friend of mine and a very fine handyman,' she said.

The woman sniffed. 'He dresses like a tramp.'

'I try not to judge people on their appearance, it's such an unappealing personality trait. What can I get you?'

The woman, trying to decide if she had just been insulted, gave her order and Annie moved to make it as quickly as she could; she didn't want that kind of customer hanging around. The woman took the proffered coffee with a huff and left. John took her place, stooping to look in through the window.

'Hello,' he said.

'Hello,' Annie smiled. She felt self-conscious and a bit giggly. Her eyes kept wandering from his eyes to his mouth. She was suddenly very warm despite the fearful draught coming in from the open window.

'You handled her very well,' said John.

'Her type are all pomp and tiny minds.'

'How's your head today?'

'Fine,' said Annie brightly. 'After twelve coffees, it's absolutely fine.'

John laughed.

'I feel I should apologise,' he said.

'Oh? Why, what have you done?'

'I can't seem to stop kissing you.'

Annie felt a flush race up from her toes and burst into her cheeks, which felt like they were pulsating on red alert. She tried to gather her wits.

'I mean, I didn't like to say anything . . .' said Annie.

'It must be a terrible inconvenience for you.'

'One doesn't like to complain,' said Annie, smiling.

John smiled back at her, an easy smile that lit his whole face and made Annie want to pull him in through the hatch and ravish him beneath the coffee machine.

'You look busy,' he said, tilting his head to look around her at the full cafe within. 'I might go around and see if Alfred needs a hand.'

'I'll be taking him round a coffee in a minute. Would you like one?'

And maybe a sex-starved forty-four-year-old woman on the side?

'I thought you'd never ask.'

Annie smiled as though her thighs weren't on fire and John unfolded himself back up to his full height.

The cafe remained steady. Billy barely had time to clear down the tables between one set of customers leaving and the next set eagerly scouring the tiny cafe for a space. There were too many orders for Annie to leave the coffee machine, so she sent Billy out with warm scones and hot coffees for John and Alfred.

Later, Annie took Emily out a hazelnut latte – she had discovered that these were her favourites. Emily leaned her placard up against the wall and took the cup gratefully, holding it between her mittened hands.

'Hypothetically, and strictly off the record,' said Annie. 'If a person were to buy Saltwater Nook to live in and keep the cafe open, what would be the Historical Society's stance on such an occurrence?'

Annie met Emily's intense gaze squarely and raised her eyebrows. Emily narrowed her eyes and then nodded her head slowly.

'In that instance, the Historical Society would cease and desist all picketing and welcome that person with open arms. It's never been about ownership; we only want to see Saltwater Nook preserved.'

'Then I can assure you, in strictest confidence, that we are singing from the same hymn sheet.'

Emily's face broke into the widest smile.

'Any chance of a piece of tiffin?' she asked.

Chapter 75

At three o'clock Annie paid Billy and he left with a spring in his step. She had enjoyed having him around; he was quite talkative once he got going and it was nice to have help with the close down. She stepped outside and let the cold air wash over her. Up ahead, she could see Ely's outline, leaning against a signpost and looking out to sea; he must be waiting for Billy. Annie smiled to herself. *You could do a lot worse than to have Ely looking out for you*, she thought. There were still quite a few people on the prom. She could have stayed open past two thirty p.m., there was business enough to do so. She decided she would stay open later next Saturday and see how it went. She was sure Billy wouldn't mind the extra hours and it couldn't do any harm to set their reputation now, before the winter really took hold. People were more likely to venture down to the coast in the cold if there was the promise of a hot drink at the end of it. She could start doing sausage rolls and pasties, or maybe even bacon baguettes for Saturday brunch. Annie pondered, *If I play my cards right, people will come to the coast for Saltwater Nook alone!*

Her reverie was broken when she heard John come up behind her.

'How are the workers?' she asked.

'Almost done. We're hungry and cold, though; well, I am anyway, Alfred's like a workhorse.'

'How about some posh fish finger sandwiches to warm you up? Ely dropped in some fresh fillets.'

'That is the best offer I've had all day.'

'How many offers have you had?'

'I don't want to get into it, you'll only get jealous.'

John went back to the garden to tell Alfred that sustenance would be within the hour. Annie went back inside and set about creating a fishy afternoon tea. While the fish fingers crackled in the pan, she cut a crusty white loaf into thick doorstop slices and slathered them with salted butter. Annie dolloped some mayonnaise into a small bowl and roughly chopped a few capers and a handful of jarred cornichons, which she stirred through the mayonnaise to create a quick tartare sauce.

John came back in just as Annie was flipping the fish in the pan – the topsides were a pale golden brown and the pan hissed and sizzled. She noticed that John's hands were lobster pink with cold.

'Shouldn't you be wearing gloves to fix the fence?'

'I forgot mine. Alfred's got skin like leather, even the splinters don't bother to stick in his skin. He's putting me to shame out there.'

Annie laughed and pulled a sympathetic face.

'Come and wash your hands before you eat,' she said.

'Yes, ma'am,' said John, sidling past her to the sink. 'I've been talking with Alfred.'

'I should hope so. It would make for a boring work environment if you were both silent.'

'I've found a shelter. It's a few miles away but they've got space.'

'What are you talking about?'

'A homeless shelter. It's a kind of halfway house really, for people like Alfred. To get them used to having a home again.'

Annie stopped what she was doing.

'What did Alfred say?'

'He says he'll give it some thought.'

'I must say, that's a better response than I thought you'd get. From what I understand, people have tried to get him help before without success.'

'But there must be a reason for that,' said John. 'Something that's happened in his past that has stopped him from being able to live inside and, at some point, it needs to be addressed. These guys have counsellors to help him get to the bottom of all that.'

'It sounds like just the thing he needs,' said Annie. 'I've been worrying more and more about him. Some of the nights he sleeps in the cave are just bitter, I don't know how he can bear it. I even thought about getting him a bed to try and tempt him to stay in the bay instead of going into the city for the winter.'

'Hopefully, this will be the answer. The shelter have booked him in preliminarily for the ninth of December, that gives me a bit of time to ease him into the idea. They're happy for me to take him to see the place first, so it doesn't feel like such a shock. Don't mention it when he comes in, you know what he's like. If he thinks we've been talking about him, his pride will get all dented and he'll take off.'

'Is that what happened last time?' Annie asked.

But the conversation was brought to an abrupt halt by the appearance of Alfred. The three unlikely companions sat together at one of the tables and ate their fish finger sandwiches in the lamplight, while outside the late afternoon grew darker and darker. Nobody spoke about the shelter, though it was clearly on all of their minds.

After they had eaten, the three of them went out to look at the fence. It was dark now and Annie was about to get her phone torch out when John stood at the gate and waved his arm towards the house. Two lamps either side of the door came on and lit the porch area, some of the light spilling down the stairs into the garden.

'Wow!' said Annie.

'The bulbs went back in August and I didn't get round to changing them,' he said sheepishly. 'I should have sorted it as soon as you moved in.'

'Well, I appreciate that you've done it now,' said Annie. It would certainly make finding the keyhole easier at night.

'Wait till you see this!' said John, darting up to the front steps and opening a small black box on the wall.

The garden lit up with strings of lightbulbs which zigzagged above head height, all the way down the path, attached to tall posts along the fence. It was like an enchanted garden. Annie felt her heart squeeze.

'I love it!' she shouted over to John, who grinned with unbridled smugness.

The shrubs were neat and tidy, mostly thanks to Alfred's continued attentions, and the new white picket fence was good and sturdy and unlikely to shift even with what the coast wind could hurl at it.

'How much help did John actually give you with the fence?' Annie asked, while John stood admiring his handiwork further up the garden and reaching up occasionally to twizzle a bulb so that they hung uniformly.

'A fair bit,' said Alfred. 'I'll give him his due. But he spent quite a bit of time fiddling about with lightbulbs too.'

Annie laughed.

'So I see. Thank you for all this, Alfred. I really appreciate it.'

'It's no bother,' said Alfred. 'One thing puzzles me, though,' he added.

'Oh? What's that?'

'Are these really the actions of a man who intends to raze the place to rubble?'

Chapter 76

Alfred didn't stay, despite Annie inviting him to come up to the flat for a cup of tea. He had 'things to do', though Annie couldn't imagine what odd jobs he was likely to be doing in the dark. He left shortly before six, his shoulders hunched and head down against the cold as he disappeared into the night. To her disappointment, John didn't come in either. He had a video call with Celeste before she went out and he wanted to work on the plans for Raye and Aiden's extension.

'On a Saturday night?' Annie had exclaimed.

'No rest for the wicked,' said John.

Is he trying to avoid being alone with me? Annie wondered. *Wouldn't any red-blooded man be up there like a shot, trying to get his end away?*

'What are you thinking?' John asked. 'You look miles away.'

Annie brushed it aside with an airy laugh.

'Oh, nothing,' she said, hugging herself against the cold evening. Even with her coat and scarf on, the wind was finding its way in.

'You know I would like to come up, don't you?'

'Do I?'

'You should.'

'Then why don't you?'

'Because I don't want to complicate things more than they already are.'

'I'm inviting you into the flat, not my vagina,' she said. *Although my vagina would welcome you too!* she thought wistfully.

John let out a laugh that seemed to echo into the black nothingness beyond the garden.

'How very candid of you,' he said. 'Then let me be candid also. If I come up now, we're going to have a very enjoyable evening and at some point, I am going to want to kiss you. A lot. I think we've already established that I can't seem to keep away from you and I'm pretty sure you feel the same way. It would be unnecessarily coy at this point for either of us to deny that we find the other attractive. However, whether we like it or not, it does complicate things. I need to make sure that the decision I make with regard to Saltwater Nook is what's best for my aunt. And you need to think about whether you would still want to be friends if my final decision for the Nook didn't go in your favour. I just think we should wait a while.'

Annie felt almost positive that she would want to be more than friends regardless of what happened. But she wasn't going to blurt that out to him like some silly schoolgirl. Though she would love to throw caution to the wind, she appreciated the care with which John was thinking through the implications for both of them. Unfortunately, his thoughtfulness made her want to tear all his clothes off and have sex with him right here in the garden.

'I understand,' said Annie. 'I don't completely like it. But I appreciate it.'

'If it's any consolation, I don't like it either. I can't stop thinking about you and it's driving me crazy. It seems like all you've done is drive me crazy one way or the other since you arrived!'

'Ditto,' said Annie, smiling.

He leaned down and brushed her cheek with a kiss.

'I'll see you,' he said and he left.

Annie watched him go until the night swallowed him. Then she wandered back through the fairy-lit garden and closed the door on the dark. She stood in the hallway surrounded by the craggy faces of fishermen past looking out of the photographs on the wall. She was falling for John; she could feel it happening and there was nothing she could do to stop it. It was more than how time seemed to pass slower when she was waiting for him to arrive; more than how each day was electric with the anticipation that he might show up unexpectedly, or how her heart leaped each time his name flashed up on her phone. It was a feeling inside her bones, like he was pulling her to him, and against her better judgement, she didn't want to resist. Wasn't it just bloody typical that the man she wanted to leave her alone was persistence personified, while the one she wanted to ravish her was keeping her at arm's length?

Chapter 77

It was Sunday, Annie's one full day off, and the weather could only be described as awful. Even the most ardent wild weather lover would be hard pressed to find inspiration in its utter bleakness. The wind and rain were sometimes working together, sometimes tag teaming, without ever stopping for a break. The windows were running so thickly with rain that Annie could barely make out sea from sky from beach. Annie didn't go out all day. Instead, she filled the slow cooker with the ingredients for a lamb hotpot and caught up on housework and reading. Though she didn't show it, Annie was sure Mrs Tiggy-Winkle was appreciative of her company. At three o'clock she had a video call with Alex and Peter.

'Are you ready for the pre-Christmas Christmas party?' asked Alex.

'I think so. I've planned the food and John's going to help out . . .'

'John again!' said Alex. 'Seems like we've heard a lot about John one way or another.'

'Is he friend or foe at the moment?' asked Peter.

Annie tried to look affronted but, in truth, she secretly

liked it when they ganged up on her like this; she loved that they had remained so close.

'Mum's walking that fine line between hate and desire!' said Alex.

Peter made retching noises.

'Anyway!' Annie cut in. 'The village council organise the rest of the festivities, the processions and singing and the fires and stuff.'

'It's a bit like you've stepped into the past, or a cult; have you seen *The Wicker Man*?' asked Peter.

Annie laughed.

'It sounds pretty insular when I talk about it but it's really not like that. It's just a community that didn't forget how to be a community. They look after each other. It's kind of nice.'

'And they have a lot of parties!' said Alex.

'They do have A LOT of parties,' Annie agreed. 'I'm sorry I haven't been up to visit either of you. It's been pretty full-on here.'

'So much for taking a step back,' said Alex.

'Don't worry about it, Mum. Anyway, we've got a surprise for you . . .' said Peter.

'We're coming down for the Christmas Festival shindig!' said Alex.

'Oh my God! That's wonderful news! I can introduce you to everyone. Oh, you've really made my day.' Annie couldn't stop smiling. 'Is Greg coming too?'

'Yep, he's coming with us.'

'Lovely,' said Annie. 'And Peter, will you be bringing anyone?'

'I'm between relationships at the moment,' said Peter with a wry smile.

'You haven't had a *relationship* since Clemmy Pearson in

Year 9,' Alex snorted. 'Your idea of getting serious with a woman is asking what her surname is.'

'He just hasn't met the right girl yet,' said Annie.

'That's because I'm not looking for the *right girl*, Mum, so don't get any ideas about marrying me off to one of the locals in some weird Willow Bay ritual,' said Peter.

After an evening relaxing with Tiggs on the sofa, while the log burner crackled merrily in the corner and Colin Firth wrote books in a roll-neck jumper on the TV in *Love Actually*, Annie scooped a good portion of lamb stew into a bowl for Alfred. She covered it in foil, then wrapped it in several tea towels to keep the heat in, poured him a large glass of wine and carried the supper down to the cafe, with a couple of extra blankets from the airing cupboard. It was cold tonight, even for a seasoned rough sleeper like Alfred.

Back in the warmth of the flat, snuggled up with a book in the soft bed, under the weight of a heavy duvet and an overweight cat, Annie counted her blessings, and wondered what the future would hold for Alfred. If he agreed to go to the shelter, she would miss him, but it would be the right thing for him – hopefully.

Her phone buzzed with a message from John.

I can't sleep. What are you reading?'

How do you know I'm reading?

You're always reading. Answer the question.

A Christmas Carol. 🎄

What chapter?

What are you doing?

I'm downloading it, so that we can read together from our separate beds.

I'm halfway through stave one.

Wait for me.

Are we reading buddies now?

In the absence of kissing, I thought we may as well share books.

Instead of saliva?

What a charming way with words you have. 😊

Let me know when you're ready, Mr Granger. Scrooge and I are waiting.

Annie smiled and waited for John to message that he had caught up. Was it weird that this felt like the most romantic thing that had ever happened to her? They read to halfway through stave two, where Fezziwig has his Christmas party, stopping at intervals to message their thoughts about a particular line or paragraph; John asking if she could rustle up a similar feast for the Christmas Festival and Annie telling him not to push his luck, and both of them googling what 'negus' was.

Do you think you'll be able to sleep now? Annie messaged, feeling her eyelids drooping.

I'll give it a try. Thank you, Annie.

What for?

Just thank you.

You're welcome. Nite nite, John. Sleep tight xxx

Don't let the bed bugs bite xxx

Chapter 78

The temperature dropped incrementally day by day and in that first week of December Willow Bay plunged headlong into winter. Sometimes Annie had to force herself out for her walk in the mornings, knowing that if she left it until after work, she wouldn't go out at all. But the swimmers kept swimming – their joy seeming to increase as the weather grew colder – and the walkers and runners still made their daily commute to the coast, and against all the odds, business at The Saltwater Cafe remained steady.

Alfred had agreed to give the shelter a try and even though she knew it was the right thing, Annie couldn't shake the feeling that Willow Bay was losing someone special. Annie found herself making two dinners each night and leaving one for Alfred in the cafe. She made herself get up extra early to give him a hot drink before he left in the mornings; once on a night when the tide was out, she even tramped a thermos all the way down to the cave. He shook his head at her, chuckling his low grumbly chuckle as he took it, as though *she* were the eccentric. It was silly, she knew, but she wanted to feed Alfred up before he left. She had inherited the need to feed people from her mum, who couldn't bear it if someone came into their home and didn't leave feeling replete; this had been known to extend to the vicar, the boiler engineer and the woman who came to check the electric meter. It was one of the reasons Annie had been so sure she wanted to be a chef.

As well as reading the books for the book club, Annie was working her way through Christmas novels with John at bedtime. They were currently reading *Hercule Poirot's Christmas*. It had become Annie's favourite time of the day. She would curl up in bed at an agreed time, with her book and her fully charged phone, and read in tandem with John. It was intimate, a thing just for them, and she often fell asleep wishing that the night hours were longer.

It drives me crazy to think of that dastardly Mr Knightley in your bedroom! John messaged when they'd finished discussing the abominable Simeon Lee.

Annie was suddenly wide awake and tingling in all the right places.

He is indeed dastardly! she replied. Particularly between the sheets! 😊

Gaaaarrghhh! What's wrong with me, I'm jealous of a dildo!

Annie laughed out loud.

Hahahahaha. Well then, let's hope my stupid husband agrees to buy me out, so that I can buy you out, and you can come over here and usurp Mr Knightley.

If he doesn't pull his finger out soon, I'm going to drive to The Pomegranate Seed and shake the money out of him! John messaged.

I'll talk to him again. Let's save the husband-shaking as a last resort, Annie typed, smiling.

Chapter 79

The much anticipated Christmas Festival celebrations were just hours away. The hob had been swallowed by two large catering saucepans, one containing a beef bourguignon and the other a rich vegetable and ale stew, which had been blipping contentedly on a slow simmer all afternoon. The Christmas tunes playing on a loop had spurred Annie and Gemma along as they cut out and baked enough sugar star cookies to sink the famous *Willow*.

John had been roped in to help Bill and Paul set the fires that would line the beach and act as both a beacon for ghost ships – mostly the ones that had been lured to the shallows by Willow Bay's iniquitous forebears – and warming posts for chilly revellers. It seemed to Annie that the residents of Willow Bay spent a lot of time atoning for their ancestors' misdemeanours. They were supervised in their endeavour by Emily, who had suspended her dislike of John for the sake of the festival and historical accuracy and winked conspicuously at Annie every chance she got. Alfred lent a hand where needed. Only a handful of people knew that this would be his last day in Willow Bay and that handful were determined – whether he liked it or not – to make it special for him.

Annie watched John wistfully as he worked. He was wearing old jeans and a knitted sweater with a Christmas tree motif and was laughing and joking with Paul and Bill, and even Emily. Though she knew they were trying to be sensible and not give in to their feelings, the lines were becoming increasingly blurred as time went on. The wildly inappropriate flirting only added to the sizzling chemistry between them and the longing in her chest grew more acute each day. It seemed both futile and necessary to deny their attraction, which Annie supposed summed up their peculiar and contradictory non-courtship.

'He really likes you,' said Gemma, when she caught Annie looking out of the window for the hundredth time.

'It feels like the fates are conspiring against us,' said Annie.

'Or maybe they're just waiting until the time is right for you two.'

Annie smiled and went back to sprinkling edible glitter over a batch of warm orange-spiced snowflake cookies.

Annie had decided to stay open all day today, so when Gemma left for the school run, Annie had a couple of hours to manage by herself before Billy arrived after school for the evening shift. At half past three Sam's van pulled up with Pam and Raye and they wrestled Charles Dickens's giant papier-mâché ghosts into the back garden. Annie hoped the sight of these leering effigies wouldn't induce Alex and Peter to turn tail and run when they arrived.

'Oh, Annie, it looks wonderful in here!' cooed Sam.

'You don't think it's too much?' Annie, swept up in the festive spirit, had added to the already bounteous decorations by interlacing more fairy lights around the cafe, which had begun to resemble an alpine chalet crossed with a Santa's grotto in Las Vegas.

'Too much?' blustered Pam. 'It's Christmas, there's no such thing as too much at Christmas!'

'I agree,' said Raye. 'It feels magical in here, with all the wood and the twinkling lights, and that view. You've created a winter wonderland.'

'And let's face it, it's bloody bleak outside!' added Sam. 'I dare anyone to walk past on a day like today and not be drawn in. Honestly, Annie, it's like an oasis of cosy.'

Annie felt warm inside. Maeve marched in.

'Hello! Crikey, that smells good. What time are we eating?'

'Not till six,' said Annie.

'Good God, I'll have withered to nothing by then. Better make me a large mocha to keep me going, and I'll take a slice of that ginger cake. And a couple of those biscuits. And a packet of crisps.'

The folk band set up beneath a hastily erected gazebo and pretty soon their rendition of 'Fairytale of New York' by the Pogues was filling the cafe as they warmed up. Alex, Peter and Greg arrived just before six o'clock.

'And what the fuck are they?' asked Peter, nodding to the papier-mâché giants stood like a grotesque welcome party by the steps.

'They are the Ghosts of Christmas Past, Present and Future,' said Annie, pulling each of them in turn into a bear hug. 'So, you'd better watch yourselves!'

'Mum, this is amazing,' said Alex, after they had given Greg the world's shortest tour around the flat. They were standing in the cafe now. It was the first time they had seen it other than in photographs.

'He's not wrong, Mum,' said Peter. 'I'm really proud of you. Is that weird for a child to say to a parent? Fuck it, who cares, I *am* really proud of you!'

'Me too,' agreed Alex.

'I concur,' added Greg. 'When my parents split up, my mum kept posting pictures of herself pissed, dancing on pub tables and draping herself across men half her age.'

'Sounds like fun,' said Annie.

Greg grimaced. 'This is a much bigger up-yours to Max than photos of you poking your tongue in Greek waiters' ears,' he said.

Alex and Peter looked as though they were distinctly glad to have dodged that particular bullet.

John came in and introduced himself.

'Good to meet you at last,' he said, shaking hands with each of them. 'Your mum talks about you a lot. All good things obviously.'

'Well, isn't that a coincidence,' said Alex. 'Because she talks a lot about you too!'

Peter sniggered.

'Okay then!' said Annie quickly. 'You've got hot drinks, now off you go outside. I've got customers to serve.'

'Does that include me?' asked John.

'You can stay if you don't cause trouble,' Annie smiled. She was acutely aware of being watched by Alex and Peter. Greg was smirking.

'You'd better come with us then,' said Peter. 'Mum says you are a bit of a troublemaker.'

'Does she now?' John's eyes twinkled as he grinned at her.

Annie felt hot.

'Come on then, lads,' said John, 'let me introduce you to the locals.'

They all four headed outside. All this flirting with no actual action was doing nothing for Annie's delicate hormones. One of these days she would spontaneously combust and all that would be left in the ash would be her pixie boots and her contraceptive coil.

'Do you fancy him?' asked Billy with his usual guilelessness.

Annie snorted.

'It's complicated,' she replied.

'People always say that but if you like someone and they like you, what's so complicated about it?'

'Billy, you are wise beyond your years.'

Chapter 80

Aiden and Bill had set up a trestle table in the patio area and were ladling steaming mulled cider from two large vats into paper cups. The little pyres along the beach were lit and the dark promenade was as busy as any sunny Saturday. John came in with a cup of hot cider.

'Come on,' he said. 'Close the cafe for ten minutes and watch the procession. You too, Billy.'

Annie did as she was told. *Ten minutes won't hurt*, she told herself.

The Ghosts of Christmas Past, Present and Future had been covertly lugged via the sand dunes, which ran along the bottom of the cliff, all the way to the end of the promenade, whereupon they were rigged up to join the procession back towards Saltwater Nook. The golden flecks of candles shimmered in the darkness like fireflies. The ghosts swayed above the heads of the procession – lit with torches from below, by the puppeteers who held them – their robes rippling in the breeze, their huge faces ghastly in the cold light of the moon. The choir sang 'Good King Wenceslas' as they processed, then 'I Saw Three Ships', 'God Rest Ye Merry Gentlemen' and 'Ave Maria'. As more people left the little fires on the beach to join the choir, they sang carols with more well-known lyrics such as 'Deck the Halls' and 'We Three Kings'. When at last they reached the cafe, the ghosts were secured facing out to sea and the folk band picked up the music. Annie felt warm despite the cold. She saw Alfred a little way along the promenade and waved. He waved back.

'Come on, Annie!' shouted someone in the crowd. 'What are you playing at? I'm starving!'

A roar of agreement went up.

'I guess that's my cue!' Annie laughed. 'Come on, Billy, let's feed the hungry hordes.'

'We'll give you a hand,' Peter called over; the boys had both had part-time jobs at the restaurant in their teens, so they knew the drill.

By the time Annie had scraped the last of the vegetable stew into a bowl and announced 'That's it, folks!' she was clean out of biscuits, cakes and hot chocolate powder. Even with Peter, Alex and Greg helping, they were still rushed off their feet. John had taken over the kiosk and had managed to soothe even the most impatient customers. There was something about his courtliness which disarmed people. It was not so long ago that Annie had found his manner overly formal and pompous, but now she found that it was one of her favourite things about him.

'Um, Annie.' John came up behind her as she was finishing off two chai lattes. 'There's someone at the kiosk.'

Annie peered around his shoulder and made a reflexive 'Urghh' sound. Max.

'Can I help you?' Annie asked.

'I thought I'd come and see you. The boys are staying with me tonight, so I thought I'd pop down . . .' he trailed off.

Annie looked back into the cafe. It was emptying out now; she would close in a few minutes anyway.

'Boys!' she called back. 'Dad's here. Go out and spend a bit of time with him. Billy and I can take it from here.'

'I thought we could talk,' said Max.

'About?'

'Everything.'

'*Everything* is not going to fit into this evening. And you may have noticed, I'm rather busy at the moment.'

'Later then.'

Annie could feel John's eyes on the back of her neck while Max made puppy eyes at her from the front. She turned back into the cafe.

'Honestly, boys, thank you but it's all right. I've got this.'

Alex and Peter finished what they were doing and headed outside. Greg followed behind them but not before he'd turned back to Annie and given her an exaggerated eye roll. She smiled and began to clear tables. She saw Max hovering at the kiosk window in her peripheral vision but ignored him.

Alfred came in and Annie brought over a slice of cake she'd held back for him.

'I'll be leaving tomorrow,' he said.

'I know.'

'You've done a good job here.'

'I think you're doing the right thing, but it won't be the same here without you.'

'I'd have been pushing off to the city before long anyway.'

'But still. I'll miss you.'

'John's right. It's time to face my demons. I've got to at least give it a try. Tide's in tonight.'

'Good job you can sleep here then.'

Alfred nodded and headed back outside.

A couple of hours later and the revellers had drifted home, the band had packed up and the makeshift bar was dismantled. The little beach fires had been doused and the wet wood piled into the back of Paul's pick-up. The beach was cold and dark and still, and it was hard to believe that there had ever been a party; if it wasn't for the presence of Max and the boys, Annie might have thought she'd imagined it all. John had made himself scarce ever since Max's arrival. He'd popped in briefly to say goodbye and tell her what time he was dropping Alfred off the next day.

'Come and see me after,' said Annie. 'Tell me how it went.'

'I will. I promise you, if there's any sign that he's not okay, I won't leave him.'

'I know you won't. You don't have to go just because Max is here.'

'He seems to want to talk to you. Let's leave our book tonight, *The Woman in Black* can wait. Truth be told, it's scaring the shit out of me anyway. I'll let you sort out whatever you need to with Max.'

Oh God! His understanding was making Annie like him even more. *Stupid Max and his relentless wooing.*

'It's all hot air, you know,' she said. 'He's not a man of great substance. Puddles have greater depth than he does.'

John smiled.

'We'll talk tomorrow when I haven't got your husband's beady eyes trained on me.'

John bent and kissed her cheek, lingering longer than necessary. Annie breathed in the scent of him, felt the warmth of him on her skin and wished she could pull him to her and stay like that, just the two of them, wrapped in one another's arms. He pulled away, his eyes held hers for a long moment, and then he left.

Chapter 81

Max took the mop out of Annie's hands.

'I'll do that,' he said. 'You crack on with cashing up.'

'You haven't mopped a floor since 2002,' said Annie.

'I'm a changed man. You'll find out if you give me half a chance.'

Annie shook her head and began counting receipts. Alex, Greg and Peter were upstairs; she could hear the rumble of their laughter through the floorboards.

'Do you like him?' Max asked.

'Who?'

'That John.'

'Yes. I do like *that John*. Very much.'

They worked for a while longer in a silence which felt laden with unspoken truths.

'This place is great, Annie.'

'Thanks,' she said idly, totalling up the day's takings.

'You wouldn't have to give it up if we gave us another try. It could be the perfect set-up.'

Annie looked up.

'What are you talking about, Max?'

'This could be like a sister cafe to the restaurant. We could

393

call it The Pomegranate By The Sea. You could stay down here while we rebuild our marriage; we could start dating, go back to the beginning. It would be exciting, romantic, me dropping you off at your door after a nice meal. You'd get the breathing space you need, and we'd be building the business at the same time.'

'I don't need breathing space, Max. I—'

'Don't answer now. Sleep on it. You can't tell me the boys wouldn't love to see us at least try.'

Max's phone buzzed on the counter and Annie automatically picked it up to pass it to him. And then she saw the message.

Ellie's mob: Hey Maxi, I'm sad I won't get to see you tonight ☹ I'm keeping it warm for you baby 🖤😳 💗 Xxx

Max must have seen the expression on her face because the colour drained from his. He looked as though he'd like to make a dash for it but he didn't. He stood frozen to the spot.

A wash of nausea sloshed in Annie's stomach as adrenalin shot through her. He was still lying even now. All that wooing. All those meaningless words. She was glad the boys were upstairs. This wasn't going to be pretty.

'You told me it was over with Ellie.'

'It was! It is!'

'I'm not sure Ellie knows that.'

'Well, she's . . . you know . . . she's not so bright . . .'

'Max!' The word snapped out of her, loud like a gunshot.

Max jumped and dropped the mop.

'You are a liar!' She began to move towards him, and he took a few steps back, hands held up in supplication.

'Annie, I promise you, I ended it. It was over. But then it looked like you weren't coming back, and she wanted to meet and—'

'Tell me the truth! For once in your life just tell me the fucking truth!'

He couldn't meet her eyes.

'I didn't want to be alone,' he almost whispered. 'But I swear, if you'd have come back, I would have ended it straight away. That would have been it!'

'You were hedging your bets!' She laughed bitterly. 'I should have known.'

'It was a stupid thing to do, I know that.'

'What about that day? Upstairs? When you told me you loved me and tried to get into my knickers. Were you seeing her then?'

'I would have finished it!' Max said helplessly. 'All you had to do was say the word.'

'I shouldn't have to say *any* words for you to not cheat on me, Max! At its most basic level, the function of a marriage is that you don't fuck other people!'

'What do you want me to say?' Max shouted. 'I fucked up! There, I said it. But you're no angel. I know about the affair you had when the kids were small.'

This pulled Annie up short. She hadn't realised he had known about her revenge affair. She shook herself. She wasn't going to let him throw that in her face, not after everything he'd put her through.

'Yes! I had an affair,' she said, jutting her chin out defiantly. 'I had an affair to get back at you and I own it, fully and completely. But you screwed your way through our entire marriage. How many were there, Max? How many more than the ones I know about?'

For the first time since she'd left, Annie could see the light of resignation in his eyes. Finally, he knew they were done. He was beaten. He straightened himself and held out his hand for his phone. He smiled, a smile that she knew from old. The one that used to fill her stomach with dread. The smile that warned of a quiet yet acidic attack. But there was no dread in her stomach now. Whatever power he used to have over her had dissolved, along with any last vestiges of feeling for him.

'Too many to count,' said Max.

Annie smiled back at him. In one fluid movement she picked the mop up off the floor, dropped Max's phone into the bucket of soapy water and gave it a good bashing with the mop.

'What are you . . . ? You stupid . . .'

Max dropped to his knees and thrust his arm into the bucket. Annie pulled the mop out and began to drape the dripping mop head over Max's head and neck and torso. He cried out in annoyance and shock, but Annie simply dipped the mop into the dirty water again and scrubbed it over his head.

Max stumbled to a stand, his phone retrieved, his hair and clothes dripping with water. He was rubbing at his eyes and spluttering curses at Annie. Annie leaned in close and said: 'You are going to buy me out of the restaurant and give me half of everything else, or I will sue your arse for everything you've got. Get a solicitor and get it done.'

She picked up the bucket and with one almighty swing hurled the contents over Max.

'Now get out of my cafe!'

Chapter 82

When Annie took to the promenade the following morning for her pre-work walk, the weather was bitter, though at least for the moment the sky seemed to have wrung itself dry. A storm had started around midnight and hadn't burned itself out until the early hours. The promenade was several inches deep in displaced shingle that had been vomited up and left by last night's waves. The roiling sea was as brown as Annie had ever seen it, churned up with sand and seaweed and frothing at the mouth. The dark clouds scudded by as though on a conveyor belt. Even the seagulls struggled to fly against the forceful air currents. They beat their wings ceaselessly whilst being pushed backwards through the air.

She considered last night as she walked. Admittedly, it wasn't her finest moment. The boys had crept gingerly downstairs after Max had left and found her mopping up the water that hadn't been absorbed by Max's clothes. She'd confessed to her outburst, which they'd more than likely heard anyway but they seemed to find it hilarious.

'We didn't know he was still seeing Ellie,' said Peter, when the jokes about her starting a new life as a bucket-wielding circus clown or taking up professional car cleaning had subsided.

'If we had, we would absolutely have told you,' Alex added, and Greg agreed.

'I'd have made him,' said Greg, ruffling Alex's hair.

'Oh my God, Greg, you know how long it takes me to do my hair!'

Peter laughed. 'You should grow it like mine, bro,' he said, pulling his mane back into a ponytail. 'Easier to handle.'

'Casual yeti has never been my style,' Alex retorted.

'So, the whole bucket then?' said Greg.

'Every last drop,' said Annie.

'And you mopped him,' said Alex. 'That's a bit weird, isn't it, angry mopping a person?'

'It was a spur of the moment thing,' said Annie.

'Spontaneous husband mopping,' Greg mused.

'In a funny way, I feel kind of bad for him,' said Peter.

'Sorry,' said Annie. 'I'm sure he'll be okay once he's dried off.'

'No, jeez, Mum, what are you apologising for? I don't mean the drenching. I mean, I feel sad that he's such a mess. It must be awful to be wrapped up in so many lies.'

'Stressful,' agreed Alex.

'Well, there's an easy cure,' said Greg. 'He just needs to stop being such a bloody liar!'

'You're not planning on becoming a psychiatrist, are you, Greg?' Annie asked.

'Life coach,' he grinned.

After half an hour she was braced for the day. She let herself in by the cafe door, flicked on the lights and made straight for the heaters. Five minutes later, with her hands thawing out nicely and the coffee machine grumbling into life, Annie began to take the chairs down from the tables, and then she stopped. The plate she'd left out for Alfred was empty, as was the thermos. A folded note next to the plate, written in a spidery hand, read, 'Thank you'. Annie felt a stab of sadness at the thought she might never see him again. She wondered how he would get on today. She hoped he would be able to settle and accept the help that the shelter was offering. It was selfish of her to want to keep him in Willow Bay but the crotchety old chap was as much a part of the bay as the gulls and the craggy cliffs; with him gone it was like there was a piece missing from Willow Bay's jigsaw.

By eleven o'clock she still hadn't heard from John. She knew he was taking Alfred to the shelter for nine a.m. and she'd been checking her phone ever since.

'He's probably caught up in paperwork,' said Gemma. 'You said he's acting as Alfred's next of kin, didn't you, so there's probably forms to fill in and stuff like that.'

'I guess so,' said Annie. 'When's Brian back?'

'Next Wednesday,' said Gemma. 'He's home for two months. I've learned not to say anything to the kids until a couple of days before he's due back. They get so unbearably excited and highly strung that they stop sleeping and start having tantrums every fifteen minutes.'

'Crikey. Don't worry, my lips are sealed.'

The door opened and a gust of wind made the fairy lights swing and the baubles on the tree jangle. Annie looked over, hoping to see John. It was Max. Gemma made a show of pushing the bucket further under the counter with her foot and Annie had to work to tamp down her smile.

'Can we talk?' he asked without preamble.

Annie looked at Gemma. All the tables were full, but they were up to date on orders.

'It's fine, go,' said Gemma, making shooing motions.

'Come through,' said Annie.

She led Max through to the hallway and pushed the door not quite closed, so she could keep an ear on the cafe.

'Can we go upstairs?' Max asked.

'No,' said Annie. 'Gemma might need me.'

'I didn't really envisage doing this in a draughty hallway.'

'I'm sure you've done plenty of things in draughty hallways, Max.'

'I came to tell you that I surrender. You win,' he said.

Annie raised an eyebrow and waited for the catch.

'I don't think there are any winners in this situation,' she said. 'I just want what's mine.'

'I'll buy you out. I've spoken to my parents and they're going to lend me the money. It'll take a few weeks to get it sorted.'

Annie could hardly believe what she was hearing.

'I instructed a solicitor this morning,' he went on. 'There's nothing to contest. You're only asking for what you're entitled to.'

Annie raised her eyebrows.

'Thank you, Max,' she said.

She darted a look at him and his eyes were glassy and brimming with tears.

'I am so fucking sorry,' he said with a quavering voice. 'So very, very sorry.'

'Okay, well, it's done now. We can both move on.'

'Do you think we could ever be friends?' he asked.

'Don't push it,' said Annie.

Max choked out a watery laugh which immediately became a sob.

'Can I have one last hug,' he whispered through his tears. 'For old times' sake.'

For crying out loud! she thought.

'Sure,' she said. 'One last hug. But no funny business.'

'No funny business,' Max repeated like a sobbing parrot.

Max reached out and pulled her into an embrace, clinging to her and making her hair warm and damp as he buried his face and wept into it. Despite feeling mild repulsion at being squeezed by Max, she found herself rubbing and patting his back as though she were soothing a giant child, which she thought just about summed up their relationship. She thought she heard the door creak but when she managed to loosen Max's hold enough to move her head, there was nobody there.

After taking a moment to compose himself, Max went out the way he had come. Annie nipped upstairs to change her cardigan and spray perfume in her hair. She didn't want to spend the whole day smelling Max on herself.

'Max has agreed to buy me out! I can buy Saltwater Nook!' Annie whispered loudly into Gemma's ear.

Gemma squealed. She threw her arms around Annie and together they did a sort of jump hug behind the counter, which earned them a few curious glances.

'Oh my God, I'm so relieved, and excited obviously. I can't wait to tell John, I wish he'd hurry up!'

'He's been,' said Gemma.

'What?'

'He came in when you were speaking to Max. He opened the door to the hall and then seemed to change his mind.'

Annie's stomach plummeted.

'Did he say anything?'

'No, he just said he'd come back later. I asked him about Alfred, and he said he's settled in and seemed happy enough. He left in kind of a hurry, so I assumed he'd forgotten something.'

Or just seen me in Max's arms, Annie thought.

Annie waited for John to come back to the cafe, in the hopes that Gemma was right and he'd just forgotten something and would come bowling back in any minute. But her realist side knew John *thought* he'd witnessed a reconciliation between her and Max, and the day rolled by without hide or hair of him. She wanted to message John and tell him he'd been mistaken, but what if he came back saying he'd never even considered that? Then she would look stupid, *and* she would have planted the idea in his head! Eventually she could stand it no longer and messaged him as though the whole Max thing had never happened.

Gemma said you popped by. She said Alfred's fine, want to expand on that? How did he seem when you left him? Come and see me, I have big news! Don't want to do it over the phone. Xxx

She got a reply – much later than she would have liked.

Yes, Alfred seemed fine. It's a big change but I'm hopeful he'll see it's the best thing for him. I said maybe in time he could get a place of his own in Willow Bay, rent somewhere. I'd help him with deposits and stuff. Anyway, fingers crossed. Big news? I'll try and get down when I have time. X

She noted the one kiss, as well as the *when I have time*. That wasn't good. She recognised a brush off when she saw one. She was going to have to face this head on.

Just so you know, Annie messaged back. *What you saw, in the hall, isn't what you thought you saw.* xx

She didn't get an answer.

Chapter 83

Annie spent most of the following day wrestling with herself. She desperately wanted to call John and tell him that she was in a position to buy Saltwater Nook, but her pride kept pulling her finger away from tapping on his name each time she got out her phone to see if he'd messaged. Needless to say, neither of them had suggested tandem reading last night.

'What is with you?' asked Gemma.

'Oh, nothing. I'm just worried about Alfred and stewing about John.'

'You've not heard from John then?'

'Not since yesterday.'

'Have you messaged him since?'

'Certainly not!'

Gemma rolled her eyes.

'Anyone heard how Alfred's getting on?' asked Maeve, strolling in with Podrick panting along at her side. 'I know it's the best thing for him and all that but it's a blow for me. I could really use his help chopping some wood. I say wood, it's more like a whole tree. Lost a yew tree last year in a storm and I've had it drying in one of the outbuildings. He's jolly good company too. Doesn't talk unless he's got something worth saying.'

Annie and Gemma furnished her with as much as they knew.

'John not been down today?' she asked, looking around as if he might be lurking in a corner somewhere.

'Not today,' said Annie.

'Oh,' said Maeve. 'I thought John pretty much had a foot in the Nook at all times these days.'

Gemma shot a look at Annie, which didn't go unnoticed by Maeve.

'What's going on there then?' she asked. 'Had a tiff?'

'No, no, nothing like that. Maybe a little misunderstanding,' said Annie.

'Well, you want to sort it out then. John's the kind of chap you want on your side. Good man. Bit like a bull in a china shop sometimes but who am I to talk!'

At five o'clock the next evening, Annie messaged the group.

The weather is atrocious, completely understand if you want to give book club a miss tonight.

The messages she received in response were pretty unanimous.

Maeve: I think we should at the very least pride ourselves on NOT being a fair-weather book club. I'll be there and I WILL judge anyone who cries off because of a spot of rain.

Gemma: Oh goodness, no, the weather is only going to get worse, we can't give up at the first hurdle. Book club is our beacon to help us through the dark winter ahead. I'll be there!

Sally: Really couldn't not turn up even if I wanted to bail after Maeve's rousing and slightly threatening message 😀 Count me in.

Annie still hadn't heard from John and rebuked herself for

the number of times she checked her phone throughout the day. She had given in and called him, but his phone had gone straight to voicemail; he was obviously ignoring her.

The weather didn't improve, and day surrendered to evening with no demonstrable effort. There wasn't – so far as Annie could see – even a discernible sunset to mark the change, only darker shades of grey and a further drop in temperature, which seemed to echo her mood.

Annie rolled out the pizza dough, spread it liberally with first tomato paste and then pesto, and layered olives, anchovies, baby plum tomatoes and mozzarella on top. She poked sprigs of fresh basil in the gaps, drizzled the whole thing with olive oil and put it in the oven to bake. Hot carbs, she decided, was the balm to soothe her fellow book clubbers when they came in out of the cold.

Chapter 84

Just before seven, the wind buffeted Saltwater Nook so hard that the locks on the kiosk shutters gave up, causing the wooden shutters to slam back loudly and repeatedly against the wall. Annie fumbled about in the store cupboard until she found a bag of cable ties. She pulled on her raincoat – though there was no chance of the hood staying up – and fought her way round to the front of the kiosk. It took three tries before she managed to fasten the shutters closed and pull the cable fast through the hooks. The rain lashed at her back as she checked the rest of the locks on the other windows, the wind undecided as to whether to flatten her to the walls of the cafe or sweep her out to sea. The crash of waves behind her was deafening; salt spray stung her eyes and lips. Half blinded, her hands red raw from the cold hard rain, she secured the rest of the windows, including Alfred's, since he was tucked up in the shelter. *Thank heavens for small mercies*, she thought and silently gave thanks for John's tenacity in preventing him from being out in this storm.

'Need a hand?' Maeve yelled. Annie hadn't heard her pull up in the tumult caused by the storm.

'I'm just finishing up!' Annie shouted back. 'Go on in and warm up.'

She heard Gemma shriek and looked round to see Maeve trying to push Sally's wheelchair against the wind, while Gemma leaned her full force against the door to stop it slamming shut, so they could get in. Annie tightened the final cable tie and pushed her way against the wind, and almost fell into the cafe behind the windswept women.

Gemma gave a kind of hysterical laugh that was mirrored by the others.

'I've not known a storm this bad for twenty years!' exclaimed Maeve. 'Had to help the girls get the sheep in the barns – poor old things were at risk of taking off.'

'I'm glad you were driving tonight, Maeve,' said Gemma, shaking her coat out and hanging it up on the hook behind the door. 'I don't think I would have been able to do it.'

'It wasn't fun,' said Sally. 'My car was all over the place coming down here.'

'God, yes!' mirrored Gemma. 'I could hardly see a thing through the rain, it was coming down so fast!'

Sally was mopping her face with her jumper. Annie handed round clean tea towels for blotting hands, faces and hair.

'Smells good in here,' said Maeve, handing her coat to Gemma to hang up and taking a seat.

The others 'Mmmm'd in agreement.

'If the weather gets any worse, I'm camping out here for the night,' Sally joked.

'You can sleep in Alfred's spot since he's gone civilian,' said Maeve.

Sally looked enquiringly at Annie and Annie explained how Alfred had been found somewhere to stay for the winter.

The women took their places. Four editions of *The Tenant*

of Wildfell Hall in various states of repair were placed on the table. Spirits were high this evening, not least because of their adrenalin-fuelled journey down to the Nook. The boisterous storm was making itself heard in the cafe, so that they needed to talk louder than usual to be heard, and the draught was enough to keep the candles permanently a-flicker, but it felt warm and cosy in the orangey glow of the lamps.

Maeve filled everyone's glass with hot dark-fruits punch, while Annie sliced the pizza and brought it steaming to the table.

'I mean,' said Gemma, pulling at a long string of mozzarella still attached to her pizza slice, 'it could have been a lot simpler if Helen and Gilbert had just been honest and frank with each other from the start.'

'Would have made for a shorter story, though,' said Annie.

'I kind of like the way the story meanders itself out, like a lazy river,' said Sally.

'Nice touch, with the whole thing being written via letters and diaries,' added Maeve. 'A good way to split narrators.'

'It was making my heart ache because Helen and Gilbert are clearly in love but there are just so many misunderstandings between them keeping them apart,' said Gemma.

'Well, you weren't supposed to leave your ratbag husband in those days,' said Annie.

'Unlike you,' Maeve guffawed through a mouthful of garlic bread.

The women laughed.

'And I won't be rushing back to nurse him when he gets knob-rot!' Annie said.

'Ooh, but who is your Gilbert?' asked Gemma, winking exaggeratedly.

Annie flushed.

'Aye-aye,' said Sally. 'What's all this then? Got a fella, have you, Annie?'

At that moment the cafe door crashed open; the wind caught it and slammed it hard against the wall. The women screeched and the candles blew out. John stood in the doorway, windswept and soaking.

Chapter 85

There was a flurry of indignant curses.

'Holy fuckwits!' yelled Sally.

'You're not in my will, John, so it's no use trying to frighten me to death!' Maeve declared loudly. 'And shut the bloody door!'

Gemma's comments amounted to a series of unintelligible squeaks.

'John, what the—' Annie began. She could tell from his face that something was very wrong. *Oh God, please don't let something have happened to Mari*, she thought.

John cut her off.

'Have you seen Alfred?' he asked her, ignoring everyone else. His voice was rough with desperation, his eyes pleading. Annie stood and looked at him, trying to read his face. John turned and, with some effort, shoved the door shut against the wind. The floor was soaking. He pushed his hair back off his forehead. Rain dripped continuously off his nose.

'Have you?' he asked, turning back to Annie.

'No,' said Annie. 'I thought he was in the shelter.'

'Sit down, my boy,' said Maeve, wrestling him into a chair. 'And tell us what the devil is going on.'

John ran his hand through his hair again; his other hand clenched into a fist on the table. Annie sat down beside him.

'Christ!' he said. 'I should've known better. I'm such a fucking idiot!'

'What's happened?' Annie asked. She put herself into his line of sight so that his eyes had to meet hers. 'Tell me.' She ached to take his hand but didn't.

'I got a call last night from the shelter. Alfred took off after a meeting with the counselling team and didn't come back. I've been driving around looking for him ever since.'

'All night? For Christ's sake, John, you could have had an accident. Why didn't you call me?' Annie scolded.

'I grabbed a couple of hours' kip at a motel, but my phone battery died.'

'You should have come to me!' said Annie. 'I would have helped you look.'

'I thought I'd find him.' John looked pleadingly at her. 'I tried the town centre, then the wider town. I've been over most of Thanet. And then I thought, maybe he'd tried to get back here; hitchhiked or something.' He glanced around the room. 'I guess not.'

The women shook their heads.

'What if he has come back and you just haven't seen him?' said Sally. 'You said he's got a kind of hideout.'

'Surely he wouldn't have gone into the cave?' said Gemma. 'He must know it would be dangerous in weather like this!'

'Alfred knows the tides better than any of us, but we can't rule out that he didn't try and get into the cave when the tide was lower, thinking he could ride out the storm in there,' said Maeve.

'And if he's panicked and bolted, he might not be thinking straight,' added Sally. 'Anxiety can make the most level-headed person act irrationally.'

'I just don't know where else he would go,' said John. 'This is all my fault.'

This time Annie did reach out to him. She took his clenched fist firmly in her two hands.

'You are not responsible for Alfred,' she said with conviction. 'He is an adult man and any choices he's made, wise or otherwise, are his own. Okay?'

John didn't look at her. Annie repeated herself in a tone that demanded a response.

'Okay?'

John looked at her and nodded infinitesimally. Annie nodded back.

Annie was first to her feet. Her heart was beating hard in her chest, adrenalin making her feel sick. She had a terrible feeling that Maeve was right: where else *would* Alfred go? The tide had been coming in fast when she'd been securing the shutters and the storm made the swell far greater than normal.

'Right!' she said. 'Coats on. Mari's got torches in the cellar. We'll sweep the beach as far as we can.'

She ran behind the counter and quickly swapped her ankle boots for the pair of wellingtons she kept there.

'What if a couple of us turn our cars around to face the beach and put our full beams on?' Sally suggested.

'Good idea,' said Maeve. 'John and I both have four-by-fours so their beams should be high enough to reach over the prom. And yours is best placed of all, being parked right on the prom itself,' she said, nodding at Sally. 'John, have you asked at the pubs yet?'

John shook his head.

'No, I came straight here.'

'Okay, lad. In that case actually, Sally, would you mind driving up to the pubs and asking if anyone's seen Alfred? Not too much of a pain to get in and out with the chair, is it?'

'Not at all,' said Sally as Gemma handed her her coat. 'Leave it with me. I'll message if I get any information.'

Annie fetched the torches and the search party set out into the night. Maeve and John moved their cars further back along the shingle path, to where the ground was slightly elevated, bringing their headlamps level with the bottom of the promenade. The white beams lit the storm. The rain was coming down in slanted sheets. The sea was a swollen foaming mass, waves built on waves as far back as it was possible to see, the front-runners crashing relentlessly against the shore. The tide was too high and too ferocious for any hope of making it round to the entrance of the cave.

'Maeve,' Annie shouted. 'You and Gemma take that end of the promenade.' She pointed beyond Saltwater Nook, where the prom ended, and the rocks climbed up the cliff. 'See if he's taken shelter anywhere among the rocks. We'll take the beach. He could be holed up beneath the curve of the promenade.'

'Right ho!' shouted Maeve. 'Everyone got their phones?'

The others gave the thumbs up.

'Any sign of rockfalls, get the hell away fast!' yelled John.

'Roger that!' Maeve called back as she and Gemma began a slow determined trudge towards the bottom of the cliff.

John jumped down onto the stones and Annie took his

hand and followed. It was harder to see down on the beach. They flicked on their torches and began to shine them around.

'Should we split up?' Annie called. The violence of the storm was stealing her breath.

'No!' John replied. 'We need to stick together. We can't risk one of us getting into trouble.'

Annie gave a thumbs up and they began to tramp along the middle strip of beach between the howling sea and the edge of the promenade, Annie shining her torch against the under-curve of the prom while John cast sweeping motions with his, out across the beach. Unease writhed in Annie's stomach. She hoped Alfred wasn't here, she hoped he had simply taken himself off to the city. She would rather he was sheltering in a doorway somewhere, relying on the kindness of strangers, than here on this beach, or worse, trapped in the cave, or worse still . . . She couldn't finish the thought. She looked out towards the cave and as she did so, the moon appeared from behind a cloud and briefly lit the water. Something bobbing on the waves caught her eye. Her stomach dropped.

'What's that?' she called, pointing with her torch to where something was being tossed back and forth between the waves.

John followed her torchlight and added his. They made their way as close as they dared to the edge of the shore, the rolling army of waves beating them back with a volley fire attack, the spray alone soaking them through. The torchlight picked out the eerie glow of orange fluorescent stripes. There was no mistaking it; it was Alfred's rucksack.

Chapter 86

Annie's breath caught in her throat and froze her to the spot. She didn't notice the foamy water running over her wellingtons. John began to yell Alfred's name but the ocean's answering bellows drowned his shouts. And then she saw it, out by the entrance to the rocky cove: unmistakably, an arm waving. Alfred was clinging tenuously onto a rock, the waves crashing relentlessly over his head.

'Alfred!' Annie hollered. John followed the line of her torch and swore. At that moment a terrific wave loosened Alfred's grip and they watched helplessly as the water swallowed him. Annie screamed out in horror. Maeve and Gemma heard the sounds and came running back along the promenade. Alfred bobbed back up, his arms fighting against the waves in some attempt at swimming. John tore his coat off and yanked off his boots and threw them back up the beach.

'Call the coastguard and an ambulance,' he shouted, kicking off his jeans and hurling them back towards the rest of his things.

'What the hell?' Annie shouted. 'You can't go in after him. John, stop for a minute! Stop! John!'

John wasn't listening. He began to wade out into the sea.

Annie grabbed his arm but he shook her off and in another second he had thrown himself into the water and was swimming against the waves.

Annie's boots had filled with water, but she didn't notice. She waded back to the shore and pulled out her phone with shaking hands. Annie could hear Maeve and Gemma's shouts as they tramped down the beach towards her, their shouts becoming exclamations of horror as they took in the scene before them.

'I couldn't stop him!' Annie shouted to Maeve, as she waited to be connected to the emergency services. Annie had to put her hand over her other ear to be able to hear the phone operator over the noise of the storm.

'Coastguard and ambulance,' she shouted breathlessly into her phone. As she spoke, she cast a look over at Gemma who had collapsed to her knees in abject horror, her hands clasped over her mouth. Maeve stood frozen, her face a grim reflection of Annie's own feelings. Annie looked back out over the water. John was still swimming hard, the water swallowing him one minute then spitting him back into view the next. The fear was almost paralysing; she was breathing so hard she felt dizzy.

'He's reached him!' yelled Maeve.

Gemma began to stand shakily. Annie felt hope leap through her. If they could just make it back to the rocks and hang on till the coastguard arrived . . . She could hear snatches of Maeve's conversation on the phone with Sally.

'Not looking good. Wait by the pub and let the ambulance follow you down. No sign yet, weather's bad, though.'

Out on the water the two men were tossed back and forth by the waves like they were partners in some horrifying Danse Macabre. Annie could see that John had one arm wrapped

417

around Alfred, but it seemed impossible that he would have enough power in his free arm to swim them both to the relative safety of the rocks. And if they got too close without securing themselves, they would just as likely be dashed by the rocks as saved by them. Annie couldn't bear to watch but she couldn't tear her eyes away either.

'They're going to make it!' cried Gemma.

The waves had taken a blessed break from crashing over their heads and John took full advantage. He surged forward towards the rocks through the roiling water. Annie could feel herself breathing for him, her limbs twitching in sympathy. She couldn't feel the rain or the cold anymore; she was outside of herself, willing and pulsing every ounce of her energy towards John, pushing him forward, hoping beyond hope that she would get the chance to tell him how she felt about him.

'Sweet Jesus, have mercy on them!' came Maeve's strangled cry.

Annie followed Maeve's horrified gaze out past the struggling men, to where a wave was steadily and stealthily building. The air whooshed out of her lungs. There was nothing she could do. There was nothing anyone could do but watch the horror slowly unfolding before them. The wave began to pick up speed, growing still higher as it slid towards the men.

'Swim!' Annie screamed. 'Swim faster!'

Gemma began to sob. Maeve's face was frozen in angst.

John looked up as the wave towered over them, a great foaming mouth of water, and then its jaws snapped shut, swallowing them whole, and they were gone. It didn't seem real; it couldn't be. She was trapped in a nightmare, a horrifying, gut-wrenching nightmare, but she was awake. She felt emptied, as though the waves had dragged her insides out to sea.

Chapter 87

The aftershocks of the wave pushed the tide in still further and all three women were drenched as the water gushed furiously past where they stood, transfixed, their breath held as they desperately clung to hope. The seconds ticked by but neither John's nor Alfred's head broke the dark surface of the water. Maeve began waving and pointing, and Annie was vaguely aware of the orange helm of a lifeboat bouncing across the waves from the other direction. But she couldn't tear her eyes away from the water; she swung her torch uselessly this way and that, hoping to catch sight of a hand or head. She reasoned that the wave could have sent them off course, it could even have propelled them forward towards the shore. The boat slowed as it reached the peninsula and powerful flashlights began sweeping the sea. Annie followed the streams of light on the water. But water was all they illuminated; miles and miles of water and no sign of John or Alfred.

Annie could hear someone crying quietly and it took her a moment to realise it was her. She began to shiver then; the full force of the cold came home to her. Her sodden clothes hung heavily on her; her feet, swimming in cold sea water inside her boots, didn't feel like they belonged to her at all. Tears stung her windburned cheeks and her nose was running. She fumbled in her pocket and found a damp tissue, and blew her nose with fingers so stiff with cold they could barely obey her commands. Across the way, Gemma was sobbing uncontrollably into Maeve's shoulder; Maeve held her tightly and though she made soothing noises, her face was grim, staring out to sea. Annie shook herself mentally. She wouldn't believe they had drowned. She wouldn't. Until the lifeboat found a body, there was hope.

The sound of a car engine behind her dragged her from her thoughts. She turned to see Sally leading an ambulance slowly along the shingle towards Saltwater Nook. As Annie made to climb back up the beach to tell her the news something bumped against her shin. Annie looked down to see Alfred's rucksack had washed up beside her. For a moment, she almost lost her composure. The pressure of not letting herself give in to the grief hammered inside her head. She looked out across the water and let the freezing wind whip at her face. Annie took in a lungful of the frigid air and pushed down the panic. She picked up the wet, heavy bag, telling herself she would dry it out for him to give back to him later, and then made her way to where John's clothes lay in a sodden heap. She picked them up, repressing the urge to hold the coat to her face and breathe in the smell of him. With her arms full of her missing friends' belongings, Annie tramped back up the beach to where Sally sat on the promenade above, the wind buffeting her wheelchair while she watched the lifeboat as it bounced above and dipped below the waves, methodically scouring the seemingly empty ocean.

Annie threw the clothes, boots and rucksack up onto the

promenade but her own clothes were so water-laden she didn't have the strength to heave herself up. She motioned to Sally that she was going to head to the steps along the way, when one of the paramedics thrust out a hand to her; the other, a woman wrapped in a dark green waterproof coat, offered her hand too and between them they hauled first Annie then Maeve and finally a still tearful Gemma up onto the promenade.

'Any news?' asked Sally.

Annie shook her head. Sally looked up the beach.

'Where's John?' she asked and then her gaze fell upon the clothes strewn at her feet. 'Oh,' she said. 'Oh no. Oh God, no, he didn't?'

'He did,' said Annie.

The four friends held hands and watched the lights from the lifeboat sweep jaggedly over the waves and up the steep cliff peninsular.

'Who lives there?' asked the male paramedic.

'I do,' Annie replied absently.

'It could be a while yet and it's not good for any of you to remain out here in wet clothes. Can I suggest we go in and wait? I'll make us all tea if you point me in the right direction.'

'He makes an excellent brew,' added his partner.

'I need to stay here,' said Annie.

'The outcome won't change whether you're out here catching pneumonia or inside warming through,' said the female paramedic with gentle but firm frankness.

'You're right,' said Annie, gathering herself mentally. 'Maeve, help me open the shutters. If we keep the lights low, we can watch from inside. I'll get scissors.'

Annie opened the cafe door and hurried off to find scissors. Gemma scooped up John and Alfred's belongings and they headed into the cafe; Sally and the paramedics filed in after them.

Gemma sat herself down at the long window bench and Sally pulled up beside her, taking Gemma's hand in both of hers and rubbing it. The paramedics – Georgina and Mark, as they introduced themselves – made small talk as they made tea and kept up a positive but idle commentary on the cafe and location. Annie guessed they must be expert at filling empty air with friendly noise to soothe people and she was grateful for their presence. Maeve stood waiting at the door.

'Here.' Annie slapped a large pair of scissors into Maeve's outstretched palm. 'I had to secure the locks with cable ties. You'll have to snip them. I've got more ties in my pocket if you think the cabin hooks will need extra securing.'

'Got it,' said Maeve. And the two women went back out into the storm and began to undo all the work Annie had done earlier. The lifeboat had broadened its search. Annie got outside in time to see it heading around the other side of the peninsula. Without its powerful beams to cut holes in the darkness the night swallowed the cliff, and the meagre light from the car headlamps only dimly lit the beach and the ever-encroaching tide.

The wind was so strong that Annie and Maeve had to work together on each window, taking a shutter each and securing it back with the cabin hooks and cable ties to be safe. As they opened the last set – Alfred's window – they were greeted by the forlorn faces of Gemma and Sally staring past them.

'Better turn the headlamps off,' said Maeve grimly. 'They'll be draining the batteries.'

Maeve went to her car and Annie to John's. As she pulled open the door the smell of John's aftershave washed over her and for a second she was winded by her fear for him but she swallowed it down and leaned in to switch the headlamps off, thrusting the beach into a darkness that felt oppressive and hopeless. Above their heads a scant moon was trying to light the sky but failing dismally beneath layers of thick cloud.

Chapter 88

'Hot sweet tea,' Sally announced as Annie and Maeve blustered back into the cafe. Several large cups of strong, dark tea were laid out on the middle table.

'Thanks,' said Annie.

Maeve picked up two cups and went over to sit beside Gemma. She pushed one of the cups towards her friend.

'Come on, old girl,' she said affectionately. 'Drink up.'

Gemma looked at Maeve, her eyes brimming with tears.

'It's just so awful, Maeve,' she said quietly. 'I can't believe it.'

'I know,' said Maeve, patting her friend's hand. 'I know.'

'There's still hope,' said Annie, taking a seat next to Sally. 'People can bob around for ages waiting to be rescued. They might have got pulled further around the bay, past the crag.'

'Absolutely,' said Sally. Though Annie felt she was humouring her more than speaking with conviction.

'John's a strong swimmer,' said Maeve.

'And Alfred's a stubborn old bugger!' said Annie. 'With that power combination they're bound to be okay.'

Annie had forgotten how wet she was until she saw Maeve shivering uncontrollably. She looked down at her hands and saw that she too was shaking as she tried to pick up her cup.

'I think it would be a good idea for you all to get out of those wet clothes if possible,' said Georgina. 'Have you got any spare jumpers? Or extra blankets, Annie?'

Annie nodded.

'Sure,' she said. 'I'll get some.'

'I can go if you like,' said Georgina.

'No, it's fine. Thank you. I'd rather be busy.'

Annie pulled off her water-filled wellingtons and her sopping socks, her feet blue with cold and her toes wrinkled, and headed barefoot up to the flat.

In the quiet of the flat, she took a few moments to compose herself before she pulled open the door to the airing cupboard and began to fill her arms with quilts and heavy blankets. She pulled off her wet clothes, threw them into the corner and re-dressed in a baggy jumper, jeans and warm knitted socks. In her chest of drawers she found a couple of jumpers that would probably fit Gemma and Sally, and hanging in her wardrobe was an old cable-knit cardigan that had belonged to her mother, which she pulled out for Maeve.

Before leaving the flat Annie scanned the dark horizon through the sitting room window, but the view was the same as she had left it. She left the light on, just in case John and Alfred had lost their bearings and needed a beacon to draw them home.

She came back into the cafe to subdued but amiable conversation and quickly pulled on her discarded ankle boots from earlier.

Wet clothes were draped over chairs and replaced with ill-fitting hand-me-downs and warm blankets. Annie was just bringing a large bell jar filled with tomorrow's cookies to the table when the lights went out. Gemma squeaked.

'Oh, for fuck's sake, what now?' Annie groaned into the darkness.

There was the sound of a match striking and Sally's face glowed yellow in the darkness, as she lit the candles left on the table from book club.

'Power cut?' asked Maeve.

'I don't know,' said Annie. 'It could just be something's tripped the fuses. I'll go and check.'

'Do you need me to come with you?' asked Mark chivalrously.

'No, thanks. I'll be fine.'

Chapter 89

Annie took the torch from the sideboard and headed out of the cafe and down into the cellar. The fuse box was on the wall, halfway down the cellar stairs. Annie opened the box and shone the torch in. Sure enough the circuit breaker had tripped. Annie carefully checked all the switches for obvious problems. Everything seemed to be in order, so she flicked the trip switch and the light in the hallway came back on; the gratified sounds coming from the cafe told her that the electricity was back on in there too. She snapped the fuse box shut and turned to leave when a faint thudding noise distracted her. She stood still and listened. There it was again.

Annie made her way gingerly down the cellar stairs. The thudding continued. The closer she got to the bottom of the stairs, the more prominent the sound became.

'Are you all right down there?'

Annie jumped and pelted down the last three steps.

'Shit, Maeve! You scared the crap out of me!'

Annie looked up to see Maeve draped in a tartan blanket, standing at the top of the stairs.

'Sorry, old girl. Was just making sure you were all right.'

'There's something moving down here.'

'A rat?'

'That's what I wondered.'

The thudding came again.

'Did you hear that?' Annie called up the stairs.

'Not really.'

'I'm going to have a look around.'

'Got a weapon with you? If it's a rat, you might need to give it a wallop.'

Annie grimaced.

Another thud, just one. Annie moved to the middle of the room and waited. *Thud, thud, thud.* It was coming from a pile of sandbags. Cautiously, Annie walked towards the pile and one by one began to heave them down onto the cellar floor. *Thud, thud.*

It can't be, Annie thought to herself. *Surely not.* But already hope was blooming in her chest. She went to the wall and thumped it hard, which was answered by three quick thuds and a muffled shout.

'Oh my God, it is! Oh my God! Maeve, get help! I need something heavy, something to bring a wall down!'

She banged on the wall.

'Hold on!' she yelled. 'I'm coming! John, is that you?'

Annie began tearing at the sandbag wall, kicking and rolling them away from her to make a space.

'Maeve said you need help?' came Mark's concerned voice down the stairs.

'We need to take this wall down. There's people behind it!'

'I'm sorry? You need to what?' Mark was coming down the stairs. 'Have you hurt yourself?' he asked as though dealing with a frightened rabbit. 'Did you bang your head?'

Annie growled in exasperation.

'Here, come here!'

Mark did as he was told, stepping over the discarded sand-bags.

'Behind this wall is an old smugglers' tunnel that leads out to the sea. Listen!'

She pounded on the wall with both fists and shouted, 'John!'

Her banging was returned by three methodical thuds and then, no longer insulated by the sandbags, a more distinct shout of 'Yes!', which made her heart leap.

'John,' Mark called through the wall. 'Is Alfred with you?'

The reply was muffled but unmistakable.

'Yes!'

Annie could have collapsed with relief.

'Well, I'll be,' said Mark, rubbing his chin before taking off up the stairs. 'Never a dull day in the ambulance service!' he shouted before disappearing out of view.

Annie could hear excited mumblings from above. She cast around for something to bash the wall with. John's tool bag was open on one of the chest freezers. She rooted around in it and found a hammer and chisel. She set at it, lining the chisel up against the cement and hitting the end of it with the hammer. *Oh God*, she lamented to herself, *this is going to take forever!* She heard Mark's footsteps on the stairs.

'Step aside,' he said, brandishing a sledge-hammer.

Annie eyed him with surprise.

'You never know what you're going to need in this job,' he said, answering her unspoken question with a grin. Mark turned to the wall and banged it with the side of his fist. 'Hello in there!' he shouted. 'I'm going to break through the wall, so I'm going to need you to move back. Do you understand me?'

There was a muted bang in response and John's distant voice came through the wall.

'I understand. We're moving back!'

Mark swung the sledge-hammer back and smacked it hard at the wall. The wall wobbled. Bits of cement flew out and skittered along the stone floor. He swung again, and again. On the fourth swing a large crack appeared, running diagonally up to what was once the door frame, and a chunk of several bricks dropped forward from two thirds up and crashed to the ground, splintering into multiple chalky pieces. Behind the hole was not, as Annie had hoped, a vision of John and Alfred but an old wooden door with iron studs.

'It's the old door,' Annie said to Mark. 'They must have left it in situ for extra flood protection.' Then she banged on the wood. 'John, we're almost through. We'll be with you soon!'

'Put the kettle on!' came John's raspy response and Annie laughed loudly, as though it was the funniest thing she had ever heard.

Carefully Mark and Annie lifted down the loose brickwork at the top and then worked their way down, scooting the remnants to one side, until the door was fully revealed. Mark reached up and attacked the top bolt and Annie the middle. They were stiff with age but with brute force and wiggling combined, eventually all the bolts were drawn back. Annie gripped the thick ring of the door handle with both hands and twisted hard to release the latch. After a few good tugs, the door hinges relented and, slowly, the heavy door creaked open.

Chapter 90

A blast of cold damp air whistled over Mark and Annie, like a wraith screeching to freedom; the force blew Annie's hair off her face. Mark called up the stairs to Georgina. The light from the cellar dappled the floor of the dark tunnel. Annie grabbed the torch and shone it into the space to find John shakily pulling himself to his feet, using the cold slippery wall to steady himself. A dark heap lay unmoving next to him, the mass of matted hair and layers of sodden clothes revealing the heap to be Alfred.

Annie rushed to John, who was shivering violently in nothing but boxer shorts and an irretrievably torn shirt, and helped him out of the tunnel while Mark moved to Alfred, whom, Annie saw when she got closer, John had put into the recovery position. Moments later Georgina rushed down the stairs with two bulging paramedic rucksacks and two thermal foil blankets, one of which she handed straight to Annie, before she disappeared into the tunnel.

'Hot sweet tea is on the way!' Georgina trilled.

'I thought you'd drowned,' Annie whispered, barely holding back sobs. She wrapped the blanket, which came down to his ankles, around his shoulders and forced him to sit on the stone stairs, despite his protestations that he had to see if Alfred was okay.

Georgina poked her head around the door.

'Sit tight there, John,' said Georgina. 'I'll be with you in a minute.'

'Is Alfred okay?' John asked. His voice was hoarse.

'We're helping him now,' Georgina replied non-committally.

Annie pulled the blanket more tightly around him.

'Are *you* okay?' she asked.

John looked at her and tried to smile through chattering teeth.

'I've probably swallowed more than the recommended daily amount of seawater,' he said and bent double, coughing hard. Annie sat herself next to him on the cold stone step and rubbed his back.

'You stupid sod!' she half laughed, choking back tears. 'Who does that? Who throws themselves into a raging storm like that?'

'Me apparently,' he replied. 'I couldn't leave him out there to drown.'

'I know,' said Annie quietly. 'I know. I can't decide whether to kiss you or punch you.'

'I think the rocks gave me enough of a beating for one day,' he said.

'I'm coming down with tea!' came Maeve's voice from above.

She reached them and Annie stood to let her pass. Maeve handed the steaming mug to John, who took it with shaking hands.

'Get that down you, boy,' she said.

John took a sip. Maeve looked around.

'What about Alfred?'

'They're still treating him,' said Annie.

Maeve was quiet. Annie knew she was worried.

'Right ho,' said Maeve. 'I'll go and fill the troops in. Let me know when you're done with that one, John, and I'll make you another.'

Annie turned her attention back to John. His legs and arms were a mass of cuts and scrapes and Annie didn't doubt that he'd have some royal bruises by morning. She put her arm around him and pulled him close. John leaned into her, his hands wrapped around his mug of tea. His hair smelled of cold winter walks. They sat that way for a while before they heard coughing and the low grumbling sound of Alfred's voice. Annie let out a breath she hadn't known she was holding, and John perked his head up like a dog who's just heard his master's voice. Above Alfred's protestations came the soothing tones of Georgina's calm voice and Mark's jolly quips. John went to get up, but Mark appeared around the door.

'Right,' he said, smiling broadly. 'Your turn.'

'I'm fine,' said John, his voice still gravelly.

'Would you mind letting me be the judge of that?' asked Mark cheerfully. 'Only my bosses get terribly narked if I let accident victims diagnose themselves.'

Annie smiled and John did the closest approximation he could muster.

'How's Alfred?' asked Annie, straining her neck to see if she could see around the door.

'He's doing really well considering,' said Mark. 'We're going to take him to hospital to get him checked over by a doctor.'

'He won't like that,' said John.

'So I've noticed,' Mark replied.

'He struggles with being kept inside,' said Annie, quietly enough that she hoped Alfred wouldn't hear her. 'He's, um . . . he's . . . well, he's homeless and he doesn't do well in confinement, if you see what I mean.'

'Gotcha,' said Mark. 'Thanks for letting me know. We are going to have to take him in, but we'll let A&E know and we'll be as sensitive to his needs as we can be.'

Annie was worried that a spell in hospital would send Alfred into another spiral like the one that had led him to this situation in the first place, but when Georgina popped her head around the door and said brightly, 'Okay, Mark. Ready when you are!' and there was no sound of Alfred grumbling, Annie surmised that Georgina had worked her charms on her curmudgeonly friend.

Chapter 91

Mark finished checking John over. He bandaged a couple of the nastier gashes on his legs and put a butterfly stitch on a cut on his head. After taking his blood pressure, pulse and shining a pen-torch in his eyes, Mark declared that John had been very lucky indeed.

'I'd like you to come in too and get a doctor to give you the once over,' said Mark.

'Do I have to?' asked John.

'No, you don't have to. We advise it just in case. You could be concussed. But ultimately it's your choice.'

'I'd rather not,' said John. 'I'm not an emergency and I don't fancy sitting in an A&E waiting room for hours just to be told I can go home and rest. No offence.'

'None taken,' said Mark. 'I wouldn't want to be waiting around either. Have you got someone at home? Or anyone that can stay with you tonight? I would feel happier knowing you have help at hand should you need it.'

'He can stay here,' said Annie. 'I'll keep an eye on him.'

'I don't need a babysitter,' John protested.

'Don't argue with me. You're staying here,' said Annie.

Mark went back to the ambulance to get a stretcher and

John and Annie followed him up the stairs, Annie walking behind to steady John if he needed it.

'I'm not wearing any trousers,' said John when they reached the cafe door.

'Worried the sight of your legs will be too much for the book club?' asked Annie. She looked down at the marks left on the wooden floor by his wet socks. 'I think you need to take those socks off. You'll get trench foot.'

'You seem determined to get me naked.'

'When you're my age and single you've got to get your kicks when you can.'

John chuckled.

'Far be it for me to deny you your kicks, Ms Sharpe,' he said, reaching down – foil blanket crinkling – to remove his socks. 'Satisfied?'

'It'll do for a start,' said Annie. 'Come on then wet-pants, let's put your fans' minds at rest.'

For several minutes John was swamped by women. Gemma clucked about him like a mother hen, while Maeve forced another cup of strong tea with two upon him.

'You look like you've just run a marathon,' said Sally.

'I feel like it too.' John tried to laugh but erupted into another fit of coughing, which saw Gemma's clucking go into overdrive.

It was warm in the cafe and Annie was pleased to note John's shivering beginning to subside a little. Then Georgina and Mark came carefully into the cafe with Alfred strapped onto the stretcher they held between them, and everything went quiet. Alfred's eyes were closed but they fluttered open as a little gasp escaped Gemma's lips.

'Thank you, John,' he croaked.

'Anytime,' said John. He turned to Annie. 'I'm going to follow him up in the car,' he said.

'You most certainly are not, young man,' said Maeve, flinging off her blanket. 'Half dressed and half drowned, you look an absolute fright! You stay here, my lad, and get some rest. I'll be accompanying Alfred to the hospital. Margate, I presume?' she asked Georgina, who nodded.

'Don't fuss, woman,' wheezed Alfred, before closing his eyes again.

'When have you ever known me to fuss, you crotchety old bugger?' Maeve retorted. 'I'm only coming to make sure they don't accidentally mistake you for a sasquatch.'

Alfred's lips twitched into a smile.

'Could murder one of your bacon sandwiches,' he whispered.

'Behave yourself and I'll see what I can do,' said Maeve.

Chapter 92

Annie stood by the door and waved until Sally's car, with Gemma in the passenger seat, rounded the bend. The rain had mercifully stopped but the cold wind still howled as though anguished and the ocean thundered in response.

Georgina had given Annie some advice on what to keep an eye out for with regards to John. For the next twenty-four hours she would be watching for chest pains, shortness of breath, dizziness or confusion and fever. Annie hadn't felt so responsible since the boys were small.

'You can sleep in my bed and I'll take the sofa,' said Annie when they got back up to the flat.

'I'm not taking your bed,' croaked John. 'I'll take the sofa, I'll be fine. I'm just glad to be warm again.'

'It's not a big sofa and you're rather a big man, you'll be squashed.'

'I'll be fine.'

It was clear he wasn't going to be persuaded. Annie went into her bedroom and returned a moment later holding her fluffy dressing gown with the cat-ears hood.

'Take that shirt off and I'll chuck it away,' she said, thrusting the dressing gown at him.

'I'm not wearing that!' said John.

'I don't have anything else that will fit you. It's dry and warm and I promise not to take photographs of you in it while you're sleeping.' John looked unconvinced. 'You've got no other clothes,' she reasoned. 'I can put your jumper and jeans through the wash now and they'll be dry by morning. I won't look,' she said, holding out her hand and making a show of turning her head and screwing her eyes tightly shut.

After a sigh of resignation, she heard the ruffle of clothing and then John pushing his tattered shirt into her hand. She opened her eyes and turned back to look at him. She quashed the laugh that spasmed in her chest at the sight of this tall, dark, handsome man looking gangly and awkward in her pink dressing gown, instead going to the kitchen and stuffing his shirt into the bin and the rest of his clothes into the machine.

Annie came back into the sitting room with her arms full of fresh linen and thick blankets.

'It's hard to look any kind of masculine in this,' John said, motioning to the dressing gown. 'Whichever way I sit looks distinctly camp.' He did look comical, the two edges of the gown constantly falling open to reveal his long hairy legs.

Annie gave a wry smile. 'Well, I think you look very becoming,' she said, directing him to get up while she laid a cotton sheet across the sofa cushions and fashioned him a makeshift bed.

'In you get,' she said when she'd finished.

John gave her a look that was halfway between amused and uncomfortable.

'You're not going to tuck me in, are you?'

Annie flushed. That was exactly what she'd had in mind.

'I want to make sure you're comfortable,' she said. 'Don't be a pain in the arse about it.'

John grinned and climbed under the blankets, pulling them up around his chin.

'Your bedside manner leaves a bit to be desired.'

'Shut up and go to sleep.'

Annie was reluctant to leave him. She'd suggested sleeping in the armchair, so she could keep an eye on him, but John had firmly vetoed the idea.

'I'm not going to be able to sleep if I think you're watching me,' he'd said.

Annie sighed, hanging around near the door.

'Can I get you anything before I turn in?' she asked.

'A glass of water, please,' said John. 'My throat feels like sandpaper.'

The paramedic had said a mixture of choking on the seawater and all the shouting would leave him with a sore throat for a few days. Annie dutifully brought him in a large glass of water and put it on the coffee table next to him.

'Okay, well, get some sleep. You know where I am if you need me, just holler.'

'Will do.'

'Well. Goodnight then.'

'Goodnight,' John answered.

Annie was at the door when John said, 'Thank you.'

'For what?'

'Worrying about me. Letting me stay tonight . . .' The words hung as if there was more to say but it didn't come.

'It's more your home than it is mine,' said Annie. She smiled at him, then turned and left.

Chapter 93

Annie couldn't sleep. She had mentally redecorated Saltwater Nook and put together a three-course bistro menu – mental organising was usually a great soother – but still sleep evaded her. The evening's events and all its possible outcomes kept playing on a loop behind her eyes. Fear and relief, fear and relief filled her chest repeatedly. She wondered if Alfred was okay. Maeve had messaged the group at half past midnight to say that Alfred was comfortable and that she was heading home. Though she wanted Alfred back to his old self as soon as possible, she hoped he was incapacitated enough tonight that he wouldn't make a break for it and disappear off into the back streets of Margate.

Annie was glad she didn't have a clock that ticked in the bedroom. Somehow a ticking clock seemed to elongate the hours when you couldn't sleep. She'd read somewhere about the phenomenon of dry-drowning and snippets of what she'd read returned to her now, despite her best efforts to dismiss it. *Is that a thing? Dry-drowning? Is it only in children?* She couldn't remember. She began to worry about John dry-drowning on the sofa. *Why wouldn't he just go to hospital like a normal person? Now I'm responsible for him!* She ran through the symptoms list

Georgina had given her. How could she check these things from her bedroom?

After several long minutes of panicking that John might be dying quietly in the sitting room, she got up and tiptoed along the hall – silently cursing every squeaking floorboard – to the dark lounge. She could just make out his silhouette. She listened hard and was rewarded with the sound of his breathing: slow and steady. Relieved, Annie crept back to her room, climbed into bed and fell into a fitful sleep. She woke with a start at a quarter to two and tiptoed back into the sitting room, where she again waited until she heard John breathing before returning to bed. After much tossing and turning she drifted off again, only to wake up at ten to three in a panic that had no meaning for twenty seconds before the events of the previous night came crashing back to her with startling clarity.

When she crept in again at twenty past four, by now an expert in avoiding all the squeaky floorboards, she couldn't hear anything. With fast rising panic, Annie stepped further into the room, holding her own breath, the better to hear his. There was a rustling sound from the sofa, and she let out her breath. She blinked into the gloom of the encroaching dawn and could make out John's outline. She took a step backwards to creep back to her room when John's outline moved, and she froze. John lifted his arm, the corners of the blankets in his hand, and shuffled back flat against the sofa.

'Come on,' he said in a gravelly whisper.

Annie hesitated.

'Neither of us is going to get any sleep if you keep coming in to check I'm still alive. Don't ever take up being a cat burglar as a career, you'd likely get pinched on your first job.'

Annie smiled into the darkness and made her way to the sofa. She lay down, nestling in against him, her back up tight against his front on the small sofa. She wiggled briefly to get comfortable before John brought his arm and the blankets down and draped them over them both.

'Are you comfortable?' he asked.

'Very,' she replied.

'I'm sorry about before. When I saw you with Max . . .'

'It doesn't matter.'

'I realised that not being with you was not an option, however complicated it makes things.'

'After tonight, I'll happily take complicated, so long as you're with me.'

'You should know, I'm useless at wooing,' he whispered, nuzzling his face into her hair.

'Good. I've had enough wooing for one lifetime.'

'But I *can* promise you I will never cheat.'

'No wooing and no cheating – I've never had a better offer.'

She yawned and John tightened his embrace around her, pulling her closer still, and Annie revelled in the weight of his arm across her body. Warm, if slightly squashed, with the slow rise and fall of John's chest against her back and his feet wrapped around hers, she drifted off to sleep.

Chapter 94

Annie woke up alone on the sofa. She was too hot under the blankets. She reached to the coffee table and picked up her phone; there was a yellow post-it note stuck to the screen which read:

Don't panic! All is well. I'm down in the cafe. Didn't want to wake you. XX

Annie peeled the post-it back and saw the time: 9.22 a.m. 'Shit!' she said out loud, kicking off the blankets and rubbing the sleep from her eyes. She stumbled out to the bathroom and found another post-it stuck to the door:

There's no rush. Calm down. XX

This made her smile. She quickly got showered and dressed and headed down to the cafe.

The cafe was full. The air was crisp and clear and the sky an innocent blue that belied the previous night's tempest. Gemma was behind the counter making drinks and plating cakes while John delivered them to the customers. Mrs

Tiggy-Winkle was following him around. Gemma looked up.

'Hello, sleepy head!'

'Thank you for opening up, Gemma. I'm sorry, I overslept. I'm so embarrassed. How did you . . . ?'

'John let me in,' said Gemma.

John finished setting a tray of drinks down for the swimmers and came over to Annie.

'Good morning,' he said and bent down to brush her lips with a kiss. Annie felt herself swoon. She heard Gemma hiccup a squeak of delight.

'I'm sorry about this, John. You're meant to be resting and instead you're running around the cafe. Sit down. I'll take over. How are you feeling? Okay? Not woozy? No shortness of breath?'

'Blimey, take a breath, will you! I'm fine. Feel like I've done a bloody good workout but otherwise I'm fine. Besides, I've got my bodyguard keeping an eye on me.'

Tiggs was rubbing herself against his legs.

'She woke me up by licking my eyebrows.' John raised his eyebrows incredulously. 'Never had *that* experience before.'

Annie made John sit down and set to with the coffee machine. Mrs Tiggy-Winkle, all indignance after having her bottom unceremoniously sniffed by a Cockapoo, jumped up onto John's lap and made herself comfortable.

The cafe was buzzing with talk of last night's dramatic events. John played the whole thing down, saying it was luck that saved them and Alfred's tenacity that kept them going, but Annie knew better. She'd heard the account John had given to the paramedics. The force of the wave had smashed

Alfred's head against the rocks and knocked him unconscious. Alfred was sucked under by the current, but John had
managed to grab him and had swum them both into the
mouth of the cave. He had half carried, half dragged Alfred
up through the narrow tunnel to the cellar door at Saltwater
Nook. John had undoubtedly saved Alfred's life.

The cafe emptied out and there was a lull, during which
Gemma flitted about clearing tables ready for the lunch rush.
John, still chair-bound under a large ginger cat, caught Annie's
arm as she carried a box of Kettle Chips.

'Can we talk for a minute?' he asked.

'Sure.'

Annie stashed the box beside the door to the hallway and
came to sit across the table from him.

'I'm going to tell my developer friend that the deal's off. I
want you to have Saltwater Nook. And if Max drags his heels,
then I'll sell my flat and take a loan to tide Mari over. We'll
work it out.'

Annie reached for John's hand.

'Max agreed to buy me out,' she smiled. 'He's got the
cash.'

'Oh my God, Annie, that's amazing!' John beamed back.

'But if my offer isn't enough to get Mari what she needs,
then go with the developer. I mean it. It won't change how I
feel about you.'

John brushed a wisp of hair that had escaped her ponytail
behind her ear.

'When I was lying in that tunnel last night, hoping to God
someone would find us, I kept thinking, this place has been
saving my life for years. How can I flatten it? Everything good

that has ever happened to me has come about in some way because of Saltwater Nook.'

He was looking directly at her, his eyes boring into hers. Annie could hardly breathe.

'Everything?' she asked.

'Everything,' said John. 'We'll make this work,' he added. 'I promise.'

Chapter 95

The cafe door flew open and Maeve entered, pushing Alfred in a wheelchair.

'Tally ho, chaps!' she shouted. 'Get me a coffee, would you, Annie, there's a girl. The coffee in the hospital tastes like sheep-dip.'

Gemma squealed delightedly and rushed at them, hugging first Maeve then Alfred, who did not look pleased at the attention but took it with good grace, only scowling minimally beneath his shaggy hair.

'How do you feel?' Annie asked.

'Like I drank several pints of the English Channel and got dragged through a cliff,' said Alfred.

'Still, well enough to be a grumpy old bastard, eh?' said Maeve.

This insult brought a smile to Alfred's weathered face.

'Thanks for saving my life, John,' said Alfred. 'I've come to shake your hand.' He went to get out of the wheelchair but was stopped by a firm hand on his shoulder.

'Stay in the chair, you daft bugger,' said Maeve. She wheeled him over to John who was unsuccessfully trying to extricate Mrs Tiggy-Winkle from his lap so that he could stand.

'You can stay where you are as well, young man,' added Maeve forcefully.

John and Alfred shook hands from their seated positions.

'If it wasn't for me, you wouldn't have been there in the first place,' said John. 'I'm sorry if I pushed you into something you weren't comfortable with.'

'I got a bit overwhelmed is all,' said Alfred, clearing his throat. 'I'm not used to form-filling and timetables. Been my own boss for too long. But nearly drowning . . . well, it puts things into perspective.'

'What's going to happen now?' asked Gemma. 'Are you going back to the hospital?'

'Ah, yes. Well, we've been talking about that,' said Maeve. 'Thing is, they couldn't discharge Alfred if he didn't have somewhere to go. You know the old brick summer house in my garden. It's not much; draughty as hell and needs a lick of paint. But Alfred has agreed to move into it, see how he gets on. If he likes it, he can stay. It's not a free ride, you understand,' Maeve went on. 'I need help in the garden and there's always things buggering up in the cottage; can't expect much else from a place that's been around since George the Third.'

'It seems like a fair compromise,' said Alfred when three pairs of astonished eyes fell upon him. 'Reckon I should be able to stay there without getting fidgety legs.'

'I'll help you get it painted up,' said John.

'Me too,' said Annie. 'You can take the old Calor gas heater from here.'

'I've got a bed going spare,' said Gemma. She looked at Alfred. 'It's really uncomfortable, almost like sleeping on a table really, only marginally better than sleeping on the floor.'

Alfred smiled.

'Don't make him too comfortable or I'll find him bunking down in the barn with the sheep,' said Maeve.

'Better than sleeping with the fishes!' said John, casting a knowing nod in Alfred's direction. Alfred nodded back.

Maeve and Alfred finished their drinks and Maeve got up to leave.

'Right,' she said. 'We're off. Cheerio!'

Gemma held the door and Maeve backed out, pulling Alfred in his wheelchair, who looked as grumpily content as Annie had ever seen him.

'Look!' said Gemma, pointing to the window. 'It's snowing!'

Annie went to stand by Gemma. Sure enough, the sky had taken on a yellowy-greyish tinge and fat flakes of feather-white snow zigzagged down on the breeze. Annie felt John standing behind her.

'There is something magical about snow,' she said in an awed whisper.

'This is a place for magic,' said John, leaning down to brush a kiss across her neck. A shiver of delight ran through her.

She turned to him and said, 'You, upstairs and put your feet up, no arguing.'

John – begrudgingly – went back upstairs to rest, with Mrs Tiggy-Winkle in tow.

Chapter 96

Gemma left at half past two for the school run. Annie switched off the heaters and let her eyes roam over the little cafe, clean and cosy and ready for whatever tomorrow would bring. She felt a sense of deep satisfaction in her bones; she had never felt surer of where she was supposed to be. Here. Here at Willow Bay, running The Saltwater Cafe, like Mari had before her. She was even looking forward to winter by the sea – the first of many, she hoped – and all the Christmas festivities that would ensue. She closed the door and turned to find John sitting on the stairs.

'You made me jump,' she said.

'Sorry,' said John, standing up and coming to meet her.

'Are you all right?'

'Not quite, but I will be.'

'Oh? And what has to happen for you to be quite all right?'

'This,' he said. He bent towards her, lifting his hand to gently cup her face, and kissed her. A long, slow, deep kiss.

It was a good kiss. Annie felt dizzy.

'Do you know what I was thinking about when that wave went over me?' he asked.

Annie shook her head slightly, searching his dark grey eyes.

'You. I was thinking about you. I was thinking that I couldn't bear to drown without seeing your face again. It was the thought of you that made me keep swimming, kept me going through the cliffs. I promised myself that if I made it out alive, I wouldn't waste another moment. I would tell you how I feel.'

Annie was breathless.

'And how do you feel?' she managed to stammer. He hadn't taken his eyes off hers and they smouldered now, with something darker. Her pulse quickened.

'I love you,' he said. 'Even though most of the time you drive me nuts. I've never met anyone like you. And now that I have, I don't think anyone else would ever compare.' He stared hard at her, as though trying to decipher a code. 'You're not saying anything.'

'I don't know what to say. You've stolen all my words.'

'Tell me you feel the same way. Tell me it's insane but you love me too.'

'It is insane,' she said. 'I hardly know you. And yet, I am utterly convinced that you are the best man I have ever met. And I am completely in love with you.'

They kissed then. They kissed for a long time in the draughty old hallway of the smugglers' favourite haunt. And eventually, when they could wait no longer, Annie led John upstairs to the flat.

'Mr Knightley will be jealous,' said Annie, turning on the stairs.

'Mr Knightley's services will no longer be required,' said John, scooping her up and over his shoulder and making

Annie squeal with laughter. 'I can promise you that anything Mr Knightley can do, I can do better!'

And as the two lovers discovered each other on that cold, bright winter afternoon, John Granger was as good as his word.

Epilogue

It was Christmas Day and Annie's tiny sitting room in Saltwater Nook was fit to burst. John had pushed the sofa and armchair against the wall to make room for a long folding trestle table which Annie had covered with tablecloths. Celeste and Peter had made several runs up and down the stairs ferrying chairs from the cafe, while Greg and Alex chatted amiably with Mari as she supervised their laying of logs in the wood-burner. John had declared himself to be at Annie's beck and call for the day and she had taken him at his word, though he'd raised his eyebrows at the volume of Brussel sprouts she'd wanted prepped.

Annie threw the window open in the tiny kitchen and fanned herself with Mari's almanac. It wasn't easy cooking a three-course Christmas dinner for seven people in a kitchen the size of a hamster cage.

'Is this the last of it?' asked John, picking up a serving platter piled with a mountain of golden crispy roast potatoes.

'Almost,' said Annie, motioning to two generously filled gravy jugs. 'Leave room on the table for the turkey.'

John grimaced. 'Much more and it'll collapse,' he said jokingly. 'There's already enough food to feed Henry the Eighth, his court and his peasants!'

'It's Christmas,' said Annie. 'If there's not far too much food, then I haven't done it right.'

Two saucepans rattled on the hob as the Christmas puddings steamed. Annie heaved up the giant platter holding a perfectly bronzed turkey and carried it into the warm sitting room. A cheer went up. 'Would you like to carve, Mr Granger?'

'It would be an honour, Ms Sharpe,' John replied, planting a brief kiss on her lips, which prompted another cheer from the party around the table.

Mari was sitting at the head of the table, flanked by Greg and Alex, the three of them engaged in a lively discussion about Buddy Holly, whom Mari had seen live in 1958. Peter and Celeste sat opposite one another deep in conversation, the sparks between them practically fizzing. Annie went around the table filling everyone's glass with champagne while plates were passed along to be piled with succulent slices of meat.

The conversation was lively and loud. Annie took a sip of her champagne. Outside the sun was setting, a giant orange orb disappearing into the ocean, and the sky was cloudless – a sure sign of more freezing weather to come. The lights on the little Christmas tree in the corner twinkled and beneath the sounds of laughter, carols were playing, and logs popped and crackled in the wood stove.

Annie glanced around the table at her favourite people in all the world and she felt a deep sense of contentment that was not just from the champagne she'd been drinking since midday. She was happy, happy to her very bones. And when John caught her eye and took her hand, lacing his fingers with hers, Annie knew there was no place in the world she would rather be than at Saltwater Nook.

Acknowledgments

This book was far harder to write than my first because it came with a host of added worries which weighed on me like the sandbags in Mari's cellar: What if I was a one-hit wonder? Would everyone be disappointed by my second offering? What if my publishers realised that I wasn't a proper author at all but just some woman who likes writing stories?

Luckily, I have the most amazing, supportive agent and editorial team around me, who reassured and guided me through all my wobbles and made me feel empowered to push on through. People often use the phrase 'it takes a village', but I can assure you that to transform my initial story idea, with all my arm-waving and overly excited descriptions, followed by my truly gigantic first draft, to the point where it becomes an actual book, *really does* take a village!

Firstly, thank you to Hayley Steed, my agent at the Madeleine Milburn Literary Agency, maker of dreams come true, who champions my work with the strength of a goddess. Thank you for reading through my story ideas and gently guiding me to focus on just one – my brain is a shocking jumble!

To Jayne Osborne, my ever-patient editor, thank you for not

running for the hills when I presented you with a first draft the size of *War and Peace*. Thank you for always being kind as you wade through my chapters; you have a way of delivering constructive criticism that never stings and always feels collaborative. And thank you for coming up with such a lovely title when my own title suggestion sounded like a murder thriller! You are wonderful and I am so happy we met.

By now the editing team are used to my bananas ways, so thank you to Samantha Fletcher and Lorraine Green for being editorial geniuses and for helping me untangle my time-bending timeline. And thank you to Pippa Wickenden for your most excellent proofreading skills. This book is what it is because of the time, enthusiasm and effort of the Pan Macmillan editorial team.

Thanks to Kate Dresser, my US editor, for all your input from across the ocean; it has been great to have you with me on this journey and I can't wait for us to work together in the future.

My thanks go to Mel Four who has once again come up with the most beautiful cover design, you are a star! You know how much I love that gold foiling!

To Rosie Wilson in publicity and Elle Gibbons in marketing, thank you both so much for your enthusiasm, your amazing ideas, and for steering me so expertly with kindness and patience through the process. You understand that I am not only a bag of nerves but also a complete techno-dipstick and it doesn't faze you one bit.

Book people are the best people! Thank you to the booky people on Twitter and Instagram. Your passion for books and kind, generous spirits have made my social media a safe haven in what has been a strange time for all . . . you are also responsible for my ever-growing TBR pile with your tantalising book reviews!

Thank you to The Bayou Book Babes for letting me join your book club. It is an absolute joy to talk books with such fabulous women, you are awesome and I'm always so excited to catch up with you all! And thank you to the Cafe on the Beach, in Hythe, for letting me spend hours writing this book in your cafe before the pandemic, and keeping me topped up with fine coffee takeaways all the way through it.

Lindsay and Jo, thank you for being my first readers and giving me the confidence to go ahead and press 'send'. I love you both so much. Aileen, you have been championing me for nearly thirty years, what would I ever do without your love and friendship? Thanks Adele, for our work-morning zoom calls where we have tried to recreate a working-in-a-coffee-shop vibe in lieu of the real things being open; you are a marvel.

To my mum and dad, thank you for being hilarious, loving and supportive in equal measure, you mean the world to me. To my brother Simon and my sons, Jack and Will, thank you for being the kind of men who inspire the heroes for my stories.

And finally, to my husband Dom, the best of men, thank you for helping me proofread this novel, even though rom-coms are not remotely your thing. Thank you for taking me out to look at leaves and fields when I feel overwhelmed, and for calming me down when I'm being an anxious-Agatha; I appreciate and love you to your very bones.